SONG OF SECRETS

TATE HALLAWAY & RACHEL CALISH

Level Up
PRESS

leveluppress.com

Published by Level Up, LLC (Level Up Press)
Saint Paul, Minnesota | leveluppress.com

First Edition 2015

Art Direction/Design: Kristin Smith
Illustration Credits: Mandie Brasington, Alexis Cooke
Photography Credits: Chris Hill, Coka Ostojic

ISBN: 978-0-9861925-0-0

Printed in the U.S.A.

ACKNOWLEDGMENTS

Tate Hallaway:
I would like to thank Naomi Kritzer, Sean M. Murphy, and Josey Walsh for their invaluable contributions to making this a stronger book. It's often believed that writers write alone, but nothing could be farther from the truth for me, in my experience. I would like to also give a shout out of deep appreciation to my family, Shawn and Mason Rounds, for putting up with me—particularly during the revision process. And thanks has to go, of course, to my co-author, Rachel, for making the writing such fun, and to the artists, Mandie and Alexis, for bringing our vision to life.

Rachel Calish:
Many thanks to Tate for being the yang to my yin and a blast to write with. A big thank you to Kristin Smith who has amazing talent and is the most calming business partner ever. Thank you to Barbara Schulz for talking us into an illustrated fiction project and being a great sounding board and guide—along with deep thanks to Alexis and Mandie. Thanks to Emlyn Chand and Falcon Storm for being lightning fast on tight deadlines and making publicity much less scary. And I can't adequately express my gratitude to my household—human, four-legged and bird-footed—for taking such good care of me.

TABLE OF

CONTENTS

THEO'S FELONIOUS HOBBY CHANGES EVERYTHING

Isn't it funny how one moment in time can change everything that comes after—a single event that totally fucks up your life, but also, just maybe, makes it that much richer... more *magical*?

Theo hadn't planned to piss off all of the most powerful demons controlling the West Coast, but then again she never *planned* to piss off anyone — it just happened. Let's get real. Planning wasn't exactly Theo's strong suit. Impulse was more her thing.

That, and instinct.

Plus, Theo cultivated a rather felonious hobby: she liked being in other people's houses and watching how they lived their lives. And, you know, once inside a house, she couldn't leave empty-handed, could she?

Maybe it was obvious that that sort of illegal behavior might end up with some serious consequences, but it hadn't so far. Theo had a special ability that made her little 'habit' harder to break—a little something magical up her sleeve that made it super-easy to get in and out without anyone knowing a thing. It was her ace in the hole. It wasn't like she was taking a crowbar to someone's window. This was art, elegance, and, Theo liked to think, a natural extension of healthy curiosity and imagination.

How different was it, really, from checking out an estate sale and spending your time piecing together life stories from what was left behind? Making up stories to explain away other people and their crazy actions was a thing everyone did.

Theo just did it a little more… aggressively.

That guy who was so short-tempered with his wife and little kid? Theo figured he totally had a crush on his super-hot guy neighbor and it freaked him out. That kid who studied until the middle of the night? That one wanted to become a famous veterinarian who only worked on pot-bellied pigs. The fragile-looking woman with all the diamonds? She was thinking about giving it all away to charity and moving to India…. And, so…. Theo just helped her get started on the 'giving away' part.

These new people that had caught Theo's attention—now, they were driving her to distraction. She couldn't figure out enough about them to even *start* a story.

So in a way, they kind of asked for it. She HAD to get in. Because, seriously, WTF?

Their house was the kind with large expanses of pure white carpet, where a guest would feel hyper-aware of any smudge, even on their underwear, which made Theo's current disguise all the more delicious.

She'd been in the house two days in the form of an Ironclad Beetle.

Yeah, so her ace? Her ability to shape-shift.

She could be a number of different animals, but the insect was her favorite breaking and entering form because it was all about the entering with minimal breaking. In this body, she was three-quarters of an inch long and almost impossible to kill. Her carapace could take the full weight of a grown man without cracking. That's why she'd hitchhiked down to Texas with the sole purpose of finding an Ironclad Beetle. She'd seen a TV special about them and just had to absorb that tiny, beautiful black-and-white body into her storehouse of shape-changing forms.

Yet, cool as it was, by day two Theo was getting mightily tired of being an Ironclad Beetle. For one, it took forever to get from one end of the room to the other. Secondly, there wasn't a lot for her to eat here, being a fungivore and all. Third, she was starting to think strangely—like, one more day and maybe her whole world might be reduced to click-clack of mandibles and scuttle, scuttle of tickity-toes—but damn if she'd leave until all the puzzle pieces fit!

These people were more than your average mystery, more than her usual just-curious/in-and-out type, which is why she'd stayed in their house so long. There was some deep shit going down here.

On the surface, the owner appeared to be an older man who spent most of his days in his huge garden. Another man and a woman lived with him, but they kept a cool distance from each other. The reason Theo had initially decided to explore their lives was that, from the outside, they seemed to be some kind of funky suburban, professional threesome. And how wild would that be? But, it turned out they were nothing like Theo thought they'd be.

Still titillating, just in a completely different way.

No sex. In fact, the atmosphere between the threesome was chilly, workmanlike. The older guy seemed to own the place. Everyone had separate beds. All three of them were ridiculously nondescript in their suburban whiteness and nearly interchangeable, but for age and gender. They didn't even seem to have any personal effects, no 'happy threesome' or 'family vacation' photos. It was like they were living in a house decorated by the FBI for the witness protection program.

Which was a possibility... except for the guns. Theo was pretty sure the FBI wouldn't want ex-criminals or Mafioso running round toting firearms. She knew about the guns because she'd seen the woman tuck one into a holster at the small of her back as she and the young guy left the house the other day.

Puzzle piece number sixty-three: the two of them went somewhere, for every day, for eight hours at a stretch... like a job? A job where guns were required? Were they some kind of cops or agents? Or maybe just fancy Mall cops or security guards?

Theo thought she'd read somewhere that your average police officer worked a ten-hour shift. She had no idea how long FBI or CIA agents worked, so that was still a possibility.

If they were law enforcement, a smarter person would get out of the house and not take anything, but where was the fun in that?

So she continued to wander, following the owner as he moved through the house. Theo waited for that thing that would be a clue to the strangeness of this fake-threesome. Finally, she hit the jackpot.

A keypad locked door!

She'd seen it in her wanderings the night before, but no one had gone through it. She'd originally figured it was nothing more than high-tech garage door, but it hadn't mapped out right. Puzzle-piece number twenty-two, but she'd set it aside because it went with nothing else.

Finally, it looked like the owner was going to go through. He pressed the code on the pad. The mystery door opened!

Theo scuttled down the stairs after him. Her tiny, simple heart beat faster; her legs clacked in excitement.

The room they entered looked like a museum. Display cases held items that ranged from books to jewelry to old-fashioned weapons. She scurried to hide behind a case and waited as the man crossed a room, opened a case, took its contents, and headed back out the door. Lights went out. The door closed.

Theo was alone in the 'treasure' room. Time to change back into a form that could do a decent amount of scouting in a short time. Honestly, sometimes she had a hard time seeing through the beetle's eyes, being so differently structured, so it was time to take a real, good look around.

It was hard to wait, but at least in this form her palms didn't sweat. To be on the safe side, she stayed motionless for another quarter-hour before she finally moved out from behind the case and shifted from beetle to human.

Shifting was weird.

Transformation always felt like being hit in the forehead so suddenly that her consciousness fell backwards out of her body.

There was a dizzying minute while she got her bearings. She'd learned not to move during that time. Theo thought the shift ought to make a vibration like a bell being struck, but without sound. It didn't, but the tingle of ionization, like the sensation and smell that preceded lightning, followed her through from whatever magic space her body travelled.

That was that: Theo was human again.

She blinked, feeling overwhelmingly thirsty and itchy. She rubbed her face with her hands and then brushed her palms over her shoulders and down her arms, already chilly. Clothing didn't change with her body, so she was bare as the day she was born.

Above, in the house, an alarm clanged.

Oh shit! Motion triggered? She should've known better. She'd been in houses where the alarm wouldn't register the cat but would pick up a human.

Cold adrenaline shot through her blood and she grinned. Time to grab and run.

Against one wall was a long walking stick with a cloth wrap on a peg. She grabbed the stick and swung it at the nearest cases, shattering the glass. Taking the cloth wrap, she doubled it up and made a pouch of it, then walked carefully amid the shattered cases, trying to avoid the broken glass and grab what she could.

The door swung open and the older man stared at her in shock. Theo returned the favor because his pupils were no longer a cloudy gray but red and slit like a cat's.

Wait, what?

What was he? A demon?

He opened his mouth and said a few words in a language Theo didn't recognize. Magic?

If magic was going down, the time to book it was long passed.

Theo darted across the room, shouldered him out of the way, and sprinted up the stairs.

Over the last few days, she'd cased the place well so she knew her exit: through the garden to the place where broken bricks made the wall easy to scale. It was early spring and the ground felt spongy under Theo's bare feet. The cool air brought goose pimples to her skin. She had tiny wave of guilt as her feet trampled the newly planted garden, but that feeling evaporated when she saw how quickly the old man moved. She figured he'd be spry and fit, but something about his movements were... unnatural. Theo didn't have the luxury to really examine him, but it was almost as if, instead of a natural run, the old guy leaped forward in too-long bounds, almost like an animal, but even then, unnaturally so as it was more jerky than graceful.

Shit. That was creepy.

Theo made for the wall as fast as she could. The bricks were rough on her hands and feet, but she'd done this sort of thing enough—even in the dead of winter—that she had hard calluses for palms and soles.

Yep, demon or magic of some kind. At least the wall slowed him.

Theo landed at a run and headed for the next yard over. These estates all had yards of an acre or more, dotted with trees and ornamental hedges. Not quite as much cover as she'd prefer, but enough for her to dodge around and hide behind as she made for her escape point.

A half-mile over was a high school—a long, low red brick building. It was the reason she'd been successfully stealing in this neighborhood for the last three months. Several months ago, she'd rigged the first-floor girls' bathroom window to not latch.

Coming from behind the school, she streaked through a patch of trees, and then along the back side of an auxiliary building so she could reach the window without being seen by anyone on the grounds. Most of the kids were in afternoon classes. Even so, someone must have seen her. Normally, she did this kind of escape at night. She could only hope that no one would believe that a naked girl was running full-tilt toward the school. At least she'd picked on that was built in the 1970s with very few windows.

Similarly, she'd lucked out that no one was out for gym, because seeing a naked girl busting ass across school grounds might have been a bit… awkward. Though, she did have a Plan B for a worst case scenario which involved crying for help.

Thank Fate she hadn't had to use that one yet.

This time cut things close, however.

Setting her bundle on the ledge, Theo pushed the window up and crawled in. Grabbing the goods just before a workman came around the side of the building, she had the window lowered again in seconds. In the second stall, she stood on the toilet seat and moved aside the ceiling tile she'd marked. Inside, she'd stowed a backpack stuffed with a school uniform. She dressed quickly and then put the cloth and the goods into the backpack next to the notebook and textbook she kept there as part of her cover.

At the sinks, she washed her face and hands thoroughly and then pulled her long black hair back into a simple ponytail. It made her look younger than twenty-two. She figured she could easily pass for eighteen.

The bell rang and she stepped out into the hall with the surge of students pouring from the classrooms. She followed half-remembered directions and helpful signage to the library. At a table in the back, she took out the textbook and notebook. She glanced at a clock. Once again, luck favored the foolish.

It was the final period of the day. In forty-three minutes, she could walk out the front door.

It was a long forty-three minutes. She was a seasoned pro at the whole smash-and-grab thing, but that guy's cat-like eyes had totally freaked her out. A demon… Theo was sure of it.

When the bell finally rang, she gathered up the notebook in which she'd been trying to sketch his eyes, packed it into the backpack on top of the stolen items, and joined the mass of students heading for the front door. She was feeling pretty calm until she spotted the old man. He stood on the sidewalk, scanning the crowd of students with the woman with the gun. Theo's skin crawled with the ache to burst into a run, but she made herself keep walking slowly with the crowd.

As they moved onto the steps, she stayed near the center of a large clot of students. Randomly, Theo touched the arm of the boy closest to her. She guessed him to be a senior so she asked: "Hey, are you in my…" she had to think for a second, but came up with, "…Trigonometry class?"

"Third period? Mrs. Adderley?" he responded. He seemed super-excited by the prospect, but then his acne-dotted face crumpled as if he was trying to place her.

"No, I guess not," she giggled flirtatiously. Then, she sighed. "Damn, I really need those notes. I totally fell asleep," she said with another little, gosh-I'm-so-dumb laugh. They were passing within a few feet of the woman in the jacket, but Theo made herself stare at the boy as if he was the only person in the whole world.

It worked like a charm. He blushed and stammered, "I could tutor you a little if you want."

She grinned at him with honest gratefulness. He'd already helped her more than he would ever know. Still, she needed one more favor. "You know what I really need? A ride home. Usually my mom picks me up and she texted to say she's stuck at the office."

"Oh," he said, his flush growing even redder. "Yeah, sure. No problem. My car is kind of a wreck, but you know, uh, yeah… wow. I'd be happy to."

"You're awesome!" She poured on the charm and took his arm. "Thanks. You're a *real* lifesaver."

When they pulled away from the school's parking lot, the man and woman were still out front, talking quickly to each other, the man shaking his head.

Theo let out a huge sigh of relief and leaned back against the passenger seat.

She'd gotten away.

Now, if only she could shake that creepy sensation that slithered along her spine when she recalled those glowing red, cat-slit eyes.

Right, so not only was there a kind of magic in the world that no one told her about, but there were also demons.

Theo wasn't sure how she felt about this, but she thought maybe she was a little pissed off. Because, for a world that wasn't supposed to have any magic at all, Theo's sure was full of it.

CHAPTER TWO

GABE SEES THINGS NO ONE ELSE DOES

Gabriel Herrera figured he was dangerously close to being one of those creepy-ass homeless guys who talked conspiracy theories and about how the devil was going to get you and eat up your soul. He could see himself now: listen, *man, seriously, there are demons everywhere. I'm telling you, a black cloud is eating your head right now....*

Christ.

Gabe pulled the hood over his head and hugged his knees tighter. Hunger and exhaustion jittered through his body in shaking waves. For the first time in a long time, Gabe wanted to go home. Too bad West Virginia was literally the other side of the country.

Too bad home wasn't really a home at all and sucked rocks.

Sheets of rain pounded the highway overpass he crouched under. Overhead, tires hissed and trucks rattled, shaking loose sandy debris that smelled of piss and exhaust. At least shadowed in pitch darkness, no one passing on the sidewalk below could see him huddled here.

The black canvas backpack tucked under his butt held everything Gabe owned—besides the clothes on his back. The contents were pathetic: two pairs of underwear; three socks (not pairs, mind, just three—one green, one black, and a white one that matched the two currently on his feet); an mp3 player that ran out of battery juice three weeks ago since someone nicked the charger; a plastic baggy containing twenty-six dollars and forty-seven cents; his grandmother's rosary, and a Gideon

Bible he stole from a hotel in Wichita.

Gabe had thought for sure that the rosary and the Bible ought to protect him against demons, but that'd been a bust so far.

Every once and a while, out of the corner of his eye, Gabe would see a pulsating, glowing blackness clinging, like an aura around certain people. If the visions weren't bad enough, yesterday they'd started talking. The librarian who'd shown Gabe to the world religion section had a blackness attached to her that constantly muttered, "sadness, sadness, sadness."

Maybe he needed a Torah or a Qur'an?

No, what Gabe figured he *really* needed was good meds. Because, come on: paranoid delusions with religious overtones and, now, auditory hallucinations? Seemed like classic symptoms of schizophrenia to Gabe. He'd done some research into that, too, and he was the perfect age for the onset of the disease: nineteen.

Now that he was almost out of money, Gabe considered the wisdom of showing up at one of the free clinics and just telling them he needed some antipsychotics stat. Worse case scenario, they'd admit him to some dreary psychiatric ward. At this point that sounded pretty good: three squares and a bed, not a bad deal.

At least it would be warm and dry.

Thunder shook the sky. Rivulets of water snaked down the steep grassy bank. Gabe hunched deeper into himself, resting his chin in the space between his upraised knees. Water dripped from one of the rebar beams, spattering the tip of his already soaked Converses.

Yeah, when the rain slowed, that's what he'd do—check-in somewhere. Long ago, he'd dumped or sold anything that could identify him. He'd grown out his hair, gotten a few new tats (not entirely of his own freewill, but that was another story), and was two thousand, six hundred, and forty-five miles from home (to be precise, Gabe'd checked Google map). No way was Asshole looking for him here, in San Francisco.

Mom and Meema had probably given up, too. That was probably just as well. They didn't do much to un-fuck-up his life, if anything his moms' constant bickering drove him further away. Even so, he kind of wished he could call just to let them know he was okay.

Who was he kidding? They probably hadn't noticed he was gone. They might even be relieved to have one less mouth to feed. It didn't matter, anyway. Somewhere on the road, time had emancipated him. The only thing that held him chained now was this weird drive he'd had toward the Pacific and… the visions.

It'd been like something called to him, pushing him to this place.

Well, he'd made it to the ocean now and it seemed fairly likely that a couple of pills three times a day would take care of the rest. Maybe he could finally get a real job or go back to school and make some friends.

Real ones.

Not the kind of 'friend' he usually picked up and used for food and shelter and a little spending money.

The rain slowed almost imperceptibly. But, after so much time outdoors, Gabe could easily hear the shift. He bet he only had to sit here another hour or so before it'd be nothing more than an irritating drizzle.

The Free Clinic was just south of the Presido on 10th. He'd have to dodge the fare on the bus, but that wasn't hard. Turns out, most bus drivers weren't paid enough to wrestle a fully-grown man over seventy-five cents in change. You just had to be shameless. Make no excuses and don't engage. It worked in a surprising number of situations.

Having a plan let Gabe's shoulders relax some. He was able to snooze fitfully until the rain slowed enough to make his move.

:: :: ::

The bus driver gave him a dirty look the whole ride, but Gabe ignored it and the snide remark the driver snarled at him when he stepped off onto the curb. The Free Clinic was a funny little building at the top of the block. It looked like someone had taken a hacksaw to one of the Victorian painted ladies that were everywhere in San Francisco. The second floor had the remains of a kind of rounded tower and some scalloping designs near the roof, but the bottom half was plain, squared-off box. Meema would have called it 'classic re-muddling.'

Thanks to the holiday, a queue stretched out the door and a few paces down the block. Gabe took his place at the end. The lady in front of him gave him a little nod of greeting. He nodded back and tried to ignore the darkness that buzzed around her head like a swarm of angry black flies.

By the time, he got into see a nurse Gabe was ready to dry swallow anything they gave him to make the whispered voices stop muttering, 'fear, fear, fear, fear.' At least when the lady moved off, she'd taken the incessant noises with her.

The nurse took one look at the color of Gabe's skin and the soft curls of his hair and said, "¡Hola!"

"Hi, to you, too. I hope you speak English because my Spanish kind of sucks," Gabe said with an apologetic smile. Mom had only taught him a few phrases, none of which came in handy when people assumed he was a native speaker. Obstinately, he'd taken Chinese when he'd had the opportunity in high school. Since being on the street, Gabe picked up bits and pieces of Spanish, but he'd be hard pressed to have a full-on medical discussion. Negotiate the price of a bedsit or a little off-the-books work, sure. More complicated than that and he was out.

"No problem," the nurse smiled back. A compact black woman, she had tight cornrowed hair. Low to the ground and solid, she reminded Gabe of a hammer. She had a voice like that, too: hard and blunt. "What can I help you with today?"

"Right, so, I need antipsychotics."

"Oh? Do you have a prescription you need filled?"

"Uh, no," he said, shifting in the hard plastic chair, slightly embarrassed now that he'd said that bit out loud. He was highly self-conscious of the dripping of his jeans and the white-knuckle grip he had on the strap of his backpack. Gabe took a deep breath. Nothing ventured, though, right? "But I've been seeing things for a while. Weird stuff. The kind of things that make a person think there're demons everywhere, you know? That lady you just helped? She had a cluster of... I don't know, demonic fear flies attached to her? That's what I mean. Not normal. Anyway, I found this book at the library and I'm about the right age and—"

Gabe stopped mid-sentence. He'd looked up just in time to see the nurse blink. Suddenly, it was like she'd lifted a second pair of eyelids. Her pupils turned to slits and the irises were an unnatural shade of red—that glowed.

"You can see," she said matter-of-factly.

"Um." Okay, this was a new development. Had he just slipped a cog? Did this really just happen, or was he in so deep in that his delusions had taken over completely and started talking back?

Reaching under her tiny metal desk, the nurse pulled up a purse. Unzipping it, she rummaged through for something.

That seemed like a normal thing to do, if a bit odd. It wasn't like she sprouted wings or something, but it wasn't quite the response Gabe would've expected either. I mean, shouldn't she get some kind of psychiatric evaluation test going? What was she after? A gun seemed unlikely, so what did snake-eyed demon nurses keep in their purses?

Gabe glanced over his shoulder at the thin, plastic curtain. Should he make a break for it? It kind of seemed stupid to bolt. If he'd just gone around the deep end, this was when he needed help the most, right?

Then again, just because you were paranoid, didn't mean they weren't out to get you.

The nurse found what she was looking for: a business card. "I'm going to call someone."

That didn't sound right, but Gabe was determined to stay hopeful. "A specialist?"

Her smile was far from reassuring, "Something like that."

Maybe if her fangs hadn't been showing at that moment, Gabe would have been more willing to stay. As it was, that smarmy, vague response felt like the wrong answer and more than a little fishy.

As soon as dialing the numbers distracted her, Gabe got up and walked out. Despite the fact that his heels itched to run, he moved slowly and steadily towards the exit.

"Hey, kid, wait," the nurse shouted, "I'm trying to help you!"

The worst part was that he felt himself hesitate. Maybe she *was* only trying to do right by him. The scary part about schizophrenia was that the lines between reality and fantasy would start to blur. How could he know what was really happening when he couldn't trust his own senses?

All the same, something about this didn't feel right, and Meema always said, "Even when you can't trust anything else, always go with your gut."

Every fiber of his being told him: *run.*

He could try a different clinic once he'd looked up the right drugs to take. Then, when they asked if he had prescription, he could lie and say he did, back in Mexico or some such crap in the hopes they'd just write him a new one. He could fake a lack of understanding of English. He'd done it before, when it suited him.

Next time, he wouldn't bring up the demons.

Never bring up the demons.

Once he was on the sidewalk, Gabe allowed himself to break into a run.

CHAPTER THREE

ERIN IS A MONSTER IN NEED OF A RESCUE

Some days, when the meds were working less well, she swore the metals whispered in tungsten and steel that there was a war between the demons—and she was the prize, the princess trapped within the tower.

To keep the pain away, Erin thought small, unnoticed thoughts. She kept her head bowed and her eyes shut. Over the dull thudding of her heart, she could hear the footfalls of the man pacing the tiny confines of the sterile white room that smelled of pine disinfectant and the musty depths of the venting system. Erin desperately wanted to shift her arms; her wrists were bound with plastic ties to the arms of the dental chair they used to put her in whatever position worked best for that day's experiment. It bothered her that her arms had gone numb, and the desire to reach under the chair and touch the mechanisms that moved it clawed at her brain like a fever.

Erin calmed herself in her usual way: reciting the periodic table of elements in order; then again with only the metals; then separating out the alkali metals, the alkaline earth metals, the transitional elements and the other metals.

When she was really little, her father sang her songs about the metals. He could sing the periodic table, like she did now in her head, but he also made up songs about common metals. She remembered being carried from room to room, small and snug in his arms. He would touch the furniture, faucets, pipes, light bulbs, pans, jewelry, cans and tiles, telling her about the metals in each one—until she knew them like the characters in her favorite bedtime stories.

Long ago, Erin made herself stop missing him. Dead was dead. Never coming back. No rescue.

But she still sang his songs in her head.

His songs of the periodic table was all that she ever told them when they tried to ask about her powers and how they worked. Not that she knew the answers they were looking for, anyway. This morning the one in the white coat had given up after FE, Iron. She hadn't passed out from the pain of whatever he injected into her, but had stopped being able to think properly. She kept repeating the atomic properties of Iron over and over and over. At first, it made him angry and he hit her. Then, he realized it was useless and let her fall into a fitful kind of dreamless slumber.

The white-coat man was back now, or at least she assumed it was him because she wasn't going to open her eyes to look. The door opened and shut and the person who'd come through had a heavy stride but carried no gun, so it was probably him. She'd have felt the gun.

He and the man left to guard her thought she was still passed out, because they didn't keep their voices hushed when they talked about her.

"It don't seem right," the guard said. "That thing might be a demon, but it's a cripple."

"You're supposed to say 'differently abled' these days," the white-coat one snarked.

"Whatever," the guard said. "It seems wrong to be messing with a girl who needs crutches to walk."

"You see that's what they want you to feel," white-coat said, his voice now darker and oilier. "It's part of their glamour. For all you know, that thing is oozing pus and popping pustules and only making you think it's a tiny crippled girl."

Was she?

Erin was pretty sure she wasn't oozing any pus. If she had had another face to show, she would have put it on years ago.

Anything to not be herself.

Someone would have seen this True Face, too, in all the clinics Erin had been through in her life.

These men weren't like the men at the clinic her grandparents had taken her to. Those ones had pretended better that they were real doctors. The clinic had been okay, no worse than most, but then they told Grandpa they needed to send her to a hospital in another town for more "treatments." The place they sent her wasn't a hospital at all, but that didn't surprise her as much as it should have. There were other kids there too, and they were as bad as the guards. It was almost a relief when she showed some powers and they said they were going to move her to this facility. Erin had almost been looking forward to it—at least until she got here.

The guards at this "hospital" had known to shave her head to expose the horns she kept carefully filed down. Of course, they'd noticed the reason she used a cane: her feet had been disfigured—the toes and some of the foot cut off by her own family—to stop claws from growing. Grandpa would probably be pleased to know that her captors had pulled her canine teeth, thinking they were capped fangs. Empty sockets still ached in her mouth.

Pretty soon she'd be carved to nothing.

Maybe that was for the best. Demons were evil. She had to work hard every day to make sure that the evil didn't overcome her. Apparently her demonic nature was like a cancer, it would keep growing and growing unless held in check. When she'd been at home, every morning before bed and right away when she woke, Erin would inspect herself to make sure nothing was growing back. If it did, she hacked it off herself before her grandpa did.

She knew that they were just trying to do what was right for her, but the first time she'd faced that axe in the barn... Erin shivered, making the chair squeak.

"Oh good, you're awake," white-coat said. "I want to try something new."

Erin opened her eyes.

She tried not to ever open her eyes since being brought here, because every time she did, her brain could never entirely parse what she saw. The place that she was being held looked so unreal, so science-fictional. Cavernous walls were covered with machines... sick machines. They didn't have strong metal hearts; the ticking parts were plastic or formed from other alien, un-living things. To add insult to injury, everything was either beige or the color of baby barf. Looking at them made Erin physically ill.

The 'doctor' wore a white lab coat. The guards wore uniforms. It was hard to look at them for very long either because it was clear they were shams… and sick, too.

But then, maybe Erin was the sick one. Her family always told her so, anyway.

"Tell me," Erin said, her voice so pathetic and weak. "What do you want from me?"

The 'doctor' turned to look at her. He was the sort of guy, if he wasn't a torturer dressed up like a doctor, who looked like he could be a suburban dad with a wife and the two point five kids. Caucasian, with salt and pepper short trim hair, handsome in an interchangeable news anchorman way, he smiled at Erin, his expression patient, paternal.

"As you're no doubt well aware, you're an abomination," he said the words in a voice as calm Mr. Rogers. "What we want from you is to understand how you can be, how something like you can even exist. We plan to discover your secrets, even if we have to tear you atom from atom."

Oh, Erin thought. Well, if that's all.

CHAPTER FOUR

KITTY IS A HUNTER, BUT NOT LIKE MOMMY WANTED

"Maternal" was a word that was as alien to Kitty, as "Sangkesh" was to most people.

From what Kitty had gathered in terms of anecdotal evidence was that the majority of people in the world—humans—had no idea about the Unseen World. They didn't know anything about the Gul, greater or lesser, Shaitans, witches, or even the great demon protectors, the Sangkesh. Stuff that, for Kitty, was completely ho-hum and every day.

But, they had moms.

Normal moms.

Moms that, if the stories could be believed, didn't just think of their only daughter as a breeding experiment to be forged into the ultimate demon hunter, a weaponized mini-me.

Which might not be so bad, if Kitty didn't suck at it—if she hadn't been a complete disappointment to Suhirin from the moment she'd uttered her first word.

With a sigh, Kitty looked at her phone again.

The text from her mother said: *Stop by my hotel, I have something for you.*

That was about as loving and effusive as things ever got.

Looking at the text, Kitty's chest tightened. Her breath squeezed up into her throat. The muscles across her shoulders and up the back of her neck clenched. She felt the gritty squeak of her molars grinding and opened her mouth, trying to crack the tension out of her jaw.

When Suhirin said "something for you" she didn't mean a present, at least not the kind normal people got. It wasn't going to be a new iPod, which Kitty would actually appreciate. It was more likely to be a weapon, maybe a katana or a gun or some kind of throwing bladed thing—or not a thing at all. It could be a test, a spell, a puzzle to crack, a little mirror holding a demon that never spoke the truth.

Yeah, Kitty still had the mirror around somewhere; hopefully, Papa or Dad didn't accidentally sell it at a rummage sale. That would get awkward.

Though nothing was going to be as awkward as seeing Suhirin and getting this sure-to-be-awful gift. Because, somehow, even though it was meant to be a 'gift,' Kitty would fail it.

Failing everything, even gift getting? That was Kitty's true superpower.

Just once Kitty would like to make her mother proud of her. She had gotten perfect grades in elementary school—the last time she was allowed to go to a normal school. But then she was whisked off to Austria to attend the secret school for the Sangkesh demon-hunters: the demons who hunted other, much worse demons.

In the high school courses she took online when she wasn't failing weapons training or failing the obstacle course or failing combat, she'd gotten high grades, even in advanced mathematics. The year before she'd been expelled from the Hunters' School, she'd been getting personal notes from some of the professors asking about her college plans. Good thing she'd applied to a few, not believing she could go. When she failed survival training by nearly dying, she got shipped back to the States and four fairly normal years with her dads until she graduated summa cum laude in math. Her professors begged and *begged* her to continue in math, but Suhirin had another plan to turn her into the ultimate demon hunter.

Twenty-one was young for grad school anyway, right? She could take a year or two and get tutored by Lily Cordoba, the retired head of the demon-hunters. Maybe she'd even make her mother proud this time, though she didn't hold out much hope.

Almost no one failed out of the Hunters' School because if they showed poor aptitude for all the stuff Kitty sucked at, they got transferred out before they could fail. Everyone except Kitty. When your mother was the mighty Suhirin, feared head of the Sangkesh demon-hunters, you did not get transferred out. In Suhirin's world, if you couldn't fight if didn't matter what else you were good at, your very best was still one rung below sucking suckage with suck sauce.

At least the school had given her some precious memories, most of which were wrapped up in Blake. In the rare moments when she decided she didn't give a shit about family pride and all that, the fact that Blake was out there, fighting the secret war, was the only thing that kept Kitty from telling her mother to find the shortest pier and take a long fucking walk. Blake was the best student to come out of the school in decades, and the first girl Kitty ever kissed, and no way was she leaving Blake out there without Kitty's brain to back her up.

Look at her! Just getting this text was making her spiral into panic. Short, shallow breaths, almost panting. Kitty bent forward and pressed her fingers hard into the cords of muscle up the back of her neck. She imagined they were Blake's fingers, not hers, and in the darkness behind her closed eyes that belief started to unknot the pain in her head and the vise grip across her ribs.

What was it going to be like to be face-to-face with mommy dearest?

Kitty considered putting her mother off. She'd composed the text in her head a hundred times, "How about never? Does never work for you?"

Except Suhirin never took 'no' very well and somehow Kitty could never stop accepting her tests and trying to pass them.

Just outside, Dad puttered around the house and his garden; Papa was at work. She could see if Dad needed help, but she wasn't so good with growing things and dirt, so she tended to lose patience with the garden stuff pretty quickly. Plus the text was already making Kitty super-jumpy and annoyed. In this state, she'd probably spear her own foot with the weed digger.

Leaving her bedroom above the garage, Kitty wandered out into the back garden where Dad was on his hands and knees at the base of a shrub. She smiled to see him.

Everyone always assumed that Papa was her biological father, because he was black and Kitty was so clearly mixed—only the humans never realized how much demon was in the mix. But, her bio father was really Dad, also part demon with a recessive gene for enhanced strength. Suhirin chose him from a database of candidates. Bonus that he was gay and she wouldn't have to worry about messy emotional entanglements when creating her perfect child.

From Dad Kitty had inherited a tendency to gather a little pudge in the middle, softer, looser curls, one-half of the genetic combo that let her lift twice her own weight and the ability to curl her tongue. Otherwise, she looked startlingly like her mother (including fangs and pointy ears), which of course was always a problem at the demon-hunting schools. She couldn't even pretend she wasn't Suhirin's daughter.

Dad wore his favorite gardening clothes: dusty, broken-in jeans and a cotton muscle shirt. Papa always teased him that he looked like one the Village People in it, the 'Construction Worker' or something like that. Kitty once looked up the Village People, and had never quite recovered from the "Indian."

"Dad, I'm going downtown to Suhirin's hotel. She has a thing."

"What kind of a thing?" he asked. Sitting back, he squinted up at Kitty. Dirt streaked across his cheek, like some kind of homey stereotype. He was doing that worried thing with his nose where it looked like something smelled bad.

"You know, probably deadly or whatever. I wish she'd quit that."

He blinked at her for a few moments as if trying to decide if she was being serious. Finally he said, "Yes, me too. I'll be happier when she leaves town again."

That surprised Kitty a little. Dad was normally more circumspect about how he talked about Suhirin. Dad told her very, very little about her conception beyond telling Kitty not to worry, that love was involved, and that she would always and forever be loved. He let out a sigh and went back to digging. "I do hope you'll be happier in the new school."

Me too, she thought, but she said, "I will. Lily has a really good reputation. She only takes one or two students every five years." Plus, Kitty had been promised that she could finally go back to school, real school, at the same time so she could finish up the language requirement to get into grad school.

"I'd feel better if you were going to Berkeley. Of course, I felt that way before," Clearly he still wasn't sold on letting her study with Lily, but he was torn by 'what was best.' Both he and Papa were awesome like that. They were real parents. Just like other people had. The kind that didn't think affection was shown by how deadly you made the obstacle course.

Kitty bent down and kissed the top of Dad's head. He smelled so much of summer and home that suddenly, she wanted to stay and try not being bad at dirt and growing things.

But, she'd decided, so it was time to drive downtown and face her mother.

:: :: ::

Suhirin had one of the largest suites at the Westin. In the living room of the suite, Kitty first saw three people—two women and a man—in nondescript clothes sitting in front of expensive laptops and computer monitors. Another man and woman sat further back at a dining room table cleaning gun parts.

Because: of course, guns.

Seeing them in the hands of strangers always gave Kitty the creepy-crawlies, even though she'd trained to assemble and re-assemble one blindfolded. A sudden blush flushed Kitty's cheek as she remembered *exactly* how she'd managed to pass that particular part of training. Even now, she could feel the ghost of Blake's hands covering hers, the press of her against Kitty's back, and the whispered instructions whispered into her ear. She could also feel, very clearly, what they did after she got that gun back together.

Kitty realized she'd stopped moving forward when one of her mother's thugs gave her a funny look. She shook herself out and stood in front of Suhirin, like she was snapping to attention.

Even though Kitty tried not to, she always hoped that one day, among these thugs and bodyguards, Blake would be there and they could exchange a knowing smile, if nothing else. Though there had been other women since, Kitty would kill to see that cocky smile of Blake's again. Blake was like her good luck charm—just thinking about her could reliably pull Kitty back from the brink of full on panic.

Plus seeing Blake or any of the other kids from the demon school again would reassure Kitty that she was making the right choice by continuing to serve her mother this way. What if they were all already dead?

And if they were, would it give Kitty the strength to tell her mom to fuck-off, or would it just reinforce the need to do this job?

Her mother got up from the couch where she'd been reading a file to give Kitty a brief, stiff hug.

Awkward hug was super-awkward.

So much not knowing how long to touch, feeling as though this should be more comfortable, and all the nerd body spasms of 'What even? How does?' that made Kitty knock into Suhirin in all the wrong ways, underscoring her complete lack of grace.

Once the hugging ordeal was over, Kitty stepped back.

Iron-like muscle and dense bone, Suhirin stood two inches taller than Kitty: a lean six feet. Her hair was, as always, shaved down to an inch from her scalp, tight leonine golden brown curls lighter than her black skin, framed a long face not often given to smiling. Her flattened nose, common to all the members of their family, her deep amber cat's eyes, and her thick fangs, increased the lion-like effect. She was gorgeous, in a frightening kind of way.

Kitty's own fangs weren't a third the size of her mother's. Some days she wondered if, rather than an effect of age, the length of Suhirin's teeth was a feature of pure willpower—she wanted longer fangs so she simply grew them. That's how it always seemed to go with her mother: whatever she wanted, the world obliged her.

Except in the rather crucial area of her one and only daughter.

Their silence stretched just long enough to be uncomfortable. Kitty wondered what Suhirin thought looking at her, but it wasn't hard to guess, not when there was that slight tightening of her expression. She must see how Kitty's breathing was shallow again, how she was standing still by clenching every muscle in her upper body—not at all the relaxed, coiled power of Suhirin's frame.

Turning, Suhirin picked up a thick file from the dining room table and handed it to Kitty. No words were exchanged, but Kitty knew what to do with the file. She scanned the label that read: Theodosia "Theo" Elektra Young.

Flipping it open, Kitty skimmed through the cover sheet: witch, untrained, shape-changer, sister of Sabeline Young who was a rising star of the Hecatine witches.

"She broke into a Sangkesh vault and took some items," Suhirin said.

Her tone was like her words: all business, no feelings, clipped, precise, and demanding. "I need you to help us find her."

What? An assignment? It was almost like Mom trusted Kitty to do something right. "Why me?"

"She's your age."

Oh, of course, Kitty thought: *not because I'm brilliant, not because I have models for this sort of thing, not because Suhirin might finally have some need for advanced mathematics, but just because they were the same age?*

To Kitty's incredulous look, Suhirin said, "You know what kids your age like. It gives you an advantage. Use it."

Like she knew anything about normal kids and normal lives.

So, Kitty ignored that. "Do you think she was operating under instructions from the Hecatine witches?"

In between flipped the pages, Kitty's hand went to the back of her neck, fingers digging into the tight muscle. She saw Suhirin watching her and dropped her hand.

Suhirin said, "They wouldn't dare move against us so openly, but it's possible there's a deeper plan. The things she stole … some are very powerful."

"When you find her, are you going to hurt her?" Kitty asked.

"Akiva," her mother said, using her given name with a tone of disapproval.

"If you want me to do this for you, you could at least call me Kitty and answer my questions."

"We won't kill her," Suhirin said with a sigh, as if both disappointed by this line of questioning *and* the fact that there would be no murder.

It was weird that Suhirin's iron fist wasn't going to close around this girl in a 'final solution.' Normally problems just got snuffed out. It was curious that wasn't the case, this time. Kitty thought that was probably because of this girl's family and her sister's connection to the Hecatine witches, not because it was the right thing to do.

Kitty paged through the file. The girl was less than a year older than Kitty, grew up in America and Greece, attended great schools (jealous!), left college after two years, seemed to hook up with both boys and girls—that was cool—and had been observed turning herself into a cat and a crow. She wasn't on any known roster of the Hecatines, not that they knew all the witches.

This Theo person seemed to keep her distance from her sister. She'd never gone any place that was associated with Hecatine training, and so it was safe to assume she was a natural witch—or that the Hecatines kept their connection to her secret just so she could pull a stunt like this.

Then Kitty looked at the list of items Theo had stolen and she felt the surface of her skin tighten, cool, and prickle with alarm.

Sangkesh vaults held some serious weapons and often items no one fully understood yet, and in rare cases, one of the greater magicks that could tear the fabric of this world. That's what this stupid girl had grabbed.

She looked up at Suhirin and nodded. She'd help. Bad enough if the witches had this, but if it was a random, impulsive, independent act, that was worse. This was some serious shit that should not be out in the open.

"Good," her mother said to Kitty reaction like she sensed Kitty was on the case, had buy-in, or whatever-the-fuck. Then, Suhirin returned to her papers spread out on the couch. Because, that was it: audience over.

Kitty stood there a moment, despite the obvious dismissal. She wanted to say something, though she wasn't sure what, like: *Okay, but this is the last job like this*, or maybe *I'll do this, but I want to get updates of my classmates, I need to know they're alive, that I'm doing this for a good reason...*

But none of that came out. Instead, all she managed was a weak, "Okay, bye then," which Suhirin didn't even acknowledge.

:: :: ::

Kitty went back to the house and the familiarity of her two rooms. Her dads had fixed this place up for her as a gift when she was 17 and started college. That's what people should mean when they said "I have something for you." They should mean that you were going to come back from nearly dying at the Hunters' School in Europe and get handed a key to the door that led from the side of the house down a flight of newly-carpeted stairs to the two rooms that had been once been for junk and old books and Papa's weight lifting equipment—and find that the rooms were clean and freshly painted and that Papa had put in baseboard heating, better electrical, and egress windows. That was a fucking "gift."

Kitty loved her quiet, cozy rooms and the little bathroom jammed in by the furnace, because so many great things happened there over the last four years. She was really going to miss this place.

The room at the foot of the stairs was her study and the back room her bedroom. She settled in the reclining armchair that used to be Dad's, pulled over her laptop on its little swing desk, and started making notes from the file.

The Hunters' School had been good for one other thing: it had taught her to track people like a pro. In fact, they had whole classes on how to by-pass the massive security needed to access police, FBI and other human governmental records and computer systems. They also gave her the keys to the secret by-ways of demon-only networks, only some of which could be traced on computers, and even then only if you knew which dog-whistle words to listen for.

Kitty hesitated to call what she did cracking or hacking, but really, that's what it was.

What she couldn't do via the net, Kitty did with math. She set out patterns, she searched for formulae, and she plugged in numbers until a picture formed, like graphing a line in simple Algebra... only on so many more vectors.

It took most of the week. Then she used a VPN to upload her conclusions to her mother. She'd narrowed the search field to eight cities and two mid-sized towns.

Her mother replied by text: *Good job, Akiva. We'll begin with these.*

"Good job?" she repeated out loud. It must have been extraordinary to have garnered that.

Kitty let out a harsh sigh and deleted it, but it took a lot more effort to get Suhirin out of her mind and the image of the dark-haired girl with the haunted, hungry eyes.

CHAPTER FIVE

THEO RUNS INTO A SPOT OF TROUBLE

Theo knew the items she'd run off with were far from ordinary, but she'd had no idea she'd get cornered this quickly, this completely.

Who the *hell* were those people she'd stolen from?

Theo was beginning to have an idea, and it involved vast networks of well-trained spies, trackers ... and hunters.

Laughing darkly to herself, Theo shook her head: for most people that would mean the CIA or some other governmental organization. But to her, it was taking the shape of something far scarier, something she'd only tangled with a few times, accidentally, and had backed away from hella fast.... Because, you know, she'd been told magic *didn't* exist. So this stuff wasn't supposed to be real. It shouldn't exist, and it sure as shit shouldn't be on her tail right now and closing in fast.

Demons.

The kind with glowing-red, cat-slit eyes.

Theo's more-than-human sense of smell picked up the scent of lemongrass soap and metal polish again, closer this time. Sometime after absorbing the dog, or maybe it was the cat, Theo found that some of the animal traits stuck around more or less permanently. One of them was her sense of smell—though it was kind of odd because it wasn't like she noticed odors all the time. It was more of a Spidey-sense; she detected the smells of danger.

Like how people said dogs could smell fear.

This scent she couldn't link to anyone in the immediate vicinity, but she didn't need to. This was the third time today and the tenth time this week she'd caught the odor stalking her—each time circling closer.

Hunting behavior.

Ducking into a shopping mall, Theo moved down the central corridor, pausing in front of shop windows and trying to catch whomever it was in the reflection. She hadn't needed to be that sneaky, she realized a moment later when a group of four people in black suits hustled in, hot on Theo's tail.

Black fucking suits! Not ninja suits, but, like, 'hello, we're some nebulous scary organization' black suits. One of the suits put a hand to her ear, talking through a hidden microphone. Awesome. They were super-organized, *networked*, nebulous scary organization suits!

As Theo watched them, two of the suits hovered near the doors scanning the faces of the people coming in and out. Two others started down the corridor towards Theo.

Time to move.

First, Theo had to lose them in the crowds, and then, with luck, she could stash her backpack somewhere safe, shift into her beetle form, crawl into the vent system, and just wait it out as they searched the whole mall and left.

Theo didn't want to lose this backpack. Problem was, like her clothes, it wouldn't change form with her. She needed to find a place to stash it. It'd been a kind of lucky charm so far, plus it had a good amount of money in it that she had plans for.

When she'd first sniffed the hunters circling in closer, she'd sold a few of the items she took, hid the especially weird and valuable-looking ones, and then bolted, like a rabbit, from her usual safe holds and contacts. The last thing Theo wanted was for the people she trusted to get caught up in this weird-ass, scary demon stuff. Especially when it was so hard to find trustworthy people amid all the liars and cheats. The good news was that she had very little but the money she'd gotten from the sales on her, distributed in thick rolls in pockets and pack. If these suits were after the items she'd stolen, they were going to be sorely disappointed.

Leaving her usual haunts, she'd ended up in Sacramento, a city she didn't know terribly well. Walking the length of the mall, Theo went up the stairs. The people in black were going store to store, slowly and de-liberately. They looked like FBI agents and the shoppers gave them odd looks and cut a wide berth around them. Theo was damn certain they weren't agents at all, but pretty clever to look like them—if they grabbed her, it was less likely that people would intervene. They probably had fake badges too.

A second pair of suits started at the far side of the mall and worked their way along toward the first. If they had a pair stationed at the far door as well as the pair that stayed at the front door. That meant there were eight of them—eight to one, terrible odds. Theo wondered if she should call her parents. They'd gotten her out of tight spots before—well, their money had.

And it wasn't like they'd ask questions. They'd just want to keep their precious family name out of the newspapers, unless, of course, it was a debut announcement or in the *New York Times* Sunday Styles Section.

If Theo leaned on them, however, it would mean she'd have to pay in her own way. She'd get flown back to Athens or wherever they were living at the moment and get stuck attending boring parties surrounded by beautiful, empty people.

Yeah, no thanks. Theo would pass on that. Honestly, she'd left that world because she didn't get people. Watching people was like reading the words on a page and getting what each individual word meant but being unable to put them together in a way that made sense.

Their houses? Their stuff? Those things usually told a more straight-forward story, built a fuller picture. People? They were always lying, leav-ing out the most important parts, pretending to be what they weren't.

Animals made sense. They didn't do all that shit.

But, maybe Theo could call her sister Sabel and ask her to drive up from San Francisco and pick her up for a few days. She missed Sabel, who wasn't all that bad for a person—though Theo didn't know her all that well. There was a huge age-gap between them, nine years. She left the house just about the time Theo could have used a big sister.

Kind of like now.

Theo's heart skipped nervously as she felt them closing in. The calls could wait. They were a game-ender, anyway. Perversely, Theo wanted to see if these suits could really catch her. It wasn't like these people could shoot her in a mall. Even if they were demons, they had no idea what *she* could do—all the animals she could shift into. Better to take it one step at a time, see if she could minimize her losses. If not, she could always just fly away.

Moving along the second story walkway, Theo looked down at the first level, at the shoppers, scanning for suits. There, in the crowd, she swore she saw a familiar flash of pale skin and dark hair, as if thinking about Sabel had called her forth. Theo rubbed a hand across her eyes and looked again but couldn't spot the Sabel-look-alike a second time. It must have been a mirage of memory... or desperation. Soon enough the suits would be searching the second floor. This wasn't a very big mall.

Heading for the food court, Theo kept her eyes open for a group of young men that she could talk into taking her bag for her. She'd just spotted a promising group of three when two suits came into the open area from the other side. Damn it! Cut off!

Without changing her pace, Theo turned right. She walked slowly along the fastfood counters, looking up at the menus, turning her face away from the suits. As she did that, she also surreptitiously scanned for an escape route.

There, at the far side of a row of storefront restaurants, a hallway led into the service area of the mall. Theo paused to look over her shoulder. The suits spotted her! Worse, they were a lot closer than she wanted them to be. She turned towards the hallway and gave into the impulse to run.

If she could just get through the swinging door at the end, out of sight for a moment, she'd turn beetle and hide. She'd have to forget about the pack and her clothes and the money. It was far too awkward changing form in her clothes, so she was going to have to start stripping. Shrugging the pack into her hands, she untucked her shirt as she ran. If she could pull the shirt over her head quickly, she'd only have to contend with scrambling out of her pants as a beetle. If the denim proved too awkward, she could just hunker down and hide.

She could do this.

She could make it.

A puff of air brushed the back of her neck and a thin blade pricked her skin. It barely grazed her, but, an instant later, she lost the feeling in her legs. They would no longer obey her. Stumbling, she fell forward onto her hands.

Shit, Theo thought as she went down, *maybe they were Ninja Suits, after all.*

Determination and fear had her pulling herself onward with her hands like a spastic marine, but it was painfully slow. A suited man caught up to her in no time. He grabbed a handful of her sweatshirt. Lifting her part way up, he dragged Theo a few feet back up the hall. With an unceremonious shove, he propped her up against the wall where she slumped like a rag doll.

Snatching her bag, he unzipped it so he could look inside.

From where he'd put her, Theo had a clear view of his face and the hallway entrance. His face was so broad it looked comical, or like one of those gargoyle faces they carved in stone on old buildings with the wide, oval mouths and tongues hanging out. Behind him three more suits entered the hallway. The leader was a tall, athletic woman with close-cropped golden-dark hair. Her skin was the color of hazelnuts.

"Is it in there?" she asked the wide-faced man.

He shook his head. "Change of clothes, couple of books. Money."

The woman knelt in front of Theo, grabbed the front of her shirt and pulled her forward. She had fangs, like a cat, and golden eyes, and she smelled like copper and blood.

"Where are the items you stole?" she asked.

"Nowhere near here," Theo slurred. She overplayed the difficulty she had in talking because feeling was returning slowly to her legs. If she could stall for long enough, maybe she could get up and run. Or, if she waited and didn't tell them where their stuff was, they'd probably take her somewhere and tie her up. As weird as it sounded, that was preferable; they were bound to leave her alone at some point and that would give her another opportunity to change into a smaller form and slip away. Theo just prayed they didn't feel the need to rough her up too badly first.

Keeping Theo in an upright sitting pose with one hand, the woman put the other hand on Theo's throat. She felt the prick of claws rather than fingernails in the soft skin under her chin.

"I will take you apart very slowly," the woman said in a purring tone.

Fear hit Theo like an icy undertow that dragged her reason down into darkness. She flailed and struggled, trying to squirm away, but the woman pressed back and down, pinning Theo to the ground by her throat and closing off her airway. Giving up the pretense of being help-less, Theo clawed at the woman's arm and at her face. Unimpressed, the woman caught Theo's wrist in her iron grip and twisted until tears rolled down Theo's face.

The service door at the end of the hall opened with a whine and a cold voice said, "Take your hands off her."

Even with lack of oxygen blurring her vision, Theo recognized that voice: Sabel, her sister.

The hand on her throat eased, but didn't let go.

Theo gulped air and tipped her head back to try to see what was going on. From her perspective on the floor, she first saw four pairs of boots: one black and heavy, one brown and well-worn, one a gray cowboy style under casual slacks, and the foremost pair sleek, black and delicate. She glanced up the skinny legs. Sabel looked down at her with eyes like gray thunderclouds in ivory skin that anger had turned the color of ice.

She was really here.

It hadn't just been a wish or a memory.

Beside Sabel stood two women and a man. A short, dark woman wore the huge boots. The other woman was tall and broad with spiky short blond hair and a cute leather jacket that did not in any way match her worn boots but looked all the better for it. The man seemed to be American Indian—smartly dressed, handsome, white-haired. Together, they all looked pretty capable, but were still way outnumbered by the suits.

One of the suits reached into his coat and flicked his hand out, throwing something Theo couldn't see. Sabel raised her hand and whispered a word. Everyone seemed to wait for something to happen, but nothing did.

The suit and his companion reached into their coats. This time they appeared to be reaching for knives. Theo clearly heard the sound of metal ringing out of sheaths, but when their hands came into view, nothing was visible in them. Knives she couldn't see? Behind them, two more of the suits had arrived and when they saw the front two draw, they did the same.

Sabel inhaled deeply, as though taking in more than air. When she spoke her voice resonated like it was part of some funky subwoofer, half-heard, half-felt. Her words were a command: "Hold your positions."

Theo's body froze. So did everyone else in the hallway.

Sabel knelt and prized the woman's hand off Theo's sweatshirt. The woman's eyes were blazing, but she didn't—or couldn't—move.

Magic.

Sabel has just used *magic.*

All this stuff had both fascinated and scared the shit out of Theo, but, now…. Now she felt betrayed.

"I knew it," Theo hissed as Sabel and the blond woman muscled her a few feet down the hall.

Theo never understood it, but she'd felt it. The way Sabel had closed off from her. It was like that fucking snowman song in "Frozen." No wonder that movie had made Theo cry like a baby. It was them, only for real.

All these years Theo had thought she was alone. Sixteen of her twenty-two years spent in wonder, fear, loneliness—all punctuated by fact that at the age of six Theo had *known*, no matter what Sabel said, that she could not be the only one in the family with magic.

Sisters were supposed to be close like that.

Share secrets.

Not keep them from each other.

CHAPTER SIX

GABE JUST RUNS (UNTIL HE CAN'T ANYMORE)

Gabe ran until he ran out of breath. Even though, a half a block away from the clinic it was pretty obvious no one was coming after him, Gabe ran and ran and ran, like, maybe he could outrun the terror that had settled deep in his gut.

Either he was insane or demons were real.

He was beginning to think maybe the answer was both.

Leaning on his knees and sucking air in gulps, Gabe tried to figure out where he was. He didn't know San Francisco terribly well yet. Unlike the natives, Gabe couldn't yet navigate by hills and landmarks. Was that Twin Peaks just over there? No idea, but he thought he might be near the Castro. A limping walk to the intersection confirmed that the congested thoroughfare in front of him was, in fact, Market Street. The cross street appeared to be Eagle.

The nice thing about 'living' at the public library was that Gabe had read a lot about the town he was living in. Tourist books had a lot of helpful information about cheap and free places you could hang out. If he remembered rightly, Gabe thought that somewhere just up Eagle was a steep, grassy park: Kite Hill? Supposedly good for dog walking, seeing the sights? Gabe didn't care so much about that, he just needed a place where no one would harass him while he sat for a while and regrouped.

Focusing on finding the park entrance helped Gabe forget about insane demons for the moment. He only had to go a few blocks before he found a few helpful signs and a rock-lined path at the end of a small, scrubby garden. The park didn't look like much, just a steep dun-colored knoll, but path was clearly marked and wooden railway tie steps lead him up. The earlier rain made the steps treacherous. Nearly worn-out Converse sneakers weren't the best hiking gear, but Gabe took it slowly. Without many tree breaks, the wind cut at him. It was easy to see how this hill got its name. It'd be a great place to fly kites.

As he climbed, Gabe tried to distract himself with the increasingly amazing view. Downtown glittered like a glass and metal jewel below. It was gorgeous, if you ignored the massive black pulse of goo over the shelters in the Tenderloin and that strange interlaced silvery net that seemed to swell up over the whole city like a protective dome. Holes had been torn in the mesh and Gabe swore he could almost hear a hiss, like air leaving a tire... or a snakes squirming to get in, to breech the defenses.

La, la, la.

Nope. He'd just turn away from that strange scene. A few families in the park, who chased after barking dogs and flapping white kites. With the sweat of his hair drying in the wind, Gabe felt conspicuously dirty and obviously homeless. Thankfully, no one took much notice of him as he found a scrubby native pine tree and pulled himself up into its sheltering branches.

He used to love to climb trees as a boy in West Virginia. Tall branches were an escape from bullies and their taunts. The odor of pine pitch was the smell of safety.

Now that he had some time to think, Gabe tried to parse out what had happened back at the clinic. The snake-eyed nurse hadn't done him any harm. As far as Gabe could tell, she never even tried to pursue him after he freaked out. Did that mean that, in his twisted psyche, the snake-eyed demons were agents of good?

He really wished he could get a handle on his mind's cosmology. From his reading about schizophrenia, Gabe had come to the conclusion that from the point of view of the mentally ill person all their crazy had an internal logic, a system that made sense... at least to them. Why, then, did he not even have the first clue who he should trust? His gut had said: snake-eyes equals bad. Had that been the right assumption? She hadn't reached for anything bad in her purse, just a business card.

What would it have said, if he'd taken it? Gabe regretted his impulse because, if he had the card right now in his hand, he might have some kind of tangible evidence. He's at least have something in his possession, something physical, that he could hand to someone he knew to be sane, like a librarian without one of those moaning clouds, and ask them what it said. Then at the very least, he could confirm that it was, or wasn't, whatever he thought it was.

And what if it was somehow... real. Like, what if it had been the address to a secret club of demon seers?

Gabe would seriously kill for some answers right now.

Answers and a sandwich.

The running had worn him out. He felt tiredness seeping into his bones. Before he knew it, he was asleep.

Songs filled his dreams, the song of metal and the Periodic Chart of Elements, and a song like a Greek Chorus, of a thousand women's voices singing, 'Seer, seeker, we seek our seer. See us some secrets, secrets of seeing...'

Gabe woke when a strong gust of wind shook him from his branch. He fell to the ground hard, but somehow remembered his martial arts training and kept his head tucked up against his chest. His back ached like a son of a bitch; he'd smacked the small of it into an exposed and knotted root. Picking himself up with a groan, Gabe looked around the emptied park. The families and their dogs and kites had all gone home with the setting of the sun.

Rubbing his face and shouldering his backpack, Gabe headed back down the hill. Honestly, he hated to leave the shelter of the pine, but his stomach had other ideas. He needed to find a soup kitchen.

Or he was going to have to hustle up dinner in some other way.

Dumpster diving.

Or, failing that, he'd have to fall back on old... tricks.

:: :: ::

Gabe missed 'last call' at the Tenderloin's soup kitchens because some old fart Muni driver decided he'd had enough of fare dodgers and threatened to call the cops over a measly seventy-five cents. Gabe had the money, but the guy was such a dick about it that it felt better to just flip him off and hoof it. He should've known that stubbornness was it's own reward, however. It was the sort of thing Asshole would have done, or those fucktards at military academy.

Long ago, Gabe had determined not to be like those men. But, somehow anger and pride always roiled just below the surface, like one of those black blobby monsters—hovering, hovering, ready to devour him.

The bad luck just kept coming.

Gabe tried to organize a dumpster diving party with some of the other latecomers in the hopes that someone else might know the good spots were mis-ordered pizza got tossed out, still piping hot (and fresh enough not to be too gross). All he got for his efforts were suspicious stares and a lot of "fuck off, creep" in several languages, including the universal single finger salute.

That whole series of exchanges depressed him and spiked his anger again.

And now....

Now he could barely see.

The whole of the 'Loin was covered in blackness. It was like pushing through some kind of photonegative of the famous San Francisco fog, except that the tendrils of smoke were alive and ready wrap around him, like tentacles of some wispy, haunted beast. Whispers floated everywhere, hissing of despair and loneliness and aching hunger.

It was hard to even see to cross the street.

A testimony to how hard up the 'Loin was, people solicited him as he hurried by. "Spare change, buddy?" and "Looking for a date, sweetheart?" called out from allies so covered in black gunk that they looked like gaping, open maws of a black hole.

For the second time today, Gabe ran. He ran for the light—a haze he could see at the edge of the intersection. Why he ever thought venturing inside this pit was a good idea, he'd never know

As he walked down the hill toward the light, he hummed a strange tune to himself, "See us some secrets of seeing, seer of secrets: Sangkesh, Suhirin, Sliver Song, Stealing Secrets.... Shaitan."

And a pathway cleared....

CHAPTER SEVEN

ERIN SINGS METAL
(NO, NOT THAT KIND)

Someone somewhere was singing her father's songs, and they brought Erin back from the swirling emptiness of the drugs. She was able to claw her way up to memories....

:: :: ::

Your daddy was a real devil, that's what they always said to her. Grammy would hold up a fresh baked cookie and tell Erin that in order to have it, she needed to recite a passage from the Bible (her choice!) and renounced her father, Satan.

That last one took the flavor out of every bite because Erin remembered her father as a handsome, dark-haired man with a broad smile and an infectious laugh. Even though Erin was too young to remember any of it; she'd heard the story often enough. It was a miracle you survived the crash, honey, the one that took our beloved daughter, your mother.

The never mentioned her dad. Except when they cursed.

She had his eyes, they said, and they didn't mean it as a compliment, though Erin always loved the slight epicanthic fold and rich, dark eyelashes she'd inherited from him. Even if Grammy had allowed her to wear any, she'd never have needed mascara or eyeliner because they were so thick and bold.

When they sawed off her horns, they'd made her repeat through the blinding pain, "Get thee behind me, Satan."

The men who poked and prodded her now kept talking about Satan, too, but there was something different about the way they said it, like they hung on to the word too long at the beginning, making it sound like there was an 'h' in there. Shaitan. Satan. It didn't matter. Anytime that word came out, it meant pain for Erin.

Satan was her curse.

The curse her father had left her. As if it wasn't fucked up enough that he'd up and died on her, taking Mama with him in the fiery car crash. It was the gift that kept on giving, because Grammy and Gramps... well, she shouldn't be ungrateful. They loved her, didn't they? They said so all the time and they cried whenever they cut her, reminding Erin they were only doing it for the good of her eternal soul.

Yet, somehow all this "good for her" always hurt so bad.

"Yes," the white coat said, "Just take your medicine. It's good for you."

As he came close to her, Erin could hear one of her father's songs. This one sang of a tungsten carbide wedding ring. Despite the pain she knew she was about to feel, Erin smiled wanly to herself. Someone somewhere else was singing her song: not getting the words right—no, not at all, but the feeling was there, the melody.

This was something she could use. The song could fill her heart and let her survive almost anything. Under her breath, she started to hum. As she did, an image began to form in her mind, take shape—a hexagonal lattice of metal atoms, one a-top another, growing, building... coming into her.

The jab of the needle nearly broke the complex song she wove. But, she finished before the 'medicine' took away her energy. She'd fight this one, though. She'd push back, using what she'd just absorbed, and, with luck, sleep pain free tonight.

It was *evil*, Erin knew it, but a necessary one.

As she slunk off into the dark to let the song do its work, Erin wondered when the 'doctor' would notice his wedding ring was gone.

She smiled. Joined somehow with that other voice, her song was strong again.

CHAPTER EIGHT

KITTY BRINGS A KNIFE AND MEMORIES

Packing for the move to Lily's school, Kitty found the folding knife that Blake had given her. The handle was scuffed but the blade was perfectly edged as if new. Blake had carried it for years as one of her boot knives and given it to Kitty during survival training as a lucky charm. Didn't work. But she kept it because it was so Blake.

For all that she loathed the Hunters' School, not every day was awful; there were people she wanted to remember. Kitty kept the knife, with its slender, deadly blade to remind herself that when Suhirin asked her to research something, she was doing it for real people, people like Blake and the others from the school, and not just because she had some crazy, impossible hope of impressing her mother.

It had been four years since Kitty's expulsion from the school forced an end to her mostly secret relationship with Blake. She'd been thinking about her a lot lately.

Maybe she didn't have to wait and ask Suhirin about her classmates. If Blake wasn't out on a clandestine assignment, maybe she was reachable now. Setting the knife on her bedside table, Kitty logged into the Sangkesh intranet, the Keshnet, to see if Blake had any kind of current contact info. She wasn't supposed to use the Keshnet to access information about field operatives, but she'd been on it so much lately for Suhirin that no one would notice.

The record was kept only under the nickname "Blake" and contained a single option for contact: a Skype name.

Kitty pulled up Skype and tried it.

The app rang and then clicked over to a black screen the resolved slowly, blurrily to show Blake's olive-tan face and tousled raven-black hair. She didn't have her contacts in; her eyes were their natural gray-gold-malachite with vertical pupils like a cat or a fox.

"Cute Kitty," she said. "You got my psychic message."

"What?"

Telepathy wasn't a power any of the Sangkesh had. Of course "psychic message" was a figure of speech ...

"I was thinking I needed to call you," Blake said. "How the fuck are you?"

"Uh. Hey, I'm okay." Kitty got tongue-tied because seeing Blake suddenly like this made her want to reach through the wires and signals, across the distance, and kiss her again. She'd dated some girls in college, but all human, so Blake was her first lover and the only one who'd been part-demon like Kitty. She hadn't realized how badly she'd missed Blake until now.

"Your mom again?" Blake asked.

Trouble with Suhirin was a much easier answer than: *gods, I miss you way more than I ever imagined.* Kitty told her, "She's sending me to Lily to get more training." Blake would know what all that meant.

"How many other students? Any chance there are three of them?"

"It's just supposed to be me."

"Good," Blake said.

"Why good?" Kitty asked.

As they talked, she was trying to get some glimpses of the room behind Blake. Tan walls, part of a curtain. Was it a hotel? Was Blake safe or at least as safe as she could be? How far away was she?

Blake said, "There was something about four people, two witches, two demons. A Shaitan said it and it bugged me. Hang on, I wrote it down."

Blake left the screen showing more tan wall and Kitty heard rustling, digging through a suitcase most likely, and then she was back, looking puzzled at a piece of paper.

"Can't read my own code," she said.

Kitty shook her head. "I'm supposed to be the one who overcomplicates things. What does it say?"

"Sing a song secrets, the song of silver," Blake said. "What the hell's the song of silver?"

"A person's surname, maybe?"

Blake turned the page 90 degrees and squinted at it. "W-74. Does that mean anything?"

"Tungsten," Kitty said automatically, though she was sure that notation could mean other things as well. "Is there anything else?"

"I wrote 'Re' like in regarding, but there's nothing after it. I still can't write while running very well."

Kitty almost said "nobody can" but realized one of these years Blake might master that skill. Instead she asked, "Where is this from?"

"An assignment in the Pacific Northwest to track down a Shaitan, big one. He'd split but there was a flunky. I bound him but he was going on about all this – about how the four must be brought together, two demons with two witches, and the song of secrets, a bunch of Shaitan nonsense. But you know how it is when they get going and you can feel there's this thread of truth? It felt like some heavy, bad truth so I thought maybe you'd know."

"Not yet," Kitty said. "Send me that page. I'll work on it."

"You're a champ," Blake replied and her grin said a lot more than the words.

"Don't be silly," Kitty told her, grinning like crazy back at her.

Kitty tried to remember the last time they'd talked, maybe a year ago in passing. Had Blake been single? Was she now? Could she be anywhere near the Pacific Northwest? Because if she was, Kitty would literally drive all night to get to her.

"Seriously, are you okay?" Blake asked.

Kitty shook her head. "I'll let you know but yeah, I think so. I'm safe."

Blake's grin went lopsided. "If I need to come down there and kick some asses …?"

"Where are you?"

"Izmir," Blake said.

Not only was that not drivable, but Kitty couldn't even pretend she could come up with some excuse to fly to Europe and "run into" Blake by accident. Izmir was just too damned far and she'd never have a reason to go there.

"Next time you're in the States," Kitty said.

"I'll come see you," Blake said. "If I can … when I can."

Blake ended the video call, but those last words of hers sounded like a promise and left Kitty grinning. What time was it now in Izmir? What would Blake be doing? Was she still sitting there, like Kitty, staring at the blank screen and thinking of her?

A few seconds later, she'd sent Kitty an image of her scribbled page of notes:

2 demons, 2 witches
Sing a song of secrets
Sing a song of silver
W-74
Re

It reminded her of something, but what?

Her fingers found the handle of the knife she'd set down and traced the titanium grip. As it warmed, the smooth metal almost felt like Blake's skin under her thumb.

Only Blake could get her to actually like a weapon. But not in way she'd ever use it. She put the knife in the box labeled "Lily's School."

She'd just hidden it under her favorite flannel pajama pants when Dad knocked politely at her door. From behind the wood, he called, "Papa needs your help again, hon. Hurry or he might strain his back."

Kitty left her packing to go help. Papa was notoriously pigheaded when it came to things he was sure he could lift. This was why he had at least one herniated disk.

"What is it this time?" she asked, and tried not to smile, because, seriously, one day the fool was going to do some serious damage to himself.

"My pot of rosemary, the one in the Greek amphora? I was talking about moving it to a sunnier spot, but I didn't think he'd just start wrestling with the thing! It's huge!"

Sure enough, when they reached the garden, there was Papa, hunched over super-awkwardly, trying to lift/roll a pot half as tall as he was. Kitty put her hands on her hips and said, "Give it up, old man. The Cavalry has arrived."

Just in time, too. Sweat already stained Papa's oxford shirt at the pits. His tie was askew, making him look less like a computer engineer and more like an overdressed gardener. Setting the pot down with a grunt, he glared at Dad. "Tattletale."

As tall and broad as Papa was, many people would have shrunk from that hard stare. But, given his past association with Suhirin, Dad apparently had some kind of affinity to and immunity from withering glances. "Sticks and stones, dove." Dad said, as he got up on tiptoes to give Papa a peck on the check. "Let our capable daughter do this little thing. What's the point of having children if you can can't get them to do your dirty work for you?" he teased. "Besides, you know she's butcher than the both of us together."

That was patently not true. She was plenty strong but that hardly made her butch, and Papa was one of those guys who looked like, in another life, he could be playing professional football. Except of course, that he was a klutz, like the typical nerd, and had zero coordination. He still worked out, though, and so was quite strong.... For a human.

Lifting the rosemary was easy work. Between Suhirin's blood and Dad's, she was a bit more than half-demon. Of course, she also inherited the pointy ears, which she mostly kept hidden under her hair, and the fangs. When people noticed her ears, Kitty had always managed to deflect them with a casual, "Yeah, weird, huh? I was born that way. They're a defect, but my folks thought I looked cute, like an elf, so they never fixed them." Her fangs? Most people never even gave them much more than a double take, since they were only slightly longer than some people's canines.

She'd been lucky. Most of the Sangkesh were only part-demon and had inherited traits they couldn't easily brush off or hide, like horns or hooves or tails. They had to be surgically altered or kept out of sight of humanity.

Kitty had heard that Lily wore contact lenses over her bird-like irises, caps on her pointed teeth and heavy boots to hide the fact that her feet resembled talons. Lily came from the Eagle lineage, not Lion like Kitty and her mother. Dad was a Lion too, but all he got were funky toenails and the barest hint of catlike points to his ears.

In total there were eight lineages of the Sangkesh but one had died out and most Sangkesh were now a blend so that only occasionally would you meet someone with pure characteristics that said: Lion, Eagle, Bull, Stag, Cat, Goat, or Fox. Kitty had seen students at the Hunters' School with goat eyes and cat claws, or bull horns and fangs. If you were the product of multiple lineages, the characteristics you got could be pretty random.

Papa shook his head, watching her. With a bright smile he said, "Show off."

Dad poked Papa in the ribs and said, "You know she's not. That's not even a quarter of her strength."

Papa agreed with a loving nod. "Too bad you inherited my nerdiness through osmosis, girl. You could be Wonder Woman."

It would help, too, if she didn't fail *all the things.*

But, Kitty pasted on a smile, "I'd look awesome in spandex."

"And a tiara!" Dad added.

"Yeah, but skip the bracelets," Papa said. "They always looked too much like manacles for my taste, and you don't need 'slave girl' accessories."

Dad bopped Papa on the arm lightly, "Maybe she's into that sort of thing. It's none of our business."

"That's not what I meant!" Papa roared in his joking way. "I'm talking about black pride here…."

Kitty smiled. It was like this every night. They'd probably argue in this kind of loving, teasing way all the way through dinner. Papa reminding them all about his youthful political activism, telling taller and taller tales about arrests and protests, and Dad just nodding happily along while slipping another spoonful of whatever awesome thing he'd concocted for dinner on to their plates while no one was looking.

It was going to be so hard to leave.

But she needed to do this. It was her last ditch effort to be someone of use to the demon hunting community. Even if she just wanted to be a mathematician like Papa, she had to do this for the names, all the people whose lives she could stand beside.

"Come on, enough of all this," Dad said finally, "I've made a nice goodbye dinner for our Kit-Kat."

:: :: ::

Later that night as she was trying to fall asleep, she got the knife out of the box and slid it under her pillow, curling her hand around it. The titanium handle reminded her of Blake's notes. The song of silver, what was that? In all her reading, she'd never come across a reference to a song of silver or a song of secrets.

Shaitan demons lied all the time, made things up just to screw with your head. It could be nothing. But Blake had pretty good instincts. If she thought it was important then Kitty had to figure it out.

Silver ... titanium ... tungsten ... the knife and the words blurred in her mind on the edge of sleep.

Re ... re: what?

Rhenium, she thought. But sleep came and covered up the word.

CHAPTER NINE

THEO WOULD PREFER MORE SEX IN YOUR VIOLENCE

The scary, clawed woman exploded into motion, lunging forward.

Sabel's magic must have worn off, because suits started to run toward Theo. Instantly, the blond woman swung into them, throwing punches. Sabel left Theo's side to move with the blond, seeming to flicker in and out of sight.

More magic.

So much magic.

The short, dark-haired woman with the big boots stepped in front of Theo, blocking her from the clutches of the scary woman. The white-haired, brown-skinned man leaned back against the wall, like he was settling in to watch a good show. Indicating the woman in the heavy boots, he said to Theo: "Smart money's on Lily."

Okay, boots = Lily.

Lily and scary lady circled each other, like a scene from Crouching Tiger, Hidden Dragon. When the scary lady struck, she moved too fast to follow. Yet, somehow, Lily was never where her strikes landed. Lily flowed in a slow, inevitable circle around her taller opponent. Finally, Lily struck with one spinning boot to drop the scary lady. She rolled onto her, like an alligator. Lily's arms folded around the scary woman's neck and shoulder, locked together. Her legs wrapped the woman's body tightly.

Scary lady was down.

It had all happened so fast.

At the end of the hall, the suits had Sabel and the blond on their knees, guns pointed at them, but they looked uncertain when they saw Lily get scary lady in a headlock.

"Call them off," Lily said.

"Fuck you," scary lady said.

"You don't want to see what Ben and Abraxas can do," Lily said. "Call them off."

The white hair guy pushed himself off the wall. Apparently he was either 'Ben' or that Greek-sounding name Theo had never heard before.

Scary lady seemed a little nervous about one of the names, but she pursed her lips and said: "No."

Lily sighed and looked up at the suits. "Let Ana and Sabel go," she said. "Or I'll knock Suhirin out and we'll make you. We really don't want to kill anyone over this."

"Don't you—" the scary lady that Lily had called Suhirin started to say, but Lily closed the hold over her throat and choked off the words.

The suit standing over Sabel stepped back. Eventually, the one with the blond, who must be Ana, did the same. Ana and Sabel got up carefully and walked back to Theo's side of the hallway.

The paralysis was wearing off and Theo sat up. Adrenaline, fear and anger still coursed through her, making her whole body shake. That, and the gut-twisting sense of deep betrayal.

"You lied to me," she spat the words at Sabel, and then louder, "You lied!"

Sabel looked surprised to suddenly find herself the target of Theo's anger. But, in a flat voice she said: "I never lied to you."

That was so Sabel, wasn't it? Probably true in some hair being split way, but fuck that. Theo snarled: "You told me you couldn't do magic. You lied. All that time. When I was six, I asked you."

Sabel bent down to brush her fingers along Theo's hair. "Theodosia, I never told you I couldn't do magic. You asked if I turned into a bird, but I didn't. And," she looked around at the tense situation, "You know, this really isn't the time to discuss it."

In the middle of the hall, Lily was slowly relaxing her hold on Suhirin. They untangled and stood up, looking like two jungle cats unsure if the fight was really over. The suits milled around until Suhirin waved them off. They went out into the mouth of the hallway, leaving them alone.

"You know what she took from us," Suhirin told Lily. "It's not safe out in the world."

Lily turned to Theo and asked, "Will you tell them where it is?"

Lily looked way too much like a hip middle-aged mom to have just taken down Suhirin, who was built like an Olympic athlete, and that almost made Theo want to answer her. But she didn't. Because what was 'it,' besides obviously one of the items she'd stolen? Anyway, her hurt about Sabel was too important.

"I saw you," Theo told Sabel, only barely managing to keep the sobs from her voice. "You turned into a bird and flew away."

Hobbling to her feet, Theo grabbed the front of Sabel's jacket and shook her. Her sister stared at her with eyes as gray as a rain-saturated sky.

"That's not what you saw," Sabel said as her fingers gently loosened Theo's grip on her jacket. Stepping away, she said quietly. "I sent my vision out from me like a bird, but my body never changed. I can't turn into a bird. I don't know any witch who can."

That made no sense.

"I can," Theo said, dropping her now-empty hands to her sides.

"You, what?" Sabel asked.

"I can turn into a bird," Theo told her. "But, you wouldn't know that because you left me. You showed me it was possible and then you just left. And you lied about it."

"Natural witch, untrained," Suhirin said in a growling voice, from across the room. "Dangerous. And," she paused and looked sharply at Sabel, "Not under anyone's protection."

Lily added, "That doesn't explain how she got in to your safe house undetected."

So that's what the threesome's house was. But, Theo didn't answer that Lily's implied question either. None of these people needed to know her secrets. Hell, Theo wasn't sure she even knew the real answer to that question.

"And I asked you about the Latin," Theo said to Sabel, because this was the stuff that mattered to her. "And why you went out at night. I asked you so many different ways. You never told me."

Sabel looked away. Like she always had, whenever Theo asked about magic. Ana, the blond, shot Theo a sympathetic look, but came over to squeeze Sabel's hand.

"We'll take her back to the compound and you can pick her up when she tells us where the items are," Suhirin said.

"You'll take her over your dead body," Sabel told her, sounding very unlike the sister that Theo was used to.

"Doubtful," Suhirin replied. "You can't take her; you'll just let her go. And if you do, I'll find her again and you won't be there to save her. But if she tells us now, she can go with you."

Theo considered the hard face of Suhirin.

Who were all these people and how badly did they want to hurt her? What would they really do if she told them where their precious items were? Once they had those, they had no reason really not to just kill her—and when Suhirin said she would take her apart, she sounded like she'd really enjoy it.

If these items were so valuable, maybe they were the key to finally getting people to tell her the truth. So far they'd already forced Sabel to show her magic.

And that was leverage Theo would keep.

"I have no guarantee that I'm safe from you if I give you your things," Theo said. "No deal."

"You would have my word," Suhirin said.

"Scary Lady, I don't know you from jack and you didn't exactly charm me in our first minutes together."

The woman with the blonde, spiky hair, Ana, snickered and then coughed lightly to try to cover it up. Sabel glanced back at her and the barest smile passed over her mouth. Must be the new girlfriend then. Was she some kind of magical too?

"I'll take her," Lily said with a long sigh brushing out between the words.

"You?" Suhirin asked.

"I'm already fostering Kitty and I'll have a second student if Ben can find the missing girl, I don't see that a third would be much extra burden," Lily said. "She needs an opportunity to learn enough that she's not a danger to herself."

"Won't she just run?" Ana, the girlfriend, asked, sounding like that's exactly what she'd do in Theo's shoes. Theo definitely liked her.

"Lily will put a binding on her, won't you?" Suhirin said.

"A what?" Theo asked.

"Like a magical house arrest bracelet with a range of a few miles," Lily said.

That sounded good to Theo. There wasn't a chain, cuff or bracelet she'd found yet that she couldn't change form and get out of.

"That sounds fair," she said. "What's it made out of?"

Lily looked her up and down and then cast a glance at Sabel.

"If I understand what I'm seeing in terms of how your abilities work," Sabel said. "It's going to have to be fashioned in ink, under the skin, like a tattoo."

"Oh, shit," Theo said before she could stop herself.

Everyone laughed, even Suhirin, Scary Lady.

"I'll come for tea when I'm in town, Lily," Suhirin said. "Just so I can experience the profound gratitude of not having to live in that house. And the next time you come at me, I won't pull my punches."

Theo had the impression that Suhirin hadn't pulled them this time either, but whatever, some people just had to save face like that.

"Wonderful," Lily said to the retreating back of Suhirin.

"Did we win?" Theo asked.

The white-haired guy nodded but Sabel said, "No. How you make more enemies in a few weeks than I could in a decade just escapes me."

"Well if you'd taught me about magic ... "

"This is going to be a long drive back," Sabel said sounding pained.

Theo was secretly looking forward to it. Despite what Sable said, they *had* won. Or, at least, Theo had. She hadn't had to give up her secrets or her stash. And, maybe, just maybe she could have a sister again... one who she could share magic with.

:: :: ::

Theo should have known better. The car ride went from awkward to awful. She expected Sabel would yell at her, but she didn't. She kept looking over at Theo like she was trying to figure out if Theo was a body-snatched alien or something worse.

The girlfriend, Ana, had opted to drive back with Lily and Ben, understanding they needed a little alone time. Or maybe she'd been with

Sabel long enough that she knew to get out of the way when Sabel was icy-pissed like this.

"Help me understand," Sabel said in a cool, measured voice. "You can turn into a bird and you used this power to break into a Sangkesh vault—without knowing the first thing about demons or witches or magic—and you don't even know what you stole?"

Theo couldn't control the roll of her eyes, nor could she resist the opportunity to jab at her own open wound: "Maybe I would've had a clue, if you ever told me anything."

"And you're angry at me because at the age of fourteen I decided it was a bad idea to tell a human six-year-old that magic exists?"

Theo hated the way Sabel could ask a series of infuriating questions that were really statements. Crossing her arms in front of her chest, Theo turned her head to watch the Palo Verde trees of the Sacramento Valley roll by. The spring had brought out their distinctive yellow flowers.

"I left when you were ten," Sabel went on and queued up another non-question. "Considering how mature you are now, do you think at the wise old age of ten you'd have been ready for that information?"

She let the words drop into the silence between them and left it there. Theo heard the subtext loud-and-clear, anyway. Sabel still didn't think she could handle this; she still thought Theo was too immature.

"Fuck off," Theo said.

Sabel gave her a glance that seemed to say, 'See?'

Silence, strained and uncomfortable, was the hallmark of their mother; Sabel had inherited it in abundance. Theo took after the loud, blustering tones of their father. Both parents and their two brothers, who now ran the family businesses, spent the bulk of their time in Greece.

Theo stretched out her toes, trying to shake off the last of the pins and needles. If they couldn't talk about that, maybe they could talk about something else, Theo decided. "So you're a witch, right? That's a thing. Please tell me that this new school thing is like Hogwart's with chocolate frogs and magic wands."

That, at least, made a smile ghost across Sabel's cold expression. "I'll bring you some chocolate frogs. But, Theo, this isn't about pranks and jokes. Suhirin could have killed you."

"I was like two seconds from going beetle and getting away," Theo said.

"Beetle means what?" Sabel asked.

There was a break in the traffic and they were able to speed ahead until they hit the next knot of cars.

"That I turn into a beetle."

"You … it's not just the bird?"

"You're supposed to know about this stuff!" Theo protested. She'd been trying to keep the emotion out of her voice like Sabel was so good at doing. But she failed like always. "Just tell me. Just anything you know about all this, for once. Anything, goddamn it!"

More silence, more traffic.

"Give me some time," Sabel said in her usual clipped way and then took a look, shaky breath and went on, words fast and loud, "I just saw my little sister almost get killed. I keep this away from the family; I keep *myself* away from the family, precisely so this won't happen. Now it has. What am I supposed to do with you now, Theodosia? How on earth can I keep you safe?"

Her voice shook at the edge of tears and Theo had to look away out of the window so she wouldn't cry. She'd wanted so much to be real sisters, whatever that was, but hearing Sabel hurt and afraid about her, she couldn't handle that.

She set her shoulders and looked at Sabel.

"Who were those people?" she asked to get them on a marginally easier track. "Who was Scary Lady and, what was it? Some funeral flower?"

Sabel gave her a little sidelong glance. There was water in her eyes but she wasn't crying. Theo couldn't think of a time when she'd seen Sabel cry and she for sure didn't want to go there while they were stuck in a car together.

"Lily?" Sabel asked.

"Yeah, her."

"Lily is an ally. Scary Lady is Suhirin. She's a protector demon, not that you'd know that to meet her."

Theo tried to get the words to make more sense than they did but finally asked, "Isn't protector demon an oxymoron?"

"Nobody hunts demons better than other demons," Sabel said. "All the demon hunters are demons or part-demon like Lily."

"Is she on the same side as Scary Suhirin? They didn't seem to be."

"Lily is semi-retired from the same organization."

That made Theo laugh. "Damn, I'd hate to see what she was like if she's out of her prime now."

"Exactly," Sabel said in a way that actually made Theo smile, like maybe they were connecting the way she'd wanted them to after all. "Even when Lily ran the demon hunters, she and Suhirin had philosophical differences."

Like Suhirin wanted to kill me and Lily didn't, Theo thought. But she didn't say it, worried that it would make Sabel tear up again.

"And you work for?"

"An order of witches," Sabel said.

"So it's like the demons are the CIA and the bad demons are, well, the bad guys and the witches are the FBI?"

Sabel thought about that for a few minutes. "Pretty close," she said. "But we're the CIA. The demons can be the FBI." She flashed Theo a wan smile and added, "I was in touch with mother earlier when I was looking for you. We should call her and tell her you're safe. I'll put it through on the car speakers."

Theo groaned. Seriously, they were calling home? "I don't want to talk to Mom right now." *I want to talk to you,* Theo thought, but left unsaid.

"You want to go with bad breakup or fell in with a rough group of kids and got caught holding stolen goods?"

"Do the second one," Theo said, wishing, just once, they could tell the truth.

When the conversation started, Theo listened to Sabel spin lies with the ease of a spider building a web. Hell, by the end of it, Theo half-believed it herself. Theo'd always thought of Sabel as the good girl.

Maybe that was a lie, too.

People were so... hard.

She almost wished she were a beetle again. Beetles had it easy. They didn't have to deal with family or any of this shit.

:: :: ::

Theo didn't remember falling asleep, but she woke to Sabel's gentle nudge and: "We're here."

Blinking the sleep from her eyes, Theo glanced around. She wasn't sure why, but Theo had expected that the magical tattooing would take place in… well, a tattoo parlor or, at the very least, in someone's house. Instead, they seemed to have pulled into a narrow back alley in some corporate part of downtown San Francisco.

Sabel's Mercedes looked out of place beside the scummy, graffiti-scrawled, industrial-sized dumpster. Theo stepped out, but held on to the door. The alley stunk of piss and industry. Smog caught the back of her throat.

The cars containing Suhirin and her thugs and Lily, Ana and the white-haired Ben pulled up behind them. The only other vehicle in the alley was a motorcycle, a Harley or one of those hardcore bikes. Theo got out of the car, feeling nervous for the first time since Sabel had shown up to the rescue.

When the car door shut, it closed with a kind of finality that made the back of Theo's knees itch. Theo's sensitive nose caught the acrid scent of sulfur mixed with danger, and she held back a shiver.

A rail-thin white guy with a shaved head swung the back door of the office building open for them. Though the evening air held a chill, he wore a white tee shirt. Theo could see yakuza-style sleeves of ink that shifted and changed every time she blinked. Seeing her, he smiled and whistled a strange tune under his breath.

Lily was two steps ahead of them stopped and lifted her nose, like she was sniffing the wind. "Sulfur?"

With that the shaved head guy's grin grew wider, more animalistic. Still looking only at Theo, he asked, "You ready for the Devil's ink?"

:: :: ::

Theo had at least hoped for a tattoo parlor of some sort. Instead, this whole weird crew had traipsed inside the office building: Suhirin, Lily, Theo, Sabel, Ana, Ben, the funky tattooist, and herself. The seven of them stood, unspeaking, waiting for the elevator to take them somewhere.

The lobby was as nondescript as such things often were. The floor was linoleum that had been polished into a dull gleam that spoke of too much traffic or a lazy janitorial staff. The walls were a riot of beige on beige. Palm trees stood sentry at the door in similarly dun-colored pots. Theo scanned the list of offices and their suite numbers hoping for a clue. Alas, none of them read: "Demon Lair, Suite 301" or even "Bob's Brilliant Tats!" Instead, they all had interchangeable names like "Business Solutions" and "Marketing Services."

Next to her, the tattooist hummed a song that, for some reason, sounded vaguely familiar to Theo. If it made any kind of sense, she would have said it was the song of the Periodic Table of Elements.

But that wasn't a real thing, was it?

The ding of the elevator bell made her jump.

Shit, when had she gotten this nervous? Even as she tried to retain some kind of cool, Theo glanced at Sabel. She wanted some reassurance from her sister that this was okay, because it felt really *not* okay.

Suhirin pressed the button for the fifth floor.

Theo actively had to resist the urge to start to babble incoherently, or worse ask Suhirin if she was enjoying the weather. In fact, she briefly considered turning into the Ironclad Beetle right now. She wanted to be small and unseen. No, truthfully, she wanted an escape. If they didn't already know she could transform, she'd do it with the hope that they'd figure she'd disappeared or something. Maybe if she held on strong enough, she could cling to the inside of her clothes while they shook them... Yeah, except Scary Lady wouldn't rest until they found her. Hell, the more time she spent in Suhirin's presence, the more Theo was convinced that if she did do the bug-in-clothes trick, Suhirin's solution would be to set the clothes on fire and wait for her to scuttle out in desperation—or something equally evil and ruthless.

Theo was trapped.

And there was Sabel, staring straight ahead, refusing to meet her eyes, like she was one of her jailors. Or did she see, in the cold set of Sabel's jaw, that she was some mix of afraid and angry?

Unable to take the silences, Theo turned to the tattooist and asked, "Is it going to hurt?"

He laughed at her. "It's a high-powered needle, sister."

She'd never had a tattoo before, but she wasn't stupid. "I meant the magic."

Again, Theo glanced to Sabel unconsciously. This time Sabel glanced back, though her lips stayed pressed together and her eyes narrowed. She shook her head a fraction, the international sign for, "Don't ask."

Theo rolled her eyes in return. It was a simple question. Couldn't she at least tell her baby sister it was going to be all right, that it wasn't going to hurt her, not permanently, anyway?

"Uh, speaking of tattoos," Theo said, "Is this permanent? I mean they usually are, aren't they?"

"No," Suhirin answered with authority. She seemed like the kind of woman used to issuing orders. She even stood like a soldier, stiff and erect. "The ink will fade once your instruction is complete. The spell we will weave is very complex. Lily and I discussed our terms during the drive. You will be excessively well cared for. Far more than I would have bothered for a thief."

Lily, who looked like a mess of curls and distraction next to Suhirin said, "You'll be able to transform. I would like to teach you more about that, once things are settled, if I can." For some reason, she glanced over her shoulder at where Ben stood, leaning back against the elevator wall, his arms crossed casually in front of his chest.

"You could just tell us where our items are," Suhirin said. "Then you would be as free as you like. Go anywhere and do … whatever it is your kind do."

Sail yachts and volunteer, Theo started to say, but the elevator door opened and Suhirin strode out, as if not expecting Theo to give any kind of answer. Well, that was fine.

At any rate, Theo was hoping to keep the stolen items hidden, as leverage.

Even though she wasn't sure what she planned to leverage, exactly, especially since it seemed like she was trading her freedom for…

For what, exactly?

Theo hung back in the elevator until Sabel passed, and she caught her hand.

"Is this a good idea?" Theo asked in a desperate whisper, squeezing tightly to her older sister's hand, begging for comfort. Sabel's cold fingers closed on hers like a vise.

"It's one solution to the problem."

The problem being, as always: Theo.

Theo flung her hand open, releasing Sabel with a push. "Fine, let's do this stupid thing."

Sabel said she was trying to help, trying to do the right thing, but this was what it always came down to, wasn't it? You're too wild, Theo. You act without thinking, Theo. Can't you be less impulsive, Theo? You've made things a mess again, Theo. You're the problem. Theo.

Fine, fix things and leave, like you always do, Theo thought bitterly

:: :: ::

The tattooing took hours.

And it fucking hurt.

A lot, though not the way Theo expected. You know when you scratch and scratch and it starts to hurt, and then you scratch a bit more and it stings like a son of a bitch but it feels almost good?

It was like that.

The tattoo itself a whole 'sock' of individual runes or letters or angular word doodles that ran the circular length of Theo's calf from her ankle, almost to her knee. There was a lot of starting and stopping for that, but then they had to pause to chant and whisper and... magic.

All the while it was happening, Theo sat in someone's cubicle in a swivel chair that was starting to hurt her butt almost more than the constant buzzing prick of the needles. She'd exhausted her usual thieving/anthropology games of piecing together this worker bee's life within the first two hours. The cubicle belonged to a woman or a gay man who really, really needed motivation in the form of chocolates and cat pictures to not quit work in a rage. What was weird, though, was that Theo had no idea what job this person did. Maybe they just answered the phones. There were enough buttons on it to suggest a busy office and the list of names with extensions printed above the phone had been annotated heavily.

The magic, when it happened, was far more interesting, though. Theo tried, at first, to understand the words. But they were foreign. She knew Greek, and this didn't sound like it. She'd watched enough Anime that she thought she might recognize Japanese, but this wasn't anything like that either. She didn't think it was Latin, even though her entire knowledge of that language began and ended with "E pluribus unum."

She gave up trying to understand the words, and instead watched for other clues as to how it worked. Theo sensed that everyone in the room participated in some way, even Sabel.

Sabel.

Her own sister added to the magic that was going to bind her to a specific place, put her under a kind of house arrest.

Right now, when she wasn't just trying to get through this ordeal, Theo actively hated Sabel.

A lot.

CHAPTER TEN

GABE CONSIDERS THAT MAGIC COULD BE REAL, AFTER ALL

It was several days later when Gabe finally felt like the eyes were off his back and the darkness finally stopped trying to devour him.

He'd slept fitfully in doorways, and, being too fearful to return to the Tenderloin, managed to blow through his money. He had about five crumbled one dollar bills and odd change left. He wandered the streets of Castro now, specifically looking to hustle.

His only agenda for today: eat a hot meal and find someone willing to pay for a quickie—or, better yet, take him home and make a boy toy out of him for a few weeks.

Spotting Delores Park, he headed up towards Sanchez Street. There was a café there, Deboce or something like that. It was a breakfast-all-day place where Gabe knew you could get a pretty decent meal for about five bucks.

The interior of Duboce Park Cafe was as airy and brightly colored as the exterior. The walls were a kind of exaggerated Spanish-style: stucco, painted ochre and lime green and with trims in an intense, almost jarring red. A large menu board hung over the register. Surrounded by all the polished chrome and glass, Gabe felt like a smudge. The lady behind the counter wrinkled her nose at him when he ordered the cheapest thing on the menu and then dug out his baggie and carefully handed over the exact amount in crumpled bills and change. She handed him a little flag with the cafe's mascot red dog slipping its leash, but she seemed hesitant

61

to touch him, like, she thought she might get dirty, homeless cooties.

Humiliated, Gabe slunk into a seat near the back, away from the window.

As he waited for the huge breakfast burrito, he ran his fingers through his mass of curls, hoping to make them slightly more presentable. He wished he had a book from the library to read, because there was really nothing more awkward than sitting in a fancy place like this staring at the walls. Especially since everyone around him had the look of tourists or the fabulously gay crowd this neighborhood was famous for. A few people gave him a hard look, like they knew he didn't belong here, or like they wanted to call the cops.

Gabe was too brown, too filthy, and too desperate for this place — but it was a perfect place to hook up with the kind of "patron" who would offer him a place to crash for a few days. And sex was an easy price to pay for a hot shower.

Finding a spot on the wall, he stared at it resolutely, determined not to let it get to him. After he had some cash again, he'd have to hit the 'Y' for a day pass, even though the staff always gave him a huge hassle. Used to be, when he looked younger, no one asked many questions. Now everyone wanted a picture ID. Thank god, he'd scored a fake license in Colorado. He just had to remember to answer to the name Jose and act like a hapless tourist.

He really should think about trying to get a student ID or something local. Now that Gabe had been here for a couple of months, he was starting to figure out where the right people hung out. Next time he stayed at the shelter, he'd slyly ask around to find out who could fix him up with a new fake ID... and how much it'd cost him.

If he could ever go back to the shelters...

Just thinking about it made a shiver shoot straight down his spine, like a splash of ice water.

Someone slid into the seat opposite Gabe. He'd been so distracted thinking about the black clouds of doom that he never heard the approach. Sitting opposite him now was a man whose white hair didn't match the youthfulness of his face. He looked like he could be American Indian. A quick assessment of the expensive style and cut of the guy's clothes and the way he kept looking Gabe up and down, Gabe figured he'd scored already... but not the kind of score he wanted.

This guy looked like he already had a husband, or a wife, and just wanted a blowjob in the bathroom.

Gabe could do that, but, normally, he preferred the kinds of guys who were a little lonely and were willing to pay for a person to hang around the pool and make them feel pretty and attractive. Sure, these were desperate times, but hook-ups in bathrooms were an easy way to get arrested or beat-up or both.

Something about this guy was making Gabe's gut reach for 'no.' In fact, he was about to spell out 'no' as 'N.' O.' but then he noticed that people were suddenly less interested in them, like maybe they were relieved Gabe had such a nice-looking, responsible friend. Okay, that was useful, plus, Gabe was down to the lint in his pockets, and, maybe with a little smooth talking he could go back to some swank apartment, borrow a clean shirt and a shower. "Okay," Gabe said a little dejectedly. "I'm up for it. What's your offer?"

The guy raised both thin, white eyebrows in surprise. "Offer? What exactly are we negotiating?"

As if he didn't know.

Ah hell, the guy was probably one of those who wanted to remind you that you were a whore at every turn. This day was getting crappier by the minute.

Just then the waitress arrived with Gabe's food. She nodded pleasantly to the new arrival, like maybe he was a regular. "I'll bring your latte over in a moment," she told him.

"Thank you," the white-haired guy said perfunctorily, though with a weird sort of self-satisfaction, like he was proud to have thought to be polite. This guy was a serious oddball.

Once the waitress had gone, Gabe started in on the burrito. It had all sorts of organic, locally-grown veggies in it, plus at least four eggs, and it was about the size of his forearm so it'd keep him okay through dinner time, probably through the night as well. So, he dug into it and stared at the white-haired guy trying to figure out how to approach this.

Gabe had hustled a bit before. He'd never intended to, but he'd been standing on a corner in Chicago waiting for the light to change when a guy had rolled up in a nice car and asked for a 'date.' What happened next wasn't rocket science and, despite the risks, not as awful as Gabe had thought it would be. It wasn't anything he wanted to get in the habit of, because it was too easy to get on the pimps' radars, but the occasional sex act-for-pay had gotten Gabe out of some seriously dismal situations and even better, landed him in some decent apartments and paid for a gym membership for a few months.

Given that he was down to somewhere around fifteen cents in change, now might be one of those times. After finishing half of the burrito, Gabe leaned in a little closer to the white-haired guy. In a low voice, he said, "No condom, no deal." With a jerk of his chin in the direction of the bathroom, which was unisex and the kind people would notice two guys going in and not coming out for a half hour, Gabe added, "This place won't fly. It's too early for the alley, so it's back to yours or a hotel."

"Oh, *that's* what we're negotiating?" The white-haired guy said, sounding a little shocked. But, then as if Gabe had offered something completely mundane, he added, "I'm afraid I'll have to pass."

Huh? Gabe blinked at the guy stupidly, totally not expecting to be turned down.

"My turn now?" the white-haired guy asked. "May I negotiate?"

"Uh, yeah, go ahead," Gabe said, not knowing what else to say.

"Your name is Gabriel Harrera and are originally from West Virginia."

Shit! Was this guy a detective sent by Asshole? Gabe glanced at the exit. Goddamn it, this person was between him and the door. "I'm not going back there."

"No one said you were," the guy sounded sincerely puzzled.

"Oh," Gabe said, relaxing a little in his confusion. "You're not a detective or a cop?"

"I do have a nose for detecting things, but, no, not in the way you're thinking." The white-haired guy said. "You have been seeing things, things most people can't, haven't you?"

Gabe's heart pounded in his ear, but he tried to act cool as he scoffed, "Yeah, I'm pretty sure that's called a psychotic break."

"Actually, no, not at all. They're called 'Guls,'" the guy said in a normal sort of matter-of-fact way. "Well, technically 'Lesser Gul,' but they're certainly not the product of any disease... well, not that kind of disease, at any rate."

The waitress came over and deposited the latte at the guy's elbow and a tall glass of lemonade at Gabe's. "Uh, I didn't order this," he said.

"Ben did," the waitress smiled.

Ben? Ah, the white-haired guy, obviously. Gabe pushed the glass back towards the waitress, "Um, I can't pay for this."

"I already did," Ben said.

Deciding she didn't need to get involved, the waitress headed back behind the counter.

As tempting as it was, Gabe couldn't take a sip of the lemonade. "Seriously, guy, I don't know what you want from me, but I'm not taking lemonade in lieu of cold, hard cash."

"What I want," Ben said, "Is for you to relax and listen to me. I don't actually have a lot of time. I've got another... errand that I've neglected, but I approached you because here you were, finally, just where they said you would be, if not especially timely."

Gabe had no response for that, because none of it made any sense to him. So he sat back and picked up the sandwich.

"Ah, excellent, you're listening. I win that one. Do you go again, or can I offer the lemonade for the rest?"

"Is the rest of what you want as easy as 'listening'?"

"Probably not," Ben admitted, "because what I'd really like is for you to stop thinking you're insane. You have the sight. That's a rare gift in a human. With the proper training you could be an excellent demon hunter, or seer, or more."

The blood drained from Gabe's face. He sat back until he felt the wood of the booth, solid against his back, propping him up. *'You can see.'* That's what the nurse had said. Gabe's voice was small when he asked, "Did she send you—that nurse?"

"Nurse?" The white-haired guy seemed genuinely confused. "No, no, the Vestals had a vision. They said I should meet you here and offer you a place. Of course, the visions aren't perfect, are they? I've been coming here every day at the same time for three weeks waiting for you. But, if what I smell is accurate, you're definitely a Talent that should not be wasted." His nose twitched like an animal testing the wind. "Yes, talent is very innate in you."

The Force is strong in this one.

Jesus.

That was so cliché he almost felt embarrassed that his delusions would sink to such a simple level. Next this Obi-Wan/Old Ben guy was going to say Gabe was the Chosen One or 'The Boy Who Lived.'

But, what the hell was a Vestal? Weren't they Greek virgins? That wasn't very consistent with the paranoid demonology thing Gabe's mind had going, because, really shouldn't he stick to the same Judeo-Christian pantheon? Weirdly, this inconsistency made Gabe a little less wary. It was so unlike his thought process, it seemed like it could be real... if that made sense.

Gabe looked at the lemonade. "So some Greek virgins sent you to offer me, what? Lemonade in exchange for not thinking I was insane? Pardon me for saying so, but doesn't that sound *more* crazy rather than less?"

"Oh, well, that's because the lemonade trade was my idea. Seems clear that I've lost that one, alas," Ben said, taking a sip from his latte. "No, what they want is for you to come with me and accept a place."

"A place," Gabe repeated, not liking how hungry his voice sounded. "You mean like a place to stay?"

"Honestly, I'd meant a place in the Order, but, you know, you're right, I should probably start with the basics. Yes, I can offer you that."

Just like that? "What's the catch?"

"You're an astute young man," Ben said. Twining his fingers together, he tapped his lips with his knuckles. "Nothing is free, is it? However, the cost to you isn't punitive. Once you're properly tested and trained, you'd become our knight, our sword-arm, as it were. All right, so it's a lifetime gig but I should think you might like the steady work. It's a chance to do some good. Besides, I would think any offer must be better than alleys and bathrooms, don't you think?"

Well, the guy had a point there.

The offer of a lifetime as a knight was about as insane as anything, but maybe it helped that, even though this guy had a weird vibe about him, there were no black clouds or snake-slit eyes. "This isn't a hallucination... right?"

"Of course, not," the white-haired man said without a moment's hesitation. "My name is Aben'eres, but most people call me Ben. I have some... special abilities, like you do, but I can assure you, like the Vestals, I'm entirely human."

Human? Were there other options?

Well, regardless, human was good, solid... normal. Gabe could cope with that. "Okay, so let me get this straight: you're offering me a place to stay, if I'll train to become a knight?"

"Yes," Ben said. "However, if you would like to be precise, I'm giving you a place to stay and the *opportunity* to become a knight, provided you pass your courses and your tests."

Gabe nodded, finally taking a sip of the lemonade.

Ben smiled to see him drinking. "Does this mean you've decided you're not crazy?"

Looking down at glass, Gabe let out a dark chuckle. "The jury's still out, but, if I am, you're way worse off than me."

And, what the hell, Ben's kind of crazy seemed way better than being on the streets, always alone.

CHAPTER ELEVEN

ERIN MONSTER CAN BE AN ANGEL AND A DEVIL

Your mother was an angel, that's what Grampa always said with a tear in his eye. When Erin was delirious from the drugs or the pain, sometimes she thought maybe he meant that literally. Like, maybe all her troubles came from the fact that her mom, an angel, had married her dad, a devil.

Unholy union.

Maybe it was true.

Erin remembered very little about her mother, and the few memories she had were polluted by the stories Gramma and Grampa told. When they talked about their daughter, they'd say things that sounded like compliments that really weren't, like, "She was a free spirit." Sometimes they didn't even pretend and muttered, "Well, we did our best. She was adopted after all."

Adopted. This was another one of those funny words that Erin knew was supposed to fill her with shame, but actually was the source of hope. Because, maybe, somewhere out there was a set of grandparents who knew something, some truth about why Erin was the way she was that didn't end in Bible verses and hacksaws.

Wouldn't it be cool if those people were out there, right now, looking for Erin, ready to swoop down and rescue her?

Yeah.

Except angels weren't real, were they?

Devils certainly were, but not angels. So, whatever Erin was she was some kind of evil half-thing. Maybe that's why her soul felt incomplete and why, sometimes, like now, she had to drink deeply of the iron from the blood of someone near her.

The guard near the door fainted. It was kind of funny to watch a big burly guy get that silly, dopey look and then fall to the floor like a rag-doll. Erin knew that giggling about it was only going to get her in bigger trouble, but she felt the flush, the influx of metal.

White-coat's eyes widened. He watched her face as the other guard scrambled over to his buddy shouting, "Pete? Can you hear me buddy? You okay? Hey, doc, Pete fainted."

The 'doc' continued to look only at Erin. He had a thin, horsey face that she didn't like one bit. Plus, he had a pimple on the tip of his nose that she kind of wanted to pop for him in a semi-violent way—no, scratch that, totally violent.

"Yes," white-coat said. "It seems the little demon woke up. Time to turn on the machine, I think, and test it out."

Oh, good, Erin thought sarcastically. No doubt this would be *pain-less.*

Sure enough, the flick of a switch seemed to electrify every cell in her body.

She screamed.

Maybe, she thought, if she screamed loud enough, angels would hear.

CHAPTER TWELVE

KITTY WISHES SHE HADN'T PACKED QUITE SO WELL

For all his bluster, Papa was always the first one to pick up on Kitty's moods. They'd been driving in the packed car for only about twenty minutes before Papa switched off the music they'd been singing along with and gave Kitty a hard stare in the rearview mirror.

"What's bugging you?" he asked gently.

Kitty opened her mouth and then realized she wouldn't know where to start to explain that questions from the Skype call with Blake and the information in the file about Theodosia Young and what she'd stolen were circling around her brain like vultures. She picked the next most troubling thing on her mind: "Apparently, it's not just going to be me at Lily's, like we thought."

Dad glanced over his shoulder at this. "Oh?"

"Suhirin sent me a message. There's a witch girl too," she said it casually, like it was no big deal. The part that had really creeped her out was how specific Suhirin was about Kitty's role watching this Theo and figuring out where she hid the items from the vault. Turning to watch the landscape rush by out the window, she asked, "Are we going to see the redwoods?"

Dad didn't drop it, though. He turned to Papa. "This better not be true. If we're going to be sending Kitty somewhere again on Suhirin's say-so, it should be as advertised, damn it. She should be going to grad school. Some place that doesn't waste her talents."

Papa nodded. "I still don't even know what that foreign school was for, but the waiver Suhirin had us sign was not cool, and, I'm still sure, not legal. With your math skills, hon, you should be going to Berkeley or any of the other schools that tried to recruit you into their graduate programs."

Kitty continued to stare resolutely out the window, because what could she say? That's what she wanted, too. If it wasn't for the people she had vowed to protect, her colleagues from 'that foreign school,' ... and the fact that no matter how hard she tried she was like a robot programmed to keep trying to succeed at Suhirin's tests.

"I need to take a year of German anyway for the requirement," Kitty said quietly.

That's what she said to placate them, but she knew it wasn't true. Her opportunities were slipping through her fingers. If she didn't move soon, she might never win the Fields Medal, which, for math was like Olympic gymnastics. But, you had to be younger than thirty to qualify.

Thirty was far, far closer than Kitty might like to consider.

Papa gave a big harrumph, but he turned the radio back on. "I suppose that's true enough."

Dad was still nervous. He glanced back at Kitty again. "What did Suhirin say? There's just one girl and she's a witch?"

Kitty shrugged.

She'd gotten a text from Suhirin explaining that there had been some changes in the plan of Lily's school. Originally, Kitty would be Lily's only student, a kind of an apprentice. Now.... Well, now things had gotten complicated.

She shifted in her seat as she tried to figure out how to explain this to her folks. "She's some girl Suhirin wants me to spy on." It didn't help matters to know that this girl, Theo, had been caught because of the research that Kitty did. Was she lucky enough that Theo didn't know it was a combination of Kitty's mathematic models and deductive online research that caught her?

On top of that, trying to spy on her from within the same house was going to be just swell. She added sarcastically, "That won't make things super-awkward or anything."

For some reason, this bit of information made Dad relax. "That sounds like Suhirin all right."

Papa sighed. "Explain to me how this is all for the greater good again, David."

Dad reached over and patted Papa's thigh. "You can't see them, but the world is full of unseen forces," Dad said patiently.

They talked about this a lot, but Dad never lost patience when Papa needed to hear it again. The nature of the material world made it hard for pure humans to remember that real magic existed or how it worked.

"There are protective forces, like the Sangkesh demons that vie for control of cities," he said. "That's who Suhirin works for and they control San Francisco, which is how we know our baby is going to be completely safe at this crazy, magic school for gifted youngsters."

Kitty laughed at his X-men reference and grinned at the rear view mirror so he could see. She took up the explanation.

"There are bad demons, really bad. So the good demons keep us all safe from them."

"But you said this girl is a witch?" Papa asked. "That's different?"

"Witches are ...," Kitty shook her head because she never really got the witches, but she tried to be sort of fair in her explanation. "Like humans with magic who spend a lot of time arguing about stuff and don't do much except sometimes show up and tell the good demons to get back in line."

"This witch girl isn't going to think she gets to do that with you, is she?" Dad asked.

"She'd better not."

"Is she at least a genius like you?" Papa asked.

"I doubt it," Kitty said, but quickly added. "She does have some pretty good abilities, though." She didn't say out loud that from Theo's file it looked like her abilities were: shape-shifting, stealing, lying, pissing people off and getting laid.

CHAPTER THIRTEEN

THEO CALLED THIS SHIT

A few days later, Theo felt like she could do a "called that shit" dance. Sabel had left her.

Again.

Just like that.

In fact, Sabel had hung around only long enough to throw money at the problem. Money enough to buy a house.

A fucking house.

With the family money, Sabel had bought Lily and company a brand-new house that Theo swore Sabel had had decorated in a style she knew would irritate Theo. It was all so fresh and new that there was no trace of any story or history or puzzle. Not that Sabel even stuck around long enough to see her reaction to it all.

They finally had magic in common, but of course there was still so many much more important things her Ph.D. doctor sister had to run off and do rather than explain them to Theo. She said, "I'm not the right person to teach you," and then, "I can't. I literally cannot teach you what you need to know," and finally, "I have to go figure out … I can't even explain. Lily and Ben can teach you."

Was she under some vow of silence like a nun? Or did she just not want to make time to explain things to Theo?

Either one could be true, knowing Sabel.

It was stupid. This whole thing was stupid, because Theo had no idea what this Lily person could teach her. Everyone had already told her that what she did was impossible and that hardly anyone, anywhere could do what she could. This one guy she met for about five minutes, the white-haired Ben, apparently knew something about something similar, but like Sabel, he'd spent exactly five minutes saying "hi; bye."

Lily knew demons and magic, apparently, but didn't seem all that interested in talking about any of it. Lily was apparently half-demon or some part anyway, because she had wicked-cool pointed teeth, kind of like a shark but without the rows, and impressive feet that looked like huge eagle talons. But when Theo had bombarded Lily with all the 'what even' and 'how' of it all, Lily just said that would come later.

It was always: *later*.

It was like Theo was under the most boring house arrest ever.

Theo considered calling her mom to see if there was some way to buy her way out of this, but Sabel had made it sound like Theo could still be in trouble from Scary Lady, Suhirin. Theo supposed she could buy her own way out this time. She still had all the stolen goods hidden and, probably, if she coughed them up, she could leave this place and go....

Where?

'Home' wasn't anywhere better. Not that she'd really had much of a thing when she was out doing her stealing. It wasn't wise to stay and prey in the same neighborhood too long, so Theo had been living a vagabond life. She couch-surfed easily enough. Whether she really understood people or not ,they seemed to like her, even be drawn to her. She enjoyed finding groups of people to hang with for a while, until their lies and bullshit piled up too high, and then she could always go find some other people, hope they'd be a bit better this time.

In between people, she'd stash her things and turn into the owl or the cat and live for a while in a world that made sense to her. Living in an animal form helped her stay a few steps ahead of the authorities—but she was beginning to realize that all along when she thought she was so free, she was actually seeking.

Desperately seeking magic.

Ha, that sounded like the title of a really cheesy movie, probably starring some washed up musician or one of those actors who was in everything.

This place, at least, had the potential to give her the answers about magic—if anyone would actually fucking tell her anything. She'd play her puzzle game on this house, pretend she was casing it, but Sabel had bought them a place so new and empty there was nothing to uncover... beyond yet another tacky doily. Doilies! Jesus, Sabel might as well have rubbed salt into her wounds!

Flopping back on the mattress on the floor of her room, she pulled her pants leg down to stare at the ink around her ankle. There were cuneiform letters in orderly upward rows, separated in rows by black lines. Like a sock, it went nearly to her knee. Whatever magic the letters contained, they didn't stop her from transforming. She'd tried that right away. She could still manage all her various animal guises with no trouble at all.

Sitting back up, Theo looked at the balcony just outside her door. Maybe one way to get answers about magic was to force them. Nobody wanted to talk to her about this stuff? Well, she could find some of them out on her own. Like, what was at the end of her leash? What exactly happened when she flew outside of the prescribed range of this tattoo restraint? Would she hit some kind of invisible wall? Was it possible that when she tried to cross the boundary, she'd just magically teleport back to this house? Or was the whole thing super-mundane and it'd just be come kind of electric shock, like those doggy 'invisible fence' things?

Time to find out.

Theo stood up and started stripping out of her clothes. Shorts, shirt, bra, and underwear dropped onto the bed in quick succession. She always felt free when she was naked—free and natural, like a wild animal. Stepping out on the balcony, she felt the wind tickle along flesh, making goose bumps rise along her arms and her nipples perk. The breeze pulled at her hair as she balanced on the top of the railing.

She stood there for a heartbeat or two, just breathing in the salt-smog taste of this new city, San Francisco.

Then, she jumped.

Spreading out her arms, she switched bodies. With a gut-swirling pop, Theo's human body slipped into the nowhere place and the crow's form unfurled around her sense of self, its glossy black wings sweeping out quickly to catch the air. She'd nearly miscalculated how fast her human body fell and she had to flap furiously in order to land softly on the asphalt of the driveway. She hopped around, adjusting her wings and remembered the feel of her bird-body. Theo often thought she should see if she could get a side-job as writer for one of those animal science-y magazines like *National Geographic* or *Discovery*, because she knew things about animals that no naturalist ever would. And, being a bird, she was pretty sure she had some serious insight into the mind of dinosaurs, too.

A sharp-eyed glance at the house showed that her change had gone undetected… or ignored.

With a powerful surge, she was airborne.

Humans dreamed of flight, craved it, even—or so they said. Theo found the real-life experience disconcerting. Even though her crow-body knew how to keep itself aloft, her brain felt as though it were always falling. In a way, it was. A flap up countered the motion of falling. Once she got up high enough, however, she could glide.

Theo loved soaring.

Now, she circled lazily in the sky, trying to decide if her house-arrest radius was a circle, column, or a sphere. Not that she could easily fly 10 miles up; the highest any bird flew was 37,000 feet, which was just over seven miles high. Most airplanes didn't even go that high.

So, it didn't really matter.

Still, better to hop those last few inches or fly very low, in case the consequences were paralysis or something disastrous like that.

As she flew she thought about that famous poem:

Turning and turning in the widening gyre / The falcon cannot hear the falconer; / Things fall apart; the centre cannot hold;

The center cannot hold, for real, dude.

Theo couldn't stay here, in this empty house, for much longer, not without answers. Sure, it was better than Scary Lady coming after her, Theo supposed, but the mystery her mind worked on now was the puzzle of magic. Once she was on a puzzle, she never let it go.

After all, that was how she'd gotten into this mess in the first place.

Plus, she thought, taking a breather in the shelter of a Spanish chestnut tree, she fucking hated silence.

Silence was the weapon of choice for the women of her family.

Sabel had bludgeoned her with silence after the whole bird thing, an act of violence as far as Theo was concerned. Then, like now, she decided to defy everyone and their silence: if it could be learned, she'd teach herself.

Taking off with a defiant 'caw' she pushed onward, toward the edge of her magical leash. She began to feel the effects. Pins and needles were plucking at her muscles and nerves, like when Scary Lady's thugs had shot her with the poison dart.

She glided lower to the ground and shied away from the busier streets. The last thing she wanted was to pass out somewhere where she could get run-over.

Or picked up by a hungry cat.

A wave of dizziness had her spiraling further down. With the pins and needles distracting her as well, Theo found flight too complex and bounced on the sidewalk, causing a group of tourists to jump up from their restaurant patio seats to point and take pictures of the world's clumsiest crow.

Several people even hazarded closer, phones pointed at her, as she shook herself out and tried to keep moving.

Great.

Theo hoped that whatever magic was making it hard for her to move didn't also revert her to her human form… otherwise that was going to make an interesting viral video. Bad enough that her crow tumble would be chronicled all over Instagram and Tumblr.

But she didn't think the magic would switch her back to her human body. She'd learned in her two years at college, attempting drunk party tricks, that she could not transform in full view of people. It just wouldn't happen. Something about them watching. And if people looking at her could do that, how much more so with them holding smartphones, right?

A few more hops forward and she started to see spots floating in front of her eyes. Her stomach pitched and swirled with the desire to vomit. Her whole body itched and burned with the sensation of a thousand fire ant bites.

Yeah, a saner person would stop moving forward now.

But… what if, it was only another inch and she'd be free?

Behind her, tires squealed as someone bumped up to the curb. She flapped forward the moment she saw who came barreling out: Lily.

"There you are, you silly bird," she said.

The tourists continued to snap pictures as Theo tried to flop away from Lily's scooping hands.

Just before the pain grew too intense and Theo passed out, she heard Lily say, "I can see I'll have to find better ways to keep you busy."

CHAPTER FOURTEEN

GABE GETS A 'HOME ON THE (ST)RANGE'

Holding the door of the MINI Cooper open for Gabe, Ben reminded Gabe of some kind of perverted prince and a tiny white pumpkin carriage, or maybe the white-rabbit from Alice in Wonderland.

Because knights and demons?

Yep, down into the rabbit hole you go, Dude.

Gabe had gotten into strange men's cars plenty of times before, but this was the first time in a long while that he was buckled in properly and staring out at the passing scenery. The white MINI Cooper convertible zipped up and down the hills of San Francisco.

In his copious library reading, Gabe had heard it claimed the city was built on seven hills, which included the most famous ones like Nob and Russian, but there were a lot more, almost too many to count. The whole city was defined by these severe, vertigo-inducing ups and downs and the odd little micro-climates they produced.

Houses and shops gradually spread out as Ben drove them out of the heart of downtown.

They passed a sprawling campus. The centerpiece seemed to be a weird-ass building that had Gabe craning to see it better. It appeared to defy gravity, with a jutting structure that rose up at an impossible angle, like a steamed open clam's shell. The earlier rain brought out the greens of the trees and grass of the quads; the more mundane glass-fronted classroom buildings shimmered in the hazy sun. Fresh-faced student-types played Frisbee on the lawns.

"I suspect you'll be enrolled there," Ben said casually, as they turned down a street. He gestured to a stone gate that had the initials, "SFSU."

"Seriously?" Gabe asked. "Are you trying to tell me they teach Knighthood 101 at San Francisco State University?"

Ben clucked his tongue. "Knighthood is strictly extracurricular."

Right, of course, Gabe thought sarcastically, everyone knew that, how dumb of him. "So, I'll go to some kind of knighthood evening school?"

"Lily will teach you at the new house. Think of it as demon-hunting homeschooling."

Lily? And who was paying for all this again? The Greek Virgins?

They passed a group of college-aged guys shouting unintelligibly at passers-by and all holding up signs with Greek letters. The Greek stuff made Gabe think of the Vestals, so Gabe asked, "Spells?"

"Rush week," Ben said, with a little roll of his eye. "Listen, when I said you weren't insane, I did not, however, mean that the entire world had suddenly transformed into Hogsmeade at Universal Studios. Things have just... deepened, perhaps. At any rate, college is still college, and, frat boys, unfortunately for us all, are still frat boys."

Ben's obvious disdain made Gabe chuckle.

Despite himself, Gabe was starting to feel at ease. He really shouldn't. Ben had promised him a place to stay, and that was something Gabe could hardly afford to think about... much less consider paying for, despite all this weird-ass talk about it all being in exchange for 'lifelong service as a knight' for some organization called Vestals, which apparently weren't virgins at all, but witches.

It was all still so weird.

On the other hand, the car was warm and dry and Gabe's stomach was full. It kind of made him sleepy and... accepting. Like, sure, Vestals and homeschooling for knights, why not?

The car pulled into a drive and Ben cheerfully announced, "Tah-dah, we're here."

'Here' turned out to be a long, modern house in a collegiate neighborhood with a terrace running along the front of the third story. It said, "money" and looked like a place where you couldn't put your feet up on anything. That was less than ideal, but, for sure, it had a shower, probably several bathrooms, heat, and running water. In other words: perfect.

Gabe wondered if the place belonged to Ben.

The car stopped in front of a closed garage door, which was under a huge bay window. Gabe noticed they didn't go in the garage. Maybe this was someone else's place after all.

"What next?" Gabe asked, part of him still wondering if this was all part of his delusions and 'next' would involve his ass in the air and a lot of lube.

"Next, we go in and I introduce you to everyone."

"Everyone?" Gabe didn't like the sound of that. Too many people were a problem—harder to fight, no chance to run. He knew he'd relaxed too soon, damn it. It was the food. He shouldn't have eaten; it always made him sleepy and stupid.

Ben must have sensed the panic behind Gabe's words. "There's nothing to worry about," he said. "Though, I should warn you about Lily. She's half-demon and half-human, but fully incarnate. She won't look like what you're used to seeing, but if her boots and her teeth caps are off, you'll get a pretty startling sight."

Boots and teeth caps? A sight of what, exactly? "Did you just say half-demon?"

"Yes," Ben said, switching off the car and unbuckling. "Half-human, half-demon."

"So demons are real?"

"Yes."

Ben seemed perfectly calm about it all, so Gabe shrugged. *Knights and Vestals and demons, oh my.* Though he felt more like Alice in Wonderland than Dorothy. "Yeah, okay. So, just her?"

Ben shrugged. "I wouldn't worry so much if I were you."

That wasn't really an answer at all, but Gabe had come this far. Shouldering his backpack, he went up the stairs behind Ben and watched him open the door without unlocking it. Who left a house like this open? But as long as Ben didn't latch the door behind them, that meant Gabe had an open exit, which might be good if this turned into 'jump the homeless kid.'

If Ben was up to no good, he was completely casual about it. Not only did he not lock the door behind them, but also Ben didn't even seem to care if Gabe followed or not. So, Gabe trailed along into a foyer that smelled of fresh paint. They moved down into a long, bright room with blonde wood floors, tan walls, looking like a showpiece at an open house. In that room was the longest couch Gabe had ever seen. The couch faced an expensive, massive, sweet, drool-worthy, he-could-stare-at-it-for-days flat screen TV mounted over a marble and wood fireplace.

Marble—yeah, this place was all that.

Gabe felt hyper-aware of his street-stained jeans and grungy, used-to-be-white-once t-shirt.

From where they stood, a dining room table with six chairs around it was visible through an open doorway. As Gabe was still trying not to stare covetously at the TV, a woman stepped neatly around the table toward the living room.

Automatically sizing her up, Gabe noted that the woman was short, closer to five feet than to Gabe's height. A bit of muscle showed under her work shirt, but sleek and toned, not strained and bulging like a body-builder, and padded with some middle-aged weight. He figured he could probably take her in a fight; she looked like she could be fast—potentially dangerous enough that he shouldn't underestimate her. Dark hair was bound at the base of her neck and her skin was just a hint lighter than his own, like, maybe she was Arabic or Italian.

"Aben'eres?" she said and her eyes narrowed under a confusion-lined forehead. "Who is this?"

She'd called him by his full name, and clearly not happy to see a guy in tow. So, what did that make her? The wife?

"Oh, this?" Ben said with a funny little smirk and a shrug. He put his hands into the pockets of his gray trousers, as though trying to look the part of an innocent schoolboy. "Well, I did tell you about him, even if you didn't take me seriously. Surprise. I brought home 'the promised one.' You don't mind another lodger, do you? Only I made a little bargain with Gabriel here...."

"The one the Vestals want? Lilith, Eve and Miriam! Ben, if you want me to train a Vestal witch ..."

"I didn't say we had to give him back to them."

Gabe was only half-listening to the answer because he'd suddenly noticed Lily's feet.... if you could call them that. As Lily came fully into the doorway, Gabe could see that under the loose pants she wore, her legs ended in something that would have looked more natural on an eagle. Three, long thick, scaly toes jutted out in the front and one off the back. They ended in wicked sharp, jet-black talons.

If she's not wearing boots....

Oh. So, when Ben had said, 'half-' demon he meant, like, the lower half was actually inhuman.

While trying to blink away the stubborn delusion of the giant eagle-feet, Gabe absently corrected Ben. "Uh, yeah, you did. You said I had to pay for all this by becoming a knight."

"Oh that's true," Ben told him. "You have to serve someone. But who you serve may be open to debate."

"If they come for him, it's going to be a bloody fucking war," Lily said. "You were supposed to get the girl. The broken one."

"Yes, well, I got distracted," Ben said with that little smirk. "Besides, I already told you this one can *See*."

"Oh great, he can *See*. You're such a damned romantic. And don't call it knighthood, you'll give the boy delusions of grandeur. There hasn't been 'knighthood' in two centuries. Can he *do* anything?"

"Nope," Gabe said, tired of being talked around, especially by a lady with eagle feet. "Not a damn thing. Sorry to bother you, ma'am. Thanks for everything. I can see myself out."

Because, seriously, Gabe could tell he wasn't welcome. Ben had promised something he'd had no right to give. In fact, Ben hadn't brought Gabe to the Vestals at all. Instead, this Lady Bird Lily was a half-demon who seemed opposed to the Vestals. Was that even good?

Demons didn't sound good. Not at all.

Demons sounded like something a guy should back the hell away from. Stat.

Gabe turned toward the door. There was a girl standing there, staring at him with a wide grin. How the hell had she snuck up on them? Ben and Lily didn't seem bothered so Gabe figured she must be another part of this messed up household.

A daughter?

Maybe, but she didn't look that much like either of them, because, first of all, she was smoking hot. She seemed to be about his age with barely-wavy brown hair that fell past her shoulders, maybe even halfway down her back. She had full, sensual lips and a classic, maybe-Greek nose

"Hey," she said in a kind of rich, musical voice. "This place just went up a notch. Where'd they catch you?"

"Uh...they lured in me with a decent meal and I got stupid," Gabe said, smiling despite himself. "You?"

"Caught me in a mall, 'cause I stole some shit from baddies. I'm Theo."

Stole from baddies... Gabe tried to process this and failed, but then he half-remembered something from a dream or a song. Stealing secrets, that was it, but what did it mean? Ben had mentioned 'seeing,' and, suddenly, Gabe wondered if maybe, in some weird way, this was part of that. But, he had no idea how to talk about magic to a stranger. So, mostly in response to admiring her again, he said: "Sweet." Realizing he hadn't introduced himself, he added, "I'm Gabe. Or Gabriel, I guess, if you want to be formal."

She laughed. "Oh, if we're being formal, I'm Theodosia Young. Well, Theodosia Ioannou if you don't Anglicize it. But let's not be formal. Are you some kind of magic?"

She just threw that out like it was the kind of question people asked each other. Hi, how are you? What do you do for a living? Are you some kind of magic? "I don't know. Maybe?" Gabe pointed at Ben. "He thinks so. Or some Virgins do."

She raised an eyebrow. "Virgins? Is that what you're into? I've got some bad news..." Then, she gave him a look, the kind that went straight to his crotch, that clearly implied that she was very much NOT one of those.

Gabe didn't usually blush easily, but he felt heat creeping up his neck. This conversation was getting away from him, but in a way that was totally fascinating. He hadn't had this much fun talking to someone in a long, long time. Especially not a girl... no, a woman, really, with those curves. Gabe wanted to reply with something that was equally clever and sexy, but all he could do was stammer, "That's not what I meant. I meant, uh... Vestals?"

"Oh, those bitches," Theo said, offhandedly. After a pause in which she blinked charmingly at him, she added, "You looked like you were leaving, but please stay. There's no one else here my age and if I keep flirting with my sister's girlfriend, she's going to kill me. You can have one of the rooms on the ground floor, big windows, hop right out and run for it if you don't like it here."

She seemed to think he'd be staying here too? So maybe this after-hours/extracurricular school thing was legit? Then, why had Lily seemed so unsure of him? He glanced behind him where the Ben and Lily were exchanging furious whispers and occasionally glancing in his direction.

It had never occurred to Gabe that there might be other students at this so-called school. Sure, Ben had made it sound all above-board, but Gabe's still skittish brain hadn't really allowed him to consider the idea that this would really be permanent and could include… friends.

To himself he muttered, "This is getting harder and harder to resist."

"Let me show you around," she said and brushed past him, close enough that the side of her breast softly grazed his bicep.

She went through the living room and into the dining room so Gabe followed, feeling like a puppy. On the far side of the dining room, a doorway led to a huge kitchen with a big island in the middle. Theo skirted this, took a sharp right and started down a flight of stairs beyond the island. The stairs descended to a long hall with four doors—one at either end and two on the long wall facing the stairs.

"Bathroom," Theo said pointing at the door at the end of the hall to their left. Then she flicked her finger the other direction, "Creepy home chemistry lab magic space and another bathroom. These two in the middle are bedrooms. I think you'd like this one."

She opened the second door in the hall, the one further from the base of the stairs. It was a good-sized room, the wood floor was cherry colored with thick boards and the walls were a creamy yellow that made him wince. The window started halfway up the wall, but it was plenty wide and she was right that he'd have no trouble getting out it.

"Why this one?" he asked as he went to the window to make sure that it opened.

"Further from the stairs, so more time to react if you hear something you don't like. The window is equidistant from the path to the side street and the front of the house, so you have your pick of directions, and you're in the middle of the row of hedges."

He looked at her and raised his eyebrows in an "and?" gesture.

"Get under the hedges and hear which way they're going," she said. "Then run the other way. Unless you're sneaking out in the middle of the night."

Did it disturb him that she seemed to have already mapped out an escape plan? Was that proof that this place was creepy? Or did she think this way regularly because she stole stuff?

"If I am, are you coming with me?" he asked.

"Can't. House arrest. I have a ten mile radius from this house and then, well, I don't know what happens after the pain, but I'm sure it's pretty bad. Didn't make it through the pain part long enough to find out."

"That's not legal," he said. It also fell squarely in the 'creepy' column.

She pulled up her right pant leg, showing a tanned, slender, muscled calf with a tattoo from the ankle to the knee. "Nope, not legal at all," she said. "Magic, though."

A house arrest tattoo? For real? Gabe looked at the window again.

"Relax, they're not going to do it to you," she said.

He was going to ask how she could be so certain when a crash came from the front of the house and the sound of a man's voice yelling about a trunk full of rocks.

"Let's try going out your window," Theo said.

She crossed the room as lightly as a cat, slid the window wide, put her hands on the sill, leapt up into a tucked posture of knees-to-chest, and vaulted out with a mind-numbing grace. Gabe put his hands on the sill, swung one leg up, tipped forward and sprawled out onto a patch of grass on his hands, one leg, and part of his face.

He shook himself and glanced up with the hope that maybe she hadn't seen his spectacular klutz-o-rama.

"Elegant," Theo snarked.

Man, he was batting oh-for-a-hundred with this person.

With a sigh and a cursory wipe of the obvious dirt stains, Gabe got up and followed her as they slunk around to the front of the house. Behind Ben's car in the driveway, with its back half sticking into the street, was a long, silver VW Sports wagon. A man by the open trunk rubbed his shoulder saying, "That has to weigh a hundred pounds."

"Papa, I told you it was too heavy for you." That came from a tall, mixed-race girl with a mane of dark brown hair tipped golden, and a broad leonine nose. She was heavy-set and chesty, but not fat, in that way Gabe figured she got called 'big-boned' or 'plump' a lot. When she smiled, Gabe would have sworn he saw sharp canines, almost like fangs.

"What is this, moving in day?" Gabe whispered to Theo. Rush week for demon-hunters?

They were crouched together in the narrow space between the hedges and the lawn. Though the branches were gnarly enough to hide them, a small gap in the foliage gave Gabe a perfect view of the action. Theo pressed up closely beside him, peering through the same opening. He could feel the heat of her body against his thigh.

She shrugged. "Works for me. Like I said, I can't go far. Company suits me better."

"Right, so if she stays, I could go."

"I didn't say that," she said with that amazingly seductive smile. "Anyway, if you've got magic, you're going to attract the wrong crowd."

He snorted. Like this girl knew anything about not falling in with the 'wrong crowd.'

Hunching together, they returned their attention to the comedy-in-progress. It wasn't fair to call it a complete farce. The two guys—the new girl's parents? —argued good-naturedly in that way that said 'long-term married couple' as they tried to negotiate the box together. There was counting and toe-smooshing and quiet, under the breath swearing that seemed to only go as strong as 'gosh-darn it all,' which Gabe found instantly endearing.

The new girl shook her head at them and, one armed, picked up the offending box. Over her shoulder, she laughed, "Dad, Papa, leave the heavy lifting to me!"

"What did you pack, sweetheart?" The one she'd called dad asked. "Everything including the kitchen sink?"

"Pretty much," she said happily.

Watching this scene, Gabe was very, very certain this was not the "broken one" Lily had mentioned. There was nothing broken about this family, nothing at all. In fact, it was almost painful how perfect they were. Gabe tried not to instantly hate everything about them, because it was like seeing what Mom and Meema could have been if Asshole had never been part of their lives. Of course, if Asshole wasn't part of their lives, they wouldn't have had him... which was something Gabe thought about a lot.

In fact, he kind of hoped that now that he was gone, they were getting to be... this. What was it even? Happy, maybe? Whatever it was, he wanted it so much it created an ache in his gut.

But seeing this third person, so clearly moving in, was deeply reas-suring about one thing. Ben and the woman—Lily, was it?—might still be married, but they weren't trolling for a third (or a fourth, if you in-cluded Theo). You didn't invite the dads to drop their daughter off at the creepy sex slave house.

This was really a school.

Even if one of the students did seem to have some kind of magical restraining order tattoo on her ankle, it was a school. A seriously weird-ass school, but hey, that was a hundred and fifty times better than the alternatives that had been roiling through Gabe's mind.

"The Dad is part demon," Theo said out of the blue, in that crazy matter-of-fact way she had. "Let's go meet them. Or are you going to threaten to leave again if I do?"

Before he could respond, she took his hand in her hot fingers, a bit of dirt left from Gabe's 'inelegant' landing out of the window rubbing between their skin, and pulled him through the loose branches of the hedge.

As they rounded the corner of the house, Gabe was very aware that they were still holding hands. He debated jerking his hand away, but that sent the wrong message. Or, at least, a message he wasn't sure he want-ed to give Theo just yet, because she was pretty much the most amazing woman he'd met in a long time.

If he'd wanted to let go, it was too late anyway, the dads had spotted them. The one with the shorter hair gave their entwined fingers a little knowing smile and nudged his husband. The husband glanced over from where he'd been pulling a bicycle off the roof rack. "Oh, hello," he said.

Theo smiled and let go of Gabe's hand to offer hers to shake. Gabe wanted to say something about how they'd better check to make sure they still had their gold wedding bands after she let go, but he thought that might be a bit rude.

If accurate.

Because today seemed to be about following people down the rabbit hole of strangeness, Gabe found himself shaking hands with the dads, nodding and saying, "Nice to meet you, sir. I'm Gabriel Herrera."

The new girl had come back from depositing the heavy package in-doors. She stood a distance away, with her hands on her ample hips, and her head cocked as if giving both of them a serious once-over.

Gabe had no idea what she thought, looking at him so intensely. He felt very aware that he hadn't showered in too many days and that he'd been wearing the same set of clothes for months. He needn't have worried, however. Her eyes flicked past him to stare hard at Theo.

"Theo Young," she said and glanced back at Gabe. "Where is he from?"

"The Vestals," Lily said from the top of the stairs. "Kitty, meet Gabe, and you apparently know Theo, they're two other members of your class."

"Why are there *two* other students?" Kitty asked. "How many total are there?"

Gabe wasn't sure, but it sounded like he'd just been insulted for being human. Theo and the new girl continued to glare at each other.

"Four," Lily said. "When Ben finds the girl."

Kitty's eyes widened and she took a step back, looked around and then settled herself as if she didn't want her dads to see that clear flash of alarm. What was so bad about them, Gabe wondered. Was it just him?

Theo's nose twitched and she asked Kitty, "Why do you smell familiar?"

"You met my mother," Kitty said. The way she said 'mother' was flat and cold.

"You're Scary Lady's kid? Well shit," Theo said. "You just stay the hell away from me."

"My pleasure," Kitty replied.

Lily sighed and suggested, "Come inside and pick a room."

"The room off the back terrace on the third floor is mine," Theo said quickly.

"Like I care," Kitty said, despite the fact that it seemed pretty clear to Gabe that she cared a whole lot.

So just to be an ass, Gabe gave Theo a poke and said, "She's into you."

"As if," Kitty snarled as she stalked off.

Though it was likely too soft for anyone else, Gabe heard Theo mutter, "Fucking demons."

Kitty's papa watched her go and said, "Well, that went well."

Her dad turned to Lily, "Two witches? I thought... that is, we were under the impression that this program was exclusive."

"I have complete discretion about how I run this program," Lily said, but her voice was warmer than the words. "Suhirin knows that Theo is here. I believe exposure to a variety of kinds of magicks will help Kitty develop her skills. Let me show you the whole facility. I think you'll appreciate the lab and the magic practice rooms."

The dad and the papa exchanged looks. They must have resolved something silently, because the dad said, "Yes, of course. Do you think we could have a tour?"

Lily's shoulders seemed to relax a bit. "Right this way, gentlemen."

Once they'd gone in, Theo turned and socked Gabe hard on the arm. "Ass!" she said, "She's a stuck-up demon princess daughter of some tight-ass super-star demon hunter."

Gabe moved out of the way before he teased, "Ha. Right."

Because that was so not a thing. Was it?

Lily poked her head back through the front doorway and looked at them. "You two, stop gawking, bring the rest of her things in from the car."

His Southern upbringing kicking in automatically, Gabe dipped his head and obediently said, "Yes, ma'am."

Apparently, he was staying. The crazy be damned. Somehow Gabe had fallen into all this, and somewhere along the line he'd decided to stay.

CHAPTER FIFTEEN

THE MACHINE THAT ATE ERIN

The machine that the 'doctor' turned on silenced the song of metals. Erin lost her voice. That thought made her chuckle darkly, because without most of her feet, she'd sometime pretend she was Ariel from Disney's 'Little Mermaid' and now she had neither the ability to walk or her song.

But, the machine had made her captors feel safer. They'd unbound her from the chair, let her pee, and thrown her in a tiny room with a plate of beans and toast and six plastic bottles of water. She ate everything like it was the richest feast and drank as much water as her cramping stomach could hold.

And then, because she finally could, she wrapped her aching arms around her waist and curled up in a tight ball on the floor and cried. She cried until the tears stopped coming. Eventually, she fell asleep.

:: :: ::

Erin dreamed of a happy place, for once.

Her grandfather had a workshop in the back of one of the outbuildings on the farm. It smelled of hay dust and sunshine and had all the tools Erin needed to build her... things. Other kids played with LEGO sets, but Erin preferred the old-fashioned Erector Set because it came with metal pieces and screws and other shiny bits. The metal was cheap and flimsy, but it still sang and she had built solar powered race cars and radio-controlled helicopters and clockwork spider-crawlers, until the barn buzzed joyfully with whirring, tiny metal toys. It was one thing her grandpa actually appreciated and fostered... at least, at first.

But that was a dark place, and her dreams, for once, stalwartly stayed positive. In fact, they seemed to be trying to give her hope... because, in the dream, the old barn workshop transformed into a new place, a place filled with even more sophisticated machines for Erin to tinker with and improve and modify. This new place smelled of platinum, palladium and gold—expensive and exotic.

And it sang.

It was singing to her now, calling her....

Home.

CHAPTER SIXTEEN

KITTY GOES TO ~~HELL~~ SCHOOL

"… four people, two witches, two demons," that's what Blake had said and now she was in a house with two witches awaiting a fourth person. If that person was also a demon … this felt like another test, only much bigger and the kind where when you failed maybe it wasn't only *your* life on the line.

Kitty walked through the second floor of the house, noting the wood floors, the gleaming dark granite countertops of the kitchen, the clean fronts of the maple cabinets, the burnished stainless fronts of the appliances.

Everything was polished and shiny, which only made Kitty miss the cramped cobbled-together hodgepodge of her private space in the basement.

Continuing her exploration, Kitty found that to the left of the kitchen was a closed door that had the look of a private room. She didn't open it. She wanted to respect the privacy of whoever the room might belong to, but also her previous school had drilled into her head that off-limits was a hard line. You didn't cross it because usually what was behind that closed door was worse than any punishment you'd get for opening it.

In front of her, Kitty saw stairs going up and down. That thief-girl, Theo, had said she had the room off the terrace. Suhirin had sent her to spy. So now the question was, did Kitty play the part of the good little girl and take the room upstairs next to Theo? What to do when she wanted to refuse Suhirin but the good girl role and her curiosity pointed in the same direction?

With a sigh, Kitty went up the stairs.

Two doors opened off the third floor hallway: the one to her right showed a smallish room with a long glass door at the end. It wasn't supposed to be a bedroom, but there was a cotton mattress, futon-style, on the floor shoved up against a wall. This was the room that Theo was willing to fight over? Not impressed.

The other end of the hall held a double door that opened into a spacious family room with sliding glass door and a large terrace. The back wall of the family room had another door, this one revealing a decent-sized bedroom with a nice queen bed and an inner door that opened into a lovely bathroom.

Kitty sat on the bed and bounced. The frame looked new, and the mattress felt very springy. Despite herself, she liked it up here. It was airy.

Her stuff was in the living room so she went back down the stairs to find Gabe trying to lift one side of the big chest and swearing.

"Honestly, what is it with men?" Kitty asked rhetorically. "Step away from the heavy boxes, dude."

He did, but his wide eyes suggested it was more out of surprise than because she asked. He was a furry one for a human with all that curly hair and the scruff along his jaw. Kind of like Papa, but with lighter skin. His hair looked dirty—or maybe that was his lack of personal hygiene. She was so not going to share a bathroom with him.

"So, um," he said. "You're... uh, so, 'hi,' I guess."

"Articulate much?" she asked, but she couldn't keep from smiling, which also showed off her fangs to good effect. "Not many demons where you come from?"

"West Virginia? No. Not nice ones, anyway," he said. "Mostly just the floating, buzzy ones. Guls?"

"Lesser Gul," she said.

"Right. Lesser Gul. Got it," he said like he was making a mental note of this new information. Kitty just shook her head. This new 'classmate' did not impress her. *Damn it,* Kitty thought, *this place was supposed to be the best. How did a moron like this pass the entrance exam? Did he even have magic?*

Theo came in through the front door carrying one of Kitty's carefully labeled boxes and set it roughly on top of another. She snorted in Kitty's general direction and walked back out the door. Gabe, looking sheepish, followed. That blockheaded natural witch of a girl probably didn't even know she was throwing off pheronomes like crazy. Even without that, she was attractive and she carried her body with that same kind of natural grace Blake had. But what was lovely on Blake was just irritating from Theo.

Kitty put the box on top of the big chest, grabbed both handles, and lifted everything. Going up the stairs with a three-foot wide chest wasn't going to happen but by turning sideways, she managed to edge steadily up them. Her balance wasn't better than human average, but she got up to her room in one piece and went back for another load. Stacking boxes two and three high, she got all of them up the stairs in a few trips. Gabe and Theo were nowhere to be seen, and with a sigh of relief, she set to sorting the boxes in her room.

Clothing boxes went into one of the long closets, book boxes went into another until she could find a spare bookcase. The bathroom had a double sink, as well as both a standing shower and a tub, but it also had another door that led to a walk-in closet that led to the room Theo had claimed and if she was going to have to share a bathroom with Theo there was no way in creation she was leaving her toothbrush and other toiletries in there. She put the bathroom box next to her dresser.

Her lungs felt tight, constricted, like there wasn't enough air in this strange new room. New places always made her nervous. Right now it was just anxiety, but Kitty knew it could flip over into something para-lyzing if she wasn't careful and smart about it. Time to sort, to move boxes and put her things in their right places. Neat, methodical. Doing a simple thing over and over, no thinking required, no feelings necessary.

She had a way of arranging her things on her dresser, near the bed, in the closet so that any room felt familiar and gave off some small sense of safety. It was working, the ritual settling her.

At least until she unpacked the knife.

Unbidden, names scrolled through Kitty's mind.

At that point, she knew she had to find a way to make this work, frustrating as it might be. She knew she could never be the hunter her mother wanted, but the Hunters' School had shown her there was a way to be *useful*. And if Blake was right, she had to get it together and *be* useful for once.

Math had been promised as well. Lily said there would be real classes in both math and German. If that was true, then this was her final stand. This was the place she could have her math back without abandoning her friends, without abandoning Blake to take on the most dangerous work alone.

She would do what she whatever she had to in order to make this work.

She would do anything at all.

CHAPTER SEVENTEEN

THEO'S PUZZLE GETS MORE PICTURE-Y

Finally, some puzzle pieces to play with!

Granted, one of them was very prickly: KittyCat, the Snotty Demon-ScaryLady'sDaughter.

Speaking of patterns and pictures, that couldn't be a coincidence, could it? No, Lily had said. She told Kitty's dads that Suhirin knew Theo was here. In fact, if Theo picked through the events of the day Suhirin's goons brought her down, she had a vague memory of Suhirin and Lily talking about Kitty even then.

Theo had ducked out of 'helping' unload Kitty's things. Gabe seemed perfectly capable, and too many chefs and all that. So, after grabbing an ice tea from the pitcher she found in the kitchen, she perched herself, like a cat, in a sunny spot in the upstairs living room. She leaned her shoulder against the wall near a window where she could look down on the unloading process and consider her puzzle pieces.

This school was starting to seem like Xavier's School for Gifted Children, only Lily was so not a balding telepath, and Theo was very, very sure she'd probably say telepathy wasn't real. Still, she wouldn't mind being that Rebecca Romijn shape-shifting chick with the blue skin—oh, wait, wasn't she one of the bad guys?

Okay not that school, then, but maybe …

Lily's School for Wayward Demons and Witches?

Looking down the hall, Theo watched Kitty muscle another box from the top of the stairs across to her door. She was so strong, but so gawky! She was sure an interesting one. Theo noticed that Kitty didn't deny the accusation of being a demon princess. So Theo's personal theories about Suhirin were basically confirmed. Scary Lady was some kind of local power, who was very, very likely connected to these Sangkesh demons she kept hearing about.

Theo wasn't sure, but she didn't think Suhirin was a full-on demon. Maybe? But, Theo had it in her head that demons were for real otherworldly. All these people with their superpowers, fangs, and weird-ass feet were part-demon/part-human. She wasn't even sure where she got that—maybe something she'd overheard Lily say?—but it felt right.

Just like you did when you were putting together a real puzzle, Theo organized her pieces by type—by features they had in common. Lily and Kitty and Suhirin were for sure part-demon. Ben? He was currently in his own pile because, if he was a demon, he didn't have any of the physical attributes that the others did, unless his white hair counted? Gabe… that dude was clearly just a doofy human, totally adorkable, but—no offense to him—not in the same league as the rest.

But he was here, so Gabe was part of the puzzle. In fact, he was in the same very important and curious pile of pieces as Sabel, because he'd talked about Vestals and Hecatines—both witches.

So among the pieces there were at least one brand of demons and two types of witches. Ben was an unknown, but he fit snug up to Lily, with a satisfying little click. Since Ben had brought Gabe, he might connect up there, too, a kind of bridge between witches and half-demons.

Then there was Theo, the piece that didn't fit anywhere.

Not yet, anyway.

But enough sitting. She slid open the patio door from the upper living room. This was the smaller of the two patios because of course if Sabel was going to use the family money to buy a house for this School for Wayward Demons and Witches, she had to go all out: three stories, two patios, at least six bedroom, five bathrooms, a creepy lab, everything except a pool.

Tucked into the edge of the patio, out of view from the upstairs living room or hall, Theo stripped out of her clothes and transformed into her housecat form. The change took a few seconds. Theo exhaled and held it. After a moment of intense concentration, followed by churning disorientation, she opened her eyes in a monochrome landscape rich with sounds, smells and another sense that human language didn't have words for.

Stretching out her forepaws, Theo pulled her cat body forward, feeling the freedom along the length of her supple back. She padded through the open patio door—she'd learned years ago not to close doors behind her—and trotted down the stairs. In this form, she was a ten-pound calico of orange, brown and black, now with a twisted design of black fur around her right rear leg.

She got outside by waiting for one of dads to open the door and darting between his feet. With Kitty and her dads out front and Gabe in the kitchen, where were Lily and Ben?

She turned her ears and smell-listened for other signs of life, then opened her mouth to draw air across the secondary scent organ there. When she'd first acquired this cat body, she could only scent the phero-mones of other cats, but over the years somehow a subtle change hap-pened that allowed her vomeronasal organ to pick up human phero-mones too. Maybe someday her human nose would catch up and she'd be able to smell emotion even in human form.

Lily's clear sound-smell-presence came from the back of the house, scented sharp with anger, and Ben's fainter signature was with her, hold-ing undertones of worry and defense. Theo trotted around to the back and leapt soundlessly onto the outer sill of the open window leading to the area that Lily called the Lab.

"... tonight!" Lily was saying in a quiet but harsh, intense voice. "How long have you known where they're holding her and you've just let them keep her? With what we've seen already, don't you realize they'll do any-thing to get what they want?"

"This may be news to you, but some days I don't feel like being your beck and call boy." Ben said casually. He leaned against the island, as if a snarling half-demon wasn't hissing angrily in his ear. "Besides, I got distracted by the boy. I already told you that."

Theo flattened along the sill. She hid herself as well as she could and yet still be able to see Lily and Ben moving in the room beyond.

Lily looked toward the closed inner door. "He could have waited," she said. "He's in danger, sure, but not that kind of pain. Ben, how can you leave her there? I've seen the Cavallo take part-demon children apart, literally, trying to figure out how to measure magic with their stunted understanding of science."

Ben sighed. "Indeed, but the Vestals were breathing down my neck. Hmmm, much as you are now. You know I dislike being cornered."

She laughed without humor, but stepped away from him and stalked across the room. "You wouldn't be cornered so often if you didn't keep overreaching. You can't serve two masters. What do the Vestals have on you, anyway?"

Ben shook his head and wagged a finger at her. "Secrets, of course. None of which I feel obliged to tell you." He let out a long breath and then checked his watch. "I suppose I have delayed long enough. I should be able to fetch her now... provided things go as they should."

"You're the only one who has a chance at it. Maybe Theo when she's older, but shifters like you are rare and ... Ben, be careful. If you leave me stuck in this house with Gabe's ... baggage ... I swear I'll track you into the All-Time if I have to."

"Oh, I love it when you talk dirty to me, darling." Ben said, and before she could take a swipe or bop him on the head, blew her a cheeky kiss goodbye.

And promptly shifted into an albino ferret.

Ben was a Shifter!

The human instincts in Theo wanted to leap into the room and chase him, find out what he was, how he could be like her. She'd never known anyone else who could do the things she could! She managed to hold back, keep her cover. Bolting from the sill, she dashed into the side yard, afraid that the ferret might have already scented her disguise.

Not that she was afraid of ferrets. But she was afraid of what happened if Lily caught her snooping. She'd already shown that she and Ben could create magic that bound Theo to a place, with the tattoo on her leg that caused unbearable pain if she went more than 10 miles from the house. What else could Lily do to her?

Crawling further back into the leaves, Theo tucked her tail around her body and went over the scene in her memory, picking out what she'd learned.

Ben could at least turn into a ferret, maybe other shapes, too. That had to give him power, something important, because Lily had said he was the only one who could get the girl—whoever that was.

Humph. As if they needed another girl in this house. Theo already hated the way Gabe watched Kitty. Not that she wanted him as a boyfriend, but he was cute in that muscle-dork way guys had when they bulked through an accident of growth and didn't realize how built they'd become. It made her want to climb all over him.

He wasn't a mystery, not like Kitty. His story seemed straightforward. Gabe'd clearly had a hard time of it, lately, but maybe always—given the way he looked around the house like it was Wonderland. She read him as a guy used to looking out for himself in a pinch, not the kind who would fuck with her mind. That worked just fine for her.

Despite Sabel thinking she was the whore of Babylon, Theo really didn't get around that much. She liked a steady thing if she could get it, if the person was decent in bed and wasn't going to get all psychological after. People were complicated; relationships made them that much more so. So really? She avoided long-term things. She'd rather be like a cat: just hook-up for fun and pleasure and because bodies wanted to do that stuff from whatever biological imperative—but no thinking involved. No entanglements after, either.

With Gabe, she figured she could have an awful lot of fun without having to go anywhere she didn't want to, or think any unnecessary things—but now Kitty was on her turf, with her ridiculous strength and a complete lack of clue about what her breasts did when she engaged her pectorals lifting heavy boxes. She had to find a way to show Gabe that Kitty wasn't all that and maybe get back at Suhirin a little in the process.

Theo padded around to the front of the house. Kitty and her dads weren't there anymore, but their scents lingered around the Sports wagon. Theo padded slowly around the vehicle and then up the stairs to the front door, picking Kitty's odor out from the others: again she smelled the lemongrass soap; plus chamomile and rosemary, probably from a hair product; a light sandalwood-style musk that could be her natural scent; and over it all the acidic bitterness of fear.

Fear? What did a girl like Kitty have to be afraid of?

Of all of them, Kitty was the one who had it made—two perfect dads and Scary-Lady, queen of demons, for a mom.

A growl formed in Theo's throat. All that perfect veneer made Theo want to poke the puzzle of Kitty until something broke, and the *real* picture showed through. Time to go human again, at least for now.

But Theo almost always had something up her sleeve. These people had clipped her wings, but she still had those items that Suhirin had been so wiling to kill her for. Tomorrow, or as soon as there was time, she would send word to one of her trusted contacts and see if he could pick up one of them and hide it somewhere within her ten mile range.

Just in case she needed something, anything to bargain with.

CHAPTER EIGHTEEN

GABE SETTLES IN
(KIND OF)

It was amazing how quickly Gabe felt at home with these strangers. *Home.* Yeah, no, that was still a weird thought.

Gabe worked up a sweat helping with Kitty's seemingly never-ending boxes. The clothes in his backpack were now officially cleaner than the ones on his body, and that wasn't saying much. He went through the house to see if he could find Ben and ask about a shower and change of clothes, but Ben wasn't around. Kitty had taken the room on the top floor next to Theo's, so the ground floor remained empty except for Gabe. He figured he'd better take advantage of a hot shower while he could, just in case.

He brought his pack into the bathroom with him and shut the door, locked it. Hot water was heavenly. It had been fourteen days since Gabe had last enjoyed this kind of luxury. All the soaps smelled nice, too. Not like that cheap, chalky stuff they had at the shelters or the too-flowery crap people had abandoned at the YMCA.

As the water sluiced over him, Gabe thought about this strange turn of events. In a matter of hours, he'd gone from a shit-ass life on the street to being some kind of student of magic at what had been called an 'exclusive' program. Even if these people were crazy cultists, it was still a step up from not knowing where his next meal was coming from.

And, speaking of crazy, he was starting to believe he really wasn't having a psychotic break. For one, everything seemed to be going well.

What he'd read on the subject of schizophrenia had convinced Gabe that a descent into madness was just that, a downward spiral. Food and shelter didn't show up when you were sick. Stuff wasn't supposed to get better, only worse.

Gabe still had lingering doubts about his sanity. How could he not, when he'd seen a woman with eagle feet and fangs? On the flipside, Ben and Lily and Theo and Kitty and even Kitty's dads had all confirmed the existence of demons.

Right now, that was going to have to be good enough for him.

Daubing out some of the shampoo, Gabe washed his hair. He felt far from settled in this strange place, but he could sure get used to indoor plumbing. It beat trying to find an open gas station or fast food joint every time he needed to take a dump. Weirdly, he'd miss spending his days at the library. Sure, people gave him that pitying look that made it clear they all knew he was on the streets, but he'd finally had all the time in the world to read whatever he wanted.

Bowing his head, he tried to get himself under control before he totally broke down and wept in relief. He couldn't let himself do that yet, because that kind of hope was too scary, it would make him too vulnerable. That was why he'd clung to the idea of delusions so long. In some ways, it was less heartbreaking to think he was insane. Because if he was crazy, then he'd already lost everything, even his mind.

If he started to have something again, something precious… he could lose it all again.

That would kill him.

Or, worse, as he'd discovered in the past, it might make him stupid— willing to do *anything,* put up with *any* kind of abuse, just to hold on to luxuries.

Twisting the faucets off, Gabe reached for a towel. He took his time drying off, focusing on returning his breathing to normal. One day at a time. That was how he'd made it this far. That was how he'd keep going forward.

He wiped the steam from the mirror. Staring at his own reflection, he was surprised by how much thinner had face had gotten. He wasn't sure it was a good look, almost a little too hollow at the cheekbones, like a hungry wolf. But, the funky little beard he had going might stay, even if it added to the lupine cast to his features.

Wet, his dark curls hung heavily, almost to his shoulders—which had broadened out at some point, too. The black swirls of the tribal tattoos on his biceps were stark against his brown skin. He'd grown to love them, but they were the reminder of how stupid he could be. The ink had been a creepy sort of possessive "gift" that one of his former 'boyfriends'—no, really he should just think of the guy for what he was, 'a trick' or a 'john.' The guy had wanted to mark Gabe, to signify a kind of ownership. That'd been a hard lesson for Gabe about trust and desperation. A lesson that continued to whisper to him now that things might seem good, but they could turn… and become frightening.

He ran his fingers over the tats, thinking of the ink that held Theo captive.

There were dangerous things about this new world. Gabe couldn't let himself get lulled by the luxuries of heat and food and shelter. He'd have to stay wary, keep his senses sharp. He needed to figure out if these were good guys or bad guys.

And he needed an exit strategy. Pronto.

When he opened the door to the bedroom, he saw that someone had set a pile of clean clothes on the foot of the bed. Ben? Must have been.

On top of the clothing was a stick of deodorant, toothbrush, and a decent plastic razor. Gabe pulled everything in to inspect it. The shirt was lavender, totally not his style, and it smelled like Febreeze, but he was able to get it over his shoulders and buttoned. It was only a little loose-fitting at the waist and too long at the sleeves—and the color looked unexpectedly amazing with his skin tone. Score.

If this was stuff from Ben's personal wardrobe, it would be way too weird to walk around in another man's underwear, so he left those. Gabe pulled a fresh pair from his backpack. The new jeans and socks he put on without hesitation. They were cotton and thick and they felt like heaven after years of mismatched threadbare socks.

One last check in the mirror and Gabe decided that, thus armored, he could face this strange new world he'd fallen into.

As he walked past the room that everyone was calling 'his,' Gabe did something he hadn't done in nearly two years. He tossed his backpack in, and walked away.

Then, picking up the backpack, he pulled out the baggie of change, counted it like he always did to make sure it was just as he left it, and shoved it into the pockets of his new jeans. The only other thing of any real value was the dead .mp3 player, so he pocketed that, too.

Thinking to hide the bag or at least tuck it out of sight, Gabe glanced around the room. When he'd first walked in with Theo, he'd really only noticed Theo, because hot, and the color of the walls, because cringe-worthy. Now he noticed that it was patently obvious that Ben had kind of fucked-up bringing him here... no one was expecting a guy. Or at least not a straight one, because there were frills everywhere. The bed had a ruffled skirt and there were even delicate looking doilies on all the tabletops: one on the end table near the bed, the other on what could only be a kind of make-up table.

And all the colors were pastel.

Even growing up with two moms hadn't prepared Gabe for this kind of overload of 'girl.'

However, the overt femininity of the room bothered Gabe far less than the sense that it wasn't meant for him. But, then he stopped himself. No, that shouldn't matter either. This was just his room *for now*. One day at a time, remember. No getting attached.

So, with those thoughts in mind, he shoved his backpack under the fancy throw pillows on the bed and shut the door on his way out.

Gabe found everyone gathered around the VW station wagon. Kitty was saying goodbye to her dads and everyone seemed to be joining in. Even Theo, though she pretended to be disinterested, inspecting her fingernails as she leaned up against the door. Gabe parked himself next to her with a, "Hey."

She gave him a double take, "Huh. You clean up good." Then her eyes darted to his shirt and she added, "Lavender, very fabulous."

He nodded distractedly, his gaze caught by how Kitty clung to her papa, their heads bowed onto each other's shoulders. You could feel the love radiating out from their body language.

"Gross, huh?" Theo said.

Gabe glanced at her sharply. He'd just been thinking about how he'd have killed for a parent like that. Mom and Meema had, at best, been benignly neglectful; Asshole was actively destructive. But, it did kind of piss him off to see someone getting what he never had, so he lifted a shoulder and said, "Yeah. Totally."

In fact, he couldn't watch this one any more. Turning around, Gabe headed back inside. "Want to see what there is to drink?" he gruffly asked Theo, both hoping for company and wanting to be alone.

No surprise, she stared at Kitty. Gabe made his way to the kitchen alone. It turned out home was a complicated thing—Gabe had thought he'd left all these feelings behind when he left without anything but his backpack. Now, it seemed home was the kind of baggage you took with you, no matter what.

That was how it had always worked, and Gabe would make it work again.

:: :: ::

Settling into this crazy house was going to take time, Gabe thought.

Watching Kitty say goodbye to her folks had put him in a rotten mood. He sat in 'his' room trying not to brood about the family he'd left in shambles back in West Virginia. A soft rap at the door made him blink away his reverie. Surrounded by mirrors and lace, he'd been slouched at the dresser, scowling. He pulled himself out of his mood enough to say, "Yeah?"

"Come to the living room," Lily's voice said from behind the closed door. "We need to talk house rules."

Finally. "Be right there."

Shaking himself out, he made his way to the room with the big TV he coveted so much. From the doorway, Gabe sussed out the mood of the room. Kitty sat on one corner of the huge couch with one knee curled up to her chest and both arms wrapped around it. Theo had jammed herself on the other end, clearly trying to act casual, but her face was scrunched into a kind of 'I'm ignoring you' frown.

There wasn't much for Gabe to do, but take the spot right between them.

Why did he have a sense this was going to be his role for a while? The person the teacher stuck between two quarreling cliques.

"Hey, ladies," Gabe said, just to get them riled up.

He was rewarded with a snort from Theo and an eye roll from Kitty.

Lily stood in front of the fireplace and awesome TV, looking at each one of them in turn. Did he imagine it or was she looking at him longer than the other two? He wanted to say, 'Yeah, I know I'm not supposed to be here. It's not my fault!' but she finally dragged her eyes from him and cleared her throat.

"House rules," she said to start. "You're each here to learn and train, both as students at the University and as potential demon-hunters or other magically useful people in the world. From your histories, I gather that only Kitty has any idea of *some* of the forces out there that can be harmful to humans and demons alike."

Gabe turned to glance at Kitty, wondering what her story was. For a girl who could lift a hundred-pound chest like nothing, she looked awfully scared. Kitty's lips pressed together firmly. Theo seemed to have snuck a curious glance too, but, whatever Lily's ominous comment was about, Kitty clearly didn't feel like sharing details.

"These rules are in place to allow us to live together peacefully and safely. I'm not going to spell out the disciplinary measures I plan to take if you break them, but I believe Theo can attest to my ability to invoke discipline as needed."

Theo grumbled and scratched her right calf over the tattoo.

Gabe tried to shoot Theo a glance that silently said, 'I thought you said that wouldn't happen to the rest of us!' but she ignored him, focusing on what Lily was saying.

"And so, we get to the rules. Rule #1, you each have your own room. Other students' rooms are private. Do not interfere with each other's things. You may socialize in each others' rooms, but I expect you to leave the door open when you do, which brings us to Rule #2: no sexual conduct with other students here."

She looked pointedly at Theo, but Gabe was the one who felt himself blushing.

"What about outsiders?" Theo asked. "Can I bring people home?"

"That's your business," Lily said. "You're an adult. No outsiders in the Lab and I expect you to mind the 10 p.m. curfew regarding *all* loud activities."

Which what, apparently included sex? Damn, the thought of loud sex was very distracting all of a sudden. Did Lily *know* Theo had loud sex? Like, had she actually heard it? Or was she just guessing? Gabe kept those thoughts to himself, and tried to focus on Lily's list.

"I expect you to keep any alcohol use moderate and legal. Kitty and

Theo, please keep in mind that Gabe is not of legal drinking age yet. Drugs are prohibited and you'll quickly learn that alcohol and magic do not mix well, so I expect you'll limit that to rare social events."

Huh, so the other two were twenty-one or older. Gabe felt a little extra awkward being pointed out as the baby of the group. He also had to tamp down on the impulse to explain that while he might be the youngest, he knew for a fact he could pass as much older. Plus, his fake ID said he was twenty-three.

Hey, wait a minute, how did Lily know his actual age? He hadn't even told her his full name!

Maybe it was magic, because he'd been trying to get in the habit of going by 'Jose' the name on the ID, and ever since he'd met up with these people, he'd been blurting out his real name everywhere.

Before Gabe could formulate a way to ask about it, Lily continued, "Speaking of social events, you are expected to attend dinner at the house on Sundays, Tuesdays and Thursdays, which will be followed by lessons in magic. The other nights are yours to socialize or study as you choose. You will also be given tests by me and Aben'eres and other tutors and are expected to perform these speedily and to the best of your abilities. You must also enroll in at least two University courses and to keep above a 3.0 average. If you are having trouble at any point, I can arrange tutoring."

Gabe sure as hell hoped they'd be "arranging" for more than tutoring, because college? He couldn't afford that! He shifted in his seat, feeling a little nervous about how he might be expected pay off these debts he was incurring. Even though it was a phantom sensation, Gabe swore he felt the tattoo needles again through the fog of drugs, that invasive, creepily intrusive feeling that had haunted his dreams even after he'd managed to escape that guy.

"So which rule number was that?" Theo asked, her voice pulling him back to the present.

Lily quirked up one eyebrow. "Four," she said. "You'll get a printed list in case you want to study it in detail. Just remember, for every way you come up with to break a rule, I can think of two ways to punish you for it."

Punish? That didn't sound good. Gabe thought back to what Theo had said so casually about passing out from pain, and wondered just what in hell's name he had signed on to. Maybe waking up with a tattoo he never wanted was nothing compared to these people.

Turning to Gabe and Kitty, Lily graced them with a softer smile. "Theo has a different arrangement than the two of you, being effectively under house arrest. Kitty, I don't expect any trouble from you and, Gabe, I trust you know which example to follow."

"Um," Gabe said. "Sorry but how am I going to take classes? I haven't registered or anything." He meant also that he had no money for it and no high school transcript or test scores or anything.

Lily's eyes brightened and she gave him a half-grin. "The Sangkesh are one of the most tech-savvy secret organizations in the world. Cooking up the right records for you is child's play. You'll be registered at SFSU this week. I'll get you a copy of your transcripts."

He wanted to ask where the tuition was coming from, but just in case it wasn't a deal he could stomach, he wanted to get a few nights sleep and a few more showers in first.

Lily went on, "Rule #5: No magic in the house outside of the Lab. Theo, for now that includes shape-shifting. This obviously doesn't cover abilities you can't turn off, like Kitty's strength and Gabe's ability to see, but let's all try to limit the amount of chaos we create, shall we?

"Rule #6: you will have chores. Do them. I'll post a chart in the upstairs family room. You will get spending money each week but if your desires outpace that amount, you'll have to come up with more cash on your own ... legally."

Without thinking Gabe blurted out, "Wait, we get an allowance? How much?"

"Thirty dollars a week," Lily said. "The School here will provide clothing, books, school supplies, and food. If you have requests for specific food items, write them on the chalkboard on the side of the refrigerator." She turned back to Theo and the look on her face was pure amusement with a hint of mischief. "Miss Young, if you write 'dick' on the chalkboard, the first thing I'll do is video chat it to your sister."

"You have something against spotted dick? I hear it's tasty," Theo said.

"That's disgusting," Kitty said.

Gabe said, turning to Kitty, "No, spotted dick is an actual thing. British, I think."

"I'm not eating it," Kitty declared. "Ms. Cordoba, what if we make something to eat, how do we keep other people out of it?"

Cordoba? So, that was Lily's last name? Wasn't that a city in Spain? If it wasn't, it sure sounded like one. Gabe had taken her as Arabic or maybe Greek, but was Lily Latino like he was?

"Just Lily is fine," Lily said. "As for your question, there's plenty of Tupperware. Put your name on it and a 'keep out' note and I trust the same courtesy you'll show each other's rooms will extend to food. We do have a cook who will put shared meals in the refrigerator, clearly marked. Now, you've heard the rules Ben and I came up with, why don't you three talk and decide if there are other rules or guidelines you'd like to request. I'm going to order us some pizzas. Who likes what?"

Not out of the back of dumpster, Gabe was thinking, but he just said, "Whatever is fine with me."

"No meat," Theo said, which sounded a little strange after the whole 'dick' interchange.

"Meat-lover's," Kitty said.

"Maybe they have one with spotted dick on it," Theo said to Kitty.

Kitty pointedly ignored Theo, which seemed to irritate Theo even more. She made a face that she ostensibly shared with Gabe. He shook his head. These two, they were making his head hurt.

Once Lily was out of the room, it got really quiet and icy. Gabe let a couple of minutes pass just to see if one of the girls was going to break the silence first. He sat there for a while, literally twiddling his thumbs and staring at the blank TV screen. Briefly, he glanced around wondering if there was a remote. Not seeing one handy, he wondered if you had to use magic to turn it on. How much would that suck?

About as much as sitting in this room with these two ladies, whose desperate attempt to ignore each other were getting on his nerves. He heard Lily moving around in the kitchen and then the back of the house. She clearly wasn't going to just bust back in and save him.

Gabe thought through about sixteen different conversation gambits, that ranged from 'nice weather, we're having' to the classic 'How about them Forty-Niners, eh?' Finally, he couldn't take it and just busted out with: "This is getting ridiculous. You two should either fight or fuck."

"I don't—" Kitty started.

"Fuck?" Theo broke in, as though finishing the thought for her.

"Fight!" Kitty insisted, but the way she raised her top lip to show her fangs kind of killed the truth of her statement.

"But you *do* fuck?" Theo said with a grin.

Kitty got off the couch, as if even five feet with Gabe in the middle was too close to be to Theo. She walked over to the fireplace and ran her hand along the edge of the mantle. It was a weird gesture, Gabe figured it was unconscious, like she was trying to dust, or clean, or somehow smooth things out.

"None of your business, witch," she said.

"You're just jealous because all you can do is lift heavy shit," Theo shot back. "It's sooo intimidating."

Her voice had an edge to it and Gabe had the feeling she was needling Kitty on purpose. Maybe testing the new girl?

The doorbell chimed and Gabe wanted to jump up and get it, but he didn't have cash for pizzas. Lily's steps sounded in the hall. The door opened and she went out onto the porch.

Theo glared at Kitty, "You demons are only strong in numbers. How tough are you on your own?"

"Oh, and *you're* tough on your own? Away from your *family*?" Kitty put a sneer into the last word.

The must have hit home because Theo actually growled.

"At least I don't need my daddies to come with me," she said.

"Really? Doesn't you sister live like two miles from here?"

"Oooh, did you look me up in your creepy demon archives? Now we know you can read, but can you do anything useful?"

"Can you?" Kitty asked. "I read in my creepy demon archive that you turn into a bug and that you have to take off all your clothes to do it. Or maybe that's just an excuse to strip in front of everyone."

"I turn into lots of things!" Theo was up off the couch now, facing Kitty across the length of the room.

"Hey, okay, I have a rule," Gabe broke in. "No name calling. I heard that whole 'mere human' sneer from you before, Kitty. Knock it off. It's not cool.... wahhhh?!" Gabe's admonishment turned into a gasp of surprise as a ripple of air currents swirled around Theo. What the hell was going on?

The space around Theo folded in on itself in a way that made Gabe jerk back from it. She was shifting, somehow he just knew. But, Theo's body didn't change like in movies with the skin shifting and all that. Instead, the whole space around her shuddered and suddenly, where she'd been standing, a huge black jaguar appeared, crouched belly to the floor, radiating heat and stinking like a tomcat.

Instinct had Gabe clambering up onto the couch. Though he wasn't quite sure why he bothered, since the jaguar could leap across the space between them in a second if it wanted. But, then again, he had a vague memory that maybe he was supposed to stand tall and act big in front of a predator, right?

Or maybe that was a bear.

Not that the jaguar was looking at him. The cat was focused on Kitty, who was backpedalling like mad. She looked shocked.

Okay, jaguar-transformation was not a normal thing in this new universe. Good to know. Because it was seriously freaking Gabe out. Maybe that was obvious, Mr. Standing on the Couch....

Theo-as-jaguar prowled towards Kitty, who continued to scramble backwards, heading for the kitchen door. Theo-jaguar paused as if calculating, one paw raised, golden eyes fixed on Kitty. When she moved again, she circled, pushing Kitty into the corner by the fireplace. Kitty's face was ashen, the whites of her eyes wide with fear as her back hit the wall.

"Whoa! Whoa! Rule number five: no magic in the house," Gabe shouted from where he was now standing on the arm of the couch, trying to see what was going on around the massive form of the jaguar.

Theo opened her mouth and growled. The deep, gravel sound went on longer than Gabe thought possible. The sound of it raised every hair on the back of his neck and arms, and his pulse thundered in his ears.

Kitty tucked herself into ball. Gabe was pretty sure Theo only meant to scare her. She could control herself as a jaguar, right? Theo padded up to Kitty on heavy black paws and started sniffing around her head and neck.

"Yeah, no," Gabe muttered out loud, "I'm pretty sure you're supposed to play dead. Cats get bored with dead things."

Of course, maybe it was different with magic jaguars? And, damn, if Kitty didn't seem kind of traumatized and frozen. Did she forget she was super-strong?

"Fight," he whispered, half-to-himself. "Why don't you fight?"

Should he jump in? Put himself between the jaguar and Kitty? Was that heroic or moronic?

From the front steps, he heard Lily say loudly, if matter-of-factly, "One sec, I think there's a big cat loose in the house. Don't go anywhere, I left your tip on the counter."

At the sound of her voice, Theo-jaguar turned and, even though Kitty had looked like she was in a completely indefensible position with her legs tucked up against her body, she surprised Gabe by finally lashing out and kicking hard with both feet. She hit Theo squarely across the top of her broad, furred chest and about three hundred pounds of cat tumbled ass over ears across the short side of the living room. After ripping out half of the doorway to the foyer, Theo crunched to a stop.

Shit was getting real. With a snarl, Theo got her paws under her and leapt for Kitty. Kitty was tough and had that super-strength, but Theo was a fucking jaguar. From where Gabe stood, the fight was too close to call. Yeah, he'd better jump in here. Maybe throw himself in front of Kitty?

Before he could react, Gabe heard Lily say some foreign phrase. In a flash, the air swirled around itself again. Mid-lunge, Theo changed back to human. She dropped onto Kitty as a naked girl.

Disaster averted, Gabe's mouth decided to show its relief with a snarky, "Elegant," at Theo's graceless fall, face-first into Kitty.

Still pressed against the wall, Kitty looked almost as alarmed to have a nude girl on top of her as a jaguar. Her ninja kick move had slid her down some, so she was mostly under Theo… like maybe they'd decided to go for option two, after all. Really, from where Gabe was standing, the view was unbelievable—breathtaking, even. Maybe it was all the leftover adrenaline kicking his body into overdrive, but his brain spazzed into 'heh, naked' territory.

Kitty's shirt had popped a button. She was pretty stacked and Theo had just about landed with her face in the hollow between Kitty's breasts. Gabe'd seen a lot of porn that wasn't nearly this well framed, especially the way Kitty's breath came in quick, heaving sobs.

"You're grounded," Lily said from the ruined doorway. Gabe wondered if she meant all of them, until Lily added, "No shifting for a week and you're doing all the household chores. Now let's see if you still have pizzas." With that, she stalked back out to deal with the delivery guy, or so Gabe imagined. He was still mesmerized by the two women.

At first, Theo looked too dazed by being forcibly returned to human-shape to realize that she was on top of a fine pair of breasts. Or maybe she wasn't into that. As Gabe watched, it all came together for Theo: the muscles along her back, ass and legs that had been startled slack, all tensed, which was gorgeous to see, even if it meant she was freaking out. She shoved herself up onto hands and knees, naked still, and straddling Kitty. Kitty curled her arms defensively across her chest.

Gabe couldn't see it, but his body informed him that the gesture probably involved a lot of Kitty's arms brushing Theo's breasts. He told his body to shut it, but it was ignoring his brain as all the blood went to more important stuff in his crotch. Then Theo crawled backwards off of Kitty, looking surprisingly cold and vulnerable, and the moment was gone. Gabe fumbled open the buttons on his shirt and pulled it off.

Hopping down from the couch, he handed it to her, "Uh, hey? Take this."

She stood with an awful lot of grace for someone who'd just crashed naked across the room. Taking the shirt from his fingers, she shouldered it on. The tails of the shirt were long enough to reach mid-thigh on her. Gabe was only mostly completely disappointed.

Lily came in through the demolished foyer doorway with a stack of three pizza boxes in her hands. As she shook her head, Gabe got a rough idea of how this might look to her: broken plaster, a cloud of white dust still settling, open boards visible in the door frame, him in the middle of the room now dressed in only jeans and socks. Next to him was Theo in a long, lavender men's shirt, under which she was still really obviously naked and either kind of chilly or sort of turned on. Then there was Kitty, who'd tucked herself further back into the corner and turned her face away from the room and seemed to be having trouble getting herself to breathe steadily again.

"Your porn movie slasher flick mash-up is never going to get funded," Lily said, completely deadpan as she walked through to the kitchen.

"Yeah, nobody'd believe the whole and-then-she-turned-into-a-jaguar thing," Gabe said. "And who is that porn for?"

"Furries," Theo said in that ho-hum way, as she walked toward the kitchen.

Gabe winced as she marched resolutely through the debris barefooted. Theo didn't seem the least bit fazed by it. Then he noticed her step had a limping-on-both-legs tenderness and figured some of the toughness was an act. Then again, maybe she did this a lot? Broke up houses and then walked out buck naked?

Gabe glanced back over to Kitty. She hadn't moved. "You okay?" he asked her, because she didn't look it.

"I'm fine," she said, but her voice shook. She suddenly seemed to notice her shirt had come undone. She tried to fix it, until it became obvious that the button was gone. "Damn it. I hate this place."

Still standing awkwardly where he'd hopped off the couch, Gabe felt like maybe he should try to comfort Kitty, even though she'd clearly lumped him in with the 'mere humans.' But, it didn't take a rocket scientist to figure Kitty for a no-touch sort of gal. So, he said, "Do you have to stay?" He glanced at her ankles, but he couldn't see any ink, and, anyway, Lily had said Theo was the only one under house arrest. "You could leave if you wanted."

Something about what he'd said, made Kitty's jaw clench. Her dark eyes flashed and she pulled herself up like he'd just called out the worst insult ever. "If anyone leaves," Kitty said, her lip curling to show off a sharp fang, "It will be her. I won't fail this time."

That sounded like another story, like the one Lily had alluded to with the demon-hunters. Because, even though Kitty sounded snotty and full of herself, Gabe could see a hardness in her face that wasn't just arrogance. Something had happened to this girl, something bad. Something she had to prove herself better than.

He could understand that. If anything, this little demonstration with the jaguar-transformation showed Gabe that he needed to start figuring out how not to be a complete waste of space. He had no idea how, but he had to run to catch up with these two. Otherwise, he was going to end up a splatter on the pavement.

Kitty stood and took a moment to attempt to straighten her blouse again. If anything, all her ministrations made more of her bra show. Lifting her chin, she seemed to decide to rock the wardrobe malfunction look and marched into the kitchen.

Gabe glanced down at his own naked chest. He figured he was just going to have to embrace the shirtless look, too.

Except, as he passed the far edge of the couch, he spotted a folded up men's shirt. It was white with blue stripes. Again, not his usual style, but, somehow, he was not surprised when he unfolded it and held it up to his chest that it seemed like it would fit. Where was this stuff coming from? When Lily said that the household would provide food and clothes, had she meant that literally, like somehow things would just appear in the house when you needed them?

Looking around the seemingly empty room as he shrugged into the new shirt, Gabe nervously whispered, "Thanks."

Before he walked through to the kitchen, Gabe turned and told the room, "But, you should have gotten Kitty one too. She needed it more than me."

The kitchen and dining room reminded Gabe of the post-Avengers shawarma scene, where everyone sat around a table, not really engaging, just munching food determinedly. Theo ate at the island, her back to everyone, staring out the window at the darkening sky. She'd gone up to her room and got a pair of jeans, but hadn't changed out of Gabe's lavender shirt.

Lilly and Kitty sat at the table in the dining room; Lily had the *SF Chronicle* in her lap and seemed to be reading the editorial page. Kitty was staring at the slice of pizza on her plate, not eating it, rubbing the back of her neck like it hurt.

The gloomy little scene would have brought Gabe down, but the smell of fresh, hot pizza made his stomach do a little happy dance in anticipation. Seeing a stack of plates in the center of the table, he took one for himself and loaded up. Once he had a slice of each kind, he plunked himself down at the table.

He looked at Lily for a long moment as he chewed a mouthful of cheese and bread. After swallowing, he asked, "How did you know I was only nineteen? I never said. Hell, I'm not even sure I told you my name."

She blinked at him coolly. "Ben got your information from the Vestals. And despite what anyone might say about them, they keep excellent records."

Records? Of stuff he'd been trying so hard to hide? Great. "Who *are* these Vestals?"

Lily looked at Kitty who straightened up and answered like this was part of some test. "They're an ancient order of witches, one of the top two orders, the other is the Hecatines—what Theo's sister is part of, which I guess makes her a Hecatine too, unless they don't want to take her. They're also sneaky record keepers."

"So who are the good guys?" Gabe asked.

"The demons," Kitty said, like it was obvious. "The Sangkesh demons who work to protect humanity from … everything else." She went back to staring at the pizza slice but didn't pick it up.

But I'm a witch, Gabe thought, *and if the Vestals want me, what does that make me?*

"So the witches are not the good guys?" he double-checked.

"Witches are good," Theo yelled in from the kitchen but didn't elaborate.

"It's not as simple as good guys and bad guys," Lily explained. "The Sangkesh demons protect humanity, but in their own way, so do the Hecatine witches, and the Vestal witches seek to guide the knowledge of all of us—and we all disagree on the best way to do this. The other demons, they can be a lot more dangerous, the Shaitans generally like to torment humans and the Gul, the ones you can see so easily, they feed off humans."

"What about the Cavallo?" Theo asked. She'd gotten up from her seat at the island and was leaning against one side of the doorway. Her half-eaten slice of cheese pizza flopped in her hand, dripping grease onto the plate she held in her other hand.

"Where did you hear that name?" Lily asked sharply.

Theo shrugged.

"I thought so. You were listening." Lily sighed. "What you need to know about them is that they're bad, really bad. You should never run across them."

'Should never' like it was unlikely, or 'should never' because, if you did you were fucked? Gabe decided the answer was probably 'both,' so instead he asked, "But what are they?"

Kitty answered him. "Humans," she said, and the disdain crept back into her voice for a moment. "Paid mercenaries, government agents, scientists, all lured by money to try to find a way to give humans the power of demons."

Taking a bite of the cheese pizza, Gabe considered this idea. It wasn't clear if these Cavallo guys could actually transfer demon power to people, but it sounded like they were willing to pay any price to do it… which meant that maybe Kitty had a reason to be stuck up. Demon power must be a seriously valuable thing. But, what all did it entail? Kitty was certainly physically strong. Gabe's arms still ached from where he'd pulled a muscle trying to pick up that heavy-ass box of hers.

So, was it like the demons preachers always railed against? The ones Gabe had seen so far, sort of fit that bill. There was Lily with her chicken-feet and Kitty with her fangs and wicked-ass looking fingernails that could almost pass for claws. In his travels, Gabe had seen the occasional person who sported snake-slit eyes, horns, or any number of typically 'demonic' features. But, was that it? A forked-tongue and super-strength didn't seem to be a big enough pay-off.

There must be more to demon power.

Yet magic seemed to be the purview of humans. The Vestals and the, what had Lily said? Hecatine. Both Greek-derived names, interestingly enough. In fact, Gabe was pretty sure he'd read somewhere that Hecate was sometimes called 'the Queen of Witches.' On the other hand, he'd thought she was kind of a nasty goddess, the kind that harbored ghosts and ushered unwitting souls into the underworld. Obviously a smear campaign by her detractors, Gabe thought with a little smile and another large bite of the pizza.

He glanced over his shoulder to where Theo had gone back into the kitchen. Shape-shifting seemed far more awesome than super-strength to him. "So who's trying to harness the power of witches?" he asked. With a little nod at Kitty, he said, "No offense, but, being a jaguar kind of kicks ass. If I'm a witch, can I learn to do that?"

"That," Lily said, with a long, dramatic pause, "Requires a very long answer, but in short, I wouldn't get your hopes up. However, with training and practice, you may discover you have some equally impressive capabilities."

Lily looked around and, seeing that Kitty and Gabe were still looking at her avidly, went on in a more lecture-oriented tone. "The Hecatine witches divide magic into eight basic energies and I've found that to be useful. Most people who can change shape are using earth energy and some, who are very skilled, take on not only the shape of an animal but a unique kind of magic associated with it. But this isn't how Theo changes shape—she's using the energy of information itself to encode the body of a specific animal and call it out as she wants. It's actually a neighboring energy to her sister's magic.

"Witches tend to be strong in information and time magic, with occasional outliers in earth or spirit energy. Demons are on the other side of the taxonomy and tend to be strong in spirit, fire, breath and earth. They're very good at moving energies around, particularly in taking it and using it to their own ends. Those Gul that you see feeding on humans, Gabe, many of them are not only eating fear or sadness, they're causing it so they can feed more fully. And if you met a greater Gul, fully-embodied ... most of them can kill with a touch if they want or worse."

"That's why we hunt them," Kitty said. "The most powerful of the Gul or the Shaitans can start wars, they can spark huge disasters, and humanity never knows, they can't know, so we have to stop them when we can, if we can."

"Shaitans," Gabe said, "That sounds a lot like 'satan.' Coincidence?"

Everyone looked at him like he was a complete boob, though Lily at least said, "No, it's not a coincidence. Shaitan is the Arabic. But," she said with a yawn, "I'm not ready to teach you all of that yet tonight. I'm going to bed. Don't stay up too late. Tomorrow will be busy."

Kitty nodded dutifully. Theo snorted from the kitchen, like it was nowhere near her usual bedtime. Gabe felt somewhere in between, because as soon as Lily yawned, he'd felt a wave of tiredness wash over him.

Kitty got up and took her plate to the dishwasher in the kitchen, skillfully avoiding eye—or any other kind of—contact with Theo. She said goodnight, presumably to Lily, who headed off down the hall from the kitchen to the closed door that must be her bedroom.

Not quite ready to turn in himself, Gabe grabbed the most-full pizza box from the kitchen counter and headed into the living room. He picked his way around the broken bits of plaster and lathe on the floor, an awkward reminder that there'd been a fight. Still it seemed a waste to let this night end without watching something on that sweet entertainment system.

He set the box on the couch cushions. Hunting around the room, he finally found the remote on the fireplace mantle. It looked normal enough. No 'press here' to engage magic, so Gabe pulled the pizza box onto his lap and fiddled with the remote until he got the screen to pop on. Mindful of house rules, he nudged the volume down to a just-loud-enough level.

As he flipped through the channels, Gabe noticed how devoid of personality the room was. Where were the family pictures? He'd first assumed the place must belong to Lily or Ben or both of them, but, if so, they hadn't lived here long at all. Despite the innate character the hardwood floors gave it, whole room had the 'real estate' open house whitewashed feel.

Like right now, Gabe could really use a crocheted afghan or a quilted comforter to snuggle into, but there wasn't one in sight. Nothing at all that said 'family heirloom' or 'old favorite' either.

He found something mindless, one of those faux documentary horror flicks, and settled in. As the evening crept in, the room had gotten dark and he sat alone with the flickering light of the TV. Gabe munched on his pizza until his stomach felt painfully full. It was hard to set aside uneaten food, but any more and he'd barf.

A shiver racked through his body. It wasn't cold, though, it was his muscles letting go more tension. He sucked in a deep breath, like he'd been forgetting to breathe all this time, too. He hadn't realized how much he missed this feeling of being home somewhere, even if it was a strange place with even stranger housemates.

The movie over, he reached for the remote only to find a fluffy blanket beside him on the cushion. The house again, giving him stuff. He flipped it out and tucked it around his lap and knees. "Thanks," he whispered.

"You're welcome," said Theo, "But I didn't do anything."

"I was talking to the house," Gabe explained.

"Sure, okay, so long as it doesn't talk back," she laughed.

After setting the pizza box on the floor, she lowered herself onto the couch beside him. The cushion sagged and their shoulders touched. Instead of pulling away or righting herself, Theo leaned even further into him. She helped herself to his blanket and the remote, too.

"Do you like those comedy news shows?" she asked, flipping.

He shrugged. "I really haven't seen TV in two years. Is it me, or is everything brighter and faster?"

She laughed. "It's just you."

"Yeah, probably," he admitted with a yawn. "I got desensitized or something."

"What kept you away from TV? Parents or lack of access?"

Gabe was glad the darkness hid the flush of his cheeks. "Oh, well, I was... unhoused, I think the term is."

"You were homeless?"

"No, I have a home in West Virginia with Mom and Meema. I just couldn't live there anymore."

"Is this a sob story?"

Gabe laughed. "Nah. I mean, I'm beginning to think my life is pretty fucking boring compared to the things you and Kitty have been through. I just got sick of Asshole abducting me and trying to send me off to military school or through church programs to 'cure' me of the queer cooties my moms apparently smeared all over me. Plus, my moms were... distracted. I don't know, it's probably not as bad all that, but at the time all their fighting just seemed too much...?" He shrugged. "Anyway, I bailed. I've been on my own since then."

Theo pulled away a little and gave Gabe a look, "Wait, queer cooties? Are you gay?"

"No, that was the ironic part to all of Asshole's freakage," Gabe said. "I hate to limit myself or rule anything out, but, so far, I get *way* more distracted by naked girl bits than guy parts."

That made Theo smile lasciviously and cuddle back up. "Good."

Gabe wanted to ask what her story was. Why did Theo steal stuff? Did she have a kind of booming trade in stolen items? Was it something she just did for herself or did she have some greater purpose? He would have assumed maybe Theo had been thieving for the Hecatines. Considering how ticked off Lily seemed to be about it all, he was guessing maybe not. Unless the story was more complicated than it seemed, he figured it was unlikely her own 'order' had put her under house arrest just for doing what amounted to her job. She didn't seem desperate, so no way she was stealing bread to eat or stuff she needed. He knew what that was like, and she wasn't that. So, yeah, no, she was stealing shit just because she could...

The more Gabe thought about it the more he could totally see Theo just doing it for the thrills. She had that kind of vibe: dangerous, crazy girl.

She was trouble with a capital-T, which, of course, just made her six zillion times hotter.

In fact, he was just thinking about maybe trying to bust that age-old move of the yawn that turned into an arm around the shoulder, when he heard her soft snores. She was out. Heh, probably an adrenaline crash after all the jaguar-excitement.

He let her doze against his shoulder for an hour. Then, very carefully, he extracted himself and lowered her gently to the couch. He arranged the blanket around her shoulders. Clicking off the TV, Gabe thought he'd done a quiet job of it, only to creak on the floorboard. Theo's head popped up, "Wha…? Oh, shit, I fell asleep, didn't I?"

"Yeah, I was just headed to bed myself."

"Oh." She blinked at the blankets he'd arranged around her shoulders. "I should get to bed too."

"Goodnight," he said, kind of hating rule number one—or was it two? —right about now. Especially since Theo had never bothered to put on anything under his over-sized shirt. He could see the swell of her breast through the gap in the buttons.

As he made his way to his room, Gabe knew what he'd be dreaming about tonight.

CHAPTER NINETEEN

ERIN WAITS FOR THE WORST

Even though her captors left her alone, Erin slept fitfully. Any time someone walked past her door, she would jerk awake, clutching the threadbare blanket to her face and wait for the worst.

The worst hadn't come for days, but that made her no less anxious. If anything it made it harder, because each time, she'd think: surely, this is it. This time will be the time they come in and bring pain instead of food.

But food kept coming.

Food and water.

There was even a bucket in the corner for her... other needs. Erin tried very hard not to think about that too hard, because it was nearly impossible for her to balance properly over it without any crutches or other support. The first time she'd tried, it had been a disgusting disaster. No one had come to help her clean up for a long, long time.

But someone did come clean her up, and they took the bucket away and brought a fresh one fairly regularly. It was mostly men. Men who either refused to look at her or looked once, long enough to sneer or spit, and then never again.

The food they brought was kind of... fascinating. Sometimes they brought her fast food—a Happy Meal box, except they took out the toy, like maybe they thought that she could fashion a weapon from a wind-up plastic kid's movie character. Or, weirdly, that they were punishing some child, which was especially strange since Erin was nearly eighteen. Yet, despite that, the lack of toy just made Erin more sad. It was a Sad Meal box, because, fuck, all that grease and chemicals and not even a damn toy.

Other times, she'd get something basic, but clearly home cooked— ramen from a packet, mac and cheese from a box, and soup from a can. The time they brought her beans and toast for breakfast, complete with a random slice of tomato, made Erin wonder if someone in this weird little paramilitary cult was English or from someone somewhere else in the UK. Because beans and toast? She'd only read about food like that in Harry Potter and British police procedural novels.

Weird.

If she hadn't noticed the penchant for military-esque uniforms, Erin would figure that a bunch of frat boys were in charge of feeding her.

She'd also finally heard a name for this cultish organization: *Cavallo*. Sounded Italian or Latin, and a little like Calvary, which they clearly were not. Not for her anyway.

She was just a monster, locked away in her little box.

Waiting for the rescue that never came.

And now her songs had been silenced.

:: :: ::

Something was making Erin's Cavallo captors nervous. Crawling over to her door, she pressed her ear to the crack to hear their chatter during a change in shift with the guards. Having not much else to do, Erin had memorized their schedule. They thought they were being random, but everything had a pattern.

Today, two of the men, the one that Erin had nicknamed 'Nasal' and the other that had a weirdly friendly, deep voice like he ought to be on the radio or a commercial announcer or something. She called that guy 'Smooth.' Nasal had been on duty at her door for the last three hours. He'd spent most of his time humming some popular song to himself on and off, checking his phone, and playing some app-game with repetitive beeping noises that made Erin's teeth itch—though less from annoyance and more from desire for the electronic bits and metal parts.

When Smooth came, the phone disappeared guiltily—Erin could

hear the quick shifting of feet and almost stereotypical covering cough. "Hey," he said to his comrade. "What's up?"

"We have to move the whole operation."

Erin put her hands in front of her mouth to stop the sound of excitement. Why would they have to move? Was someone actually coming for her? Was this a chance for escape?

"How the fuck are we going to do that?" Nasal asked. The more she listened to Nasal, the more she thought maybe he was from somewhere out East, like Massachusetts or Vermont or one of those places where 'car' became 'caaah.' "We got to move all this? The girl? The equipment?"

"Everything," Smooth said. "There's a tracker after us."

A tracker? Erin's mind repeated silently, jittering with excitement.

"One of those demon hunter types?" Nasal asked, sounding nervous.

Smooth made a sound of exasperation. "Let's hope not. We've been operating under the radar of those Sangkesh freaks for a long time. We don't want those killers coming after us."

"Jesus fuck," Nasal swore, "Is this little girl really worth all this? What's she got anyway?"

Erin craned to hear. This was a question she'd been wondering, too.

While she held her breath, Smooth seemed to consider it for a long time. "I don't know, man," he said finally. "I really don't. But, I think it's because she's got that ability with the metal. It's a Shaitan thing, I heard the boss saying, and from what I can tell, those types don't breed often, especially not with the Sangkesh."

Satan? Had Smooth really said "Satan"? Could it be that grandma was right about her all this time? She really was the spawn of Satan?

Well, it would explain the horns.

And the clawed feet.

Still, Erin had always hoped for... metaphors. She wasn't quite sure what to do with reality.

Reality stung.

KITTY SOLVES (AND CREATES) PROBLEMS WITH CAKE

The house was silent, but outside Kitty heard a car and very faintly a person's voice asking a question. She jerked alert, but the voice was far away. It wasn't Theo, she wasn't under attack, she was okay, safe. Lily had assured her that through the magic in the tattoo she could control Theo's shape shifting in the house—the grounding wasn't in name only; Theo would now find it impossible to shift inside the walls of the house.

Lily had also pointed out that Kitty hadn't been in real danger because she could have turned Theo human at any point, but that she wanted to see how they handled the situation. It was the same kind of "test" her mother pulled, and it made Kitty's neck ache with tension. She did appreciate Lily's willingness to leave her alone when she was freaking out so that she could get it back under control. When people fussed over her, especially ones she'd just met, it only made her fear worse.

There was silence again, but she couldn't sleep. Every time she closed her eyes she either saw the jaguar's open mouth growling at her or Theo's confused, dark eyes as she looked down at Kitty from on top of her. Her body had a burningly clear memory of Theo's breasts pressing into her upper belly and it wasn't a stretch to rewind from there to Theo grinning at her and saying, "But you do fuck?"

That was just adrenaline stirring up the lingering feelings from her call with Blake a few days ago—plus Theo's stupid pheromones. It wasn't like she would ever actually contemplate Theo that way. Though if she did … No. She missed Blake. She missed home and her dads.

And her head hurt like the jaguar's teeth had gone through her skull. She sat up in the bed and put her face in her hands, tears slipping between her fingers. Weakness, fear, again. Always. She missed the smell of Dad's books, she missed her bed, she even missed the girl she'd most recently had in her bed, an on-again off-again situation of the last couple of years. Not the same as Blake, but fun.

Kitty didn't make a lot of time for relationships, but she'd had a few in college. And that thought brought another wave of fear because Gabe and Theo were starting undergrad in a week and they had no idea that Kitty had graduated college last spring. What would they think when they found out that she'd started college at 17 and just got her B.S. in Mathematics? She couldn't start grad school until she was able to read in German, and her language skills sucked, so she was taking undergrad German at SFSU in the fall along with a grad-level physics course, but come spring she wanted to be taking classes at UC-Berkeley.

What if she did great here with Lily and learned to use magic and fight demons? Would her mother still let her go to grad school? Or would she drag Kitty back into the heart of the demon hunters and expect her to dedicate her life to that?

From the edge of the bed, she looked out the window at the dark night sky. A thick film of nausea edged up under her ribs. The room was too small but it was also the only place in this strange house that felt familiar. She stood up and moved to the window. Sliding the glass to the side, she pressed her nose to the screen so she could smell the clean night air and see the few stars bright enough to shine through the miasma of city lights.

The air didn't smell right. It was all piney and wet, and it reminded her of being in Europe with mother, in those big, old forests, everything rotting and crumbling. She was supposed to learn to track and fight among those old giants, but she only learned to hide and to run.

Her chest hurt, ribs clenching, her breath ragged. The darkness wasn't helping. She felt closed in, not protected. She knew she was panicking, that happened often enough, and at least now she knew enough not to panic about the panic. This awful tight, sickening pain would go on until she'd worn herself out and then in a few hours she might sleep a little. But now she had to move. If she stayed in this closing room she'd start to hyperventilate and that was exponentially worse.

She slid open her door and padded barefoot across the soft wood of the family room floor to the hall. Theo's door was closed. Kitty slipped down the stairs, staying to the outside of the treads and the outside of her feet, preventing anything from creaking and groaning, until she reached the second story and the kitchen.

She would make tea. Simple, clear, a goal to focus on. Make tea, breathe as slowly and evenly as she could, not hyperventilate, not scream, not make the panic worse. Find a cup, that was the first thing. Now, where was the tea?

"What'cha looking for?" Gabe asked. He kept his voice low but she jumped anyway, startled to hear another person.

"Tea," she said. "I'm making tea."

"It's over by the fridge in that skinny cupboard," he said and sat on one of the stools on the far side of the island, resting his elbows on the counter. He looked rumpled, the neck of his orchid-colored t-shirt slightly off-center, as if he'd been asleep for a while already.

"You want a cup?" she asked. It was good having him there. He seemed the most lost in this place, other than her, and his presence focused her. It was easier to hold it together around another person, especially a near stranger. She was so used to that.

"Yeah, thanks. Whatever you're having."

Kitty was much better at reading patterns than reading faces, so it took a while of watching someone's behavior to know if they were truly friendly, but she remembered him putting himself on the couch between her and Theo, joking, trying to get them to lighten up.

Plus he'd been willing to literally give Theo the shirt off his back when she needed it. He had a good chest for a scruffy guy, but Theo … how did she end up with a body that looked like a *Sports Illustrated* swimsuit model crossed with a semi-pro athlete? Was that her magic, did she actually run a lot, or was it just incredible good fortune? If it was the magic, if her ability to turn into powerful animals also gave her an ideal human body, than that was despicably unfair of the Universe to give Theo all that and to load Kitty up with so much useless strength.

She filled a second mug with water and nuked it while she looked through the cupboard with the tea. Sleepytime felt a little too ironic, so she selected a light mint flavor and picked out tea bags for her and Gabe.

After she put his mug in front of him and settled onto the other stool, he got up and started rummaging in the fridge. A minute later he was back in his spot with an open pizza box in front of him and a cold slice in his hand.

"Want one?" he asked.

She shrugged but pulled the box toward her and tore a slice in half so she could have something to nibble on. The panic was flowing out of her now and having something in her stomach would probably settle her further.

"You okay?" he asked.

"I don't know how to answer that," she said, exhaustion making her more honest than she might have been.

"I hear that as a no," he said and chewed on his pizza for a while.

"I'll survive," Kitty told him. The lingering fear was turning into more pain in her shoulders, her neck, her jaw and head.

After a pause, he asked, "What's the problem with humans?"

"Oh, humans are fine. I've dated some very nice humans. It's you and Theo."

"We didn't do anything. Or, at least, I didn't."

She couldn't tell him about what Blake had said, about the four people, that was still bothering her. And she couldn't tell him that her mother had given her an assignment to spy on Theo, so she picked the third most irritating feature of this situation and went with it.

"That's actually the problem," Kitty said.

Because it was the middle of the night, and the pizza was making her feel sleepy, and because he had this puzzled, a little hurt but mostly curious look in his eyes, she went on. "I was designed to be a demon hunter, to be the ultimate demon hunter. My mom picked my dad because of his physical strength, to breed it into her kid. She named me 'Akiva' because it means 'to protect,' Kitty comes from my dad calling me 'Kivi' and it drives my mom nuts. They started training me to hunt demons when I was eight."

"Damn," Gabe said, letting out a little breath.

"And mom finally admitted that I was a complete failure at it when I was seventeen and let me go live with my dads." She turned on her stool to face him fully. "I was supposed to succeed and follow my mother and lead the demon hunters and be amazing. I'm supposed to be the chosen

136

one. And then I get here and there's you and fucking Theo—and you're human witches who haven't even been trained."

"Not my fault," he said, but he gave her a little smile.

"Immaterial," she countered. "Because every time Ben looks at you it's like he expects you to start walking on water any moment now. I don't know what he knows about you, but there's something powerful about you. And Theo … Lily walks around her like she's trying to figure her out. Lily—the retired head of the demon hunters, who should have just about seen everything—and she can't figure out Theo's magic. And when she looks at me, you know what I think? I think she's afraid *for* me. She's afraid that even she can't teach me what I need, that I'm just going to fail again. So I'm not okay. I'm supposed to be The One but here you and Theo are the fucking golden children and I just want to go home but I can't."

Gabe leaned his elbows on the table. Having polished off his slice of cold pizza, he held the steaming mug of tea up to his face. "Finally, you said something that makes sense."

Kitty shot him an exasperated look. Everything she'd said made sense. "What?"

"About wanting to go home. I get that," Gabe said. After taking a sip of the tea, he set it down on the island. The granite top made a loud clink, and he looked a little chagrined and moved the cup over to a part of the pizza box that was empty. "Not to be a dick or anything, but I think I get a lot about you."

Before she could stop it, Kitty barked out a harsh laugh. "How is that not being a dick? It's pretty ballsy to think you know anything about my life."

He shrugged. "You're right. I'm a total newb when it comes to demons. But, I have an Asshole in my life and two moms." Then he laughed at himself. "Yeah, no, what am I thinking? Having queer parents really isn't a huge bonding point, is it?"

Kitty was taken aback. "My mother isn't an asshole," she said, but she tried to keep her words soft. She could get how much it would suck to have a parent that you referred to just with an epithet. Another piece of the pattern about Gabe fell into place for her, though: asshole parent, showing up in worn and dirty clothes. She wanted to offer some information back to him, but not too much.

Kitty finally settled on adding, "But she really doesn't get it—doesn't get me. The things that are important to me, like math. And I miss my dads so much. Do you … what are your moms like?"

Gabe gave Kitty a wan smile, like he knew what she was up to. "I'm not sure what you want to know. My mom, the one that gave birth to me, she's a nurse. She moved from New Jersey to be with Meema in West Virginia." He laughed again, as though to himself and sang: "I was a coal miner's daughter…" When Kitty gave him a blank look, he explained, "Meema is an engineer. She works in the coal mines."

"I didn't know people still did that," Kitty said honestly.

"It's different now. Less pick axes and more technology," he said, taking another sip of the tea and stifling a yawn. He looked out into the open part of the kitchen, which was shrouded in darkness. They sat in the pool of light from the single lamp hung over the island. "Asshole followed us down from New Jersey. He said Mom had no right to move me out of state without his consent. That's when everything started."

He didn't say any more and Kitty got the sense it was very complicated.

Finally, Gabe picked up the pizza box and got up to return it to the fridge. "Last chance," he offered.

"No, thanks, I'm done."

After putting the pizza back, he stood in front of the refrigerator for moment before saying, "Your dads seem cool. It's neat that they're a proper family."

"Yours aren't?" Kitty asked before she realized it might be rude.

"Not really," Gabe said, as he returned to the island for his tea mug. He took it over to the sink and rinsed it out. "West Virginia isn't the most liberal state. Not the parts I'm from, anyway. Laws might have changed, but people don't. Mom and Meema have to hide a lot and it made them fight. A lot. They didn't even live together since Asshole started sniffing around. If it came out they were a couple…" He shrugged. "Well, it doesn't matter now. I hope they moved in together the second I turned eighteen."

Something about the way he said that had Kitty agreeing: "I hope so too."

Looking around for a place to put his mug, Gabe finally gave up and set it back in the sink basin. "For Theo," he smiled. "Since she's on clean-up."

Kitty couldn't help but grin at that thought. "Yeah, maybe I should stay up and make a cake or something that uses *all* the dishes."

"Knock yourself out," He said encouragingly. Gabe let out another long yawn, this time accompanied by a bone popping stretch. "Well, I should try to sleep. It's weird in this new place, isn't it?"

Kitty nodded and watched him go.

CHAPTER TWENTY-ONE

THEO REWARDS HERSELF BY BREAKING AND ENTERING

Theo lay naked in bed, watching the moonlight stream in from her window. She thought about a girl she didn't know being taken apart by people with a name she'd never heard before: Cavallo.

Cavallo. It was another puzzle piece that didn't go anywhere.

At least it seemed, reluctant or not, Ben had gone after this girl.

Yeah, but then there was Ben. Ben, who didn't just know 'something' about shape shifting, but was actually a shifter!

God, the silences! They made Theo so furious. Oh, Sabel had said all imperious and full of herself like usual, NO ONE can turn into an animal. You're the only one with that power, Theo. No one has ever heard of anyone, anywhere who can do the things you do.

Nope.

Lies.

Everyone in their family lied, whether by silence, like Sabel and their mother, or very loudly like her brothers and father—as if volume equaled truth. Once she'd started turning into the crow at six and the cat a few years later and could sit outside of windows, like she had with Lily and Ben, she had a much clearer picture of what actually went on in her family.

Animals didn't lie, not much anyway. Crows had a way of misdirecting when they had to and there was a lot of posturing, but you always knew where you stood and what was what.

These human lies and silences, and she couldn't pull them apart. What had Sabel said to her so many years ago? How much of it was pure lie and how much was omission? No matter how she tried to puzzle it out she kept coming back to how it was all so fucking unfair.

Theo rolled over and buried her face in pillows that smelled of newness and nothing personal. Even that irritated her, so she spent two minutes randomly fluffing them up, though really she just kind of punched at the pillows uselessly, trying to work something out.

Maybe Sabel hadn't known about Ben. Maybe shifting powers were as rare as she said they were. Maybe it was an unintentional lie, the lie that's really more of a mistake than anything else.

Or maybe Theo was just in a mood because of that irritating Kitty Cat.

What was it about that girl that got so deep under Theo's skin? Because, normally Theo wasn't the type to use her superpowers to bully someone—in fact, she'd never transformed like that just to scare someone before. Oh, well, that was technically a lie. She'd transformed into the jaguar once to scare the shit out of a creeper who'd followed her from her bus stop and was the sort who 'only wanted a hug.' Ducked into an alley, switched and came out making that guttural rattle that made grown men piss themselves—and that guy deserved to piss his pants in fear.

But what was it about Kitty that turned her into such a raging bully? The smell of fear? The way Gabe looked at her? The fact that she had the same nose as her Scary Lady mother? All that and more?

She hadn't expected Kitty to just collapse into herself like that. She'd expected a fight. A wrestle, fisticuffs, a bitch slap, something—didn't Kitty have the demon-strength of ten men or whatever? Hadn't there been talks of elite demon hunting school? What the hell did they teach at those places, if the first thing Kitty did was collapse into a quivering ball?

A ball that had shivered underneath Theo, too, when she'd ended up sprawled naked on top of her. That had been... memorable—all that quivering flesh. Kitty'd smelled so good up close, not like her horrible mother at all—yeah, there was still lemongrass, but there was a note of something deeper, spicier. Something that smelled... tasty, like hot Thai takeout.

Theo flung herself over again. She frowned up at the ceiling. God, what was she doing, thinking like that about such an annoying bundle of prickle! Kitty was like that puzzle piece you kept picking up because you were sure you knew where it went, only to be irritated over and over.

Theo should be concentrating those kinds of thought in the direction of Gabe. He seemed very amenable, and, despite his doofus first impression, he didn't cower from a panther. That was either hot... or extra stupid. Theo laughed fondly to herself at that thought.

Hot and extra stupid: that was actually kind of her type in men.

Smiling, Theo was able to let out a breath.

Everything might have seemed like a disaster, but she'd learned a lot tonight, too. For people who said they had no idea how Theo's shifting magic worked, they certainly had a counter-spell already in their arsenal. When Lily forced her back to human, she'd felt it in the tattoo. Did they put something in the ink and the words that allowed Lily to control her shifting?

Sabel was the one who told them to make the binding magic into a tattoo. Had she also told Lily how to make Theo shift human? Despite her protests about the great mystery of Theo's magic, did she know how it worked?

More lies.

However, Theo was willing to entertain the possibility that Lily's magic spell had been something more general, like a negation or a 're-set' button. Maybe she didn't know it would work to undo Theo's shifted form, but had tried it anyway. If that was the case, that was interesting, too, because it meant Lily was a little... reckless, maybe? Because how would Lily know if Theo could get pulled back from the other side without any damage. That was huge risk. Even if it was the sort of thing that normally worked against all sorts of magic, because then that was like assuming water always put out a fire. Sure, it was a pretty good measure until you hit your first grease fire. You throw water at that shit and it only makes things worse.

You'd think, though, if you didn't know what you were facing, there'd be some hesitation, like—*oh, damn, should I use canceling spell number 43 or banishing spell 741??* Lily hadn't acted panicked or seemed at all reaching, like she wasn't sure what would work. No, in fact, she'd just waltzed in all 'hang on, pizza boy,' and said some things, and, pop, Theo was human again.

That put them back at square one, then. She knew how to operate Theo's magic, therefore: *lies.*

The lies were getting juicier, at least, more meaty—no more of these garden variety, "Oops, when we said we didn't know anyone who could change shape, we *really* meant no one other than Ben," types. Now things were falling into the category of "when we say we know nothing, we really mean everything, and we're lying to you for some reason," which made Theo think back to that other thing someone had said when they heard about her shifting. They'd called her a natural witch. Or was it feral? Either one was interesting because they'd gone there right away after hearing about her abilities.

Was shifting something untrained magic-users did… instinctively?

Learning to do it certainly hadn't required any memorized incantations or special hand-gestures or the sort of things that you might find from book learning or even from secrets passed on through the generation. Theo had simply seen—or thought she'd seen—Sabel do it, and wanted to try it for herself. Absorbing the first animal had been more of accident than intention.

So, maybe shifting wasn't actually a difficult skill to attain. Maybe, instead or being so rare and unknown, it was *forbidden* magic.

If shifting was a forbidden art, that would better explain the reaction Theo kept getting and why Sabel *insisted* that she hadn't done it. Maybe Sabel had become a bird that day and she was denying it, not because Theo had imagined it, but because it was against the law.

Theo had discovered, too, by accident, that she killed any living animal she absorbed. This was slightly less problematic for things like beetles, but when it had happened with the cat? She still felt a twinge of guilt, even though she'd thought she was helping… she was still too young to understand how it all worked. Honestly she still didn't, but at least now she knew to pick animals already in their death throes or just a few hours dead. Beyond that, her magic wouldn't take them in.

Even so, there was a reason she was a vegetarian now… yeah, this was starting to seem like a very likely candidate for banned magic.

Especially since the more you killed the more forms you had in your arsenal. Theo could easily see a twisted version of that Merlin / Morgana La Fey fight, where one witch would be all, "Ha! I'm a bear" and the other would be all, "Ha! I'm an alligator!" and there'd be no end to it.

Outlawing shifting would control those kinds of power wars.

Theo felt like maybe she'd finally gotten an edge piece or a corner of the puzzle in place.

To celebrate, she decided to break into the neighbor's house.

Lily said she couldn't shift in the house now, but did it extend to the balcony? She went onto the balcony still naked and tried shifting to her owl form. It worked!

She soared silently over the driveway and landed on a nearby fence post. A shiver and pop-that-wasn't-a-pop, and she'd transformed into cat. Quick, graceful bounds brought her to the backdoor. She paced the premises, padding on grass already moist with evening dew. The crickets silenced their constant evening song at the approach of a predator. She laughed to think at what they might have made of the jaguar she'd been a few hours ago.

She was just making her second circle around the house, considering giving up for now, when the backdoor opened. A woman stepped out into the night, carrying a bag of garbage. Theo meowed softly from the shadows and then slowly, cautiously stepped into the light, pretending to warily watch as the woman took her garbage to the alley. Theo was met with the usual, "Here, kitty, kitty"s and the woman even knelt down and held out her hand.

Theo obliged by butting up against her and flopping over to expose a soft belly for rubs. Maybe she should feel weird, but something about a hand on her fur always felt right, instinctual.

The woman who happily stopped to pet her was a white woman, probably in her forties. Theo couldn't say for sure why, maybe the tie-died tee-shirt coupled with the reading glasses perched in a nest of gray-black curls, but she seemed like she could be an aging hippy, maybe the sort who'd settled down to teach art at the university or maybe even women's studies.

No one came out to ask after the woman, not even after ten minutes of belly rubs. When she offered a bowl of milk, Theo tried to slip in but was told to wait. She sat down primly to watch. The kitchen was clean and tidy enough, though there was a pile of unwashed dishes in the sink, and, remarkably, no dishwasher. The house was older than the one Sabel had bought Lily and the crew, then. The hardwood floor looked swept, but not mopped. It was a comfortable kitchen, it looked lived in, loved, and possibly lived in… alone.

Theo formulated a plan.

She would be That Cat, the one that always came begging. Maybe, if she played her part right, she'd be allowed in and maybe, if necessary, adopted.

It could be her escape, should she need one.

As she drank her milk she purred and purred and purred.

CHAPTER TWENTY-TWO

GABE'S HOUSE GHOST IS FABULOUS

Despite the mint tea, Gabe slept fitfully. Finally, sometime after 3 am, he pulled the blankets off the bed and slept on the floor, with his back pressed against the wall and his arms wrapped tightly around his backpack.

Morning's first light and birds twittering in the eaves woke him from a dreamless, un-restful sleep only a few hours later. He dragged himself upright, made a cursory attempt to make his bed up, and then lumbered off to the shower.

This time when Gabe stepped out and toweled off, there, on the toilet seat, was a fresh set of clothes. He stared at them for a long moment trying to decide if it was creepy or cool that stuff kept showing up for him like this. Finally, he decided this was a gift horse he really didn't want to think too hard about. So, with a little shrug, he unfolded the clothes and put them on.

This house spirit, or whatever it was, picked out the gayest stuff for him. This time the button-down shirt was actually kind of pink, though Gabe supposed it could pass as 'mauve'—not that he wasn't okay with pink, because, really, the cut and color looked sharp on him.

After trimming up his face to a more intentional scruff, he made his way upstairs to the main kitchen. He knew someone was awake because halfway through his shower the water pressure had dropped significantly.

He tried to decide what to say if it was Kitty who was awake. While he lay awake last night tossing and turning, he'd thought a lot about what she'd said about how she was supposed to be the Chosen One. It felt so strange to him because, having seen her strength and Theo's ability to change shape, he felt like the most useless part of this oddball household. Sure, Ben had said all that, but Lily seemed completely underwhelmed by his ability to 'see.'

He hadn't seen anything lately, either. Not even a tiny bit of those dark buzzing things, the... Lesser Guls? Yeah, them.

Still lost in thought, Gabe couldn't process the sight that met him in the kitchen. Usually so pristine that it glowed, every surface of the kitchen seemed to be covered in a fine film of something... flour, he guessed after seeing the pile of batter-coated mixing bowls that rose in a precariously leaning tower from the sink.

Holy crap, that crazy Kitty had actually made a cake.

Sitting at one of the stools at the island was a bed-headed Theo, which in her case meant there were a few waves and tangles in the loose black hair that fell to her mid-back. On the plate in front of her was the entire half of a thick chocolate layer cake. It had been frosted white and, in cheerfully looped, pink piping cursive, was the word "Fuck." The other half of the cake sat on a fancy glass cake platter, and now only read, "You."

If any of this bothered Theo, it was difficult to tell. In fact, she sat there, unfazed, alternately sipping coffee and eating cake.

Kitty was going to be so pissed she hadn't even gotten a rise out of Theo.

Theo neatly ran her fork across the top of the cake between the frosting layer and the baked part. "Kitty made it kind of dry," she said. "But the frosting is sweet."

She held the fork out to him. The plate held, neatly separated from the cake, two letters: "F-U" in looping pink on white. "Maybe I can tempt you?"

Surprising himself by not stumbling over his own tongue, Gabe said, "Tempt? Nah, you just have to ask and I'm there."

Theo seemed as shocked by his smooth reply as he was himself. Then she laughed, not unkindly. "I know you said last night that you aren't, but I keep worrying that you might be gay."

Gabe glanced down at the button down which, in the light of the energy-efficient bulbs of the kitchen, really was more pink than mauve. "The House dresses me kind of... fabulously. I'm normally more of a jeans and t-shirt sort."

She nodded like she could see that, and then, once she had his full attention again, used her tongue to lap at the creamy frosting suggestively. At the sight of her delicate pink tongue covered in white fluff brought all sorts of naughty associations to Gabe's mind, and he found he had to grab for the counter as his knees shivered a little. He was going to have take another shower in a minute if she kept this up. This time it would have to be a cold one.

"Rule number two," Ben said casually as he strolled past Gabe, making a beeline for the coffeemaker. Theo looked surprised to see him. He clucked his tongue. "I see it's going to be very interesting for you to be the only male in a household of young women."

That was kind of a funny thing for the other guy in the house to say, Gabe thought. Especially since the other guy looked like something the jaguar dragged in. Ben's normally pressed shirt was furrowed with wrinkles and stained with mud in a long patch along his side as if he'd slid hard over wet ground. His short hair was wet and half-standing, probably from quickly washing his face and hands, then running them through his hair. Where had he been?

It was too early in the day to ask, so Gabe just shrugged and made his way over to the fridge and the remains of the pizza. Seeing him bringing out the box, Theo sighed, "No sharing a fuck after all, I guess."

"Oh I'll have 'you' for dessert," Gabe said before realizing how that sounded. "Er, I mean, I'll have the 'you' part of the cake..."

"Cake?" Ben asked, saving Gabe from further embarrassment. Theo showed him what remained of the 'fuck,' and gestured at the 'you.' "Mmmm," he remarked, his eyebrows still arched as he pulled the coffee beans from the cupboard, "I see we're all getting along famously already."

"What the hell happened here?" Lily demanded from the doorway.

"Cake!" Ben cheerfully replied.

She grunted as though that explained everything, and then went to stand anxiously in front of the coffeemaker that was now making loud grinding and gurgling noises. Gabe watched the machine in fascination

as he leaned against the island and ate his cold breakfast pizza out of the box. He'd never seen anything so fancy. It said 'Cuisenart' on the side and apparently ground and brewed coffee all at the same time. Impressive. Mom would love that.

Now that Ben and Lily were in the room, Theo focused on her cake, her head a little bowed and her expression carefully neutral. Gabe ate his pizza in silence as the kitchen filled with the homey smell of strong, black coffee. Gabe glanced over at the living room and noticed that while Kitty made a mess, someone had fixed the doorframe. Glancing down at his magically appearing clothes, Gabe wondered: or some-Thing? Maybe their houseghost fixed things, too. Theo was going to be bummed that it didn't do the dishes, though. No one else even seemed to notice, however.

Ben was focused on his caffeine; he didn't wait for the coffee to finish brewing before stealing a cup. He took a long drink of the hot coffee and Gabe thought it had to burn his mouth, but it seemed to perk him up a little.

Leaning back against the counter, mug cradled in both hands, Ben said to Lily, "I'm leaving again in an hour. The location was right, but they moved her. I think they're on the move. Maybe they've sensed me somehow."

"I thought you could track anything," Lily replied, her tone worry laced with snark.

"If it was only humans, I could. They have help. Smells like Shaitans."

"Do they know that?"

He laughed dryly. "Assuredly not. At least not the rank and file, who knows what their leadership is willing to do. Don't worry, I'll find her. They don't say 'to ferret something out' for nothing, you know."

Theo's head came up sharply and she stared at Ben with a kind of intensity Gabe had never seen in her eyes. Ben caught the motion too and looked over at her.

"Focus, cunning, hunting, stealth, ingenuity and the ability to see what's hidden—those are some of the ferret powers," Ben said. It didn't make sense to Gabe because Theo hadn't asked about ferrets, but Ben went on, "Each form has its power and to master the powers you must commit completely to that form, which is why most shape changers don't take four or more forms willy-nilly."

"Most shape changers, eh?" Theo shrugged but her mouth was an unhappy line and her forehead wrinkled with worry. Lily put a hand on Ben's arm.

"Later," she said. "Tell me what else you need." The casual way she touched Ben and the note of concern in her voice gave Gabe a strange sense of homesickness.

"I'm going to take the box out to the recycling," he said because he didn't want to see any more.

"You can put it on the porch," Lily offered. "You don't have to go all the way out."

"I might take a little walk," Gabe admitted. He held his breath, half expecting a protest or some kind of warning that he wasn't allowed to go far.

Lily nodded. "You might want to be back before lunch. I've got some questions for all of you."

Gabe felt his stomach drop a little. Like an interrogation?

Seeing his expression, Lily shook her head. "Just an interview. Nothing to worry about. I need to know your capabilities."

"Right," Gabe said. "I'll be back in a sec."

Ben stopped him before he could open the door. He thrust a twenty into Gabe's hand. "There's coffee shop at the end of the block. If you get me a Vanilla latte, you can buy yourself something with the change."

Gabe looked at the money. His stomach tightened a little. No one had made any moves on him. Outside of the weird discussion of 'punishments' that the still hadn't quite felt right, despite Lily's assurances that they were only aimed at Theo, no one had done anything untoward at all.

As if reading his thoughts, Ben shrugged, "I'm only asking for a latte, but if you're not going that way—" he started to reach to retrieve the bill, but Gabe stuck it into the pocket of his jeans.

"It's fine," he said, hand on the door again, he double-checked, "Vanilla late? You want whole milk or skim or what?"

"Whole," Ben said. "What's the point otherwise?"

Gabe tried to laugh at was clearly supposed to be a jokingly light comment, but he couldn't. His hand on the door was white-knuckled. He couldn't get out fast enough.

He stepped out into morning fog. Cool fog kissed his cheeks wetly as he started up the sidewalk toward the coffee shop. Though he'd been in San Francisco for a couple of weeks now, his leg muscles were still adjusting to the steep hill he climbed as he made his way toward the business district. Gabe felt like a tourist as he gawked at the closely nestled Victorian houses with their almost-garish paint jobs.

A noisy squawk had him scanning the sky and he was surprised to see three brightly-colored parrots bobbing on the overhead electrical wire. They had lime green bodies and red heads, visible even through the thick fog. As he watched, several other parrots joined in the growing flock. San Francisco had feral parrots?

That was kind of cool.

It wasn't far to the coffee shop, a Starbucks, the ubiquitous kind that you could find anywhere in the world and the interior and music and baristas were nearly always the same. As Gabe waited to place his order, his fingers kept caressing the twenty, smoothing it over and over, as if trying to feel the edges.... Like, was this just a gift, or was it some kind of leash?

One day, would he be asked that question he heard so many times? The one that always started: "But I've given you so much. I only want this one, little thing…"—only that one thing was never just one, and it was never, ever *little*.

CHAPTER TWENTY-THREE

ERIN IS DECAMPED AND HAS A MELTDOWN

The frantic decamping was the best thing that had happened to Erin in a really long time. Oh, it had meant manacles and hoods and all sorts of pushing and abuse, but she'd gotten her hands on someone's phone.

An iPhone.

The two guys who had her jammed between them in the backseat of the car were busy arguing with the driver about which route was best. When the guard to her left, a man Erin had nicknamed Fuck, because it was his favorite word and because he kind of was one, shifted to lean between the seats, his phone had slipped out of his pant's pocket and literally fallen into her hands.

It was hard to see under the burlap sack they'd thrown over her head, but Erin didn't hesitate. Her fingers flew over the keypad as she texted one word, 'help.' In a second, she'd sent it to the one person she trusted over everyone, even though she only knew them from a game forum and by the name 'gravejelly.' Gravejelly had helped Erin before, when she'd been stuck in that horrible Bible camp.

"Fuck, what are you doing?" Fuck said, when he sat back. "Oh, fuck, that's my fucking phone!"

As his meaty hand closed over it, Erin tried something. The machine that made her head hurt was in the car right behind them, but there was so much steel and chrome surrounding her. Never had she tried to direct any of her power, but now she focused her mind on a single, desperate command: *melt.*

She heard the pop from the phone at the same time the brakes squealed and something broke deep beneath her seat. The car jerked to a halt, pushing everyone forward. The phone tumbled from her grip as her head slammed into the seat in front of her.

"What the fuck?" screamed Fuck.

The other guard, one Erin called Silent Bob, spoke. His voice was ironic and intelligent sounding, with a hint of an Ivory Tower or maybe even high-class British accent, "From the smell, I would guess that something in the car melted."

"Well, fuck," said Fuck.

CHAPTER TWENTY-FOUR

KITTY IS SHARP, BUT IS SHE A TOOL?

Kitty sat on the floor of her new room trying to decide how much of a tool she was.

And then, whose tool?

She'd been in the hall that morning and heard Ben saying he'd be going out tracking again. He'd said, "They moved her."

The other girl, the fourth one. Two demons, two witches, like Blake had said. But what happened when they were all together? Was it a plan of the Cavallo to use the last girl as bait to catch all four of them? Did some faction want to capture Kitty and use her as leverage against Suhirin? (Not like that would ever work.)

Blake said she'd gotten the information from a Shaitan flunky, so probably not Cavallo who wouldn't be caught dead working with demons. When the Shaitans got in the mix, they could be up to anything. It didn't give her much to work with.

Kitty thought that if she *was* going to be anyone's tool, she wanted to be Blake's—and that thought got her laughing and then almost crying. This place, this "school"—it didn't feel like any of the others she'd been sent to. Every place she'd ever been before had a single message for Kitty, "Toughen up, kid."

So far, the vibe here was "Lighten up."

It was messing with her.

She called up Blake's file online but the contact info was gone, which meant she wasn't reachable. Kitty logged into her Skype and set her public message to read: "walking among the ancient trees."

It was a line from the William Blake poem "Hear the Voice," and Kitty knew Blake would understand that they needed to get in touch again as soon as possible.

She needed to send some kind of report to Suhirin, something that helped her figure out if Blake had talked to her mother. Because if she hadn't … if she was concerned enough to talk to Kitty and not Suhirin, then something was wrong inside the Sangkesh.

Kitty wrote up a tightly-worded email, very emotionless and detailed—just like Mummy wanted things. She mentioned that Lily and Ben were worried about the Cavallo operating in the city and that they were holding a demon girl. Did she want Kitty to follow up on that? (i.e. Did she already know and have someone on it?) Then she wrote up a description of Theo turning into a jaguar but didn't include the circumstance.

But she didn't hit send.

Instead she cut-and-paste it into a new file. She labeled the file Loki/Ironman because she had a ton of fanfic on her laptop. Most of it was downloads from AO3 and other sites, but some of it was her own sad attempts. Gods, her mother would be so ashamed to see what Kitty had spent precious free time doing. Even so, Kitty guessed that even Suhirin could appreciate that fanfic made a good cover for these kinds of reports, actually.

That done, she sat back against her chair. For a long moment, she stared at the wall, just thinking about everything, and about Theo. She remembered being new at the Hunter's School and being the target of other kids because she was Suhirin's daughter. She remembered how shit that felt and how Blake had protected her. Was she about to do to Theo what the other kids did to her?

:: :: ::

Kitty had been twelve when she first arrived at the hunters' school in Austria. She'd spent three years at a Sangkesh boarding school in the States, so she was over the homesickness and missing her dads. Then she had a bit of culture shock to deal with, but it wasn't all bad. The bad part was the other students. They knew she was Suhirin's daughter and when it became apparent that she couldn't fight her way out of a wet paper bag—due to a tendency to both close her eyes and freeze with fear—she became the target of cutting remarks, jokes, covert shoves and nerve pinches.

For about a year it got steadily worse, to the point where she actually considered telling her mother about it, and then it started to fall away. It didn't stop all at once like it would have if someone in power told the kids to quit it. It tapered off. When she noticed first one kid and then another not giving her any of their terrible attention anymore, she started to get curious. Almost without conscious thought, her mind began tracking the patterns of interactions.

Months passed before Kitty figured out who'd declared her off-limits. By then she was well into fourteen and getting thoroughly sick of this place that called itself a school but taught her so little that was useful. It made her less careful than she'd been, and so when she thought she had it worked out, she decided to talk to the strange, black-haired girl.

They had social hours when students could wander around the dorm buildings and common areas, and Kitty found her sitting on a stone bench with her back against a wall reading a book.

"Why are you protecting me?" Kitty asked without preamble.

"Hey," the girl said. "They call me Blake. What do they call you?"

"Kitty," she said. Everyone knew everyone else's given name. It was easy to look up. At least their current given name. But nicknames could be precious. "From Kivi."

"From Akiva, I get it," Blake said. "Mine's from the poem, you know, tyger tyger and all that business."

Kitty sized up Blake: a girl on the short side, stocky but not muscular looking, and yet there was a coiled power in her. She considered the words of the poem and picked the ones that most fit.

"'Did he who made the Lamb make thee?'" Kitty quoted.

Blake's eyes lit up. "Yes! Finally someone knows more than the 'burning bright' part. How do you know I'm protecting you?"

Kitty sat on the bench and detailed out all of her observations totaling nearly a year of patterns and relationships. At the end of it all Blake nodded and grinned at her and said, "That was incredible."

"Is that why you're doing it?" Kitty asked. "Because I can think all that through?"

"Nope, though it's great," Blake said. "You remind me of someone."

"Oh."

"A kitty and a tiger," Blake said. "We should make t-shirts."

Kitty had no idea what to say to that. She thought about asking something dull and ordinary, like what was Blake reading, but Blake was already rising from the bench and tucking her book under her arm.

"See you around, Kitty," she said and headed down the walkway.

After that they weren't friends but they were friendly acquaintances. Kitty had a little group she hung out with, kids her age who were also smart and thoughtful and not particularly good at hunting and fighting. But friends from that group kept getting transferred to the strategic school and Kitty knew she never would. Suhirin wouldn't let her.

She couldn't remember now if she and Blake even had a full conversation about anything before they kissed that first time. There were short exchanges. Blake would show her fighting moves in practice if she was one of the student coaches, enough so that Kitty started asking her for help specifically. And when they were practicing together—or rather when Kitty was falling all over herself and Blake was dancing through the moves like she'd been born doing it—Blake would ask her tactical questions and get Kitty's opinion on various scenarios she had as her schoolwork.

It was always easy being around Blake. Even that night when Kitty was sixteen and Blake seventeen—and they ended up being the last two going for showers after practice. Kitty hadn't really thought about it; she just stripped and turned on the spigot next to Blake's and asked what she was working on. Blake sketched out the latest scenario and Kitty walked her through a few ways to think about it.

And then Blake turned off the water and got her towel and rubbed her hair with it until wet, dark strands were standing out all around her head. She looked across the room at Kitty, holding the towel in one hand but not covering any part of herself with it. And she grinned, the biggest grin Kitty had ever seen on her. A look that said, "Come get me."

Kitty shut the spigot of her shower with a jerk, not even looking back at it, not taking her eyes off Blake. She crossed the room and kissed Blake, more roughly that she planned, but Blake met her with equal force.

They kissed until they heard the door handle turning and then leapt apart and started throwing on clothes. It was impossible at the time for Kitty to tell if kissing in the showers really meant anything. Plenty of students hooked up when they could. Time alone was rare, but the students were innovative. Kitty didn't bother. She still didn't trust most of the other kids there. She wondered what Blake had meant with the kiss and if they'd do it again, but weeks passed before she found out.

There was a practice weapons storehouse for the students. A little outbuilding full of slightly dull blades and guns without ammunition. It was an ideal place to work on disassembling, cleaning and reassembling guns, or sharpening blades, or drawing a blade without cutting some part of yourself, and so on. Kitty thought she'd sneak in late at night for extra practice but it turned out she wasn't the only student with that idea, so once a week she'd get up at 4 a.m. and get in a couple of hours working with the guns, which she hated, and the knives, which she hated only a little less.

Which is how Blake found her in there one morning, crying a little while she tried to figure out what she'd fucked up on a rifle she couldn't reassemble.

Blake sat down on the bench next to her and reached across her body to pick up a metal part. She put it in Kitty's left hand and then, with her hands around Kitty's, helped her fit it into the part she was holding in her right. They put the whole gun back together in gentle silence with Blake's hands guiding Kitty's, but always Kitty's hands on the parts of the weapon. She wanted to believe that would help her remember, but she knew that all she would remember from this morning would be Blake's scent and her touch, the rough and soft calloused landscape of her hands.

"In the shower …," Blake said when they were done and Kitty set the rifle on the far side of the bench.

"It's okay," Kitty said. "Things happen."

"Do they?" Blake asked. She stood and picked up the rifle, carrying it to the gun locker to hang it with the others.

Kitty watched the balanced movements of Blake's compact body. "No," she admitted and stood up and didn't know what to do with herself. "I can't stop thinking about you."

Blake shut the locker and turned around, grinning. She didn't have to say anything. Kitty went to her and they kissed until the birds started chirping outside the little building and then, realizing they weren't going to have forever, Kitty pushed her hand down Blake's pants and felt her knees buckle.

She wrapped her other arm around Blake's waist and held her up, grateful for her inhuman strength for the first time since she'd gotten to the school. Blake was wet and burning hot so Kitty positioned her hand to touch as much of her as possible, while Blake ground down against her, and she pinned Blake to the locker. She felt Blake's teeth in her shoulder as she tried not to make noise. Kitty made that as difficult as she could, pressing with her fingers, rubbing with her thumb.

She brushed her face against the side of Blake neck and kissed everywhere that she could reach in between waves of trying to make her scream and feeling wetness cascade over her hand.

The only sound Blake made at last was to gasp and say, "Footsteps."

Kitty pulled away in a flash, grabbed a towel used for cleaning swords and wiped her hand. She heard the gun locker open and shut behind her as Blake hid in it.

The door opened and an instructor blinked at her.

"What are you doing here?" she barked at Kitty.

"Working on the SCAR rifle," Kitty said. "I just put it away."

She walked toward the front door, shoving the cleaning rag in the pocket of her sweatshirt and praying the instructor didn't notice.

"You got it back together?" the instructor asked.

"Took me two hours," Kitty said and let real bitterness creep into her voice. Only some of it was for the rifle. Most of it was because she hated having to walk away from Blake.

"I'm impressed you stuck with it. Help me carry the practice swords. We're going to need them this morning."

Kitty carried an armload of wooden swords to the gym building and then went to get breakfast. She was staring at a plate of eggs and sausage, seeing only the inside of the weapons building, when Blake dropped onto the bench next to her.

"Got out about four minutes after you left," she said. "Sorry. Wish we could have stayed."

"Hah, yeah," Kitty said. "All day."

"Bet you'll never see an FN SCAR-L the same way again either,"

CHAPTER TWENTY-FOUR

Blake said.

Kitty looked at Blake's fingers wrapped around a fork, and remembered how Blake's skin felt on the outside her hand, guiding her to put the gun together. She wanted to put Blake's fingers in her mouth so badly her teeth ached.

"I have to get up," she said. "I have to go or …"

Blake nodded. "Yeah, I know. You stay, I'll go. I'll see you."

:: :: ::

Kitty wanted to stay in the memory but she had to get downstairs to do the interviews with Lily. Although Lily had her file, Kitty was curious to hear how Gabe and Theo would answer Lily's questions.

She read over the email to her mother, still burning on her computer screen. It was a very fair description of the jaguar and the magic Kitty suspected Lily had used to turn Theo human again. It might be enough information to tell Suhirin how to repeat that particular, useful trick.

But while Theo was older and better equipped and not under attack here, she was still new. And this school might be fucked up, but it was already worlds better than the Hunters' School. Being around Lily actually felt a little like hanging out with Papa and Dad—no pressure to be anything other than what you were. The house "rules" were so permissive. She felt something… peaceful… tugging at her. It was nothing at all like the last few places she'd been.

"A kitty and a tiger," Blake had said when they first talked. And now a jaguar. Theo was an ass, but she was *their* ass, not to be ground up in Suhirin's machine-like organization. Kitty deleted Theo out of the email and hit send.

CHAPTER TWENTY-FIVE

THEO ADMITS TO TRANSFORMATION DYSFUNCTION

At least it wasn't like some stupid test in college, Theo thought as they sat around the dining room table. Lily had a leather-bound tablet computer in front of her and a stylus. She also had a short but ominous stack of file folders with plenty of pages in them, some pretty ragged around the edges where they stuck out from the gray folders. Theo thought the thick one was probably hers.

Gabe and Kitty both sat back in their chairs, unlike Theo who let herself slump forward and folded her arms on the table. Her finger pads were still waterlogged from doing all the dishes Kitty had dragged out and dirtied in the middle of the night. Considering how long that must've taken, Kitty looked much too awake, her dark eyes clear and hard.

Gabe's expression was softer than Kitty's, poorly veiled suspicion on top of sleepy satisfaction. He'd polished off at least one whole pizza on his own in less than a day. Theo had sat herself on his side of the table, turned toward him and Lily. Although she was directly across from Kitty, she didn't have to look at her.

"Kitty, I have your scores and we'll be doing some other tests next week. Theo, what are all the forms you have?" Lily paused with her stylus paused over her tablet and waited.

It wasn't really fair that she had to disclose all her magic stuff when Kitty just got glossed over like that, but she answered anyway.

"Black jaguar," Theo said, but she looked down as she did. She still felt kind of dumb about leaping at Kitty like that when she'd only meant to scare her, not to mention the part about landing stark naked. "Crow, owl, beetle," she considered mentioning the cat, but decided to keep it a secret, "And mixed-breed dog."

"Nothing that swims?"

"Nah, it freaks me out, all that water. I mean, I swim okay as a human, but gills? I'm not sure, but I've been thinking about something like a turtle or a terrapin."

Lily looked at her and tapped the end of the stylus against her closed lips, then asked, "What kind of owl?"

"Great Horned."

"Explain," Lily said like she already knew right the answer and was testing Theo's reasons for the choice.

"It can carry two to three times its body weight, so if I have a really light pack, I can carry my clothes and some cash. It flies silently and the claws are pretty serious. It's a really good shape to escape in or just hide out."

Theo noticed Gabe watching her as she talked and straightened up in her chair. She'd never talked to people about her forms before and it felt weird, like she was in a dream, but also this sense of deep relief, like small muscles in her back that she'd never known were tense could suddenly let go. She stretched up and cracked her back and saw peripherally how Gabe's eyes followed her movements.

"I gather the jaguar was as carefully thought out?" Lily asked.

"Oh yeah, great climber, super muscular power, deadly, and it comes in a dark color so I can hide at night. It took me forever to get one. It … um, see, if the animal's alive when I learn its shape, it kills the animal, so I don't do that. But if the animal has been dead for more than a few hours, it's too far gone and I can't learn it. So for the jaguar I had to stalk poachers until they made the kill and then steal it. Thankfully no one notices an extra crow hanging around, especially if there are dead animals."

"Which ones weren't intentional?" Lily asked.

"The crow, but that turned out to be great. It was dying and I went to see if I could do something … I couldn't. The dog was sort of intentional, I mean I figured out by then how it worked. And then I didn't add anything else for a while. I picked up the owl when I left school and then it took me about a year to get those other ones. I was thinking about a wolf too, but animals that scare people aren't really that useful except to scare people."

Theo pointedly did *not* look at Kitty.

"What else is on your list to acquire?"

"I want something with good digging power, but I haven't settled on which animal."

"We'll work on that," Lily said.

Theo turned a little away so Lily couldn't see the extent of her smile. It was kind of cool to have people in on this with her. She'd been so focused on Sabel when she was a kid, on getting her sister to acknowledge her and trust her and teach her, that it hadn't really occurred to her that there could be a whole world of magic—of women with eagle feet and men who turned into ferrets—and now that she saw it, she wanted to make it her home.

Lily's next question caught her off guard, "Have you ever had trouble changing back to human?"

Theo blinked at her, glanced away, decided if she was going to tell anyone the truth it should be Lily. Not that she wanted to do it in front of Kitty and Gabe, but if she tried to deflect one of them was sure to catch it. Probably Kitty. And then she'd be all about trying to figure out even more of Theo's business.

"A few times," she said, downplaying it. "I mean, it was hard to tell because I'd change when I was angry and then was it hard to change back or did I just not want to?"

"Which forms?" Lily asked.

"The owl mostly."

"How often have you used the jaguar form?"

"A few—," Theo started but realized Lily would want her to be more specific so she counted back and said, "Five times."

Now that she thought about it with Lily's question in her mind, it had been hard the last two times to go human again. Well, not the very last time because Lily did that for her, but the two times before that it felt like she had to wrestle herself back into her human body.

"Making it easier to change, that's something you can teach me, right?" Theo asked.

Lily shook her head. "I'm hoping Ben can. Five forms are a lot to master. More than a lot. At least here with the tattoo we can keep you out of trouble while we work on it."

Theo nodded and scratched her calf through her jeans. She didn't want to feel even a shred of gratitude for the binding magic, but she kind of did.

She only felt a little guilty that she hadn't mentioned the cat.

But, to be fair, it wasn't like any one here had been a hundred per-cent honest with her, either. Like them, she'd just tell them *later*.

Just because she really, really wanted this to be a true home, didn't mean she trusted that it would be. She'd been burned before, after all.

CHAPTER TWENTY-SIX

GABE WONDERS WHAT HE CAN DO

Lily looked at Gabe next, "And what can you do?"

It took him a second to catch on that the conversation had moved to him because he was trying to look at Theo's smile without seeming to. "Um, see demons, I guess," he managed to say.

"Can you talk to them?" Lily asked.

"I never tried. When I saw one I tended to go the other way." Then, he glanced in the direction of where her feet were hidden under the table. "No offense."

She shook her head. "It was probably for the best at the time. As for the rest, we'll test that. Also we need to find out if you can influence them in any way. You could turn out to be a very adept banisher with that natural sight."

"What's a banisher?"

Lily reached across the table and snagged Kitty's notebook—pausing just long enough to see Kitty nod before she pulled it over in front of herself. She ran her thumb across the edge, rifling the pages.

"The Unseen World is like this, realms and places and landscapes all jumbled up together because it's not physical."

She pulled over an empty plate and tipped it toward Gabe for a moment.

"The material world is like this. Solid and well defined. It has rules and some covenants that limit magic and determine what can and can't

166

happen in it."

She put the notebook on top of the plate.

"But all the worlds really occupy the same space. Many places in the Unseen World overlap the material world and often denizens of the Unseen World can operate or even come to stay full time in the material world. A lot of those are little demons, like the Gul you can see feeding on people, and once they get here, they generally like to stay. A banisher has the raw talent combined with the training to figure out where those demons need to go back to in the Unseen World and send them there."

Gabe scratched the back of his ear. "So...," he said, after a long moment and guilty glances at Kitty and Lily. "Are demons like people— some good some bad? I guess I understand that the little ones feeding off people are bad, but what about... Uh, okay, you're just going to have to forgive my ignorance if I'm rude here, but how did y'all get to be so solid? If you were notebook stuff."

Kitty surprised him by leaning forward and answering. "About three thousand years ago, we were all the notebook stuff, but then a bunch of really powerful demons worked with King Solomon to create the Lesser Covenant that allowed them to, you know, interbreed with humans and have physical bodies in the material world. See, if you have your own body, you can't be banished or compelled, so you're way more powerful. That's why most of the demons you see who have bodies are really only part demon. And it's why I have fangs and Lily has talons. The eight families took on animal characteristics to always remind us that we promised to protect humanity from the other demons."

Kitty looked at Theo, "But the witches also got to Solomon and persuaded him to fuck up demon physiology, so it's hard for demons to reproduce with each other in this world."

"Yeah, sure, blame the witches," Theo said.

"Right, so that's my other question," Gabe said. "If the demons come from the notebook stuff, where do the witches get their power from?'

"Let's call it the Unseen World," Lily said. "Otherwise it sounds like you're saying demons come from The Notebook and I'm not that big on romance movies. As far as we can tell, witches are simply humans who evolved the ability to work with the Unseen World as a survival trait."

"Cool, like mutants," Gabe said with a smile.

"Oh my god, I love those movies," Theo said. "But I am not wearing X-men uniforms."

Gabe's mind suddenly flashed to the red corset and fishnet stocking outfit that the Scarlet Witch wore in the Avenger's comic books. He wanted to point out that Theo would look super-hot in that, but then he'd have to reveal the depths of his nerdiness. So instead he just made a reference to the Incredibles movie: "Yeah, no capes, darling."

Which, given the blank stares he got, was plenty nerdy.

"Uh, anyway, so I seriously was just born with a superpower?" he asked Lily. "I didn't inherit it from my parents? Is that common?"

"Magic inheritance is similar to DNA but not the same. It's similar in demons." She paused and looked around the table, probably thinking through what props she could use but not really finding anything because she continued without moving the salt and pepper shakers into epic battle poses or anything. "There are three main kinds of demons as far as we're concerned, you'll recall: the Sangkesh, who are the protectors like me and Kitty; the Shaitans who are the adversaries; and the Gul who feed on humans. Even if two Sangkesh have a child, sometimes that child will turn out to be one of the other types. Magic has a wild, random streak to it, or at least it looks random to most of us—Theo's sister Sabel would probably tell you otherwise. Similarly with witches, the power can skip generations and tends to gather power to itself when it does."

"So Sabel could be a witch and I could be totally normal?" Theo asked.

"That's a lot more common than two witches in the same family," Lily told her.

Theo made a grumbling sound and looked away again.

Gabe nodded in Lily's direction, hoping like hell this didn't mean he'd gotten any of this cool shit from Asshole. Well, no matter, it was his now.

Lily wiped her hands together and gave each of them a long look. "Now, let's see what you can really do. Time for some sparring."

Gabe glanced up just in time to see Kitty and Theo share what could only be described as a withering glance. Oh, joy.

Lily seemed to see it too. "Yes, that's it, exactly. I think we all have some tension to work out, wouldn't you agree?"

Pulling himself to his feet, Gabe shook his head in dismay. Well, if nothing else, this would be fun to watch. Lily did have a point, letting these two hash things out physically was probably far better than trying to get either of these stubborn women to talk it out.

CHAPTER TWENTY-SEVEN

ERIN SMELLS FREEDOM

They'd had to take the hood off of Erin's head in order to call the tow truck. She was surprised to find that Silent Bob was not nearly as 'handsome' as his voice. In fact, he was a little toady—bald and pudgy in all the wrong places. Consequentially, his uniform didn't quite fit him. He looked mismatched. Erin felt weirdly disappointed. With that voice, she'd been hoping for someone much hotter.

Fuck, on the other hand, was almost good-looking. He had long auburn hair that fell loose to his shoulders and a foxy, sharp face. A couple tattoos that looked like the sort you might get on the way in or out of prison were visible on his neck, but he was trim and fit. They sent Fuck out to deal with the tow truck guy because, unlike the rest of them, he wasn't in full paramilitary uniform. He had the shirt, but wore jeans and cowboy boots.

The driver kept eyeing Erin from the rearview mirror, like maybe he suspected she'd caused the meltdown. He'd gotten on his cell right away and informed the bosses that they were delayed by a freak accident. The car carrying the machine that jammed up the songs that metals sang to her waited around the corner to take them away once the car was taken care of. They'd all be bustled into that right now, except that the equipment took up too much room. So, they had to wait for someone to circle back for them.

Erin kept trying to think of something to do, some way to signal for help. She didn't know how to blink "S.O.S" in Morse Code and she had no idea what American Sign Language might be for "Help, I'm being held captive by these men."

After the incident with Fuck's phone, the driver had collected everyone's cells and kept them on the passenger seat, far away from Erin's easy reach. She tried to use the "Force," but apparently her attunement to metal only allowed her the ability to either absorb it or melt it.

She did take some pleasure in absorbing anything she could, though. The jammer might only be around the corner, but she was incased in steel. It was impossible not to hear some simple, strong notes. They comforted her. Plus, she took the opportunity to try to puzzle out where they were. She could almost read the street signs, but they were fairly innocuous. Didn't every town have a Main Street?

What fascinated Erin was the palm tree. She'd never really seen a tree like it before. The leaves were more like fronds and the trunk looked... pokey. The air smelled of something, too. She noticed it when Silent Bob rolled down the window. It was warm, but not so much that Erin thought she was in some tropical state like Florida.

California, maybe? She'd seen palm trees in movies about Los Angeles. Was that where they were?

Of course, they might be going anywhere. They were pretty freaked out by whoever was chasing them. They could even be heading to Mexico for all she knew.

Silent Bob watched the proceedings with the tow truck. He clicked open his door and said, "I should get our bags from the trunk. We're going to have to figure out how to move the girl without rousing suspicion."

"I don't know why we didn't dump this car," the driver said. He surprised Erin by being black. She felt a little chagrined because in her mind bad guys had equaled white guys. "We should have just left it on the side of the road."

Silent Bob shook his head. "Don't be a fool. The police would have to tag it and eventually the car could be traced back to us. If we take care of it properly, no one will bat an eye."

It made a weird kind of sense to Erin. Hide in plain sight. You were less likely to be noticed if you acted the part of an upright citizen. Hell, how many times had she used the same trick to survive? Just keep your head down and hope no one notices the freak you really are.

Fuck came back and leaned in the window. "Hey," he said to Erin, "Why don't you and me walk down to the other car?"

Erin did not want to go. She was afraid he was still angry at her for stealing his phone. What if he decided to beat her up or something? Then again, he probably couldn't do that in front of the tow truck guy. Maybe she was safe for the moment. "Okay," she said, surprised how weak and cracked her own voice was.

He opened the door. Silent Bob got out and Erin scooted across the seat and did the same. She had to use the car to steady her feet, and she was shocked when Silent Bob handed her one of her crutches from the opened trunk.

"Thank you," she said automatically.

Fuck shook his head, "Stockholm syndrome already? Two minutes ago you still had some spirit left."

He sounded like he'd appreciated that. His smile was weirdly encouraging too. Fuck offered his arm.

Since she only had the one crutch, Erin was forced to take it.

Surprisingly, Fuck didn't rush her. If anything, he seemed very careful and respectful of her feet. When they were quite a distance from the car, at least half way down the block, he gave her a broad smile. "Sun feels nice, doesn't it?"

What was she supposed to say? "Uh, yeah, when you've been locked up for God knows how long, fresh air is kind of precious."

He laughed. This close, he smelled of something familiar, an element maybe? Pointing up, Fuck said, "Yeah, but that up there, that's fire. Solar fire. And you and I, we're made of fire, aren't we?"

Erin blinked at him. What did that mean?

Then suddenly, she placed the smell: sulfur.

Brimstone.

CHAPTER TWENTY-EIGHT

KITTY FIGHTS AND DOESN'T FUCK IT UP

Sparring, oh joy, Kitty thought with zero enthusiasm as she went to change into her workout pants and put on a bra with more support. She really hoped Lily wasn't going to ask her to physically fight anyone. Kitty didn't want to know what Lily did when she discovered Kitty's tendency to close her eyes and not move.

But if Gabe ended up studying Banishing, that could be a lot of fun to watch. She'd always wondered about the level of Banishing Lily did. With the demon-hunters, she'd learned the very basics, but she'd have had to pass basic combat to get the advanced lessons. She'd heard that Lily recently bound Ashtoreth, a demon prince of the Shaitans that had raised herself almost to the level of a demigod. That had to be a beautifully complex piece of magic.

Speaking of magic, what had Lily used to create the tattoo that kept Theo bound to within ten miles of the house? She'd never seen a demon bind a human before. That was definitely on her list to learn.

She went out into the back patio space. Lily and Gabe were unfolding thick black mats over the concrete. Her chest clenched at the familiar sight; she hated getting hit and she got hit a lot when it came to fighting practice.

Theo came out of the back door in dark gray yoga pants and a tight, sleeveless shirt. At least it had a high neckline, but in exchange it showed off her sleek, powerful arms. Kitty felt like even if she miraculously lost fifteen pounds, she'd never look that svelte. And then Theo started stretching, which made Gabe's eyes just about fall out of his head. Kitty thought maybe she could really hit something … no, probably not.

She rolled her shoulders and did some of the light stretching forms.

"How many of the forms do you know?" Lily asked her, meaning the martial art that all the Sangkesh practiced.

"Sixteen," Kitty said. "But the last few are really rusty."

Lily looked at Gabe. "You've had some physical training, how much?"

"Well, I didn't die in the semester I had at military school. Plus, I might have picked up a little boxing here and there," he said, and, for some reason, looked embarrassed about it.

"Theo?" Lily asked.

"Ten years of dance," she said wryly. "Oh and I can turn into a jaguar. That seemed like enough."

"It isn't," Lily said. "Ok, Gabe and Kitty, you two first. To three strikes, non-contact. Stay on the mat."

Lily picked up two pairs of gloves and handed one to Kitty and one to Gabe. Of course they fit. Suhirin probably sent a pair in Kitty's size the minute she signed her up for this school.

Kitty stepped up to where the mats had been laid out and bowed in. Gabe watched her and, despite a confused look on his face, did the same. "Uh, I should tell you," he said, as they began to circle each other, "My fights were all sort of… unrefined."

Kitty nodded, but she was watching how he moved. She held one hand up, ready to cover any strikes to her head, the other stayed near her chest, in case he got close enough.

Her breath was already too high in her chest, her center was way off, but maybe it wouldn't matter this time. His guard was really high too, boxer style. He'd probably come at her head. She circled slowly, sliding her feet, watching him move.

He must have been testing her too, because he jabbed out a few times, not serious, watching how she'd block. The first jab she stepped away from, closed her eyes, made herself open them again. The second, she moved her hand to knock his blow aside easily, but flinched back by reflex and took herself off balance. The knotted tension across her shoulders made her as graceful as a board. He could have nailed her with a second strike and she knew he saw it so she pushed herself forward and aimed a strike at his gut. He blocked, a little ungainly, and her other hand stopped just short of tapping him on the side of the head.

"One," Lily said, and pointed in Kitty's favor.

"This is better than Ultimate Fighting," Theo quipped.

Kitty stepped back and got her guard back in place because now Gabe looked mad. Not crazy-mad, but that kind of focused, fighting mad that was dangerous. She was blinking hard with the effort of not just closing her eyes completely. And at didn't matter how much she told herself not to flinch, when she saw his punch coming at her face, she jerked back and almost failed to block the gut-punch he followed it with. She got that blocked but was badly off balance and his right fist came through her guard and stopped millimeters from her nose.

She closed her eyes. There was a brush of air on her face as Gabe struck again, just short of contact.

"Two, Gabe," Lily said.

She wanted to back away but she couldn't. When she opened her eyes, Gabe was there waiting with his guard still up. Her chest ached but she had to push through, do anything.

The Ultimate Fighting remark may have been a joke to Theo, but Kitty heard it as a good idea; on the ground, he'd have less space to come at her. She crouched low and swept out her foot, catching him behind the ankle and dropping him. He fell loose and kept his guard up so he was protected even on the ground, but he didn't kick out with his feet and she rolled into him, grappling close so he couldn't strike her.

She wanted him to spin and try to get up so she could get a lock on him, but he didn't seem to know what to do on the ground. He just curled into himself and protected his head. This seemed real, not like a fair fight, like he'd been beaten on the ground before. Kitty jumped up and backed away. She offered Gabe a hand up.

He blinked at her over the boxing gloves, as if coming back from somewhere, he shook himself out and took her hand.

"Game," Lily called. "Win for Kitty. Gabe, would you go get us some glasses and a pitcher of water from the kitchen? I think we're going to need them. Kitty, show me your form sixteen."

Kitty assumed the starting pose for the form, but she watched Gabe walk into the house, a little unsteady at first, his shoulders slumped. She wanted to run over and hug him because he looked so much like she felt, but that would probably make it worse. Instead she started the flowing sequence of the form. About a third of the way in she lost the sequence because she had to focus so hard on getting her breathing back to normal.

Lily stepped up next to her on the mat. "Follow me," she said and started the form over again.

CHAPTER TWENTY-NINE

THEO FAKES IT
AS USUAL

Theo watched Lily and Kitty move through some kind of flowing martial arts thing and felt significantly out of her depth. Kitty had clearly been studying this for years. Theo had a few years of ballet and more years of hip-hop and belly dance. That just wasn't going to cut it on the mat—though if she got paired with Gabe, maybe she could just distract him.

Seeing him curled up on the ground like a little kid in a big man's body made her want to lick him, half like a momma cat with a kitten and half very much like a human. Maybe she had spent too much time as a cat. If she ever felt like carrying him around by the scruff of the neck, she was definitely staying human for a year.

Speaking of, Gabe came out of the house balancing a tray full of glasses and a pitcher of ice water. He moved slowly and seemed to be muttering to himself about 'expensive crystal and hadn't these people ever heard of plastic cups?' That made her smile again. He seemed to have gotten his feet back under himself a little. Though, seeing Kitty and Lily going through their form, he gave them a wide berth.

"What the hell is that even?" He asked as he carefully set the tray down on the grass. "That doesn't look like anything I've ever seen."

Theo shrugged. "No idea. Some kind of demon karate I guess."

"Jesus Christ, you mean demons have their own martial arts? I had no chance," he said, as though to make himself feel better.

She resisted giving him a pat on the thigh when he sat down next to her cross-legged in the shade of the house.

Lily and Kitty finished their epic kung fu moves and Kitty came over to get a glass of water. She was breathing hard and sweating a little, but Theo thought she should have looked a lot more worn out. Freakish demon strength probably.

"Gabe, Theo, you're up," Lily said. "No shape-changing. I want to see what you can do in human form."

Clearly it was time for the belly dance moves, right? Yeah, no. Theo got on the mat and put her hands up in front of her face. She shuffled a little to the side like she'd seen them do. Would it help if she just let Gabe nearly-hit her and get this over with? Would he like her more or less for that? Probably less because he might see it as her calling him weak, so she'd better make it harder for him to win.

Gabe frowned at her, as if fully aware that she wasn't nearly as skilled as his previous opponent. She got the sense he didn't really want to go for it, though he did chase her around the mat a bit.

She flipped her hair back over her shoulder; she'd kept it long for this instead of pulling it back in case she got a chance to use the combat hair-flip. He blinked and she thought she saw his pupils dilate slightly. Licking her lips, she advanced, keeping her gaze locked with his. She was pretty sure you weren't supposed to do that in fighting. He looked puzzled. She reached out slowly and traced a line down the center of his chest.

His eyes cleared, like he realized if she had a weapon he'd be in serious trouble, and his fist shot out and paused just short of her face.

"One point each," Lily said. "Fascinating tactic, Theo. Gabe, I trust you won't let her do that a second time."

"Uh, yeah, I mean, no, er …"

He came at her with a more determined pace now. His fists actually seemed to be trying to hit her and she had to dodge and backpedal quickly to get away from them. Then she saw her opening. He swung at her and she held her ground but purposefully flinched back the way Kitty had. Her gesture was a second too slow to be a reflex, but he didn't realize that. He backed up.

Theo turned sideways and kicked like she'd seen on TV. She pulled it, but she still kind of hit him in the stomach. He made an "oomph" sound and staggered back a step.

"Oh shit, sorry," Theo said.

He came forward and aimed two rapid-fire punches at her face before she could react.

"Game," Lily called. "Win for Gabe."

"Yeah well try that with my jaguar," Theo said.

"Oh, I will," Lily replied.

Theo left the mat and went for the water pitcher to give herself something to focus on. She wasn't really sure how that went, but she thought probably slightly in her favor. She'd wanted Gabe to win. And she liked seeing what he could do. He was really cute in his boxer stance with his hands up and his shoulders bunching under his thin t-shirt. She wanted to see more of that. Maybe she could ask him to show her some of his moves. No, that was too obvious. She had to say it right....

"So," Gabe said, sidling up to her. "You know, I could show you some boxing moves if you want."

She rested her hand on his rock-solid shoulder. "Would you? I feel pretty out-classed here."

He actually blushed. "Sure. Any time."

Yes, she'd definitely won that match no matter what Lily said the score was.

CHAPTER THIRTY

GABE WATCHES THE JAGUAR FROM A SAFE DISTANCE

Gabe was still feeling the warmth of Theo's hand on his shoulder when the full understanding of what Lily had suggested hit him. "Are you really going to fight as a panther next? Can Lily change shape, too?" Because the idea of a human, even one that was half-demon, fighting a full-on wild animal seemed completely insane to him.

"I can't," Lily said from behind him. She was sitting on the patio, taking off her boots. "And I don't need to. I'm not quite as strong as Kitty but I've had a lot more practice. Theo, go change when you're ready."

"Uh... aren't you worried about the neighbors?" Gabe asked no one in particular. "Because, you know: jaguar."

Lily pointed up at the second story windows of the neighbor's house. "That's the only view into our yard over the fence and they work weekdays. Their car's gone. We checked. And I'm trusting Theo to have enough control not to go through the fence."

"Right, jaguar," Gabe said, and as for the rest, he should have known Lily would be prepared for all this. For all he knew she already knew the neighbors were 'friendly' to witchy-stuff. But, speaking of fences: "Maybe I'll watch from the terrace. You coming with me, Kitty?"

She looked from him to Theo to Lily and back to him. "Yep," she said. "Let's get iced tea on the way. My money's on Lily."

"What? I'll totally put..." Gabe tried to remember how much money he had left, and finally said, "Five on Theo." Which was pretty much

180

all he had left, so he was feeling pretty confident.

They went through the kitchen, pausing to fill glasses, and up to the terrace where they could lean on the waist-high railing and see the yard below pretty well. Lily had dragged the mats toward the back of the yard so they were completely visible from above. The panther … er, black jaguar came padding out of the back of the house looking massive and dense and kind of cheerful with its tail swishing back and forth.

Lily went to the mat and bowed in. Her body moved as loosely as Theo's, no tension in her arms or shoulders, legs bent slightly at the knees, her talons pressing into the mat enough for a good grip but not hard enough to tear it. She was grinning.

Theo circled, the heavy muscles in her four legs bunching as she prowled. Lily didn't even raise a guard and she didn't step in any direction, she just turned where she stood so that she always faced Theo. Lily looked to Gabe like she could have been a woman waiting in line for a cappuccino except that a thick power gathered inside of her; he could almost see it if he turned his head a little sideways. It wasn't like the demons, not smoky, not having any color at all really or anything visible form, but it felt like a pressure in his eyes.

Theo leapt at her. From up here and not inside a room with the jaguar, the leap was gorgeous—her body was about six feet long and fluid as water. Lily spun, lowered her left shoulder and directed Theo's body past her with a shove at the end that caused Theo to hit the ground on her side rather than her paws.

Theo was on her feet in an instant, her growl so deep that Gabe felt the wooden railing vibrate. She leapt again, aimed at the center of Lily's body. The jaguar's paw hit Lily's shoulder, its back paws still on the ground, stepping forward as Lily went down under her.

"Oh shit," Gabe said. He didn't want to win the bet badly enough to see Lily mauled.

Lily's legs went around the jaguar's hips. She had one arm across Theo's broad chest, holding her paws to one side and gripping the underside of her jaw. The other hand had the top of Theo's jaw and held it open.

Theo struggled to claw or bite in the hold and then reversed course and tried to scramble backward out of it. Lily caught the change in momentum, rolled sideways and shifted her grip until she had one arm around Theo's throat. Her other arm came back and delivered three sharp punches, without contact, to the side of Theo's face.

"Game," Kitty said and then repeated the word as a half shout to the fighters below: "Game!"

Theo didn't seem to care. She succeeded in backing out of Lily's hold. Lily jumped to her feet but miscalculated and staggered sideways. She was clearly off balance, one hand almost reaching to the ground to catch herself.

Theo ran two steps to get behind Lily and leapt again, mouth open.

Lily's stagger vanished and Gabe realized with a flash of awe that it had been a feint that left Lily in a deep, wide, legged pose. She dropped below the level of Theo's jump and surged up under her to add force to the movement and change the trajectory. Theo ended up six feet up in the air torqued sideways and falling hard.

At least this time she didn't land as a naked human, but Gabe thought it had to hurt. The mat wasn't thick enough to help when it came to a 300 lb. jaguar crashing down on concrete.

Theo didn't get up. She lay on her side panting hard and blinking at Lily, lip raised enough to show part of her fang, but the fight was clearly out of her.

Blood ran down Lily's forearm where the jaguar's teeth had caught her during the wrestling, but she didn't pay attention to it. She went and knelt by Theo and ran her hand along the side of her broad, dark head and then along the length of her body. Theo made a gruff, repeated coughing sound and Lily laughed.

Slowly, Theo pushed up on all four legs and headed for the house, limping badly on her right forepaw.

Man, Gabe thought, *these women played for keeps.* No more pulling punches. Not that he really had, but, damn.

CHAPTER THIRTY-ONE

ERIN KNOWS FUCK

Erin clutched the arm of her captor, the one she'd nicknamed 'Fuck,' and asked, "Are you...? Who are you?"

"Well, I'm not exactly your enemy, not like those guys," he jerked his thumb back in the direction of the car that Silent Bob was unloading as the driver paid off the tow truck guy and handed over keys for repairs. They were moving slowly toward the car that held the machine that ate Erin's brain, made it hard for her to hear the song of metals. "These guys, if they fuck up in front of you, will call me Zach, but my real name is Azazel."

Azazel.

Erin had read enough of the Bible to recognize one of the names of Satan. Her heart felt ready to burst out of her chest. She felt something akin to cold sweat dripping down her back. "What do you want from me, Satan?"

"Shaitan," he corrected. Then he flashed her a wicked smile as he slipped something into her hand. "I want you to cause the trouble you were born to cause."

Erin's fingers closed around something the size of a pack of cards. It was a phone. His phone. The one she'd gotten her hands on before and used to contact GraveJelly.

"It's what we do," he said, as they neared the car. "We break things, wreck them, and tear them apart, widening the gyre so the center can not hold. You just do whatever comes natural, little one. It'll be the right thing. Or the wrong one. But wrong is right sometimes, isn't it?"

They were too close to the car now for anything but whispers. Even so, she had to hiss, "Why? Why are you helping me?"

"Because these fuckers fuck it up. They want sterility that only comes with too much order. I'm breaking this up."

"Like a double agent?"

"Like an agent of chaos," Fuck said quietly. But, then he turned to the guys in the car and said loudly, "Special delivery. One creepy fuck of a demon spawn."

Erin was able to slip the phone into the pocket of the clothes they'd dressed her in as rough hands shoved her into the car, far too close to the machine for comfort. Her head started throbbing immediately. He'd given her a gift, this Satan, but she was going to be hard pressed to use it. Pressing her fingers to her temples, she moaned. In fact, she was going to be hard pressed to think at all.

Still, if nothing else, she could let the cell phone feed her, keep this evil, plastic machine from devouring her soul completely.

Rescue was on its way; Erin could hear it singing to her.

:: :: ::

The noise the metal-magic-eating machine inside Erin's head was like the booming hum of MRI machine. In a weird way, the only way to get away from it was to go into it, accept it, and let it roll over her. The cell phone she clutched was like a teddy bear, a comfort, and, so, despite everything, Erin fell asleep.

When she woke up, all Hell broke loose.

Her drivers had pulled into a gas station to refuel and go to the bathroom, probably. All Erin knew was that suddenly, out of the air, an albino weasel fell onto the hood of the car.

But the weasel was only a weasel for the split second that Erin watched it hit the hood. Then, just as suddenly, it was a white-haired man who looked very, very surprised to be a man. The man looked past Erin to the machine in the back and swore. Though muffled by the windshield, Erin could hear him mutter, "Ah, hells. How did they...?"

He never finished his question before people started yelling. Her captors burst out of the convenience store attached to the gas station. They had guns out. The white haired man, who was still pressed onto the hood, saw them. Sliding off, he slipped into the front of the car. To Erin, he said, "Hello, love. I'm Ben. I'll be your rescuer for this trip. Please fasten your seat belt, I'm afraid this might be a very bumpy ride."

Ben-the-rescuer was dressed in a nice shirt and jeans. From his pocket he pulled a screwdriver, and he frantically did something to the steering wheel column as the Cavallo thugs rushed towards them. There was a crack and a "Got you." Ben stuck the screwdriver in the place where the key should go. Giving it a hard twist, the engine sprung to life.

As they jerked into motion, Erin paused to wonder how a tiny weasel could become a fully clothed man. Didn't that defy 'conservation of mass'? Before she could think too hard about it all, Ben tossed the screwdriver at her. It fell heavily into her lap.

"Get yourself free, my dear," Ben said. Then, giving her a broad smile in the rearview, he added, "And then see what you can do about that infernal machine. A wrench in the works, eh?"

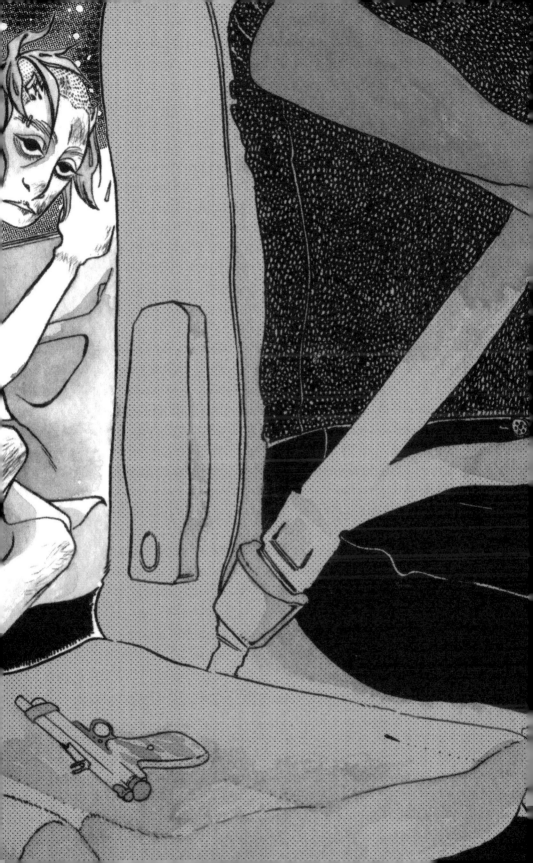

CHAPTER THIRTY-TWO

KITTY GETS INSTRUCTIONS

After sparring and cleaning up and eating, Kitty saw that a message was waiting on her private account on the Sangkesh intranet. Her heart leapt with hope, but it wasn't from Blake.

The message from Suhirin read:

The Cavallo take as many demon children as they can. Find out which one this is that has Lily so interested. Also I'm waiting for your report on the witch girl. What are her other forms? Has she mentioned the stolen items?

That was it. Kitty wanted to delete it. Or to write back a message that was all lies, but she couldn't. Suhirin was more than capable of trapping her by asking a question she already knew the answer to.

It was a miracle that she and Blake had kept their relationship secret from Suhirin as long as they did. Probably she'd been distracted at the school by Kitty's incompetence in all things physical.

But also Blake had been very good at finding ways for them to be alone, like the time at the obstacles course and then in the library …

:: :: ::

"Do it again, Akiva," Suhirin said pointing to the start of the obstacle course.

Kitty groaned and pushed up from the ground, ready to fail once more. It wasn't that she couldn't make it through the course, she just wasn't fast enough for Suhirin's standards. She was big for her age and heavy and slow, for all that strength. She'd heard the phrase "do it again" so often, she felt like it was tattooed inside her skull.

"Or," Suhirin said. "You can run the forest track."

"I'll do that," Kitty said. The forest track was a rugged three-mile run, but it was private.

Suhirin started her watch again. "Go," she said.

Kitty started running, a slow lope at first and then a little faster as she got to the trees. Her legs hurt and her lungs burned, and she wondered if she could walk the back mile and still get back in an amount of time her mother deemed reasonable.

Footsteps sounded behind her and she flinched. If it was another student, or worse, Suhirin herself, she'd probably start crying. But the steps were light, almost dancing.

Blake ran up next to her. It had been almost two months with no way for them to get time alone and Kitty's already-pounding heart felt ready to burst just seeing her. They could talk alone for short moments in the public areas, but they were careful about it. Kitty didn't want to know what would happen if Suhirin found out she liked another student. Suhirin had a way of using her likes against her.

"Hey," Blake said. "Keep running."

Kitty laughed. "You're the only person I can stand to hear that from."

"Just to the start of the bluff," Blake said. "Can you throw me up the bluff?"

"Throw you?"

"Yeah, super-Kitty, you're going to throw me straight up that bluff."

Kitty contemplated the landscape in her mind, especially the way the trail curved around the rise. It made it so you had to run all the way around the jagged stone bluff, so you couldn't cut through the woods and turn a three-mile run into a three-quarters of a mile run. But if you could get straight up sixteen feet of rock … that would cut two miles off the circuit.

"You might be crazy," Kitty said.

"Innovative," Blake said.

They reached the base of the lowest edge of the bluff and Blake stopped. Kitty came to a halt a few paces on, turned and doubled back to Blake. She was panting too hard to kiss her, but she put her arms around her and hugged her as close as she could. Blake laughed and hugged back, then pushed her away.

"Interlace your fingers and get ready to do the hardest, fastest squat plus dead-lift move you can. I'm going to run a few steps and jump and you throw and don't worry about me, got that? Right here, so we're well away from the overhang."

Kitty tried not to think about what would happen if Blake hit the underside of the bluff. It had to be not quite as bad as the things she normally faced in the field. She did know what she was doing, right? Kitty crouched and laced her fingers and prayed a lot.

When Blake's foot hit her hand, she shoved upwards as hard as she could. Blake went up like a missile, beyond the edge of the bluff, spun in the air, caught an overhanging tree branch and flipped herself out of sight.

A minute later her face peered over the edge and she threw down a thin but strong rope.

"Climb up," she said. "But wrap your hands, that cord's skinny."

Kitty pulled the sleeves of her sweatshirt over her hands and scaled up the rope. It was one of the few obstacle course challenges she excelled at since her own body weight wasn't much compared to her strength.

Blake grabbed her shoulders and helped her pull herself over the edge of the bluff. Or at least it started as helping but turned into Blake rolling Kitty onto her back, straddling her hips and kissing her deeply.

Kitty put her hands up under Blake's shirt, but Blake pulled away and looked at her watch.

"You have somewhere to be?" Kitty asked.

"You do. The most Suhirin will accept is a nine-minute mile. If you sprint part of the way back, you have fourteen minutes."

As she talked, she was pushing buttons on her watch. It gave a last, satisfied beep, and she turned her attention back to Kitty.

"You planned this?" Kitty asked.

"No."

"But the rope."

"I always carry that," Blake said. "I don't think ahead like you do, so I carry things. You hush, we now only have thirteen minutes and they're my thirteen minutes."

She put her hands up under Kitty's shirt and Kitty lost her mind for a while. The beeping of the watch alarm brought her back to an unwelcome reality.

Blake groaned and rolled off her. "Go," she said. "I'll find a way to get to you again."

Kitty sat up and pulled her bra and shirt back into place. Blake was watching her, breathing hard, and it took every shred of will she had not to go back to her. The will wouldn't even have been enough if she wasn't also so scared of her mother.

"Promise," Kitty said.

"Yes. Go."

Not quite sure how, Kitty got her feet under her and took off running through the trees. She poured all her frustration into her legs, pounding against the ground, wishing she was back with Blake. All of their time together was priceless, but she loved most seeing Blake on the ground staring up at her, eyes wide and bare and wanting her.

That was more than enough to keep her going. She sprinted down the worn track and back to the obstacle course.

Suhirin turned and clicked her stopwatch. "Good time," she said.

"Thanks," Kitty said and put her hands on her knees to catch her breath. "Showers?"

"Yes," Suhirin said.

Kitty went to the showers and stood for a long time with her face in the water and her hands on the tiles, thinking of everything Blake.

:: :: ::

Kitty saw Blake around for a few days but then didn't. Days stretched into weeks. It was harder to focus on class assignments. She went running on the forest track on her own just to stand under the bluff and remember being up there with Blake. She even went to the weapons locker and took apart and reassembled the FN SCAR-L a few times. And lucked out the week that was their weapons drill, taking second place in the contest to reassemble it.

She dove into her own projects, the study tasks she set herself, spent more time in the library, worked on getting herself ready to go to college in case by some long shot she actually could go to a school in the States and study math like she wanted. The library was part of an old building that used to be entirely a storehouse and was now only half-used for storage. It didn't have that many books in it, but it was full of computers with access to a variety of archives. Kitty had a space she liked in the far corner of the second-story room. It wasn't particularly warm but if she put on thick socks, she could handle it.

The other students left her alone in the library and most of the instructors as well and so she spent more and more time there. She started thinking about sleeping there. She could probably bring in a sleeping bag, but the security guards walked through once or twice during the night and it would be at least as disruptive as trying to sleep in the dorms. Now that she was sixteen and among the older students, she only had to share her room with one girl.

But she liked the quiet of the library. This upper room was small, with only two tables and a single row of bookshelves. She had it to herself and stayed past the closing time of the building. The guards were used to this; they'd leave her, knowing she'd make sure the doors locked behind her when she left.

Only tonight the quiet of the library wasn't completely quiet. There was a sound outside like branches in the wind scraping the walls and then a series of low creaking groans. Kitty stood up from the table and looked at the door. Was someone doing work on the building at 10:50 at night?

There was another long creak and then a rustling sound, scrabbling followed by a heavy thunk and a gasp of pain. Kitty hurried around the one long row of bookcases in the room. Blake was sitting half-propped against the wall under an open window, one hand pressed to her upper arm where blood was seeping through her shirt.

"Tore my stitches," she said. "Not serious. Hi."

"Hi," Kitty knelt next to her. "What do you need?"

"Something absorbent."

Kitty went into the hall, into the bathroom, and found some maxi pads so old they were in individual little cardboard boxes. They probably hadn't been touched in two decades. When she got back with them, Blake had her jacket off, arm free of her shirt, and undershirt sleeve pushed up. She'd exposed a long, stitched wound torn open at one end and bleeding down her arm. She laughed when she saw the pads.

Kitty unboxed one and Blake pressed it over the wound.

"What happened?" Kitty asked.

"I got a little shot."

The wound was on her left arm, where a bullet would have gone if someone was aiming for her heart and missed — or Blake had dodged but not far enough. Kitty felt shaky.

Blake pulled her jacket into her lap and started opening the pockets one-handed and digging through them.

"I climbed up okay," Blake was saying. "But the window stuck. Should've brought oil. Meant to get here before the place closed and just hide somewhere but I worried about the camera out front and then there was a thing at the dorm with all of us, since we're all back now."

She pulled cord out of one pocket and a small knife out of another.

"Okay here," she said and pushed them toward Kitty. "Pull my sleeve down over the pad and tie it in place. Tight enough to stay but don't cut off my circulation."

"I took first aid," Kitty said. "Like nine times."

But Blake was grinning at her and she realized Blake wasn't seriously telling her how to tie the bandage. She probably knew Kitty took the first aid courses over and over to get out of other courses she didn't want to do. It only took a minute to get the pad secure but Kitty fiddled with it longer because she liked hearing Blake's breath catch when her hand accidentally grazed the side of her breast.

When she was done, she got up and closed the window. It wasn't winter yet, just cool out. She sat down against the wall next to Blake and to her surprise, Blake scooted over to sit across Kitty's lap. She put her head on Kitty's shoulder and Kitty held her tightly. Blake wasn't that much smaller than she was, about three inches shorter and leaner, but almost as broad in the shoulders. Still, holding onto her and feeling her muscles relaxing in waves, she felt small.

"Where were you?" she asked.

"I don't want to say," Blake said. "I don't want to talk about that. Tell me about you. What are you doing here tonight?"

"Calculus," Kitty said. "And peeking a little at game theory. I think I'm going to like that."

"Tell me about it."

Kitty laughed, but she talked about what she'd been reading, what she'd been thinking, about the online course she was taking and the questions she'd been asking the professor. She talked until she got tired of hearing herself talk and then she just sat with Blake in her arms. Blake wasn't asleep, but she was relaxed and soft in a way Kitty hadn't felt before.

Sometime after midnight, closer to 1 a.m. Kitty guessed, the door of the room clicked open and a voice said, "Akiva?"

Her notebook and jacket were at the table with the computer she'd been working on. Kitty quickly and as silently as possible, scooted Blake off her lap — with Blake doing something to help that made it feel like she levitated to the side.

"I'm here," she said and grabbed a book from the lower level of the shelf before walking around it into the larger part of the room. "Just trying to remember where I saw this citation. I should have written it down."

Here at the Hunters' School, the campus security guards were full-fledged demon hunters, usually those recovering from some injury in the field. This one had a set of scars on the side of his face that Kitty didn't want to think about, but couldn't help wondering if someday Blake would have similar.

"How late are you staying?" he asked.

"Can I stay a few more hours? I'm not sleepy and I really like what I'm reading, it's all about finding the limit of a function."

"Sure, okay," he said and backed up a half step. "Don't stay all night and lock up when you go."

"Thanks," Kitty grinned at him.

She put the book by her notebook. It was a thick tome about the history of the crusades, from the Sangkesh perspective. Good thing he hadn't asked to see the title. She waited and listened to him check the other second floor rooms and then descend to the first floor. There was the echoing click of the front door closing. She made herself wait another five minutes, just to be sure.

When she walked back around the bookshelf, Blake was sitting up, eyes bright, grinning. "How long do we have?" she asked.

"Three or four hours."

"Does that door lock?"

"No, up here the only locking door is the bathroom," Kitty said and followed that train of thought. "Cold tile, but it's further from the top of the stairs. Nowhere to hide in there, though. Still, the guard won't check inside. I think there's a blanket down in the reading room on the common floor. I'll be right back."

She jogged down the stairs and got the worn, wool blanket someone had thrown across the back of the couch in her other favorite room. Blake was standing in the hallway at the top of the stairs, carrying her jacket. Kitty opened the door to the bathroom and Blake followed her in. It was old but pristine. All of the the students had to be assigned chores, so, even though it was rarely used, the room got cleaned several times a week. Stone walls, tile floor, and wide enough to easily accommodate a wheelchair, or two girls with a blanket.

Kitty spread the blanket on the floor, thinking they could pull half of it over them, but Blake said, "Double it up. I have another."

"You have a blanket? In your jacket?"

Blake held up a plastic wrapped packet only a little bigger than an index card that said "Emergency Blanket" on the front. Kitty tore it open and shook out the ultra-thin, metal-colored sheet.

For the next few hours, every sound in the small room was accompanied by the rustling and crinkling of the emergency blanket and then, usually, laughter.

:: :: ::

Kitty wanted to do that again. Could she get Lily to request Blake come to the school to teach them something? Anything?

She'd have to work on figuring that out too. For a second she considered just asking Suhirin where Blake was, but she couldn't. First off, Blake did the kinds of a assignments that were super classified, and secondly if Suhirin knew how Kitty still felt, she'd probably make sure they could never talk to each other again. Not out of malice, just because she thought that less emotion was more efficient and safer.

That was the thing, Kitty could have hated her if she was malicious. But Suhirin always thought what she was doing was right and sometimes it was. In fact, Kitty really wanted to be able to trust her now, to tell her everything and to get her take on the information from Blake

and the fact that Kitty seemed to be in the middle of it.
But not until she talked to Blake.

CHAPTER THIRTY-THREE

THEO JUMPS TO THE RESCUE

Theo found the next couple of days to be surprisingly peaceful. She and Kitty signed up for some classes at the university, and Gabe kept looking through the catalogue trying to settle on what he wanted to study. At night, she cuddled up to the neighbor lady while no one was watching. She'd even found time to go and collect an item from her contact: a ring. It was hidden in the house now.

Kitty seemed to be want to left alone with her books, so she and Gabe watched TV when she wasn't scrubbing anything. She planned to wait a respectable amount of time before putting the moves on him; she figured the weekend would be about right since they'd just met on Tuesday.

But, that plan got put on hold.

Friday night, in the blackness of early morning, the chime of Lily's phone pulled Theo out of sleep. She'd been sleeping with the door to the terrace open so she could feel the night air. The slight breeze carried noises up from Lily's room below her. At first Theo couldn't hear what Lily was saying, only that she sounded upset. Her voice kept rising in volume as the conversation went on, until Theo could deduce that she was talking to Ben, and it was an emergency.

"Mother Lilith, don't lead them to the house!" Lily's raised voice carried up through the screen door. "I know, Ben, but you can't come here. Take them to the gun range by the lake. I'll meet you there in ten."

Theo threw on her jeans and a shirt and hit the stairs at a jog. If something rough was happening, she wanted to be part of it: to move, to do, to be inside the action.

She caught Lily moving quickly through the hall and followed her down to the first floor and into the Lab.

"Take me with you," she said.

"No." Lily unlocked a long cabinet and pulled out weapons: a one-handed crossbow, a thin Asian sword, a soft leather case of knives, a long-barreled gun.

"How far is it? If it's less than 10 miles the tattoo won't stop me. I'll follow you. You know I can."

"Too dangerous."

Anything that was too dangerous for Theo had to be trouble for Lily alone. Lily had seen her jaguar form, she knew what Theo could do. And she owed Lily, didn't she? Lily had backed up her sister when Sabel saved Theo from the demon hunters. Lily fought Suhirin for her and she was the only person who'd ever faced her jaguar without fear—with something more akin to joy. Lily was the one who offered to take her in, to teach her and look after her. She'd still complain about it, but Theo liked it here; it wouldn't be the same if something happened to Lily.

"You need back up," Theo insisted. "It's you and Ben against how many of them? And you know what I can do. Take me with you."

"I have backup," Lily said, but she looked up from the process of tucking the weapons into various sheaths and pockets on her clothes and considered Theo for a minute. Something in her expression changed and she let out a sigh. "You'll do exactly what I say? Swear it."

"I swear I'll do what you say," Theo said. "Just tonight, though."

Lily chuckled a little at that.

From the hall behind Theo, Gabe said, "If she's going, I'm going too."

The sound of their conversation must have woken him too. Or maybe it had been Theo's feet going down the stairs, since she'd made no effort to be quiet. A glance behind her showed that he'd put on a light peach t-shirt and a navy sweatshirt, the zipper open. Who kept getting him those fey shirt colors?

"Did you learn to shoot a gun during those few months you stuck it out at military school?" Lily asked him.

"Sure did. It was one the only things I was any good at."

Lily pushed past them and headed down the hall toward the door to the garage. Kitty was standing in front of it with her arms crossed. She was in a dark tunic-style shirt over indigo jeans that tucked into knee-high black boots, looking like a combat movie extra.

"Let me drive," Kitty said. "You need to focus on telling us what to do."

"You know where the gun range is, on the west side of the lake?"

"Your GPS does."

"My GPS lies," Lily grumbled.

"Not to me." Kitty held out her hand and Lily dropped the keys into them.

In a minute they were all out the door. The night air smelled alive to Theo, her senses thrumming, on edge. Kitty got into the driver's seat with Lily up front and Theo slid into the back next to Gabe. As Kitty pulled into the street, Lily turned in her seat and handed a gun back to Gabe, the muzzle carefully pointed down and away from all of them. It looked like a large pistol but with an extra long barrel.

"This is a dart pistol. It works a lot like a regular gun, but the darts are mixed anti-human, anti-magic tranquilizers. You have six shots in the gun. There are more in the glove box but I don't have time to show you how to load it, so try not to need them. It will pierce clothes but not body armor and any place on a human or animal body will work."

Gabe took the gun and looked it over carefully. Theo noticed his jaw unclench when Lily said "dart pistol." Likely he was relieved that Lily wasn't going to ask him to try to kill anyone.

Lily pulled out her cell phone and hit a speed dial number. The conversation was brief: "Ana? I know ... Yes, and Sabel. ... The gun range two miles southwest of the house. I don't know how many. The kids are the top priority. ... Thank you."

Turning in the seat again, Lily looked at Theo, "Are you using the jaguar form?"

"Are there trees?" she asked.

Lily blinked as if surprised by the question, but nodded. "Lots."

"Then, yes," she said.

"Good. Keep them distracted and try to separate them. Force them off balance but don't worry about doing damage. They may be using infrared goggles, so don't count on darkness to cover you. If things get bad, go small and get away. Fly back to the house when you can or find Sabel. She and Ana are on their way."

Kitty turned onto 35 and sped up.

"As soon as you turn onto the side road to the range, cut the lights," Lily told her. "I need you and Gabe to do something very important."

"What's that?" Gabe asked.

"Cover our escape route. Stay with the car, keep it hidden, and ready to go. There may be more Cavallo on the way. Also, if we're not out in 20 minutes, I need you to go for help." She reached up and tucked a piece of paper above the visor. "That has contact information for other Sangkesh in the city. Can I trust you to get out of here and use it?"

Kitty didn't answer, but Theo saw Gabe's jaw flex again in the dim light as he said, "Yeah. I'm a good judge of a hopeless situation, too."

Kitty pulled off the freeway and shut off the lights. The car ghosted along a narrow road until Lily whispered, "Stop here. Theo, let's go."

Theo slid out of the car, pulling off her shirt as her bare feet touched asphalt. She hadn't wanted to strip in the back seat next to Gabe, since it sort of took the mystery out of things, but she was ready. Sweatpants came off in a flash now that darkness covered her.

A moment later, four padded feet stalked silently toward the man in body armor. He stood by the first of two cars at the close end of the nearly empty parking lot. She circled around toward the trunk of the car. She'd never killed anyone before and she wasn't even sure how to do it, but this body knew: bite through the back of the neck, not the throat, break the neck. Her jaws were strong enough to do it, but was her stomach? How do you prepare for a thing like that?

Her paw moved a stone on the asphalt. It was a tiny sound, but the man turned toward her and raised his gun. Lily stepped neatly out from behind the front of the car and put a hand over his mouth from behind at the same time that she slid needle into the side of his neck and depressed the plunger. His body went limp and Lily lowered it to the ground in silence before moving into the trees.

Theo ignored Lily and opened her mouth, scenting the locations of the men in the trees. She circled and went toward one who'd knelt in cover, holding a gun. Jaguar instincts took over and she sprang at his back.

CHAPTER THIRTY-FOUR

GABE GETS A GUN

The dart gun felt heavy and familiar in Gabe's grip. The place Kitty drove them to was a rocky, wooded point that jutted into a lake just off the highway. The sound of water lapping against the rock was almost as loud as the sound of his shallow breathing. He'd left the car door open in case he had to use it for cover, and he kept most of his body inside, in case they had to book it.

From his seat in the back Gabe looked into the rearview and saw Kitty's face. Her eyes were wide. Her knuckles whitened where they held the steering wheel in a death grip. She stared at the spot where Lily had dropped that guy.

"It could be that the needle was laced with the same drug that's in these," Gabe suggested, tapping the gun for emphasis.

"Or she just killed a guy."

Or she did. Gabe was about to say that maybe they should just assume the best case scenario until they had proof one way or the other, when a gunshot had him instinctively ducking.

Then, he remembered he was supposed to be covering the car, and he pulled the gun up and wedged in the space behind the open door. Someone was running through the trees. A flash of white—could it be Ben? But, then there was a popping sound—not like a gun, more like that universe sucking-in sound that had happened when Theo transformed—and Ben was gone.

Poof. Just like that. Disappeared.

"What the fuck? Where did he go?" Gabe whispered, not sure where to sight his gun now. Then he saw someone crash through the woods in the same direction Ben had come. He wore camo like some kind of redneck and had a huge gun, like an uzi. Must be one of the bad guys. The camo actually made it hard to get a good bead on the guy. He was still too far away for Gabe to make the shot. Gabe was just about to tell Kitty to hit reverse because they were seriously outgunned when there was another pop.

The camo-guy stumbled.

He dropped his gun. His hands went up like he suddenly had a world-class migraine.

Then his head exploded.

Gabe was so shocked he could hardly even process what had just happened. It was so dark, too, that it was hard to believe what he thought he saw was true. Gabe would have sworn that out of the guy's head came a gore-covered, albino ferret. At some point, the ferret disappeared and, where it had fallen, Ben stood up. Glancing down at the body, Ben straightened his shirt and said, "Pop goes the weasel, motherfucker."

They were too far away. Gabe should never have been able to hear anything Ben said, especially nothing casual like that, but there it was, like some new form of 'sight,' as clear as if Gabe was standing inches from Ben.

Reaching down, Ben grabbed a gun. He took off running before Gabe could signal to him.

Gabe glanced at Kitty, but she seemed to still be focused on the one Lily had taken down. Her eyes darted between his body and the car that blocked the road. Her face was gray and she was looking up, mouth slightly open, breathing fast. Her hand came up, index finger raised, and she drew a line in the air, a square, another line, a semi-circle. She touched her thumb to her third and then second finger. Was it some kind of magic?

"We have to move the car," she said after a few minutes. Her hand moved to rubbing the back of her neck.

"Lily said—"

"Protect the escape. We're in the wrong place. There's only one road in here and we're on it. We're exposed the minute more people show up.

We need to be around the other side of that building and ideally we need to set a trap."

"Um." He didn't know how to tell her they'd nearly been spotted a second ago, only Ben blew apart someone's head.

"Can you see if that guy had car keys on him?" she asked. "I can't … I just can't."

"Yeah," Gabe said. "I can do that."

Slipping out the open car door, Gabe raised the dart gun in front of him. He checked all directions before slowly advancing on the body. Every creak of wind through the woods made him jump internally, but Gabe remembered his lessons and kept his finger off the trigger and parallel to the barrel of the gun.

A shout had him turning to the left, but it was just an echo off the building wall.

Finally, he stood over the body. At least this one still had his head. In fact, the closer Gabe got, the more obvious it became that this guy was still breathing. In the moonlight, Gabe could see that this man wore a similar sort of camo outfit. It looked very military, including a beret, steel-toed boots, and a Sam Brown belt. But, it was also the sort of 'uniform' you could pick up at any hunting store. The guy would never pass muster in a real army, though, not with that beer belly and oddly hipster beard.

Training his gun on the guy's chest, Gabe carefully nudged him with a toe. When the guy didn't move, Gabe knelt down and, well, rolled him. He took the keys, his wallet, the semi-automatic, his hunting knife, and the walkie-talkie radio that he'd dropped when Lily had drugged him.

Kitty gave Gabe a funny look when he scooted into the front seat of the car with his bounty. "You stole a dead guy's wallet?"

"He's only passed out," Gabe said, trying not to think about the other one Ben had dispatched. "And, I believe in a military operation it's called 'commandeering.'"

"We're not the military," she said stiffly.

"Neither are they." Gabe said with certainty. "Now, where do you want me to put the car?"

She explained, but before he could get out and move it, she grabbed his arm in a vice-grip. "Put the wallet back."

"It makes more sense to take it. What's he going to do? Report it missing? Besides, remember, that one is going to wake up. He'll be a lot more scared if he thinks we know where he lives." Gabe said. "Besides maybe it will help. Especially if this goes deeper into the shitter and we have to run to the whats-its."

"Sangkesh."

"Them," Gabe nodded, patting the spot where he'd stashed the information in his jacket. "Now, let's get this car moved so you can use that brain of yours to get us all out of here alive."

She finally let him go. "Okay."

Gabe approached the car with the same caution as he had the body. He came along the backside, like cops always did, and checked to make sure there was no one napping or hiding in the backseat. He set the gun on the roof within easy reach and used the key to unlock the door. Once he had it open, he retrieved the dart gun and slid in behind the drivers' seat. He set the gun carefully in his lap.

It was weird, but Gabe felt grosser about sitting in another man's car than stealing his wallet. Probably because the car was far more personal. It smelled of Doritos and stale beer. There were crushed cans in the passenger side floorboard, Bud Light. Jesus, this guy really was some kind of paramilitary Hipster. When Gabe started up the engine he nearly had a heart attack when music blared on the radio. He quickly nudged it off with a shaking knuckle. After buckling himself in, he checked the rearview and over his shoulder, and, textbook like, backed the car deep into the woods. Bracken crunched under the tires and saplings whipped at the window. But, he got it deep enough off road that no one would spot it right away, at least not until morning.

After turning the car off, he stared at the steering wheel. His prints were all over it now weren't they? He hadn't killed anyone, but Ben had, and this was some kind of crime scene at the very least. Gabe's own prints were in the system, he knew that, so if they could lift them, the cops could track him... maybe, since it wasn't like Gabe'd had a permanent address until yesterday. Even so, he used his sleeve to smear at it half-heartedly. If a CSI team came out here, they were all fucked anyway.

Gabe opened the car door and nearly tripped on the body Ben had left behind. Actually, all the Gabe could see clearly was a hand, the palm up and fingers open. The rest, thankfully, was obscured in the thick undergrowth. Gabe squeezed his eyes shut, like he'd done any time he was confronted with shit he just didn't need. He made sure he had the dart gun, and stepped over the body like it wasn't even there.

That'd just go in the 'deal with it later' box. Fuck, maybe that'd go in the 'deal with it never' box.

Concentrating on just getting through the night, he took a deep breath, opened his eyes again, and watched the woods carefully as he got back to where Kitty had the engine running.

She, on the other had, seemed to have snapped out of it. Her mouth worked fast, "Okay, so I've got a plan."

Thank god someone did. The more he thought about it, the more Gabe realized how clever it had been of someone—Ben or Lily, probably—to lead the bad guys to this gun range. They were cut off from an easy escape route by the shore of the lake, but that worked both ways. Even a cop patrolling the highway wouldn't think twice if they heard gunshots and any muzzle flares would be hidden by the trees and the high wooden wall separating this area from the highway.

Shit, it was like they did this stuff all the time.

CHAPTER THIRTY-FIVE

ERIN MONSTER SMELLS BLOOD AND STEEL

Iron.

The smell of blood.

The sharp scent was everywhere in the darkness, but there was another smell—salt air and freedom. Erin was away from her captors, the Cavallo. Ben, the new, white-haired magic man smelled of earth and strength. "Pop" that was the sound he'd made when he'd fallen out from nowhere suddenly. Now the song stuck in Erin's head was that nursery rhyme that went, "All around the mulberry bush the monkey chased the weasel…"

Too bad the monkeys had guns.

All she and the weasel had was a screwdriver. But, Erin had used it to break the plastic binders on her wrists and she'd driven it into the heart of the machine that made it hard to think and killed it. Ben had called someone on his phone because he couldn't shake their Cavallo pursuers… when they'd skidded into this gun range, he apologized, said he had to draw them away.

He'd left her.

Because she couldn't run.

He'd said, "hide. I'll be back for you."

So now Erin huddled in the foot well behind the driver's seat, trying to think small thoughts, gathering her strength, as she prayed that her sorry white-haired weasel would keep his promise to come back for her, and to get them both out alive.

CHAPTER THIRTY-SIX

KITTY CALCULATES
A GETAWAY

Kitty heard shots in the trees through the open car window. Gabe had the gun he'd taken from the downed guard and crouched in the backseat, pointing the barrel out the window. The dart gun Lily had given them lay on the seat by his foot where he or Kitty could grab it, but she never would. Her body shook with tremors, but not so hard that she couldn't drive, otherwise she'd have asked Gabe to take her spot behind the wheel. She knew when she'd become a liability.

Cars came along the road to the parking lot with their headlights up full so Kitty couldn't see the number. Gabe fired off a burst of shots at the level of the tires and she heard the bang of a flat and then a crunch and breaking glass as one of the other cars hit the lead car.

Gabe breathed intensely, counting under his breath, squinting into the gun, waiting for something that Kitty couldn't figure. She kept her hands on the wheel. How many were they? They couldn't hold out much longer.

At least this was the kind of combat situation where she could be useful. She had rough estimates in her head of the number of people moving in the trees, the number of guns firing, the time it would take them to cover the area and find this car, and how quickly they could make their escape.

Gabe's count ended and he fired another round of shots. They were shooting back now but it would be awfully hard to hit their car because the building and a line of trees covered most of it. Of course all they had to do was get out of their cars and cut along the back of the building and the escape route would be cut off. How long would it take them to figure that out?

A boom, like thunder, came from the ground in front of them and a ball of fire outlined the cars at odd angles where the road emptied into the lot. It was the back car on fire—not Gabe's shot then. The cavalry? Ana and Sabel? If not, they were screwed.

"Lily," Gabe hissed. He his arm jutted between the seats, finger pointing at the right corner of the windshield. In the dark, Kitty saw a familiar figure lit gold by the fire, carrying a heavy bundle over her shoulder, big enough to be a person. She'd paused at the last line of trees, staring toward the fire.

Kitty hit the horn. Lily gathered herself and sprinted across the lot. Gunshots followed her until a second explosion ripped through the cars.

Gabe had the doors open and positioned himself in the front passenger seat. Lily shoved her burden, which was now very clearly a girl, into the back seat and climbed in after, saying in a harsh whisper, "Go, go!"

"Ben and Theo?" Gabe asked.

Lily ignored him, her hand on the girl, who had curled into a ball in the backseat "Kitty, now. Drive."

Kitty threw the car into reverse, backed up about twenty feet and swung it 180 degrees. She'd practiced that exact move in her head a hundred times in the last 20 minutes and it went mostly right, putting the car at the far corner of the building, facing along the back. She barely registered Lily's words as she braced herself for the hard part.

"Ben and Theo can get out on their own," Lily was saying. Her hand was still resting gently on the person, who seemed thin and... abused. "They'll meet us at the house."

Kitty let out her breath, put on the lights and hit the accelerator. There was just enough open space between the back wall of the building and the trees to drive the car. When the building ended, she had to cut a hard left and then a sharp right.

She'd worked it out in her head, over and over: $V - 9 \text{ km/h} = 2 \text{ m/s} *$ $10 \text{ s} = 20 \text{ m/s}$; convert 20 m/s into km/h — so that was $20 \text{ m/s} = 20 \text{ m} * (1\text{km}/1000\text{m}) / (1\text{s} * 1\text{h}/3600 \text{ s}) = 16 * 3600 / 1000 \text{ km/h} = 72 \text{ km/h}$, and convert that back to mph ... This meant she could come around the edge of the building at 5 mph, dodge the trees going slowly, and then ramp up to 45 mph in 10 seconds to break through the wooden wall between them and the freeway.

In theory, anyway.

In practice she flinched left, nearly plowed into another tree because she'd gone too far around the first, swerved right, closed her eyes, forced them open, slammed on the gas and made for the sheer blackness of the wooden wall.

The wood cracked. A post nailed the front of the car and skewed them sideways, the tires churned dirt. Finally, the front wheels caught traction on the sidewalk and leapt them forward. The front wheel dipped over the curb. She glanced back but there wasn't an oncoming car, and she pressed the gas again and they were out on 35 and accelerating.

"Shit damn, that was some driving," Gabe said.

"It was just an approximation," Kitty said.

"Of what?"

"I was off by at least 10 percent. I wonder what the tensile strength of the wood was."

"Uh," Gabe said.

"Get off at that exit," Lily said. "Pull over and park."

Kitty took the next ramp, drove for a block and pulled into a parking lot. Lily got out to do who knew what, though she seemed to be making a hurried set of calls. She kept glancing back at the girl in the backseat. Gabe looked at the girl too, who, for her part, didn't move at all to the point the Kitty was worried she might be dead.

Gabe let out a shaky breath and muttered, "I need to get out. I'll look at the car."

Kitty just sat in the driver's seat and let the shaking move through her body until it started to slow down. Her ribs burned in tension and it was hard to breathe well. Focusing on dropping her diaphragm, she counted really slowly to four on the in breath and four on the out. The girl in the backseat made a tiny sound. "You okay?" Kitty asked.

The girl froze, like she didn't want to be talked to.

Kitty understood the feeling. She wanted to curl up right now, too, but they had to get through this first. She told herself that once they got home she could freak out all she wanted, but right now they needed to get this person somewhere safe.

"You kinda fucked up the car," Gabe said when he got back in, but his tone made it a compliment. He glanced back at the girl again. To Kitty, he mouthed, "She okay?"

Kitty shook her head, but surprised herself by saying, "She will be though. We're all going to be okay."

A few minutes later Lily joined them again. She tucked a phone back into her pocket. "Are you okay to drive us home?" she asked Kitty.

"Yes," she said, and it was the truth. She still felt shaky inside, but her hands were steady.

When they pulled into the garage, Ben was waiting in the doorway to the house, his white hair and shirt spattered with dried blood. All the humor was gone from his face and he looked like a ghost of himself.

Lily opened her door and got out of the back, saying, "Lights off." He cut the overhead light in the garage.

"You set the wards," he replied, not quite a question.

"Of course, but everything helps."

Gabe opened his door but then leaned back toward Kitty for moment. His fingers pulled the slip of paper from above the visor and tucked it into his jeans pocket. They didn't need it now, the contact information for the head of Sangkesh in the city, but Kitty didn't feel like bothering to explain that to him. If the paper worked like a talisman or security blanket for him, she couldn't begrudge that. She got out of the car and stood with her hands on the hood, trying to see if her legs were steady enough.

"Theo was with you?" Lily asked Ben. Her eyes flicked nervously between the girl cowering in the back seat and the darkened neighborhood.

"We left the trees together," he said. He looked at Gabe and Kitty. "You two walk around the outside of the house and look for Theo. She can't travel as fast. She's not wounded but she … might need help."

Lily looked to the two of them as she said, "I need to get Erin situated."

"Got it," Gabe said. He went past Ben into the hallway and Kitty followed.

"I'll take east and the terrace, you look west and meet me on the patio," Kitty said.

He nodded and ducked into his bedroom. Kitty went down the hall to the outer east door. The walkway to the back patio was empty and she crossed it quickly and stood on the patio looking around. What shape would Theo be in? She wished she knew more about how her powers worked and what happened in the woods. What kind of help did Ben think she needed and how were they supposed to give it without really knowing anything?

The only light in the yard came from a neighbor's back porch light on the other side of the fence, and from the half moon high in the sky, but it was enough that Kitty saw the shift in luminosity as a dark form crossed above her. She looked up and saw the owl bank, wobble slightly, and come down to the dark-colored concrete of the back patio.

The owl roiled and coalesced into Theo, naked and streaked with dirt, on hands and knees, her hair tangled. She crawled toward the back of the house.

"Theo?" Kitty said softly.

Theo's face turned toward her, eyes wide, dark, glassy with shock, her mouth ringed with drying blood. She tried to speak, choked, turned toward the house and vomited. Kitty saw the spasms along the bunched muscles of her back and her heaving ribs.

Gabe came around the other side of the house and Kitty motioned to him to come into the back yard. He had a blanket draped over his arm and came toward her but paused as soon as he saw Theo. She'd stopped being sick and finished her halting journey to the back of the house where she opened the spigot sticking out of the wall and put her mouth under it.

Gabe shoved the blanket into Kitty's hands and went to Theo. It was a throw blanket but thick and warm. Good thinking that. She watched Gabe kneel in front of Theo, who was gulping water and gasping and washing it over her face and hair. She looked at him and then over at Kitty, her expression not entirely human in the half-light, a wild darkness in her eyes, as if she was trying to remember them but hadn't yet placed who they were, or who she was.

"That your blood?" he asked her.

She shook her head, turned away from him and vomited again. He'd managed to catch most of her hair as she turned and held it back from her face with a flash of pained sympathy in his eyes.

She scooped more water into her mouth and spat repeatedly. Kitty moved forward and handed the blanket back to Gabe, who gently wrapped it around Theo's shivering body.

"You hurt anywhere?" Gabe asked.

Theo shook her head.

"Can you talk?" Kitty asked.

"Don't .. want to," Theo said with obvious effort. She coughed, choked, spat again, and crawled back against the wall, away from both of them.

Curling her knees to her chest, Theo tightened her hold on the blanket, put her head down and started to cry.

"Go get Ben," Gabe said.

Kitty went into the house, glad to get away. She found Ben in the first floor hallway, looking through the doorway of the bedroom that had been empty until now.

"Hey," she said. "Gabe sent me to get you. Theo's back but she's … she looks like she's having trouble being human."

He stepped back and sighed loudly. "Kids. Think you're invulnerable. Think you can just kick Brother Jaguar and he won't kick back. Can you get her up to her room?"

"I think so."

"Do. I'll meet you there when I have what I need."

Kitty walked back through the house. The fear inside her had ebbed to slight waves of discomfort and overtop that she felt dread. She didn't want to see Theo like that, didn't want it to replace the version of Theo that was so easy to dislike. In the back yard, Gabe was sitting against the wall of the house with his arms around Theo who had curled into his lap, still crying.

Gabe's expression was frighteningly blank, reminding Kitty of her mother, except, unlike her, his hand was methodically and gently stroking Theo's back, like you might a child. Even though his eyes looked dead, he kept murmuring, "Just hang on. Hang on."

"Ben said to get her up to her room," Kitty said.

Theo turned her face up toward the sound of Kitty's voice. "Can you walk?" Kitty asked her.

Theo rolled forward out of Gabe's lap onto hands and knees, then pushed slowly up with her hands, rocked back on her feet, straightened her legs, stood for a precarious moment and then staggered sideways.

CHAPTER THIRTY-SIX

Kitty caught her before she could fall.

"Fucking biped," Theo muttered under her breath.

"Pursuit predation is more efficient," Kitty said and Theo gave a single cough-like laugh. "Can you walk?" she asked again.

Theo paused and then shook her head.

"I'm going to pick you up, okay? Don't go all jaguar on me."

Feeling a slight nod, Kitty took that as permission. She bent her legs, left one arm behind Theo's back, put the other under her legs and lifted. It wasn't elegant, but they'd make it up the stairs.

Gabe went in front of them and opened the doors. Kitty focused on not hitting Theo's feet against anything. Her head wasn't a problem because she'd tucked it in under Kitty's chin and Kitty could smell raw earth, pine sap, acrid bitterness, coppery blood and feline musk. It held her attention in a way she wasn't the least bit comfortable with.

She got Theo into her room and set her down as gently as she could on the futon mattress on the floor that she used as a bed. Theo rolled away from her, toward the wall. Kitty straightened up and backed out of the room. Gabe waited in the hall. He could watch over Theo until Ben showed up. He seemed to have an aptitude for it.

She went into the bathroom, but that was still too close to Theo's room, so she went down to the main floor and used the bathroom off the living room to wash her hands, and then her face, and her hands a few more times for good measure.

A small light was on in the kitchen, so she went in and saw Lily at the island slumped over a steaming Tupperware of soup.

"More in the freezer if you want," Lily said. "Split pea."

"Sure," Kitty said. She pulled a marked, single-serving bowl out of the freezer and stuck it in the microwave, hoping that something warm and thick would settle her down enough to make sleep possible.

Lily spooned soup resolutely into her mouth. Kitty had seen plenty of people look like that after hunting—trying to get calories back into their system after the hard burn of their demon metabolism.

"What happened to Theo?" Kitty asked. "Ben said she kicked Brother Jaguar?"

"The man's a poet," Lily grumbled sarcastically into the soup. "Different traditions describe it differently, but fundamentally I think she hasn't taken that shape often so she hasn't integrated it. The jaguar's mind is still there alongside hers and normally she can control it."

"But?"

"She took a man's arm off. Likely, the jaguar ate some of it and wanted to go on eating the rest of the man, made it hard for her to change back, and probably scared the shit out of her."

"Does anything scare Theo?" Kitty asked.

"You know what scares me?" Gabe asked, as he passed by the table and took a bottle of water out of the fridge. "Weasels popping out of guys' heads."

"You weren't supposed to see that," Lily said.

Kitty glanced at Gabe. She really wanted to believe he was being metaphorical, but a sinking feeling in her gut suggested he meant that literally.

He just shook his head, like he wished he hadn't seen anything. "Yeah, I get the feeling we weren't supposed to see a lot of that. Is that girl okay? The one we…" he seemed uncertain of the word choice, but settled on an angry sounding, "…rescued?"

Lily arched an eyebrow. "I told you not to come."

"Things would have been much worse if we hadn't," Kitty said. Then, because she was curious, too, "Is she?"

Lily sighed. "Her name is Erin Nakano. And she'll be… she'll live. But she has deeper wounds than the physical ones."

"The broken one," Gabe said.

"Yes," Lily acknowledged.

"Great," Gabe said, downing his water in a series of deep gulps. "Just fucking great. Well, I'm going to think about that tomorrow. For now, I'm going to stand watch over Theo."

Out he stomped, leaving Lily and Kitty alone again. Lily stood up slowly, like her bones ached. "We're all afraid," she said as she walked out. "We just show it differently."

Kitty appreciated the sentiment but still, she thought, some of them were definitely more afraid than others.

CHAPTER THIRTY-SEVEN

JAGUAR THEO WANTS TO EAT

Jaguar hungry.

Smells blood.

Theo tried to be human, but it wasn't working. She could feel the shift trying to take back control. She could still feel tendon ripping, taste sweet, sweet meat, smell the hot scent of fear, and hear the sound of flesh rending underneath powerful jaws.

Jaguar eats.

Theo watched the big cat crunching merrily on a bone, fascination and horror mixing in her. The bone was part of a leg torn open at the thigh. But not the man's arm she remembered. This had to be some kind of dream, right? Because Jaguar was eating a well-shaped female leg.

And the more she watched, the more Theo realized the woman's body that was face down under Jaguar's paws was her body.

She turned away but a hand caught her shoulder.

"Wrong way," Ben said.

"I'm dreaming," she told him, as if that said everything she needed to say.

"Of course. Now come, you have to make friends with Brother Jaguar before he starts on your head."

CHAPTER THIRTY-EIGHT

GABE ISN'T SURE ABOUT ANY OF THIS ANYMORE

Gabe tromped up the stairs. When he approached Theo's room, he could hear voices, or rather Ben's voice, speaking lowly.

The door stood open and Theo lay on her back on the futon with Ben sitting cross-legged next to her. His pale hair and shirt were still spattered with brown blood, but Theo didn't seem to care. She shivered, though she clearly tried not to; her eyes shut and her jaw clenched.

Ben bent down and said a few more things to her, and then picked up an iPod and stuck it in one of those fancy Bose speakers. When he pressed play, a steady double drumbeat filled the room. Grabbing the blanket shoved down at the foot of Theo's mattress, he uncrumpled it and pulled it over Theo. Then, he lay down next to her with his arms crossed over his chest.

A minute later, Theo's body went slack. Like sleep, but more still than that.

It seemed clear they'd gone into some kind of trance or hypnotic state. Gabe half-expected to see some kind of magical special effect— sparkles or flashes or something cool like that. If he squinted and didn't look at them directly, he almost could see a shimmering, but it wasn't terribly exciting, which was probably for the best given what they'd all just been through.

He wasn't surprised that Theo was in shock. Gabe could tell he was coming down, too. Nerves jangled and, despite promising to stay on

216

watch, what he really wanted to do was pace. He peeked into the darkened room again. Still a lot of nothing going on and, anyway, Ben was there.

Gabe let his feet take him wherever they wanted to go. He wandered in the direction of his room, back down past the main living floor, towards his bedroom the floor below that. Yawning, Gabe considered trying to sleep, but he noticed that they'd stuck the 'broken one' in the bedroom across from his, close to the stairs. Curious, he looked in.

For such trouble, she was a tiny slip of a thing. She couldn't weigh much more than a hundred pounds. Honestly, his brain said 'she,' but, really, it was hard to tell. Her—he decided to stick with that for the moment—hair was short, like, unnaturally so. Someone had shaved her head to expose some kind of bony protuberances in her hairline just above her eyebrows. Gabe would have said 'horns,' but if so they'd been hacked off with a saw.

Despite the hardcore hairstyle, her features were delicate and had an Asian cast to them. In the semi-darkness of the approaching dawn, Gabe could see a lot of piercings glittering. She had hoops in her ears, over one eyebrow, and maybe through her nose…? He'd have to get a lot closer to check on that last one and, even though she seemed to be sleeping soundly, he didn't want to surprise her by looming over her like some kind of creeper.

He already felt weird enough staring. But, this was someone they'd been willing to kill for, so he felt he had a bit of right to at least check her out a little.

The room they put her in was as 'girly' as his. The way she curled into herself, she looked very fragile among the frills and lace. Yet, even with his nascent non-powers, Gabe could sort of see the power she contained. Even without being told, he knew she was going to turn out to be part-demon, like Kitty. Except… redder.

Huh, that didn't make sense: redder. Yet, it was right, because the impression he got was of a completely different type of demon energy than any he'd seen so far. Granted, that wasn't many, but somehow Gabe knew she was special, different from anything he'd seen so far. The power that emanated from her in smoky swirls, glowed hot and burning bright red, like fire.

For a demon, she was the most conservatively dressed of all of them. Well, maybe not so much more than him now that the house was in charge of his wardrobe, but she was all buttoned up in a long-sleeve shirt and almost prim pants. He'd have thought it might be a high school uniform, except that he doubted they'd bring an underage girl here.

When she made a little noise, Gabe decided he'd better not be standing here when she woke up.

Gabe made his way back upstairs, slowly. The glow of the television came from the living room. He saw Kitty deep into some sports video game; he considered joining her, but the last thing he wanted was to simulate anything even vaguely violent. So, he kept moving up. The restless spirit of the stairway.

Soft drumming and chanting noises still came from Theo's room. The music was going a little faster now. A quick check, however, showed that Ben and Theo were still just lying on the floor, looking asleep.

Gabe settled his back against the wall, crossed his arms in front of his chest, and stared at the stairway. Something jabbed him in the back. Twisting around, Gabe discovered he'd stuck the empty dart gun into the back of his jeans, like some kind of action star. He looked at it now, its metal dark and sinister in the half-light. The weight of it was lethal, too, like all the guns he'd held before.

Growing up in West Virginia, Gabe had hunted animals as par for the course of growing-up. Your first kill was just one of those coming of age things expected of boys. Once you've dispatched Bambi with a hunting knife, something changed... it wasn't necessarily a bad thing, but you weren't the same after, either.

It wasn't ever discussed as a thing, but a person developed a 'hunting' philosophy, a set of ethics.

You hunted for Reasons. Sometimes the reason was sport, but that meant that you were probably doing something to give the animals a leg-up, as it were, like hunting with a bow. Some people had fucked-up hunting ethics, like they said it was sport, but used AK-47s. Those people were bad people.

You just knew.

Military school had been the same. The reasons were creepier, in a way, because they tended to be far more vague, like, for 'brotherhood' or 'country,' neither of which was ever a thing Gabe could get behind because they seemed to want some twisted up version of both that was controlling and bullying and exclusive.

Not his 'brothers,' at all. Not his vision of the country, either.

Plus there was always so much hypocritical bullshit. The guy who espoused all the 'brotherhood' talk, would be the first one to organize the flush-the-weird-kid's-head-in-the-toilet hunting parties.

Bad guys.

He'd gotten out from under that at the first opportunity. Because their 'badness' was more subtle, it was the kind that could get under your skin when you weren't paying attention, because so much of what it was about *sounded* right.

Turning the gun around in his hand, Gabe considered the fact that he never doubted there were things out there he'd be willing to kill for. He'd kill Asshole to protect Mom or Meema, no question. In fact, it was one of the reasons Gabe had left; they were heading for that, him and Asshole, like two trains on the same track. If he'd stayed any longer, he'd have killed Asshole. And, as satisfying as that would be short term, dude was not worth 99 to life.

Not a lot really was.

And that was the problem.

Unless, somehow, Gabe had imagined it, they'd left at least one body behind tonight. There was no statute of limitations on murder. He didn't even know—did the Sangkesh or whatever they were have the kind of power to make a body disappear? Could they hush up whatever family was left behind?

And, if they had that kind of power and used it that way, were they still good guys?

CHAPTER THIRTY-NINE

ERIN LIKES THE DEVIL'S MUSIC

At first Erin didn't think she could sleep in this new place. The woman who had pulled her from the stolen car hadn't had patient, apologetic hands at all. In fact, at first Erin had thought she might be one of the Cavallo and had tried to fight her. But she had said that she came with "Ben." Erin had managed to croak out the question, "Weasel?" to which she'd chuckled and said, "Yes, weasel."

It had been a nice moment, but then everything turned Iron and violence again, and violence made Erin hide deep, deep inside.

Now, however, she heard a song. It wasn't her father's song of the Elements, but it was a good one. It had the right scent, the right... magic.

Clutching the comforter they'd tucked around her shoulders, Erin listened to the song and tried not to think that she might have fallen into a nest of devils and their magic. She'd thought, after all, that the weasel's lady friend had shown off fangs.

Despite herself, Erin's eyelids fluttered closed. A small smile formed on her cracked and bruised lips.

At least devils had good music.

She could rest and in the morning if the door was still open, she would go. She would find a better place to hide. For now, she was going to dream a dream of metal and magic... and maybe, with luck build herself some new crutches.

CHAPTER FORTY

KITTY STILL HAS THE JITTERS

While Kitty sipped her soup, her whole body quaked. A full field operation was something she'd trained for at the Hunters' School, but she'd never been in a situation where she could have been asked to kill a person.

Dead people.

Kitty was pretty sure she'd seen dead people.

In the movies, after harrowing moments like this, people always threw up on their shoes. Kitty's stomach was the opposite. It didn't seem interested in rebelling at all. In fact, it growled from hunger, like it'd finally had a taste of something it wanted.

The soup wasn't doing it for her. She opened the fridge door again to find that of course there was a cooked steak in there. Of course. She nuked it and tore into it when it was lukewarm. The heavy meat settled her stomach, even as she felt wrong about eating it now.

When had some part of her grown into her mother's daughter?

After she ate, she knew there was no way she'd get to sleep and dawn was only a few hours away. She ended up in the living room playing FIFA Soccer on the Xbox with the sound off for a few hours. She might have dozed off and dreamt one of the matches in the middle, but she was awake at 8 a.m. when she heard a soft knock on the front door and some saying, "Let me try her cell phone."

If they were willing to announce themselves and courteous enough to knock rather than ring the bell so they wouldn't wake everyone up, they had to be on Lily's side. Kitty got up and opened the door.

Two women looked at her from the front stoop, the first holding a big white box from a bakery. She was an inch shorter than Kitty, but no less solid, with spiky blond hair and a broad, handsome face with a Midwestern white girl tan. The woman behind her looked like a slightly older version of Theo with straight black hair, stormy blue eyes and a prettier face. Kitty had seen a photo in Theo's file — this was her big sister Sabel.

"We brought donuts," the blond woman said.

That struck Kitty as the funniest thing she'd ever heard and once she started laughing about it, she wasn't sure how to stop. The woman stepped inside, put an arm around Kitty and drew her into the living room like she'd been there before.

Through the weight of the arm around her shoulder, Kitty felt the energy of an old demon, strong and protective. It reminded her of the very best aspects of being in the Sangkesh—of what Suhirin could be, if she only knew how.

Kitty let this woman return her to the couch and managed to stop laughing before it went over the edge into completely hysterical.

"I'm Ana," she said. "I'm guessing you're Kitty. Have you eaten recently?"

"When we got back," Kitty told her. "But I could eat."

Ana opened the box of donuts. "Go for it," she said.

Kitty hadn't felt hungry until she saw the donuts and then she was ravenous again. She had a chocolate frosted bismark and Ana had one as well. They ate in warm silence, but mid-donut Kitty became aware of voices from the dining room.

"—supposed to teach her, not throw her into a fight with the Cavallo," an unfamiliar voice said. Kitty assumed it came from Sabel because it sounded like a more refined version of Theo.

"The fight didn't hurt her," Lily said in return. "The problem is how she changes, not anything they did."

"But you could have gotten her shot."

"You need to trust her more," Lily said. "She may not understand how her magic works, but she's good at using it."

"Trust her? You didn't grow up with her. She is the most reckless…"

"It's not your fault," Lily said, almost too quietly for Kitty to hear.

"And they can all handle it. Theo got herself the body of what has to be one of the biggest jaguars in existence as her fighting form. Gabe knows his way around a gun and how to sit tight and cover an exit. And Kitty has all the basic Sangkesh demon-hunter training and one of the finest systems-thinking brains I've seen. They did good, Sabel, and they need to. If the Cavallo ever find this house, do you want them unpracticed? There may be times when they're all they've got."

"Theo will always have me," Sabel said.

Lily didn't answer and her lips were very thin, in a judging sort of way. Kitty wasn't sure who Lily was sitting in judgment, but she sure wondered what it was like to have Theo as a little sister. Probably a terrible pain in the ass, so Sabel's determination was doubly noble.

Kitty also warmed to hear Lily's pride.

No one had ever been proud of her work before—at least, not in a fight. A fight where she'd used math to help them escape.

Next to her, Ana pushed off the couch and walked into the kitchen. Kitty picked up the box of donuts and followed.

"We'll watch the kids. Abraxas says, 'go to bed.'" Ana told Lily.

The tired lines on Lily's face eased and she laughed. "Is that an order or an invitation?" she said, but she didn't wait for an answer. She got off the kitchen stool she'd been sitting on and walked stiffly down the hall to her bedroom.

"We're not kids," Kitty muttered, but she didn't put much emphasis into it because she was wondering who Abraxas was. Did Lily have a boyfriend?

"Figure of speech," Ana said. "Not an insult. Can you cook?"

"Some."

"Good, help me make breakfast." She crossed the kitchen to Sabel and kissed her temple. "And you, go check on Theo."

"Wait," Kitty said and Sabel turned back to them from the doorway to the stairs. "One question: Theo, is she Hecatine? It's inherited, isn't it? Even though everyone calls her a feral witch."

Sabel nodded and said, "It's inherited. Why?"

"Just curious about how that works," Kitty lied.

It was a pattern, she was just too tired to see it all. She needed someone to help her see it, but who? Could she trust Sabel? Or was it time to call her mother?

CHAPTER FORTY-ONE

THEO AND SABEL
FINALLY TALK

The weasel sang the big cat to sleep.

Then, the man taught the girl to speak to the big cat and put the big cat in a box. Luckily, kitties liked boxes, even big ones.

But the girl still felt torn up, chewed apart inside, so the man and the weasel had to dance the dance of putting things in place. Mending. It was a slow, measured dance. The steps were hard to follow at first, despite a patient teacher. After an hour or so Theo felt her inside-house was in order.

"Now," Ben said kindly, "It's time for your physical body to rest."

"Sing to me," the girl whispered. "Sing to me my name, I can't remember it."

A soft and smoothed the hair from the girl's face. "I don't know the Greek, but I will give your name in my language. Hopefully that will be enough."

:: :: ::

When Theo woke, the sun was shining in her window bright and hard. She smelled cooking meat and crawled from her futon to the terrace to choke and gulp air until she wasn't in danger of puking. Who was the asshole making meat for breakfast?

She had clothes on, sweats and a t-shirt, and she was pretty sure that had been Ben's doing and not Gabe or, worse, Kitty. The shifting landscape of the trance Ben took her through was still trying to sort itself out in her mind, but her body knew what had changed. She felt solid. The jaguar mind was still there, but it didn't keep pushing itself over her human mind and driving her down under its hunger.

The worst thing about that had been how much she wanted to let jaguar win, to slip away into the peace of the animal world. Only the feeling that she'd never make it back to control kept her from giving the jaguar full reign. She could crave days or weeks of peace, but she wasn't into obliterating herself.

With the patio door open and a little breeze blowing into the house, she could go back into her room. Now she caught another scent: Sabel had been up here in the last hour or two. Was she still here? Part of Theo wanted to run down the stairs and find out and the other part didn't want to see her now with the jaguar so raw in her mind. Sabel, who'd known there was magic and told her otherwise—what could she say to her now?

Theo went into the bathroom that she shared with Kitty's room, opened the window and turned on the ceiling fan. Then she filled the huge bathtub, stripped and lowered herself gratefully into it.

She and the jaguar didn't share the same body. When she changed, her body went into nowhere and the jaguar's body came out of nowhere, so whatever happened to the jaguar didn't really happen to her—though she had a feeling that if the jaguar ever died, she would too. Surface elements often translated roughly: dirt on the jaguar would sometimes show up on her skin or, in the case of last night, blood.

The leaps and attacks of last night's fight weren't etched out in her human muscles and bones. The soreness she felt was from the repercussions when she came back human and tried to puke out the human meat that wasn't in her stomach—it had gone into nowhere in the jaguar body—and then to shake herself near to pieces from shock and horror.

She'd done some things in animal form that she wasn't proud of, and a few that she had kind of liked but would never repeat, and nothing came close to the feel of crushing a man's limb in her teeth and the bone-deep pleasure of feeding while her human self reeled and revolted and tried to jerk away.

The hot bath water almost buffered her enough to think about it, but not quite, so she turned her mind forcefully away and dunked her head under the water to get the grit out of her hair. She wanted to feel completely human again. Ben had warned her about changing shape again soon and in particular told her to avoid the jaguar, but he didn't need to because she already felt what a bad idea that would be. She didn't want the inhabited sense of that body now. She didn't want to be an animal.

What she really wanted was someone to lie her back on her bed and trace the whole shape of her body with their hands and mouth so she could feel every inch of her human skin. Gabe, preferably. He'd be perfect with his scruffy half-beard to brush against her skin and his thick weight to press her down and outline her. Stupid Rule #2.

She'd have to make do for now. She picked up the loofah, rubbed it with soap and set to briskly scrubbing herself, starting at the tips of her toes. When she got up to her scalp, she started over again. Then she let the water out of the tub and rinsed her hair and skin again with clean water from the faucet.

She was sitting in the tub wringing the water out of her hair when the door from Kitty's room opened and Kitty walked in, jerked suddenly when she saw Theo in the tub, started backing out until her thigh hit the edge of the sink and she winced. One hand went to her leg and the other to her head.

"Hey," Theo said. "I'm about done here."

"Uh."

Theo stood and pulled the towel off the rack. "Seriously, everyone sees me naked eventually, it's no big deal. This is like the third time for you anyway, right?"

"But who's counting," Kitty said. She might have been trying for humor, but her voice came out monotone and strained.

Standing by the tub trying to both dry herself and wrap the towel around her naked body, Theo saw that Kitty's skin had an ashen look to it and her hair was a little lopsided, like she'd been resting against something that crushed the curls on the back and part of the side. Her jeans were streaked with dirt at the knees and she was wearing a single sock.

"Did you sleep?" Theo finished her super-quick drying job and wrapped the towel around herself. It was plush and long, rendering her completely decent.

"Not yet. Your sister's downstairs, and her girlfriend, they brought donuts."

"Then who's the fucker cooking meat?" Theo asked.

"Oh, uh, that was me."

"Do you know how disgusting that is after ..." Theo swallowed hard.

"I'm sorry," Kitty said. "I wasn't thinking. I've just been so hungry. It's a demon thing."

Her shoulders were slumped forward and she still had a hand pressed to her forehead like she was trying to hold back an epic headache. There wasn't an ounce of fight in her anymore and weirdly it made Theo want to go over and hug her—or maybe that was just her human skin craving touch.

Theo opened the medicine cabinet, took two Advil out of the bottle and handed them to Kitty who filled one palm with water, popped the pills in her mouth, sipped and swallowed.

"Thanks," she said. "It kind of snuck up on me, in my eyes, you know, and then all over."

"Bath's all yours," Theo told her. "I recommend it."

She left through the door to her room because it was about to get weird with the two of them in the little bathroom. It wasn't even like she liked Kitty, just, you know, trauma and whatever. She put on a pair of grey yoga pants that hugged her ass, in case Gabe was up, and a merlot-colored t-shirt.

The meat smell had abated somewhat or Theo's nose was getting used to it enough to make it non-revolting, so she went carefully down the stairs. Ana was in the kitchen, her back to the door, rinsing dishes in the sink and loading them into the dishwasher. Gabe sat at the island shoveling scrambled eggs into his mouth like they were going out of style. From the dark, bruised-looking circles under his eyes, she wasn't sure he'd slept, but his hair was wet from a shower and he had on a fresh set of gay-dorky, clothes. Theo smiled at him and went to make herself a cup of coffee.

"Where's my sister?" she asked Ana.

"Downstairs seeing if the new girl wants something to eat. How're you doing?"

"I'm in one piece. Is there anything not disgusting to eat?"

Ana gave her a sideways look and put another plate into the dishwasher. "Depends," she said.

"I think she means non-animal," Gabe said and Theo flashed him a grin. So, he had been paying attention to her well enough to get her eating habits. Or maybe he just remembered her pizza order. Either way, it was a good sign that he'd retain the knowledge of her other preferences if they ever figured out a way to explore them.

"Oh," Ana said. "Kitty baked some almond scones. They're in the oven keeping warm."

Theo opened the oven. There were eight triangular scones on a baking tray with a space where four more had been. They were dotted with slivered almonds and an enticing golden brown except for one on the end that had a darkly burnt edge. She grabbed two from the middle, put them on a plate, and went to get the almond butter and honey.

"Ben left you a note before he went to bed." Ana pointed to a folded piece of paper that said "instructions" in a florid masculine scrawl on the front.

Theo picked it up and carried it to the island where she sat on the stool next to Gabe and opened it. It read:

Never expose her to bright light
Never get her wet
Never, ever feed her after midnight.

Theo waved the note. "These are the fucking instructions for gremlins," she said.

"Uh-oh," Gabe said and touched the edge of her damp hair. His heavy fingers brushed the back of her shoulder and she shivered. "What happens when you get them wet?"

"They multiply," Ana said darkly. "Heaven save us. Theo, try the back of the note."

On the back it said:

No booze
No drugs
Hands off Gabe
Don't turn into a jaguar

She crumpled it and jammed it under the side of the scone plate so Gabe couldn't see it. She liked the gremlin instructions better.

"Let's go into the dining room," Ana suggested. "I haven't heard the details from last night." She picked up a mug from the counter and went into the other room so Theo took the opportunity to toss Ben's note in the trash, then got her plate, mug and jars, and followed. Gabe brought up the rear and chose the chair closest to Theo. She tried not to look too pleased about that, at least not while Ana was watching.

"Not much to tell," Theo said when they were sitting again. "Ran around in the trees, knocked some guys over, bit one, tried not to get shot. How about you, Gabe?"

"Uh, I moved a guy's car and shot at some tires and covered Kitty so she could get us out of there."

"She what?" Theo asked. She'd assumed Kitty would have been in a quivering heap in the back seat.

"She drove the getaway car, or whatever," Gabe said. "Did a pretty sweet job of it too. Went down the back of the building and through the wooden barricade thing. Had it all planned out in her head and it actually worked."

Ana laughed. "Having a plan that works is so much better than just having a plan, isn't it?"

"We saw a car blow up," Gabe said. "Maybe two. Was that you?"

"It drew their attention away from you pretty well and then we were mostly on clean-up. Lily and Ben got the majority of the guys in the woods and some ran after the explosions started, so we just tidied up for morning."

"Tidied up?" Gabe asked. "Like got rid of the bodies?" He leaned forward and creased his forehead as he asked, and Theo wondered how much he'd been thinking about this.

"We did," Ana said. "There weren't that many. Most of them actually got out. We try not to kill them, especially the amateurs. I'm guessing there were about fifteen or sixteen of them and when they scrambled out with their wounded in the working cars, there were five dead. We destroyed the dead and the remnants of the burned cars. Then we tossed around some beer bottles and tried to make it look like a car full of drunk kids came through shooting off guns for kicks."

Theo was about to ask how they'd blown up cars and destroyed all that evidence, but Sabel came into the room and sat next to Ana. The only sign that she'd been up since 3 a.m. was a hint of darkness under her eyes, like a smudge of eye shadow out of place, otherwise she looked as perfect as always. She looked like a fucking pre-Raphaelite painting of a Greek goddess, even though Theo was the one with the long face and the big nose and the thick lips — the one who actually looked Greek and not like some Western art romanticization.

Not that she was jealous. She couldn't be. Sabel had fussed over her and taken care of her from before she could remember. Until she went to college, Sabel spent more time with Theo than their parents did. She never begrudged Sabel anything … except the magic.

"Why did you lie to me about all this?" Theo asked her now.

Gabe looked decidedly uncomfortable and got up off the couch. He muttered something about second breakfast and headed to the kitchen.

"Theo, I didn't actually lie to you. And I don't mean that like some sneaky way out. I was fourteen years old and just starting to figure out what I could do. You asked me to show you how to turn into a bird and I can't do that. And then you asked me about a lot of stuff that I'm fairly confident came from Disney films, which I also can't do."

"I thought I saw you do that Cinderella thing once," Ana said. Theo thought it was a lame attempt to lighten the tension between her and Sabel, but it made Sabel smile and lean toward Ana slightly.

Theo ignored all that. "You could have told me magic was real," she said.

"If Father heard you saying anything about magic, he would have flipped. He threatened me for wanting to talk to grandmom about it."

"Seriously?" Theo asked. She'd never heard this story.

Sabel leaned back in her chair and pushed her straight, dark hair back from her face. She said, "You were out in the islands with Mother. I was thirteen, so you'd have been almost five. It was quite the fight. I wanted to visit grandmom to ask her about the family magic and father lost it worse than I'd ever seen. He grounded me for the whole rest of the year and said if I ever mentioned it again he would send me to a madhouse. I think that's the word he used."

"What? You had a fight about magic? I never saw you fight with Dad about anything, much less magic," Theo said. She'd seen her older brothers fight with him rarely, and never win, but she thought that Sabel, like her, had been exempt.

"I learned not to. Didn't you?"

"No, … it never came to that." Of course she never fought with her dad. He brought her gifts and wanted to hear about her school day and see the pictures she drew. Only after she'd learned to change shape did she start to see how differently he treated her. She'd always assumed Sabel got the same treatment she did … but if he treated her like the boys, or worse …

"He let you have a lot more freedom," Sabel said, actually sounding a little sad, a little jealous. "Because he had his sons by then. But believe me, magic is not something you can talk about around him. Great-grandmother was thrown out of the family because they believed she was a witch and one of his aunts did spend a few years in a psychiatric hospital."

"Were they witches?" Great-grandma? Would the surprises ever stop?

Sabel smiled a little. "Probably, given how we turned out, don't you think?"

"If you didn't turn into a bird, what did I see?" Theo asked, a little worried now that she could be both a witch and crazy.

"I was trying to learn a way to get information by sending my vision out from my body. To a regular human it wouldn't be visible, but I guess to you it looked like a bird. I probably sent it up and you watched it and in the mean time I'd just sat down or something so when you looked at where I'd been, you didn't see that my body was still there in the shadows."

That almost made sense but Theo wanted proof. "Can you do it again? Now?"

Sabel shook her head. "I wasn't good at it then and I'm worse at it now. It's not my strength."

"You could have told me something, anything," Theo said. The old feeling of betrayal welled up.

"What would you have done if I told you magic was real and you found you couldn't do any of it?" Sabel asked. "And all I'd done was put you in the way of dangers you had no defense against?"

"Except I got in trouble anyway, didn't I? So you kind of fucked that up," Theo said, angrily. Theo looked away. She wanted to think Sabel had just fallen into being Ms. Perfect again. That she'd taken a vow of silence or bowed under the pressure from her order of witches or from their family. Not that she'd really thought she did the right thing for Theo.

"I just spent last night coming back from something that might have… that I might have lost myself to, forever. You could have … ," Theo trailed off . "God damn it, Sabel. That's not okay!"

Sabel bowed her head. Her hands rested in her lap, but they were clutching, almost desperately. Theo knew that posture. It was 'I won't cry, but I really want to.' When she glanced back up, Theo was not surprised to see dry eyes. But, Sable's face looked pained.

"I know," she whispered. "And I know it's far too late, but I'm sorry, Theo. I'm really sorry."

An apology and… an explanation—it wasn't everything Theo wanted, but it was getting so much closer. She could really see now that Sabel had done the things she had because she was trying to protect her baby sister—hell, their whole family. It was so much like that stupid movie, *Frozen*, wasn't it? Sabel had shut herself off, locked herself away—and ultimately for all the wrong reasons, too. She hadn't been able to save Theo from any of it. If anything, Sabel's silence had done far, far more damage than good.

Sabel continued to look at Theo with hopeful eyes that seemed to beg, "Will you forgive me?"

Part of Theo wanted to say "No, forget it, despite everything it's still too little, too late," but this was her sister, a sister who had tried to be with her, even while bearing this tremendous secret she'd thought so well hidden—but which had really been the very wedge that drove them apart.

Theo nodded and said, "Yeah, of course, I forgive you." But, when Sabel started to breathe out in relief, Theo added, "But I want something from you, something more."

"Oh?" Sabel exchanged a very nervous glance with Ana.

"Can we try to be sisters?"

"We are sisters," Sabel assured her.

"No, I mean the kind that are closer."

Sabel seemed to be struggling to understand what this might entail. "Aren't you a little old for us to be making playdates?"

It was weird how much that stung, even if it was true. "I guess," Theo admitted. "But, we could… I don't know, text? Sometimes? More…?"

Sabel still didn't seem to get it—not entirely, but she nodded, "Yes, why don't you come by my office when you start classes and we'll have lunch."

"Yeah," Theo agreed, feeling something unwind a bit that had been coiled up tightly in her heart. "That'd be cool."

"And if that works, we can go shopping for wands and I'll indocrti-nate you into my secret coven," Sabel said with a wry smile. Was she joking? Since when did her sister have a sense of humor?

"Wands nothing," Theo said back. "I was promised chocolate frogs."

They smiled at each other after that, but neither of them seemed to know quite what to say now. At some point, Ana got up and took her coffee mug and Sabel's into the kitchen to refill them. She came back a half-second later.

"I think the new student's up," Ana said. "The scone plate's been raided."

"I'll go see," Sabel said and got up from the table. She went down the stairs and then Theo heard fast steps along the first floor hall in one direction and then the other.

Sabel returned with tight worry thinning her lips. "She's not down there. Lily said she wasn't the most mobile. I guess she usually uses a cane, but they didn't have time to grab one in... all the excitement."

"I'll check the third floor," Ana said.

Theo ignored the two of them and went down to the first floor. Ben said no jaguar but not to avoid changing completely. She shucked off her shirt and yoga pants, stepped outside the side door, and changed into her dog shape.

Now she could smell in four dimensions. There was a trail of fear and metal-edged determination and something darkly bitter that after a minute she decided was shame. Bad combo. She could smell where the girl had moved around on the first floor, but also where she'd come out this door and started down the street away from the house.

Theo looked through the hedge but didn't see anyone. She wasn't just looking for the girl, but for anyone who would make trouble for a dog traveling alone without a collar. Note to self: ask Lily to get a collar with tags that identified her as belonging at this address, just in case. She pushed through the hedge and started slowly down the street in the direction of the fear/metal/shame scent.

And demon — the girl definitely smelled like a demon, but not as much of the hardwood plus leather smell that came from Lily or Kitty, and more something like sulfur? Brimstone? What the literal hell?

The girl had made it almost half a block then turned off the sidewalk to go along the outer wall of a small apartment building that faced the side street. With the way the scent grew in intensity to her canine nose, Theo suspected the girl had gone just around that corner of the building and was sitting in the sheltered area in the back where four trees shielded most of it from view. Not that she knew about the trees because she'd scoped this out a couple of days ago to see if it was a decent make-out spot or anything like that.

She went very wide around the building, putting a thick tree trunk between her and the girl, and then stepped out where they could see each other and lowered her canine belly to the ground. Curled back against the wall, the girl held a dirty scone to her chest in a way that wrecked Theo. She whined and thumped her tail back and forth on the ground.

The girl was little, scrawny, could easily use another ten, fifteen pounds even on her small-boned frame. She had mismatched hoops of metal through her ears in a dozen or more places, a few through her eyebrows and one in her nostril. Her hair looked like it had been cut with hedge-trimmers or shaved really badly by someone who had no skill with an electric razor whatsoever.

Theo whined again and flattened herself down, looking away, putting her ears up and wagging her tail lightly. She inched toward the girl but turned her face away. She could feel the girl watching her intently.

When she'd been stealing for street kids, Theo met a few who weren't comfortable letting people touch them, but they'd pet her if she came up to them as a dog. Kids who had trouble processing inputs or reading facial expressions, kids who'd been through horrible shit, kids who had brains that just didn't fit in to the norm, they all seemed to understand the fundamental body language of a dog.

The girl let her get closer now without an increase in the already high level of fear radiating from her. Theo paused a few feet away and panted contentedly, her body positioned perpendicular to the girl. She rolled on her back and wriggled on the dusty ground. It felt good on her back, but it also made a pretty amusing spectacle for humans with her paws flailing in the air and her lighter-colored underbelly turned up. She showed the girl her throat and looked quickly at her and then away, resting on her back with her throat exposed.

They stayed that way for a while. Theo heard the voices of Ana, Sabel and Gabe in the distance. They were outside the house now, moving outward, looking.

A few minutes later, Ana came around the side of the building as if she'd been guided there. Theo rolled onto her paws, crouched back by the girl and growled at Ana.

"Whoa," Ana said and put up her hands. "Theo?"

Theo barked once and then remembered to nod her head human-style. Then, just to be clear, she growled again, low and rough. Ana took a step away.

"It's not safe for her here," she said, but her voice was quiet and gentle. "If she comes back to the house we can protect her from those guys who took her."

Theo wanted to say that she understood that, but that it had to be the girl's choice, which of course wasn't easy to communicate from dog to human. She was backed up almost to the girl now and if anything the scent of fear was a touch less overwhelming — so there was no way she was moving.

Ana looked from her to the girl and back to her. Theo flopped over on her back again and hoped that communicated. Ana raised an eyebrow, shrugged and then lowered herself to sit on the ground. She scooched over to put her back against one of the tree trunks and stretched her legs out in front of her as if she was going to tip her head back and take a nap.

"Okay," she said. "Your call. I'm just going to stay with you guys so that you've got more protection, okay? But you let me know how you want this to go."

CHAPTER FORTY-TWO

GABE MEETS A MONSTER AND BACKS AWAY SLOWLY

In the middle of Theo's big heart-to-heart with her sister, Gabe decided it was time to get out of the house. Just to walk around the neighborhood and be away from Theo's too-perfect sister and her eerie girlfriend. And just in case Theo wasn't ready for him to know all that stuff about her family yet.

We destroyed the dead and the remnants of the cars...

'Destroyed the dead'...? When Ana spoke those words Gabe had felt a chill shiver down his spine. There was something very alien about that word choice, destroyed, like, maybe it was more than just Mafioso-style acid baths or cement overshoes. 'Destroyed the dead' felt like it resonated on a deeper plane. Gabe got the sense that nothing would rise from those ashes ever. Not even a memory.

Even the way Ana talked about 'remnants of the cars' weirded Gabe out. Something about her phrasing made her sound very Old World, like she should be saying all this with some thick, babushka accent.

Except she wasn't.

And nothing else about her seemed typical of a first or second generation immigrant. In fact, she was otherwise pretty hip and cool with the language, but when she talked about the 'clean up' of last night's drama, the oddness became far more pronounced. It was as if someone else were speaking through her.

It's a good thing they convinced him that he wasn't insane, because it sure as shit would be easy to imagine that people getting messages from things in their heads was all part of some huge paranoid delusion.

Nope. It was magic.

Because that made more sense.

On his way back to the house, coming down the short end of the block, he saw Ana sitting on the ground tailor-fashion under a tree. It took him a few minutes to process the scene, but it seemed as if she were just patiently watching the new girl petting a dog—no, wait, Theo. He hadn't seen her dog form before and she looked like a small, dark German Shephard crossed with extra furry.

The girl's hand shook where she rubbed it against Theo's belly fur. Was she crying? It was hard to tell at this distance, but, even if there were no actual tears, her body heaved with sobs of some sort.

Jesus.

Something really bad had happened to her. It didn't help that she looked like an escapee with that roughly shaved head and starved, fragile frame. Something was wrong with her feet, too. It was like they were too short, somehow—had someone cut off her toes? Holy mother of god.

"Erin isn't sure she can trust us," Ana told him. "Can you go tell Lily, Sabel and Kitty that we need a bit more time here? I think a crowd would be too much for her right now."

Gabe backed up, but kept his eyes on Ana. She seemed to have a pretty good read on the situation, though. He didn't want to trust Ana after all that 'clean-up' talk, but... well, she was doing all the right things, wasn't she? Hell, she was handling it better than he would. It was kind of breaking his heart a little to watch this girl weeping like that. He'd probably have leaped the distance and wrapped her in a giant, smothering bear hug—no doubt, the wrong thing: the very last thing she could cope with in her state.

In fact, Ana had a good point. He should find the others and tell them to back off. The last thing the new girl needed was for well-intentioned folks to come barreling in too close and spook her.

With one last watchful glance at Ana, Gabe turned away.

CHAPTER FORTY-THREE

ERIN MONSTER WANTS TO RUN (BUT HER FEET CAN'T)

The puppy wasn't a puppy, Erin knew it because of the little bits of metal in its body that real dogs didn't have. There was metal up under the skin of its right rear leg in a pattern that she often felt from human tattoos. It didn't matter, though, because it was like the scones: she needed the comforting feel of the short belly hairs like she needed air to breathe. She wished she could stop crying, though. But the sobs wracked though her, shaking her entire body.

If this was a trap, she was fucked because the tears—they were relief. She let something go with each one… Erin wasn't even sure what, but the tightness in her chest, the heaviness in her heart was loosening.

She just kept stroking the fur, feeling the firm tautness of the dog's belly. The big puppy wriggled happily under her pets. The warm softness of the animal was like a balm, just like the smell of the pine trees and the sunshine on her face.

The woman hadn't moved even an inch since sitting down. Erin looked at her carefully, cautiously. It was a little unnerving how strong she looked. She smelled of power, and ancient metals like bronze. She'd talked about 'protection,' but Erin knew all about the kind of protection most people offered—the kind that came with pain and chains and restriction. 'For your own good' would be the next thing someone would say.

But no one had said anything yet, despite the fact that Erin sensed the others starting to converge.

Only... they'd backed away.

Another unexpected move. If these were the same captors, they were far more subversive in their torture.

The puppy licked her hand. Erin glanced down, realizing she'd stopped her petting. She managed to give the not-dog a smile and resumed ruffling the belly fur. "Magic," she told the puppy. "I know you're magic."

Which meant these couldn't be the same captors.... because those men hated magic. But, then, Gramma and Grandpa hated magic, too. That was why she wasn't allowed horns or claws—because the devil had marked Erin's body and that pollution had to be destroyed, banished.

She frowned at the puppy and then looked up at the patient woman. "Magic... bad?"

Erin looked at them hopefully. She'd wanted to be more articulate, but she had no words for what she was trying to ask... and she was so afraid to even be asking, anything more seemed blasphemous. She flinched. Glancing up at the sky, she half-expected for God Himself to strike her down for daring to hope that they'd say 'no.'

She pulled her hand away from the puppy and curled up into herself. "Magic bad," she reassured herself over and over. "Magic. Bad."

CHAPTER FORTY-FOUR

KITTY SEES WHAT'S MISSING BUT NOT WHAT'S THERE

Kitty had been dozing when the sound of her door opening and closing woke her. She jumped up and opened the door on Gabe's retreating back.

"What?" she asked.

"Keep sleeping," he said. "Just the new girl's behind the house with Ana and Theo so don't go back there."

Kitty raised her eyebrows at him but he just shrugged. His weird had gotten a little weirder since last night, but she didn't much blame him. She went into her room for a sweatshirt and then descended both flights of stairs to the room that had been empty until the night before. The new girl's room.

If she was out behind the house—though Kitty couldn't figure how she got there with her feet like they were—then this was a good time to have a look around and see if there was anything hinting at why she seemed so important to Lily and Ben.

At first the girl's room looked almost untouched, except for a nest of blankets on the bed. Then Kitty saw that parts of the room had been very carefully deconstructed.

She stepped through the doorway and tried to understand what she was seeing. The curtains were pooled on the floor, their curtain rods and hardware gone. Where a mirror had been hanging over the dresser was now just a piece of glass. The glass bowl of a lamp was resting on the bedside table with nothing underneath it. The electronic clock by the bed was dead and when Kitty went to pick it up, it felt hollow.

Most of the metal in the room was gone.

She'd never heard from a demon who could—she didn't even know what to call it. Had the girl dissolved the metal thinking that would help her escape? Was it unconscious? Did she somehow eat metal the way the Gul ate emotion?

Lily had said this girl was also part-demon, but metal magic wasn't anything the Sangkesh could do. Could the girl be part demon and part witch?

Kitty's head was still much too fuzzy to work it out. Time to rest more, then ask questions and then, if called for, panic.

CHAPTER FORTY-FIVE

THEO DOG
DOES GOOD

Theo had no idea how to get from where they were emotionally to a point where Erin would want to go back to the house. All she knew was that she wasn't leaving this girl and she wasn't letting anyone get near her until she was some kind of operational.

Ana surprised her by replying to the girl's repeated mutterings of, "Magic bad," by saying, "That's right. Some magic is very bad. Some magic hurts, doesn't it?"

The girl nodded but didn't look up.

"I've seen some really bad magic," Ana said, her voice distant, looking off between the trees. "I've seen bad people too. The ones who like to hurt and the ones who justify it."

The girl reached out and put her hand on Theo's side again, rubbing down the long, soft fur there.

"Sometimes when the bad people come for you, you're alone," Ana went on. "And if you're alone and you're small, then you just have to hide inside yourself and try to get through it, you know? But then other times there are good people, people who care about you or maybe they just care about doing the right thing."

The girl muttered a little to herself and Theo really hoped she'd had some people in her life who'd actively cared for her at some point. Not the ones who mutilated her feet, but real, nurturing care, like Sabel cared for her, no matter if she'd fucked up about the magic, no matter if Theo was still pissed about that, nothing changed the foundation of their relationship. Did this girl ever have that?

"When I had to go up against bad magic, I was lucky," Ana said. "I had some good people on my side. And what I'm asking you is … give us the chance to prove to you that we're good people. Please."

The girl sat still, absently stroking Theo's flank, her head cocked to one side. Her other hand reached up and touched the rings in her ears in some order that seemed to make sense to her but that Theo couldn't interpret. Ana had been watching her covertly, but when she touched the earrings, Ana's look got distant for a minute and then focused with abrupt understanding.

"Metal," she said. "Something to feel at home in."

She pulled her phone out of her pocket and held it out to the girl. The girl's head turned and her eyes focused on the phone faster than anything Theo had seen her do to that point.

"You like this?" Ana asked. She flipped the phone over, opened the back and pulled out the SIM card, which she stuck back in her pocket, then got on her knees and shuffled slowly toward them, holding out the phone. She stopped half-way across the distance between them.

The girl inched forward. Her petting hand trailed up Theo's body until it rested on her head, but the girl wouldn't break contact with her. Ana leaned the last foot forward and put the phone in the girl's out-stretched hand.

The girl sat back, both hands on the phone now, her fingers moving across the touch-screen with surprising speed for someone who seemed so deprived. Theo had assumed she was kept in some backwater, anti-everything town until the Cavallo got her, but she'd definitely had a smartphone before.

"Erin," Ana said. "It's safer if we go back in the house. You won't be locked in, okay? But I want to take you back there, maybe get you more to eat. Can I carry you?"

Erin didn't look up, but she nodded. One hand reached out and touched Theo's head.

"She's coming with us," Ana said. "She lives in the house too."

Erin nodded again.

Ana moved from her kneeling posture to a low crouch and shuffled forward the few feet to Erin. She picked her up easily and Erin didn't look up from the phone screen as she was lifted, but before Ana took a step, she dangled one hand down. Theo got up and bumped it with her head. Erin flashed her a quick smile of blinding sweetness, then went back to the phone.

They went around the corner of the building and to the side of the house with Theo walking at Ana's side. Ana managed to get the side door open without jostling Erin too much and then held it open with her foot for Theo.

"Do you want to go back to your bedroom or up to the dining room to get something to eat?" Ana asked.

Erin pointed up.

"Good call," Ana said. She went up the stairs first with Theo on her heels.

Sabel, Lily and Gabe must have heard them come in because they were all standing in the kitchen staring expectantly at the stairs and then quickly trying to look busy when Ana walked through the kitchen into the dining room. Ana set Erin in a chair facing the kitchen doorway and Theo curled up at the foot of the chair.

Erin's feet wouldn't have reached the floor, but she rested them on Theo's back easily. Theo felt them moving slightly, making little, reassuring brushstrokes across her fur. She tried to block out how truncated they felt compared to regular feet and focus on the pattern of the gesture.

"Soup or sandwich?" Ana asked.

Erin didn't answer her. She was still working on the phone.

"Okay then, both it is."

CHAPTER FORTY-SIX

GABE TRIES TO RELAX

Gabe was glad they were able to bring the new girl back into the house, but everything was very awkward as they pretended to go through their normal morning routines as if a girl with sawed off feet and horns wasn't sitting at the kitchen island.

Moving around the crowded kitchen, he made himself a sandwich with the leftover bacon from breakfast. He almost ran into Ana when he reached for the fridge door to get out the mayo. They did that awkward dance made more so by the small pot of soup in her oven mitten covered hands. As he stammered out yet-another apology, she smiled up at him and said, "Don't worry about it."

For a brief second, Gabe saw something fiery flash behind her eyes.

It wasn't like the time that the nurse's eyes went full-on cat mode, but the feeling of seeing something hidden was the same. Gabe got the impression in the 'otherness' of the eyes that there were actually two sets of irises—as though there was another person looking out of Ana's eyes, someone older.... Alien.

"You okay?" Ana asked, her smile faltering a little. "You look like you saw a ghost."

Not even glancing up from her paper, Lily said, "He probably saw Abraxas. Gabe has the Sight."

"Is that a real thing?" Ana wanted to know, "Seventh son of the seventh son?"

Flicking out her newspaper as she turned the page, Lily yawned. "Apparently."

Ana gave Gabe a knowing look and shook her head. "You know, Lily, we would all like you better if you actually slept for longer than an hour." To Gabe she said, "I share my body with Abraxas."

Gabe thought that sounded insane, but on top of everything he'd seen recently, it didn't make a dent in his overall shocked muddle.

Patting Gabe's arm, Ana said, "You'll get used to it."

"How am I supposed to sleep with all this excitement?" Lily grumbled with a little glance over at the new girl, Erin.

Ana finally moved past Gabe pour the soup into various bowls that she'd set out on the counter. "I feel for you Lily," Ana continued as she divvied up the soup. "A house full of young adults is going to be bad enough. All this magic too? Abraxas thinks you're going to need a lot of R&R and I'm way too embarrassed to say *exactly* what he suggested."

Gabe had stuck his head in the fridge to hunt for the mayo and almost smacked his head on the shelf in surprise. Was she suggesting what he thought she was? A glance at Lily confirmed it. Her face was an obvious combination of desire and slight embarrassment. Ana looked the same, only her face was more… split, as if one half was totally ready to go, and the other… a little more chagrined or even exasperated.

But not completely opposed to the idea.

If Abraxas was into Lily … did Ana …?

Gabe did not want to contemplate that. To break up the mounting sexual tension, and also because it was driving him insane in general, Gabe cleared his throat and asked, "Okay, so who is Abraxas and how'd he get into Ana?"

"Abraxas is an older…" Ana glanced in the direction of where Erin was focused on her phone and dropped her voice to a near whisper, "… 'force of nature' let's say, like Lily says," Ana explained, as she handed Gabe a bowl and set another one in front of Erin. She paused and looked to one side and muttered under hear breath, "Did you want me to describe you as 'ancient?'"

Lily chuckled and Gabe wondered if Ana had to speak out loud to this other demon guy or if she just said it for Lily's benefit.

"Anyway, he's Sangkesh and … it's a really long story."

Sangkesh? Ah, 'force' meant: demon. Pulling up a stool, Gabe settled himself on the island, but he tried to give Erin her space. He watched her carefully, but she didn't even look up from the phone. What was she even doing to it? It looked like she had the back off, but she didn't have one of those tiny screwdrivers, did she?

Turning his attention back to Ana, Gabe kept his voice low as he asked, "Okay, I'm not sure I get how this works. Some people are part.. uh, well they're, like Lily and Kitty. I guess I figured that happened the old-fashioned way. But, this 'force' of yours? He doesn't have a body? Do most?"

Lily made a jagged sighing noise and said, "Didn't we cover this? In the lesson with the notebook?"

"You watched The Notebook educationally?" Ana asked with a laugh.

"No, it's a metaphor for the way the Unseen World overlays the material," Lily replied. "The full demons don't have bodies like us. Those of us with human-style bodies, we're all some mix of .." another glance at Erin and a more pointed one at Gabe to make sure he understood her meaning, "... other and human. But even old, powerful 'forces' need a place to anchor themselves if they're going to operate in the material world. Ana serves as the anchor for Abraxas."

"It's like two people riding in a car together," Ana said. "Because only one of us can drive and it's almost always me."

"Almost?" Gabe asked because that sounded creepy as hell. And wasn't this woman the girlfriend of Theo's big sister? How did that work? Was it like a perpetual threesome with a demon?

"Sometimes he has better superpowers," Ana said and flashed him a grin.

Okay that nearly sounded cool. Gabe decided he could worry about the whole two-people-in-one-body thing some other time when he wasn't still processing ferret-bombs and exploding cars and girls with the stumps of metal horns on their foreheads.

While the girl, Erin, finished her soup and sandwich, Gabe went around to the living room and sat on the couch where he could watch her peripherally but not crowd her. Lily looked a lot better for having had a nap. She wore a clean sweater and the kind of loose-legged pants she preferred to jeans, and her black hair was pulled back in a messy-style bun at the base of her neck. She had her boots on and, looking at the girl's fucked up feet, Gabe could see why: this wasn't the time to bust out the human-sized eagle talons.

He only half-listened as Ana and Sabel said goodbye to Lily, relieved that they were going. On the surface they looked more normal than anyone else in this house, except him and Theo, but that made them all the more disturbing. He had wanted to hear more of the conversation between Theo and Sabel, but Theo seemed like she was staying in dog form for now.

Sabel went over to her and bent down to say good-bye and Theo leaned up and licked her face. The look of pure shock on Sabel's face was eloquent—clearly Theo had never licked her before. And, put that way, was that really something you should do to your sister? Maybe for dogs, yeah, but what were the rules for shape-changers?

Sabel ran a hand across her damp cheek and said, "I love you too, but yuck." She stood up, out of the range of any future possible licking. Theo panted cheerfully at her, tongue hanging half out of her mouth, and tucked herself back under Erin's chair.

When Ana and Sabel were gone, the house settled into an unsteady silence, punctuated by the sound of Erin's spoon scraping the sides of the bowl and her heels drumming lightly on the cross-bar of the chair, combined with Theo's tail lazily thumping the floor. Lily sat down at the dining room table, diagonal from Erin, and picked up her newspaper again.

Erin was peering sideways at Lily and every so often her eyes would roam over to Gabe and quickly dart away.

He got the Xbox controller and TV remote from the coffee table and turned them on. It had been a while since he'd touched a video game. Guy he stayed with for a couple of months had a sweet setup, but it was all combat games. The soccer one Kitty had been playing looked kind of cool but complicated.

When it was all started up and connected to the Internet, he flipped through a few screens, trying to figure out if there was a list of games that he could pick from. Buffered chair legs swished on the wooden floor and then he heard halting, heavy steps.

He didn't look up directly, just a little sideways. Erin was standing with a hand on the far couch arm for support, looking from the controller in his hand to the TV screen and back.

He put the controller in the middle of the couch and pushed it toward the far end. She sat, very carefully, and reached for it, watching his body the whole time. When she had it in her hands, Theo jumped up between them, turned around twice and lay down with her back pressed lightly along the side of Erin's thigh.

Erin reached down and ran a hand along Theo's back—and then her hands and her attention went fully to the controller and then TV. Gabe watched as the menu flicked through a dizzying array of options. She was changing settings and paging through games. Within minutes, she had a game loaded in which people fought each other using giant robot bodies. Her face was rapt, eyes intensely focused, mouth slightly open with the tiniest hint of a smile at the edges.

Gabe decided he liked seeing Erin's smile.

A lot.

CHAPTER FORTY-SEVEN

ERIN TARZAN, MONSTER OF THE APES

Erin was having trouble with words. Everything that came out of her mouth made her sound like some bad Tarzan movie. It was the emotions. She wasn't used to them.

Safety.

The feeling that she might actually be safe somewhere was unnerving and she didn't really know how to cope with it. Like, she wanted to believe these people when they talked to her, but all the darkness of her life welled up and whispered to her not to dare trust, trust only led to hurt and pain. The dog helped because: dogs. Dogs were like the most trusting thing ever. Not only did they trust, they also protected. Even though Erin knew this dog was a magic dog, it still worked like a kind of anchor.

Dog good.

Sheesh. That was what her brain had melted into.

The game and having her hands on the controller, that was also good. That, in fact, was almost humanizing. Having someone just sitting next to her and watching the game and not staring at her horns or her feet was also amazingly… normalizing.

She was starting to be able to breathe.

And it scared her a little.

CHAPTER FORTY-EIGHT

KITTY FEELS ALMOST HALF-~~HUMAN~~DEMON AGAIN

Kitty woke after three hours of napping, realized it was mid-afternoon, and went to go see how bad her hair was since she hadn't bothered to put it up when she crashed that morning. The bath and ibuprofen had worked to quell her headache and helped her pass out from exhaustion. She felt much better, but her hair was beyond hope. One side looked like it had lost a static electricity fight and the other side was mashed nearly flat. She pulled it all gently back and tied it in a short ponytail.

She pulled on a dark gray Pasadena City College sweatshirt her dad had given her and light gray capri pants, then went down to the kitchen to get something else to eat. Sounds of video game-style automatic weapon fire came from the living room and through the doorway she could see Lily sitting at the dining room table reading a newspaper. Domestic tranquility? Rock on.

There were sandwiches in a big Tupperware in the fridge from whatever source was providing food when no one was looking, including some thick roast beef on wheat with what she hoped was horseradish sauce. How did the invisible chef know what she liked? She put one on a plate with some kettle chips and wandered through the dining room to the doorway of the living room.

Gabe was on the far side of the couch, slouched back with his eyes half-closed like he was both dozing and watching the game on the TV. Erin had her feet tucked up under her and was leaning forward, her fingers dancing on the Xbox controller as a man ran and leapt across the screen, dodging bullets and firing his weapon back at his pursuers. Between them was a dog, mostly black but with buff highlights under her chin and a speckled blue and white ruff.

"That's just great, she gets a cuddly dog and I got a jaguar. Thanks tons," Kitty said. She turned and pulled a chair out from the dining room table with her foot to where she could sit and see the game while eating.

Erin was dominating her opponents. Kitty had never mastered the kind of twitch reflex needed for that level of first-person play, which was one reason she liked sports games and Civilization-styled strategy games. Erin's avatar executed stunning leaps and spins, landing with deadly precision and unerring aim.

She won the game, paused for just long enough to pat Theo's head and started another round.

When Kitty was done with her sandwich, Lily folded the newspaper and came to stand in the doorway to the living room, where everyone could see her.

"We'll get another TV for the upstairs family room," she said. "I can see this is going to be popular."

She continued, "You all did very well last night. Gabe, Theo, I appreciate your help in encouraging Erin back to the house today. Erin, this place is a school for exceptional students. We'd like you to join us, but that's ultimately up to you and you don't have to make up your mind right away. I hope you'll spend a week with us and see if you like it."

Erin didn't look up or respond, but the slight tilt of her head showed that she was listening to all of it.

"For the rest of you, I think you understand that Erin has had a very rough time recently. As far as we can tell, she was in a more clinical setting for about a year before being taken by the Cavallo about three months ago and moved through a few of their facilities." To Erin she said, "I'm sorry it took us so long to find you. Your friend who asked us to look for you didn't have a lot of information after you were moved."

Erin looked up for a half-second. "Friend?" she asked.

"I don't know who it is," Lily said. "We got a message that you were being hurt and to please find you."

Erin didn't respond to that, so Lily went back to what she'd been saying to the room at large. "We have just over a week before classes start at SFSU and there's still a lot I want to learn about each of you, not only what you can do but what you want to learn. But I think we also need a break, so tomorrow do whatever you like and on Monday I may have some errands and shopping for you, but nothing crucial so if you feel you need more time to rest, let me know. Erin, your participation in any of this is completely voluntary. You're going to need more time to catch up on your sleep and nutrition. I trust the rest of you not to push her and to watch out for her, help her feel at home here."

"We will," Gabe said.

CHAPTER FORTY-NINE

THEO IS A REAL BITCH

Ben's note had said not to turn into a jaguar. Theo hoped that didn't mean that shifting was out altogether. As she worried at the fur between her nails, she had to wonder, because having four feet firmly planted on the ground felt so much less... unsteady. And, while she could still understand the words being spoken, they interested her less and less.

She kind of wanted to chase something. Like a squirrel. Or her tail.

She took a little nip in the direction of the wagging thing. Damn it, missed! She barked at it as it thumped against the hardwood.

Going back to her toenail, Theo considered magic. She finally got some information from Sabel. It was more tangled family stuff, but everything was a puzzle piece.

Or bacon.

Someone dropped bacon on the floor.

Yum. Yum. Yum.

Wait, did she eat meat?

CHAPTER FIFTY

GABE ISN'T A PLAYER

Gabe leaned back into the cushions of the couch and admired the way Erin's video mech slaughtered all the enemies in her way. She seemed far more confident inside the gaming world. It made him wonder about her life... before.

Theo, meanwhile, had fallen asleep under the constant, repetitive petting. Her little doggy snores were cute. Out of the corner of his eye, Gabe noticed Kitty standing on the other side of the room. She had her phone out and pointed at Theo. She was taking film? Ah, shit, Theo was going to hate that! Especially considering the doggy drool coming out of her... muzzle.

When their eyes met, Kitty shut her phone and shook her head. "I still can't believe *she* gets cute puppy mode."

"Yeah, well, who knew Theo even had a cute mode? I'd have figured everything would be ass-kicking." Gabe said around a yawn.

If Erin was listening, she was good at pretending not to be aware.

After tucking her cell into the front pocket of her sweatshirt, Kitty came over and sat on a near-by chair. She pulled up her long legs and tucked them under herself. Taking a deep breath she said, "Last night, huh?"

Gabe nodded. "It was a doozy."

He wasn't sure what Kitty wanted to talk about, but it was clear they were all still kind of processing everything that had gone down. For

257

himself, Gabe continued to be stuck on the idea that Theo's sister Ana and her girlfriend, Sabel, were some kind of 'demon clean up crew' that could 'destroy the dead' or whatever freaky-ass thing they'd done.

Looking over at Erin's hacked-up hair, however, Gabe thought maybe it had been worth it. He really wished he could reach out a hand and touch the shaved stubble. It looked painful; like maybe someone had even used a razor. The sawed off horns… it was hard to tell since, whatever they were made of was also dark, but he'd have sworn the flatten tips of them were blackened scabs.

Yeah, maybe it was okay that Ben blew someone's head off.

When Kitty continued to sit there in silence, Gabe said, "You're a good driver. If I ever need a getaway, I know who to call."

She smiled at that. "It's a skill my mother insisted on. And I'm pretty accomplished at running away."

Now that sounded kind of fraught. "The mom that's not an Ass-hole?"

"Yes. My mother just happens to have a vested interest in my… education."

Gabe put two and two together in a hurry. "Oh, so she's the demon?"

Beside him, Erin flinched violently and her game-avatar suddenly faltered, the TV's sound system exploding with the crashes and bangs of 'game over.' Erin threw down the controller and clutched at Theo, who woke up with a startled 'yip.'

Kitty and Gabe exchanged a look and then Gabe turned to Erin and said, "You know there are good demons, too, right? I didn't."

Erin forcibly pulled Theo into her lap. She started rocking back and forth. Theo licked her forearm slowly and repetitively.

"Sometimes they're nicer than the humans," Kitty added.

Gabe almost said, 'yeah, look at Lily and Kitty,' but then thought better of it. Instead, he picked up the game controller from the floor and held it out to Erin. She rocked and rocked and rocked. Theo continued to tolerate the strangle hold and just nuzzled her.

Man, whoever broke this girl was a number one dick, Gabe thought.

"It's okay," he said, trying again. "Maybe Kitty and I will just go in the kitchen and give you some space, huh?"

He left the controller where Erin could reach it and stood up, intending to make good on his promise.

"No," Erin said, her voice quiet, but firm. "Stay."

"Really?" Gabe asked, but he lowered himself back down onto the cushions.

Erin took in a shuddering breath and slowly unwound her arms. Theo stayed in her lap. Erin's arms shook where she clutched at the material of her pants. She seemed focused on just breathing evenly instead of hyperventilating.

Kitty watched the scene with wide-eyes. She seemed to be holding her breath, too.

With effort, Erin reached for the controller and slowly, methodically went through the motions of starting up the game again.

Gabe watched this, thinking, this girl might be broken, but she's tough, too.

Like all of them.

They sat there, not saying much, as Erin's mech began the process of kicking monster asses and making game progress. Theo did that dog thing where she sighed and rolled over on her back with her head still in Erin's lap.

Kitty seemed to relax a little too. She leaned back enough to rest against the back of the chair and her shoulders dipped a fraction.

Gabe thought maybe he should try another conversation gambit, but he wasn't sure what was safe. However, it wasn't like he really knew her. He supposed he could just ask some innocuous questions. "So, Kitty, what are you thinking about taking for classes?"

She shifted a little in her seat, as if surprised by the question. "Oh, um… I'm not sure yet, you?"

Gabe tugged on his ear, a little embarrassed. "I never graduated from high school, so I should probably do that first."

"Oh," Kitty said, as though she had no idea what to do with that information, or like the idea of not graduating was utterly foreign to her. "You… dropped out?"

He could almost hear the unspoken corollary: 'Or did you fail out?'

"I left," Gabe said. "That is, school took a second seat to survival."

Kitty's finely shaped eyebrows arched up momentarily. Then, she surprised him by nodding, "I get that." She chewed on her lip, and then added, "Sort of."

That made Gabe chuckle. Somehow he doubted Ms. Perfect Life

Kitty could really understand, but then he chided himself. It was clear she'd faced some shit, too. It was just on a different, more-demon-y level than he had. Something was clearly up with that mother of hers, something that had made her kind of judgmental and prissy. Probably she had one of those super-exacting moms, one of the ones that'd kill you if you came home with an A- instead of an A. Only, as a demon, maybe she put your average 'tiger mom' to shame, having a set of real, really sharp teeth to bare.

"Anyway, I was on the street until a few days ago," Gabe said, trying to sound casual about it. He never used the word 'homeless,' because he did have a 'home.' He just couldn't go there. Lily had said she was going to get him some made up high school transcripts and he still wasn't sure how he felt about that.

For a while, he'd wanted to take the test to get his GED, but the thing that stopped him was that some states required you to be over eighteen. Others you could test at sixteen. But, none of that really mattered, because since he'd dumped his ID, he'd had no way to prove his age either way. Would the Demon Mafia, as he was starting to think of them in his head, also magic him up a driver's license?

Kitty seemed to be trying to figure out a way to ask Gabe an awkward question. Her mouth kept opening, only to close right away. Finally, she just said, "You're over 18, why not go back? Why not get a job and take some classes?"

Gabe shook his head. "A few days ago you didn't want to be in the same room with me. Who do you think's hiring?"

"Humans?" she said and raised an eyebrow.

For some reason that made him laugh and then she grinned back at him and he could feel how last night, the fighting and the running, had shifted things. He decided to tell her some of the truth of it all.

"I left my home in West Virginia because Asshole kept abducting me, and this last time he beat up my mom so bad... I just decided I couldn't keep going back home, it was hurting Mom and Meema too much, making them fight," he said.

"You're from West Virginia?" she asked. That wasn't the usual question he got at this point in the story.

"My mom is American by way of Cuba... a long time ago," he said.

A frown deepened on Kitty's lips as she listened to him. "So... when does the magic come in?"

"Huh? What do you mean?" he asked.

"Which one of your parents was the Witch? Was it your dad? Is that why he kept abducting you?"

Gabe looked at Erin, worried she'd freak out again, but the only change he saw was a slight tightening of her grip on the controller. She was frowning in a way that made him think she was listening intently, but she didn't seem otherwise upset… or at least no more than usual.

Considering the question, Gabe leaned further back into the cushions and tucked his hands behind his head. "I sure as shit hope not. If that was what Asshole was up to, he was doing an awesome job disguising it. Mostly, he seemed worried that I might be catching the gay from my moms, so he'd send me off to military schools and Bible camps."

Kitty blinked. "He really thought that? I can't imagine. My mother picked out my father in part because he was gay. No entanglements."

"Dude. Asshole thought Rush Limbaugh was God. That man is nuttier than a squirrel turd, and meaner than a skillet full of rattlesnakes."

Both women were now looking at Gabe askance. Even Theo had raised a curious ear.

Gabe smiled, "Too Southern? Sorry, we used to make a game out of coming up with funny phrases like that to describe Asshole. You know, to try to make it okay."

"They sounds nice, your moms," Kitty said.

"Some days," Gabe nodded. They sat for a while in the relative silence of Erin's video mayhem. Kitty stood up with a yawn, "I'm getting something to drink from the kitchen. You guys want anything?"

"I'd take a Coke," Gabe said.

"Me, too," Erin said, sounding so normal that Kitty started for the kitchen with a nod before pausing and doing a double-take.

When their eyes met over the back of the couch, Kitty mouthed, 'She talked!' Gabe smiled and nodded vigorously. Seemed they were making progress with Erin, just by being normal.

Kitty came back with some kind of fancy coconut water for herself and two cans of Coke. "What about psychology?" she asked as she handed Gabe his.

"You think that's my thing?" He asked, taking the ice-cold, sweating can from her. "I was thinking maybe social work."

She nodded, going back to her chair and curling back up in it. "Yeah, something like that, don't you think? Working with people?"

"Maybe," he agreed. "I'm thinking I should finally take Spanish."

"You don't know any?"

He shook his head as he popped the top. "Just some love words mom used to say to me and you know, a few of the swear words."

"That's hilarious," Kitty said, twisting off the top of her bottle.

"You never said what you were going to take," Gabe pointed out.

"Math," she finally admitted.

The robot crashed and burned again, but this time when they looked at Erin she had a huge smile on her face. "What kind?"

"Probabilistic combinatorics," Kitty said, the words falling out of her mouth in surprise. "I got a book about it to study up, do you want to see it?"

Erin nodded and Kitty bolted out of the room, returning a minute later, having pelted up and then down the stairs. She had a thick text-book that she opened on the arm of the couch between her and Erin. Erin's face looked even more absorbed than when she was playing the game, which Gabe thought was just weird, but really adorable.

CHAPTER FIFTY-ONE

ERIN UNRAVELS IN EXCITEMENT

Math made Erin so excited, she had the game controller taken apart before she even realized what she was doing. With the book open on the couch arm between her and the tall girl, Kitty, she'd also been talking about a mile a minute, something she hadn't done in forever.

But now that the controller was in pieces in her hands, the old dread started to sink into her stomach. Gabe's eyes were wide and Erin waited, her breath caught in her throat, for what he was going to say.

Because she didn't have a screwdriver.

The controller had come apart because she'd… "asked' it to, because metal sang to her, because this was her curse.

But, even though his eyes were wide, Gabe didn't seem scared or angry. He just seemed, of all things, fascinated. When he did speak, he said the strangest thing: "You stopped mid-sentence," he noted. "Not that I was following all that, but were you done?"

He wasn't going to ask?

The newness of this situation made Erin start fiddling again. She could feel herself conjuring the things she needed to improve the controller and she wanted to hold back, like grandpa always said she had to, but the feelings were too strong. To ground herself, Erin glanced over at the math textbook on the arm of the couch. Kitty was absorbed in it, too, the smile on her face like a beacon.

"What do you want to study?" Kitty asked.

"Do you have information theory?" Erin asked. "I remember some Calculus, but I need advanced differentials and information. The energy gets hazy in the wires sometimes. I'm not sure I graduated from high school either. I mean, I don't remember."

They looked at her again. This time their feelings were easier to read: shock and pity.

Gabe was shaking his head. "That sucks."

It was so simple, those words of—Erin wasn't even sure what: sympathy, maybe, or solidarity? They nearly brought another wave of tears to the surface. With effort, Erin pushed them away. Her hands worked on the controller. Shifting. Sifting. Changing.

"I don't have information theory here," Kitty said. "But I can get it for you. I think I have my Calculus book. Your high school …."

"There was a gifted student program," Erin said. "I remember a year or two maybe." She smiled a little because it was one of the good memories of the last dark years, being in the classrooms with her friends, with the equations that made sense to her when nothing else did.

The wires in the controller were knitting themselves together in a pattern close to what they had been, but faster, more elegant. The fraction of a second of lag in the key press would be gone now. If she spent more attention on it, she could get it to register changes in skin conductivity, but she'd need more metal for that and she'd used most of what she had to make her crutches. If they could get her math books here, and they were willing to, could they get her the metals she needed?

Could she afford to trust them enough to ask?

Fingers reached up and touched the tungsten stud in her left ear. There was copper in the hoop through her nose, but not enough.

Erin pulled herself into a ball, dislodging the not-puppy/puppy everyone called 'Theo.' Pulling her knees up to her chest, she hugged them. It was too easy to take. Erin had to try to remember what happened when she took.

:: :: ::

It had been that first summer after her parents died, when she moved to grandma and grandpa's ranch. Her horns hadn't started growing yet and her feet... those long, clawed toes that mama and papa told her were so clever and cute… hadn't been discovered yet. Grandpa had been different then, so kind and understanding. He'd made space for her in his workshop—her own space to build and tinker!—and had told her she could borrow anything she needed so long as she asked.

So long as she *asked*.

Erin never thought to ask because it always seemed she had just what she needed. But grandpa started getting angrier, "What did you do with the tablesaw?" he'd demand. Because just when she needed a lot of steel for her project… things like that would just…well, they wouldn't disappear, like poof!, but they would slowly hollow out, weaken, empty.

He started accusing her of selling things on eBay to get the money for the supplies that seemed to just materialize for her.

He stopped appreciating the work she did. Told her that even if she made his tractor run better, it wasn't right if she stole from him to do it. In fact, he'd refused to use it. He'd sold it to a neighbor rather than benefit from her "sin."

Dinners became horrible interrogations. "How come when you need copper wiring it disappears from the barn's walls? How are you even getting in there to do that!?" He screamed at her to stop. Begged her just to tell him what she needed. She'd tried. She didn't understand it herself. She didn't know it was her curse, leaching from her surroundings, pulling into her hands with her devil's magic the metals she craved like food.

It started causing so many problems. Grandma crying because of the money they'd had to spend to replace everything. Grandpa raging at her to stop going behind their backs. It wasn't until school started did Erin understand what was happening.

Because it followed her.

In shop class, which, despite the 'burnout' crowd that tended to favor it, she'd loved, the same sort of things happened. There was an accident that nearly cost the instructor his right arm when the drill press gave way thanks to a hollowed out and weakened support.

She'd tried to stop building things, but… she found out that didn't matter. She would leach them even if she wasn't doing anything intentional. In fact, when she didn't build, the horns grew.

Erin still shuddered to remember how stupid she'd been. It had been months since she tinkered. She'd sometimes wake up from a dream with a chunk of steel in her and or a lump of nickel, but it seemed to stop after her thirteenth birthday. Other parts of her body were changing, too, so... well, it seemed like the sort of thing you could ask woman-to-woman.

And.. they were sort of pretty.

Pointed, sure, but they were like coils of shining metals: iron, magnesium, copper, magnesium, molybdenum, silicon, zinc. Considering how little sex education she'd gotten in the rural, private Christian school, it wasn't that unreasonable to think...

...no, she should never have shown them to anyone. But, she had.

And the composition of them... it should have been a clue. If only she'd thought about it for a second! Put two-and-two together, especially with the strange wave of anemia that had been raging through her classmates and their church group.

Her horns were made from all the metals contained in the human body.

The screams, the recriminations, the "what else are you hiding, demon child?", the feet being discovered... and the axe falling.

And the hack saw.

So bloody, so horrible.. that even now, so many years later, Erin could only remember the coppery smell of it mixed with the scent of drying hay. The anxious lowing of the cows—a sound she still couldn't stand... the Lord's Prayer repeated over and over in grandpa's strangely firm, if melancholy voice.

Erin had been weirdly grateful, shortly after that horrible day, when they'd started moving around—town-to-town, trying to find exorcists, cures, treatments... all of which had finally brought them to the city, to the clinic.

The clinics had been their own kind of hell, of course. She'd tried to tell the nurses to leave her piercings in—but when she explained they protected them from her evil, well, they just upped her dosage, didn't they? Then it would happen again... beds would crumple, people would fall sick... her horns would be so beautiful and shimmering, like deadly twin swords of pestilence and war.

The horns would scare them.

Even the most rational doctors would freak to see them growing there. When she hadn't tinkered in too long, her eyes would be like hematite, quicksilver—shining, alien orbs, deadened by drugs. Sometimes she'd laugh at them and tell them there was nothing that they could do, the demon in her soul would suck the lives from their bodies!

Then she'd be transferred to the next place, usually with a surreptitious trip to some back room where the hacksaw would come out and there would be pain and restraints and "well, there. now that's better isn't it's."

It was never, ever better.

At least these last captors had figured out that the earrings and the nose ring and the bits and bobs had to stay. In fact, sometimes she was sure she'd woken up to see them leaving her little offerings—as though to feed the demon with little broken clock radios and other electronic detritus.

:: :: ::

A hand on her shoulder, gentle, concerned made Erin start. It was Gabe with a glass of water. "Do you need aspirin or something? Should I... should I get Lily?"

Erin took the glass with shaking hands. The puppy nudged her legs with the top of her head. Kitty stood just behind her with a Calculus book in her hand as though to offer it to her.

Setting down the glass carefully, Erin took the book. "No, I'm okay. This is... nice." She didn't know how to tell them that it wouldn't be long before the demon came to devour them. So, she just stuck her nose into the book and tried to read. Quietly, she whispered, "I'm sorry. I'm sorry for everything I'm going to do to you."

CHAPTER FIFTY-TWO

KITTY ASKS WHAT THE ACTUAL FUCK

Kitty heard Lily moving around in the kitchen and got up from the chair she'd dragged to the side of the couch. Her Calculus textbook was open in Erin's lap and she was flipping back and forth through the pages while her other hand idly stroked Theo's furry head. Who knew the broken girl spoke math? At least she'd have someone she could learn with.

But Kitty wasn't at peace with the newest member of their household yet. She'd looked forward to having another demon student, but something really wasn't right.

She went through the kitchen and leaned against the wall furthest from the doorway that led to the dining room and then living room. Background music from the video game was playing at a moderate volume and that should cover the sound of her conversation with Lily.

Lily had a sandwich on a plate. It was also roast beef, the meat in the middle thicker than the two slices of bread that surrounded it because she was still packing on protein and fat until her metabolism recovered from its hard burn. She set the plate on the island and looked at Kitty, her dark eyes patient.

"She took the Xbox controller apart," Kitty said.

"We'll get another."

Kitty shook her head. "No, she put it back together." She paused and then repeated that sentence more slowly, "She put it. Back. Together. With no tools, just with her hands."

"Probably works better now," Lily said and took a bite of the sandwich. While chewing she went back to the fridge and got out one of the coconut waters.

"I'm sure it does. But she also stripped most of the metal out of her room and, if I'm not mistaken, those crutches weren't here yesterday. You know as well as I do, that's not a Sangkesh power. What's her lineage? Who sent you to get her?"

It was a risk asking outright. Lily could tell her it was none of her business. After all, Kitty held no formal rank in the Sangkesh. Any power she had came from her unfettered access to her mother, and that wasn't a power she liked to use.

"We don't know," Lily said. "But the Cavallo sought her out because she has the body of a Sangkesh mixed breed but the power of a Shaitan."

That was a highly dangerous mix. Almost none of the elder Sangkesh demons had physical bodies of their own, but among the Shaitan it was impossible to get any of their signature powers combined with the strength of a physical body. That's what helped keep the world in balance. Unless a demon had a physical body of its own, it could be banished, bound or controlled. The Shaitan demons often had greater power than the Sangkesh, but also greater vulnerabilities because of their lack of bodies. If this girl had the abilities of a Shaitan and her own body, a built-in freedom from control, how powerful could she become?

"Does Suhirin know?" Kitty asked.

Lily shook her head and grinned. "I don't tell her everything. After all, what would she think if her precious daughter was slumming with a Shaitan?"

Kitty glanced through the open doorways, though she couldn't see the couch from where she stood. Erin could easily become the most powerful of the four of them. What would she do then? Would she be loyal to them? And if she wasn't, whose job was it to stop her? Could that be Lily's long game, pairing Kitty with Erin and knowing that Kitty could figure out how to neutralize her power if it came to that?

That wasn't the sort of thing you asked out loud, even if you thought no one was listening, so she picked another question: "What are you going to do when they come for her?"

Lily set the coconut water on the island and took another bite of her sandwich. When she was doing chewing and swallowing, she said,

"Hope you've learned everything I can teach you."

"Is she worth that risk?" Kitty asked. Because Kitty had learned: Failure was one thing. Death was another.

"You all are," Lily said. "Each one of you. I don't take students at random."

They stood in silence for a few minutes, Lily eating and drinking from where she leaned against the island, looking more relaxed than Kitty thought she should. Already Kitty's mind was reviewing what she already knew of Erin and what she would need to find out in order to know how to stop her.

When the sandwich was half gone, Lily said, "You don't have to worry, this house is very well hidden. I've yet to meet someone who knows how to get around Weasel magic combined with the power of the City."

Kitty didn't respond and Lily took the other half of her sandwich into her bedroom. Weasel magic was great for hiding but what if the person looking already knew they were here? What if the Shaitan who ranted to Blake about the four people, the two witches and two demons, was part of a group that wanted Erin to be here? Lily said they kept getting anonymous tips to go look for her.

Kitty had looked at the note from Blake about what the Shaitain demon said so often that she could call it up from memory:

2 demons, 2 witches
Sing a song of secrets
Sing a song of silver
W-74
Re

Insight flared through Kitty's brain. The last notation wasn't "re:" as in regarding. She ran up the stairs two at a time and called up the periodic table of the elements.

74 was W for Tungsten

75 was Re for Rhenium, a silvery-white metal.

Was the song of secrets a song about the metals of the periodic table? A song about how to use the metal powers of the Shaitans? What could Erin do with that song and her freedom?

CHAPTER FIFTY-THREE

THEO IS CALLED BACK HOME (AGAIN/FOR THE FIRST TIME)

All the people-words made Theo sleepy. Tucking her nose under her leg, she fell asleep. Brother Jaguar's drums echoed in her mind, telling her she wasn't really a dog.

A big cat, then? No, they told her, you're Theo.

She explained that she was sorry, but she was quite sure she was a crow. Or an owl.

Theo.

Theo.

Theo.

"Theo." Instead of Brother Jaguar, it was Gabe. He tucked a quilt around her shoulders and said with a crooked kind of smile, "You're going to catch a cold, sleeping naked on the couch."

"Fur," she said and blearily looked down at her very naked, very human self. She'd never turned human in her sleep before. She remembered the drums. Must have been residual magic from Ben. Either that or Lily was being a real ass with this tattoo.

He patted her shoulder. "No, I think you look better in skin, even if fur is warmer."

She made a face, sticking her tongue out. "Fuck, I think I ate bacon."

"Dude," he said, his arm still resting on the curl of her hips. It felt nice there, like a weight that held her spirit in place, "I was thinking we were going to have to buy you kibbles and rawhide." She must have

271

looked briefly interested in the prospect because he shook his head and laughed again. "Should I get you a squeaky toy?"

"Shut up," she smiled, kicking at him lightly with her legs.

He nodded, and picked up the controller that Erin had left on the couch. After turning it over in his hands a few times, he pointed it at the screen and the game flicked on easily. He seemed surprised by that.

"Magic is real," he said, apropos of nothing.

"Yeah, no one told me either," Theo said.

"No?"

"No," she said. Pulling the comforter closer around her head, she curled her body into a tighter ball. "But I guess my sister is finally talking about it. She broke her vow of silence."

"She's a nun?" Gabe glanced over at Theo as he moved his body around trying to control the mech on the screen. "I thought she was a witch?"

"Sorry, inside joke," Theo said, though really it was more of an inside-her-own-head kind of joke and more sad than funny, really. "Point is, she's talking to me and even apologized, so that's progress, right?"

Gabe nodded seriously. Even though his eyes were on the game, he said very seriously, "Every day we're above ground is progress, sister."

It shocked Theo how true that felt today—how true it felt after tearing a man apart with her jaguar teeth and almost getting lost in the comfort of four legs again. It suddenly hit Theo, too, that maybe she was the one being selfish, wanting to push so hard back with Sabel, to recreate a childhood, a 'sisterhood,' that never was. Maybe, it was okay, the way things were. Sure, there had been lies and silences, but what family doesn't have its secrets? Perhaps Theo was the one who should 'Let it Go,' and truly and sincerely accept Sabel's apology, accept that Sabel was who she was, and that that was okay.

Like Gabe implied: go forward from here, each day alive is a precious gift. After everything with the animal transformations, Theo kind of understood that this complication, this relationship shit, it was part of being human.

She might not like it always, but she was human. It was time to start acting like one—put down roots, make amends with her family, and start having real friends.

"Where are the others?" Theo asked.

"Kitty sort of wandered off. I thought she was talking to Lily but then when I went into the kitchen they were gone. Their rooms, I think, cause I heard Kitty walking around upstairs. Erin played for a while and went back to bed. Thinking about doing that myself in a few."

"Will you wait a bit?" Theo asked. "I should eat so you won't try to feed me kibbles."

Gabe nodded and Theo went into the kitchen wrapped in the blanket and got the first thing she saw in the fridge, which was some kind of garbanzo bean salad. Back on the couch, she snuggled up next to Gabe and he put an arm around her. She liked that despite his little blush, his hand was firm and confident, like he really had no doubt at all that he could hold her in place, keep her safe.

She let herself just sit and breathe. Like a human being.

And, right now, being human felt really… right.

Above her, Gabe muttered quietly, "Stupid House Rule #2," and he leaned down and kissed the top of her head. She turned her face up, half reflex, entirely wanting to kiss him, tried to stop herself and ended up just licking the front edge of his chin.

She ducked her head, "Gah, sorry. Too much dog."

Oops, not quite human enough!

But Gabe didn't seem bothered. He laughed . His arm was still on her and that made her smile. Tomorrow, she decided, she would come clean, like Sabel finally had. She'd tell Lily about her house cat form and give back that ring as a show of good faith.

The puzzle was together… and she finally fit somewhere.

CHAPTER FIFTY-FOUR

GABE CALLS HOME
(FROM HOME)

After Theo got done eating she said she was going to check on Erin and turned back into a dog again. For a second that seemed totally natural to him and then he had to shake himself hard.

Watching her eat had made him hungry again so he grabbed one of the many plastic containers out of the fridge, plus a fork, and headed to his room.

Shutting the door, he sat cross-legged on his bed. It no longer surprised him at all to find authentic enchiladas inside the Tupperware. Tupperware. Of course, they were the exact heat to his liking, too.

Just like Mom used to make.

He'd call home. Erin had that phone. She'd finally let it out of her hands once Lily had taken her to the lab and told her she could play with all the metals in there. He'd seen it on the kitchen table. Once he was finished, he'd call.

But, as he ate, Gabe's mind kept going over everything that had happened and tried to jam it into the box labeled 'good guys' in his head. He was having some trouble with that. Certain bits kept poking out. Particularly the whole 'destroyed the dead' part. He couldn't quite get over the ominousness of that phrase, especially since he'd wondered last night if the Sangkesh were the kind of power that could cover up a murder.

Because, like it or not, that's what they'd done: murder.

Gabe had been in that guy's car, smelled the leftover fast food, seen the beer cans on the floorboards. That was a person, who'd been living a life. Yeah, sure, okay, so that dude had carried a gun and tried to kill people Gabe—well, Gabe couldn't say he loved these people yet, more like he was randomly associated with them.

Which just made this whole thing squishier.

Setting the empty container on the doily-laced bedside table, Gabe let himself fall back onto the mattress. A wave of exhaustion rolled over him. His whole body felt heavy. He should just close his eyes and crash, but some weird part of his brain said 'you don't have to sleep in your clothes any more.' So, despite the deep ache in his bones, Gabe pulled himself upright and started undressing.

He kicked off his shoes and threw his socks into the corner. Belt came off and got flung in the same direction. But, then he started to feel weird——was he making more work for the 'house elf'? Where did last night's clothes go? Had they been laundered or…? No, there they were, just where he'd left them, slung over the chair by the reading desk.

Gabe retrieved the stuff from the corner and set them on the chair, thinking it was the least he could do for this mysterious house spirit: keep everything in a single pile. His body was so clumsy from tiredness that he managed to stumble into the chair when he tried to put his shoes and such on the seat. He caught the chair before it completely hit the floor, but last night's jeans slipped off. With a groan, Gabe righted the chair and bent down picked up the jeans. As he blearily flailed around with the stiff denim fabric, trying to fold it semi-neatly, a crumpled note rolled out of the pocket.

Giving up on folding, Gabe let the jeans fall to the chair as he examined the note. What was this? Smoothing out the paper, he read a name and an address:

Asilal, 011-210-001-4151
600 Montgomery St., #4800-B

What was this? Then, through the fog, it hit him. This was the phone number and address of the people he was supposed to run to if things had gotten more fucked-up than they already were.

The Sangkesh.

He had the address to their… lair? Headquarters? Whatever it was, seeing it made Gabe's muscles tense with determination. There was one sure way to find out if these creeps were the good guys. He could see for himself. It wouldn't be idly sitting here waiting for another dark night when he stupidly volunteered to do 'just one little thing.'

So, with a certain amount of determination, Gabe got up. He made a show of returning the Tupperware to the dishwasher, and casually picked up the phone to bring to his room.

He sat on his bed. Pulling out the note, he looked at it again. What was that after Asilal's name? Was that some kind of international phone number? Gabe thought maybe he'd try that next.

But, first....

Taking a deep breath, he punched in the numbers for Mom's cell, remembering to add the one and West Virginia's area code.

The phone rang.

Gabe held his breath.

It rang again.

He felt ready to pass out by the time it got to the recorded message that told him this number was no longer in service. He listened to the repeat, because he couldn't believe it. Why wouldn't Mom take that number to a new phone? Why disconnect it completely?

Fuck.

He'd wanted to tell them he was okay and that he loved them and... and ask them if they would trust a demon ever, or something like that. Mostly, he'd wanted some reassurance.

Gabe listened to the silence of the dead line and the sound of his pounding heart for what felt like forever.

Then he hung up.

He sat there awhile, almost feeling too tired, too shell shocked to do anything more, but he had that other strange number.

He decided to dial it.

The phone barely finished its first ring when a cultured British voice swiftly answered, a note of panic in the voice, "Lily?"

"Are you the good guys or bad guys?" Gabe blurted before he lost his nerve.

There was a decidedly unsettling chuckle on the other end of the line. "That rather depends on who you are."

At that, Gabe lost his nerve and hung up the phone.

He tucked the address into his battered backpack, but he decided that he'd done enough for now. If it depended on who he was, the last thing Gabe wanted to be was "the enemy."

:: :: ::

A few days later, Gabe got another shock. School had started but he was only taking two classes while he got used to regular schooling again, so he was around during the day more than Theo or Kitty. Lily asked him if he'd be willing to do an errand for her. Since he already felt like he did nothing to earn his keep, he agreed. She dug through the drawers in the kitchen until she found a stack of business cards.

"Use the bike in the garage," Lily told him, handing over the cards. "Or, if you want, I can give you money for the MUNI, but there're a lot of stops. Shall I assume you're familiar with the free clinics?"

He laughed and didn't think much more of it until he propped the bike up against a scraggly Ginko tree and walked into a familiar re-muddled clinic and handed a small bunch of cards to the nurse built like a hammer with snake-eyes.

"Oh," he said.

"Yep," she agreed.

CHAPTER FIFTY-FIVE

ERIN PLAYS GAMES ON US

When Theo-dog was with her, Erin slept pretty well. Mostly. Thing was, it was much harder to keep the nightmares at bay when she wasn't awake to build cages around them. The scent of fur and the metallic sweetness of tattoo helped, but sometimes the dark slithered out of its confines and Erin would wake up with a cold-sweat drenched start.

This time, even after Theo sleepily licked her cheek, Erin couldn't fall back to sleep. She lay there, staring at the ceiling, until she heard the soft huffs of Theo's doggie snores. Once Erin was a hundred percent sure that Theo was out, she pried herself out from Theo's sprawling embrace.

She'd left the smartphone upstairs and there was something she wanted to do... even though the idea made her gut clench just a little. But, Lily had said "friend." Could it be? Had someone actually missed her?

Upstairs, Erin snuggled onto the couch. She liked this big room with all the electronic things humming happily around her. It smelled new and fresh, nothing like her grandparent's farmhouse. She found the communal iPad on the on the end table next to a math book. Opening it up, Erin paused.

Was this a good idea?

No one in her life had ever been trustworthy. Her parents had died on her. Her grandparents had turned into monsters. People at school all hated her and called her names and threw rocks at her. Doctors were always ready to cut her up or send her away or drug her into oblivion.

But…

Lily had said "friend."

Did Erin really have such a thing?

Swiping through the options, Erin found her way back to her old hang-outs. One account had three asks, one was about some show she hadn't kept up with, the other was random hate, but the third one… Erin's heart jumped to her throat. It was him. He was asking where she'd gone, was she okay?

Trembling thumbs called up the keyboard. She hesitated for a few seconds, trying to remember how long she'd been under this time. Months? Eventually, she let out a long sigh and just typed:

Bk now. Sorry you were worried.

Then she backspaced over the 'sorry' part, rewrote it, and then back-spaced again. What she really wanted to know was this: Are you my benefactor? Are you my 'friend'? But, she didn't know how to write that in a forum like this, so she retyped the bit about being sorry he'd been worried and left it at that. She considered about sixteen hundred other things she could say, but eventually gave up and just hit send.

Even though she knew better, she waited for a reply.

It was silly. She wasn't even sure what time zone GraveJelly was in. He could be asleep right now. So, she spent some time catching up on all the things, scrolling through her feed and letting the datastream wash over her like a flowing river, cleansing her.

She followed several links and caught up on missed episodes of things she'd started watching at various hospitals, checked out game screenshots, read a few articles and reviews of the latest things, and felt herself relaxing into a giant yawn. Erin stretched the length of the couch and decided, just because, to go back and check. The red "1" next to her mailbox made her sit straight up.

Opening it, she found it was GraveJelly. He wrote:

We've missed you in the game. Are you coming back soon or are you stuck in a hospital again?

Erin smiled at that. Of course he remembered the time she used a hacked hospital account into order to help finish a campaign. That was legend in certain circles.

It had also been a tremendous ego-boost. Because no one had given a shit about the fact she was in the loony bin—in fact, that had made the hack that much more epic for them—what they loved her for was her prowess, her skill…

…her magic.

Erin hadn't really thought about it that way, but that was what it was, wasn't it? It was her magic, her superpower.

Feeling buoyed, Erin typed:

Busted out for good. Am in SF now. Maybe we're in the same time zone finally? IM me! I want to play again.

Then, she hummed the theme song of her favorite game as she got up to find a bowl of cereal. As she hummed, the song shifted from the game theme to the one her father used to sing her, the metal elements. Maybe today, she'd even go for a walk with the dog. Like, all the way to the end of the block or something.

Yeah, nothing could stop her now.

CHAPTER FIFTY-SIX

KITTY GETS TO MATH (AND GERMAN)

The start of school was perfect to help Kitty calm down and settle in. She loved the feeling of new textbooks and notebooks, new pens, a host of other office supplies she didn't need but loved to organize on her desk anyway. She'd called one of her old professor contacts and gotten into two graduate-level math courses in addition to German.

Theo was taking classes at the same school, probably something frou-frou like psychology, but that was Theo, wasn't it? Kitty tried to ignore her when she was on campus because it seemed Theo was always flirting with someone, boy or girl. To be fair, however, Kitty had noticed a change. Theo seemed to be trying to be... human? Maybe that wasn't the right word, maybe she just wasn't quite as dickish as she used to be... or maybe it was even that Kitty was finally getting used to Theo, who knew? At any rate, she was easier to live with.

Erin still mostly kept to herself, but Lily told them that was to be expected. She did come down and play games with Gabe. He seemed to love to watch her play, like some kind of opposite stereotype of the guy gamer's girlfriend. It was cute, anyway.

In fact, for the first time in her life, away from her dads, Kitty felt like she... belonged. Lily didn't expect Kitty to strangle demons with her bare hands, in fact, she'd signed Kitty up for a stunt driving class because, she said with a wink, "You never know when we might need more of your fancy driving."

Kitty just had one more thing to do before she could settle into her school work. She borrowed Lily's car and drove down to the Westin where Suhirin and her team were still holed up. It wasn't as bad as last time. Maybe because she wasn't being summoned, because she chose to come, or because she had a place where she could be useful as a demon-hunter and still have her math and her time to herself.

The guard at the door let her in and she wasn't surprised to see roughly the same collection of people and guns that she had weeks before. Still no Blake, though.

"Akiva," Suhirin said, raising her eyebrows and crossing the room to her.

Yep, she definitely wasn't as bothered this time. Her chest tightened only a little and she barely ground her teeth at the sound of her given name.

"Did Blake talk to you about the Shaitan prophecy or whatever?" Kitty asked. "About the two demons and two witches?"

"She did," Suhirin said and her face was open and curious as she said it. This was the reason Kitty had to come in person to ask her questions and see if Blake's concerns were really being heard and acted on.

"You're looking into it?" Kitty asked.

"I have a research team on it," Suhirin told her. "You can stay on your original assignment—find out where the shapeshifting witch hid the items she stole."

Kitty nodded. She was ready to be dismissed and wander off again, back to her schoolwork and the quiet of her room, but Suhirin wasn't done.

"I think Lily's doing a good job with you," she said. "I'm putting a field team together to investigate some of the Shaitan activity on the west coast. I'll give you access to their work."

That would have been surprising enough, but after a pause Suhirin added, "I'm bringing Blake in to be the covert arm of that team."

"Oh," Kitty said. She was still trying to figure out if she'd sounded too eager when Suhirin gave her a parting nod and went back to her work.

Math and demon hunting and Blake? Kitty waited until she was in Lily's car and driving out of the parking garage, but then she put on her favorite music and sang along with it all the way back to the house.

THE MONSTER GETS
A LABORATORY

Erin's horns grew larger every day.

The fire of the sun fed them, as did the metals in the lab, the ones Lily told her it was okay to absorb.

"You have to learn to control it," Lily told her kindly, "But for now, you can take what you need here."

She sampled the metals of the lab and took the ones she liked best to put in her horns and her jewelry. She strengthened the crutches she'd made herself so she could get around the house easily. All the metals in the house were known to her now, familiar and comforting, so she didn't take any of those, just the ones in the lab.

Except for one. It sang to her from the third story of the house. From near Theo's room. She went up one day when Theo was doing her chores and followed the taste of magical metal to the little balcony behind Theo's room.

It was there above the trim on the sliding door. Erin had to balance on one crutch and slide the other along the top of the doorframe, but she knocked the little parcel loose and it dropped to the floor with a little thump. She tucked it into a pocket and carried it down to her room to unwrap. A little ring, thin and pretty, with a red stone in it.

She wanted to absorb it, to pull the magic out of the metal, but she didn't know how. She tucked it back into her pocket, unwrapped now. In time she'd learn how to draw the metal and the magic out together.

Now that the Monster was free, Erin thought maybe Azazel was right, because she didn't feel so timid any more. What she wanted was to embrace this siren call, the one that hungered for the Iron of blood, and to become Chaos.

THE END *of* BOOK ONE

ABOUT THE AUTHORS

Tate Hallaway leads a double life. By day, she's Lyda Morehouse, a mild-mannered science fiction author of the Shamus and Philip K. Dick award-winning AngeLINK series. By night, she's the bestselling paranormal romance and urban fantasy writer, Tate Hallaway. She's written and published over a dozen novels (five as Lyda and nine as Tate), and together her two identities have over a decade of professional publishing experience. You can find both Lyda and Tate all over the web, but most easily at: @tatehallaway on Twitter and tatehallaway.blogspot.com.

Rachel Calish lives in the Twin Cities area of Minnesota because it's so cold you just have to sit inside and write novels. She obtained her Master of Fine Arts in Writing degree by writing stories about sexy demons. A fan of games of all kinds, you can find her playing anything from the latest video game releases to Checkers with half the pieces missing. Under the name Rachel Gold, she writes LBGTQ Young Adult fiction. You can find Rachel at: @rachelcalish on Twitter and www.rachelcalish.com.

By Tate Hallaway

PRECINCT 13 (Berkley Trade, 2012)
ALMOST EVERYTHING (NAL Trade, 2012)
ALMOST FINAL CURTAIN (NAL Trade, 2011)
HONEYMOON OF THE DEAD (Berkley Trade, 2010)
ALMOST TO DIE FOR (NAL Trade, 2010)
DEAD IF I DO (Berkley Trade, 2009)
ROMANCING THE DEAD (Berkley Trade, 2008)
DEAD SEXY (Berkley Trade, 2007)
TALL, DARK & DEAD (Berkley Trade, 2006)

Writing as Lyda Morehouse:

RESURRECTION CODE (Mad Norwegian Press, 2011)
APOCALYPSE ARRAY (Roc, 2004)
MESSIAH NODE (Roc, 2003)
FALLEN HOST (Roc, 2002)
ARCHANGEL PROTOCOL (Roc, 2001)

By Rachel Calish

THE DEMON GABRIELLA (Bella Books, 2015)
THE DEMON ABRAXAS (Bella Books, 2013)

Writing as Rachel Gold:

MY YEAR ZERO (Bella Books, forthcoming 2016)
JUST GIRLS (Bella Books, 2014)
BEING EMILY (Bella Books, 2012)

ABOUT THE ARTISTS

Together, **Mandie Brasington** and **Alexis Cooke** formed Obsessive Comic Dames (OCD), a comics collective. OCD publishes women-centric comics that explore dark, domestic narratives often with a magical realist twist. You can find OCD projects at ocdamz.tumblr.com and other work at cargocollective.com/mmbrasington and alexiscooke.com.

Made in the USA
San Bernardino, CA
21 February 2015